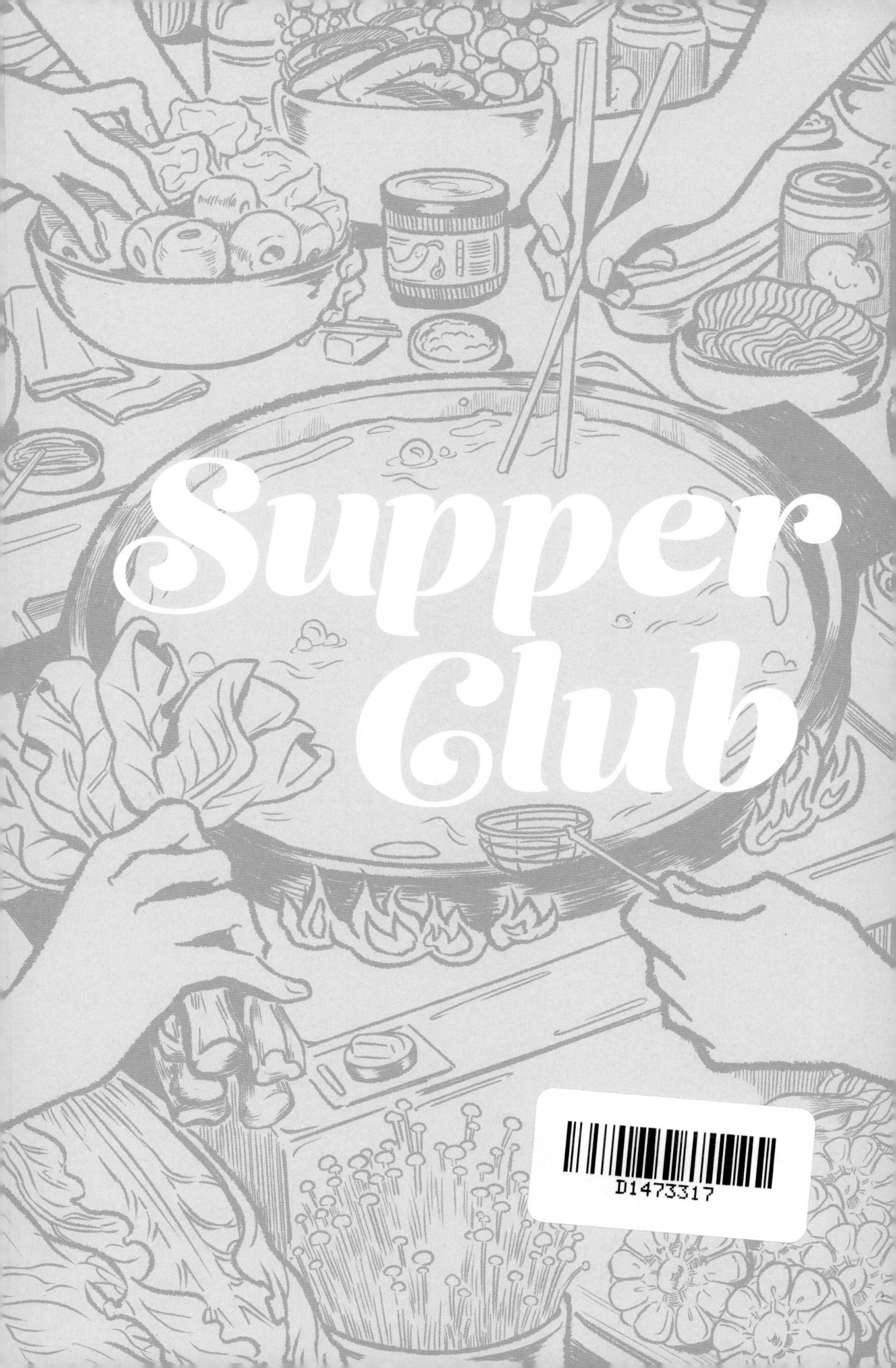
Supper
Club

IMMENSE THANKS TO MY EDITOR AND COLORIST, ALLIE, WHOM I CANNOT EXPRESS ENOUGH GRATITUDE FOR. WITHOUT HER, *SUPPER CLUB* WOULD NOT BE WHERE IT IS. SHE HELPED MY VISION COME TO LIFE ON THE PAGE.

TO MY FRIENDS AND FAMILY FOR THEIR UNWAVERING SUPPORT AND LOVE. EVERY TIME I STEP IN THE KITCHEN TO COOK, I THINK OF YOU.

TO MY FELLOW PARTNERS AT CLIFTWOOD, WHO SUPPORTED ME ENDLESSLY WITH LAUGHS AND UNLIMITED CAFFEINE. THANKS TO SABLE, WHO HELPED - AND HINDERED - MY LONG DAYS AT HOME. TO KEVIN, FOR HIS PATIENCE AND ENCOURAGEMENT.

FOR MY FRIENDS.

SUPPER CLUB. First printing. September 2022. Published by Image Comics, Inc. Office of publication: PO BOX 14457, Portland, OR 97293. ISBN: 978-1-5343-2421-3.

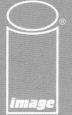

Supper Club™

CREATED BY

JACKIE MORROW

EDITED BY
ALLIE PIPITONE

COLORS BY
ALLIE PIPITONE
WITH
JACKIE MORROW

Chapter One

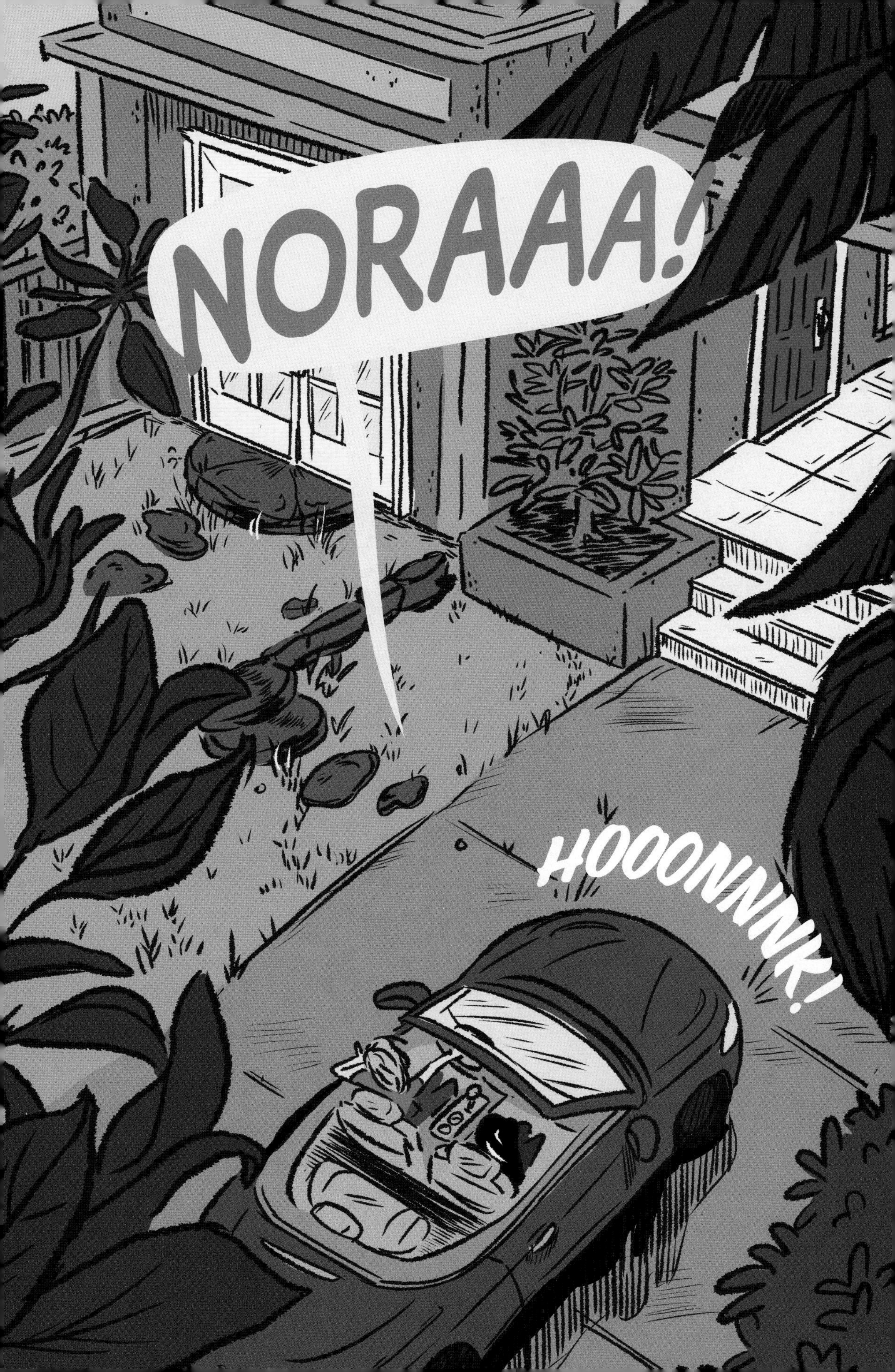
NORAAA!
HOOONNNK!

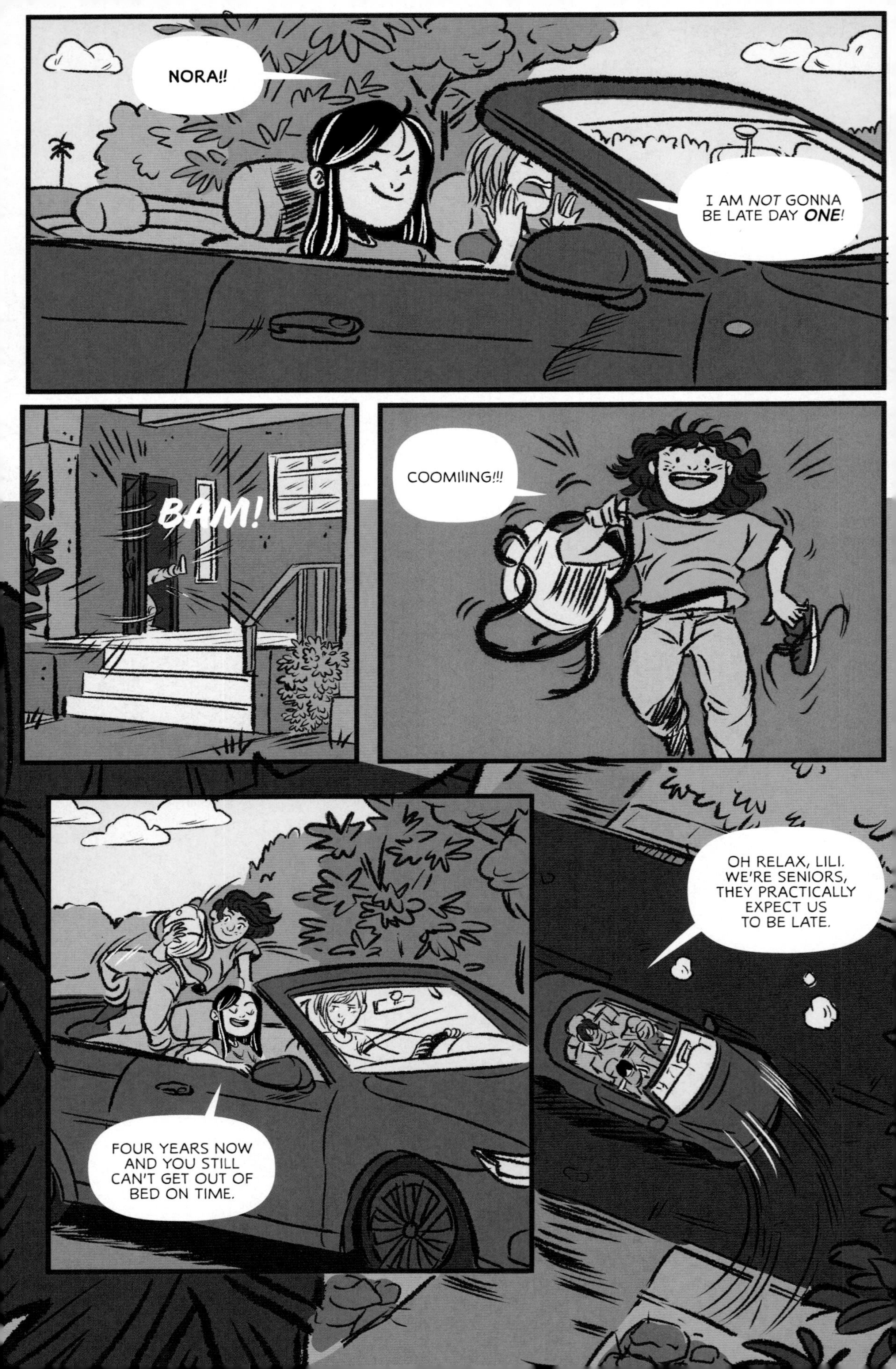
NORA!!
I AM *NOT* GONNA BE LATE DAY ***ONE***!
BAM!
COOMIIING!!!
OH RELAX, LILI. WE'RE SENIORS, THEY PRACTICALLY EXPECT US TO BE LATE.
FOUR YEARS NOW AND YOU STILL CAN'T GET OUT OF BED ON TIME.

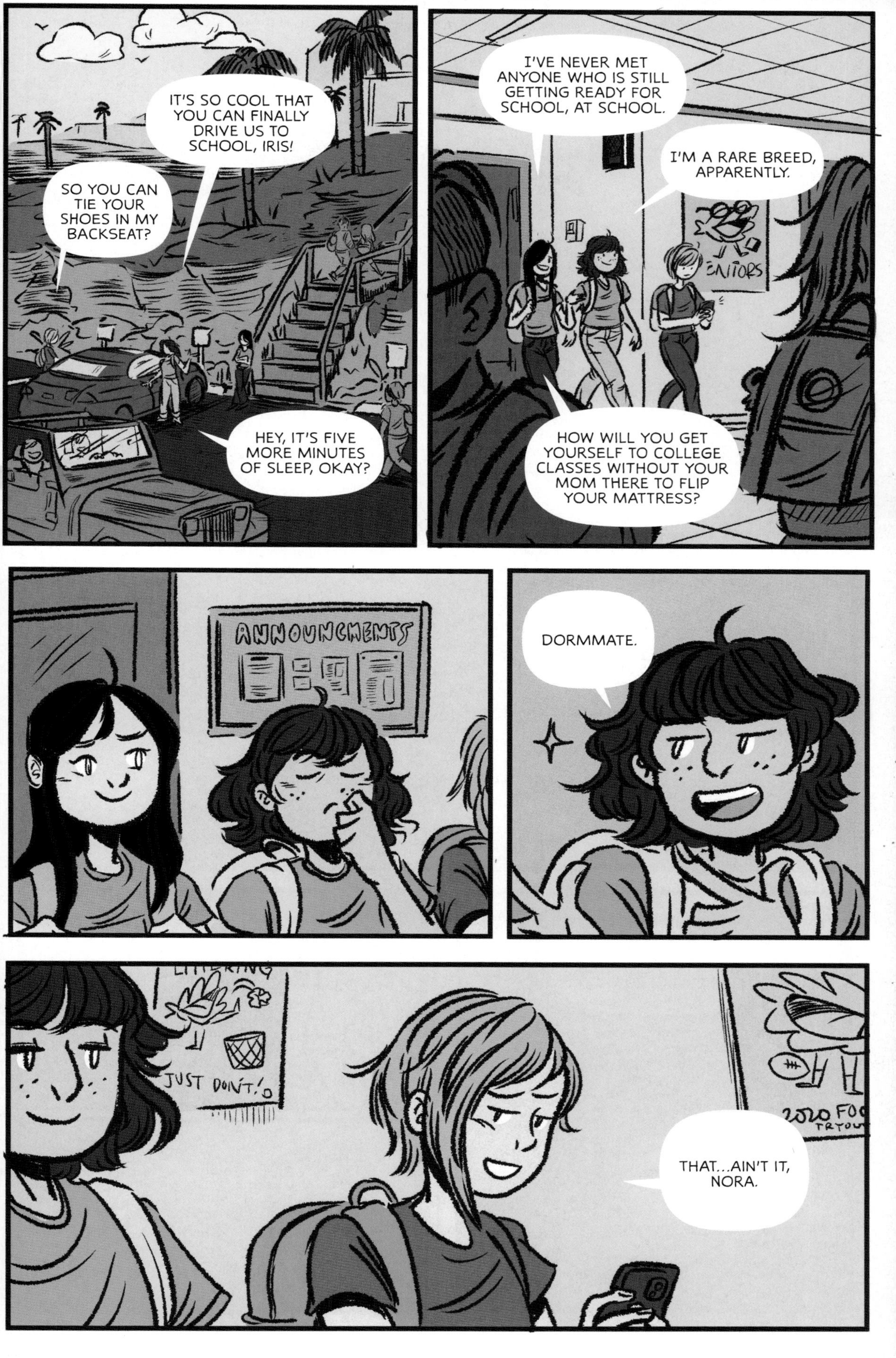
IT'S SO COOL THAT YOU CAN FINALLY DRIVE US TO SCHOOL, IRIS!
SO YOU CAN TIE YOUR SHOES IN MY BACKSEAT?
HEY, IT'S FIVE MORE MINUTES OF SLEEP, OKAY?
I'VE NEVER MET ANYONE WHO IS STILL GETTING READY FOR SCHOOL, AT SCHOOL.
I'M A RARE BREED, APPARENTLY.
ENIORS
HOW WILL YOU GET YOURSELF TO COLLEGE CLASSES WITHOUT YOUR MOM THERE TO FLIP YOUR MATTRESS?
ANNOUNCMENTS
DORMMATE.
JUST DON'T!
THAT...AIN'T IT, NORA.

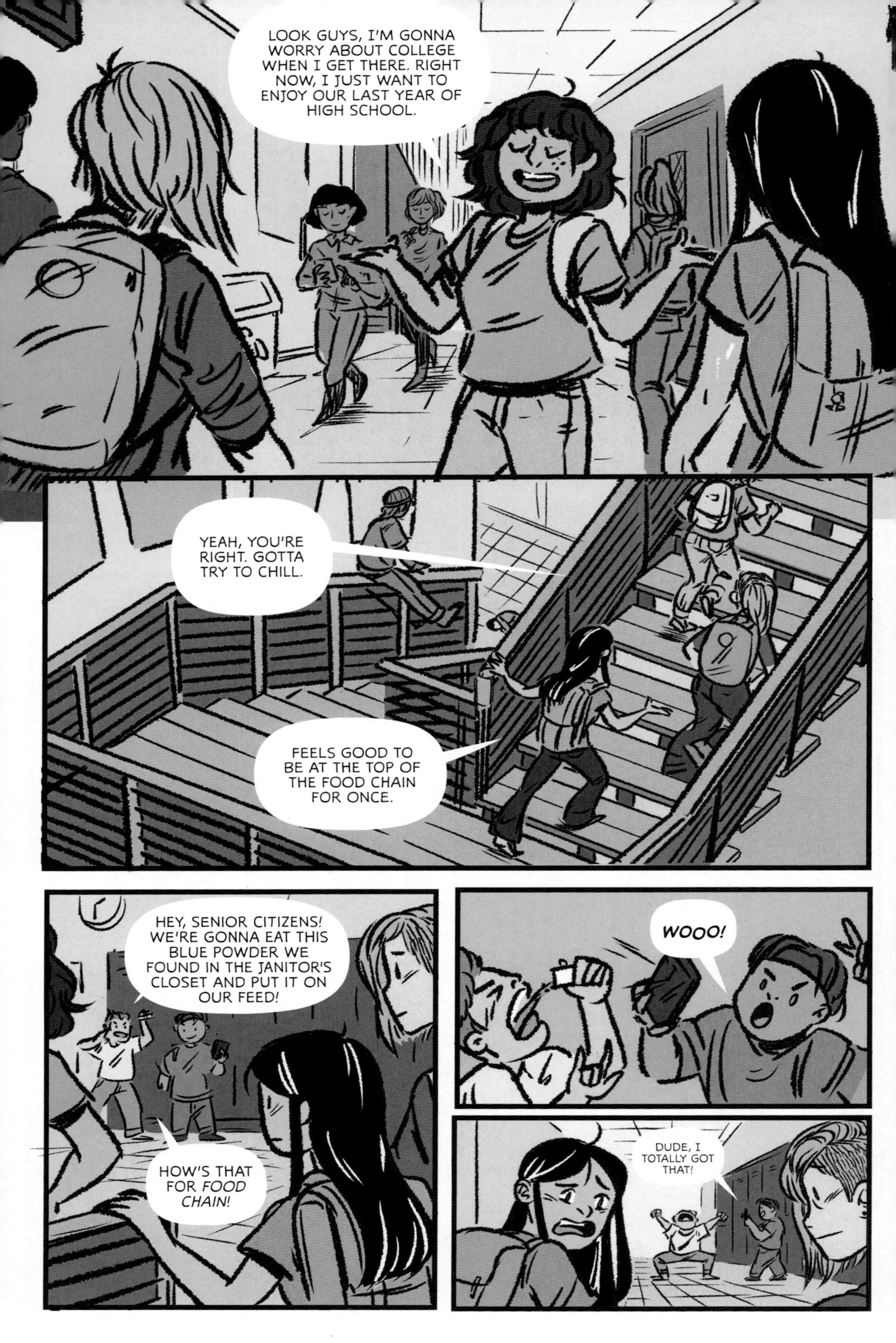
LOOK GUYS, I'M GONNA WORRY ABOUT COLLEGE WHEN I GET THERE. RIGHT NOW, I JUST WANT TO ENJOY OUR LAST YEAR OF HIGH SCHOOL.
YEAH, YOU'RE RIGHT. GOTTA TRY TO CHILL.
FEELS GOOD TO BE AT THE TOP OF THE FOOD CHAIN FOR ONCE.
HEY, SENIOR CITIZENS! WE'RE GONNA EAT THIS BLUE POWDER WE FOUND IN THE JANITOR'S CLOSET AND PUT IT ON OUR FEED!
HOW'S THAT FOR *FOOD CHAIN*!
WOOO!
DUDE, I TOTALLY GOT THAT!

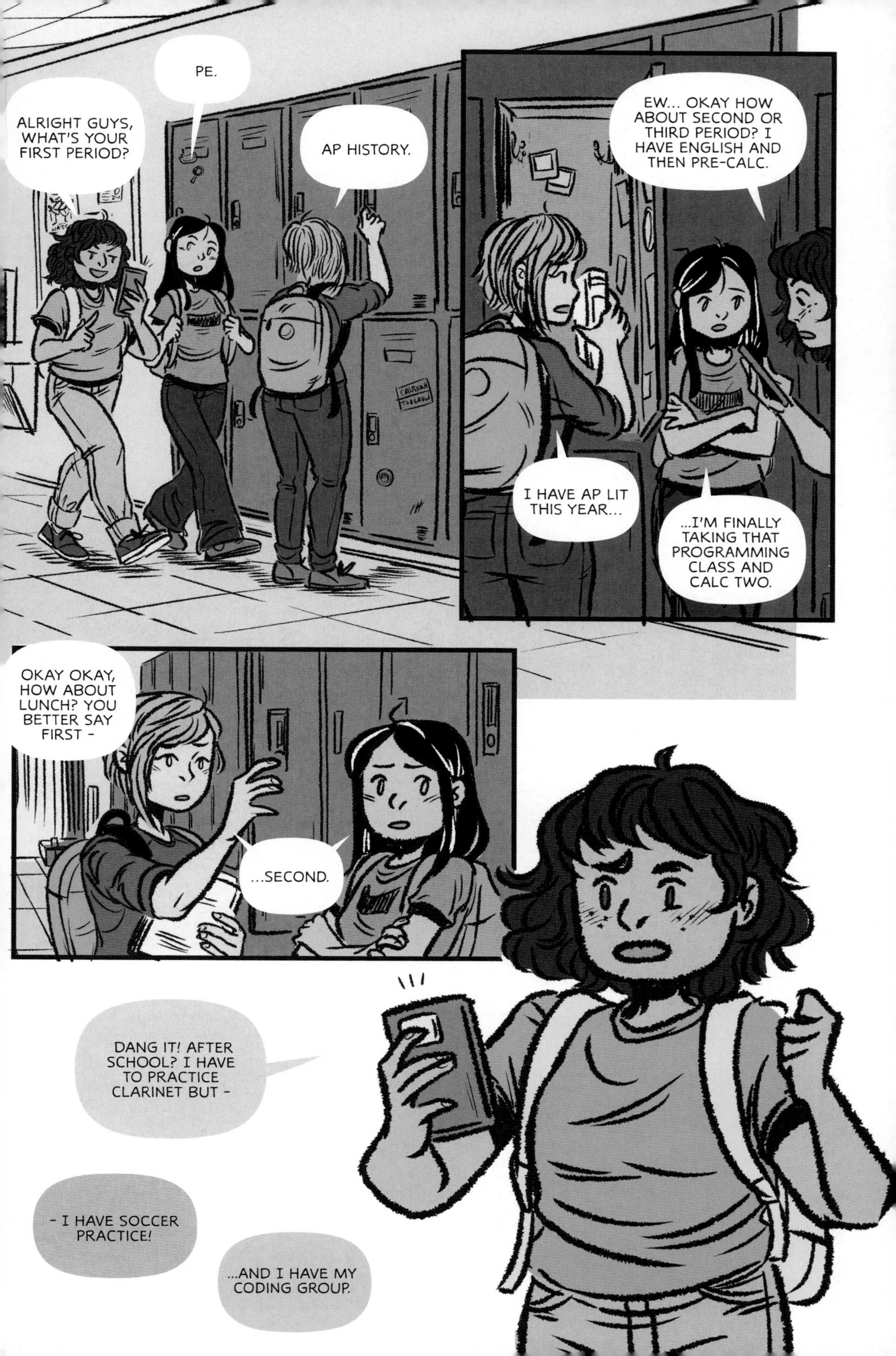
ALRIGHT GUYS, WHAT'S YOUR FIRST PERIOD?
PE.
AP HISTORY.
EW... OKAY HOW ABOUT SECOND OR THIRD PERIOD? I HAVE ENGLISH AND THEN PRE-CALC.
I HAVE AP LIT THIS YEAR...
...I'M FINALLY TAKING THAT PROGRAMMING CLASS AND CALC TWO.
OKAY OKAY, HOW ABOUT LUNCH? YOU BETTER SAY FIRST -
...SECOND.
DANG IT! AFTER SCHOOL? I HAVE TO PRACTICE CLARINET BUT -
- I HAVE SOCCER PRACTICE!
...AND I HAVE MY CODING GROUP.

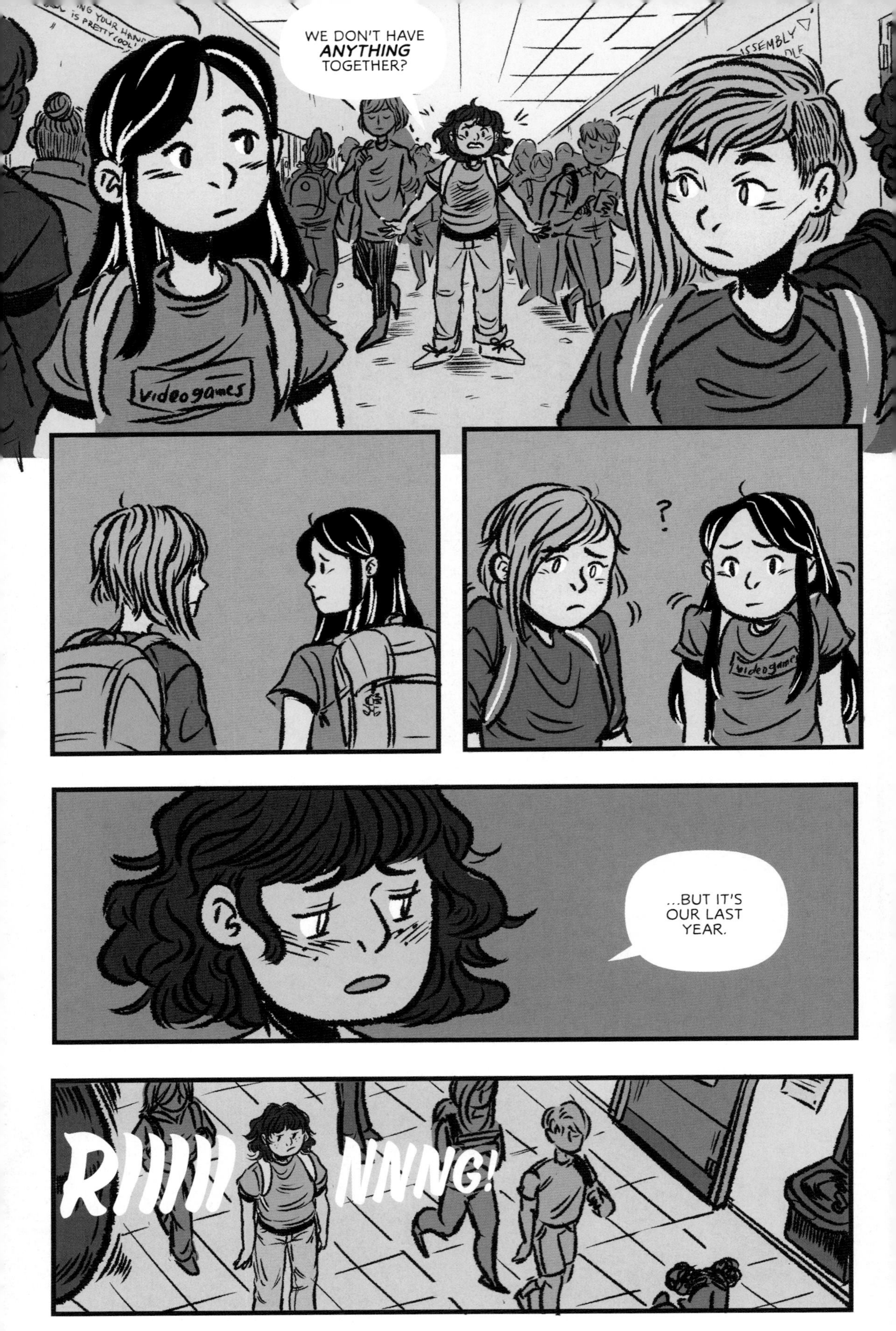
WE DON'T HAVE ***ANYTHING*** TOGETHER?
videogames
?
...BUT IT'S OUR LAST YEAR.
RIIIII NNNG!

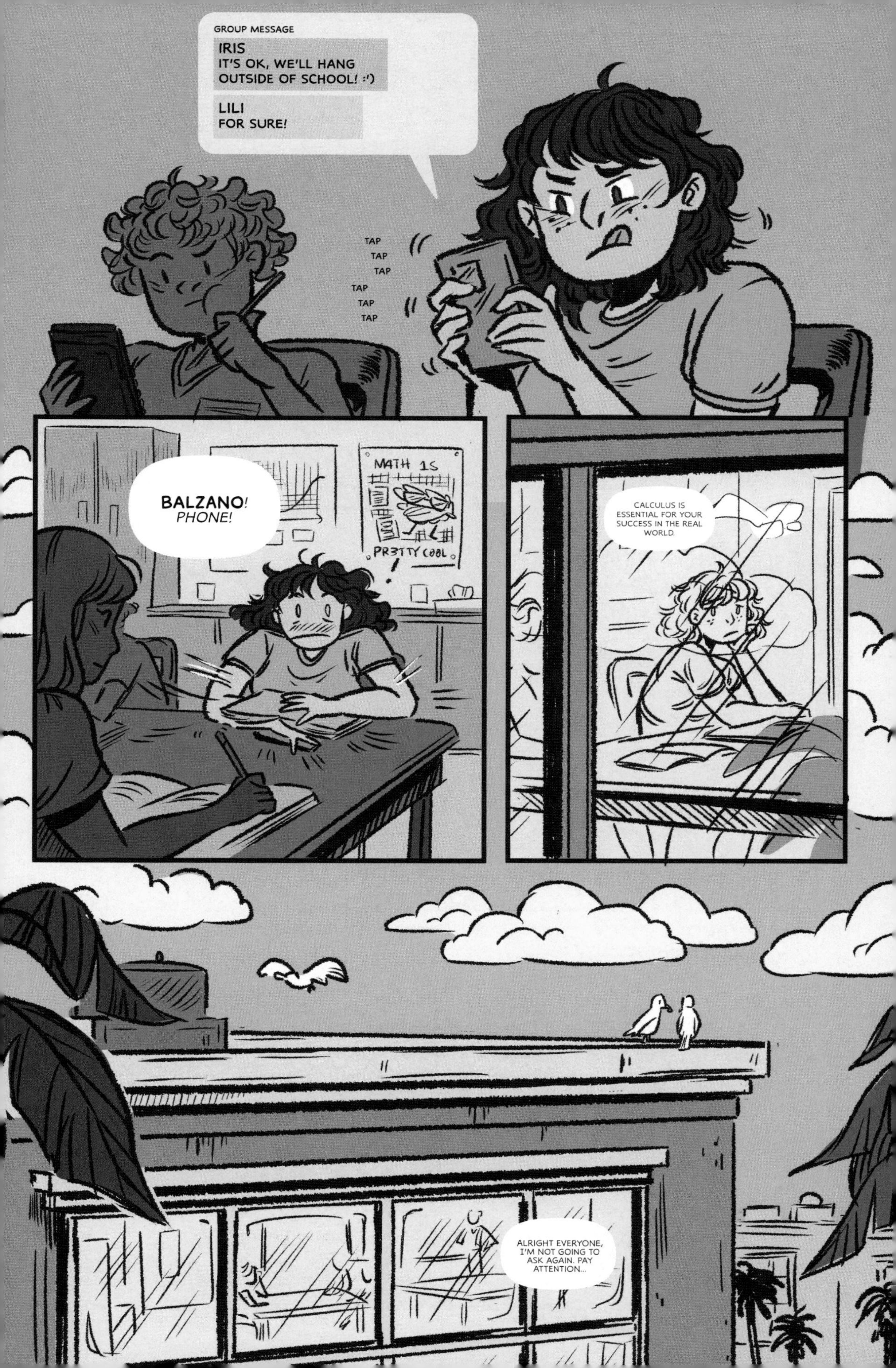
GROUP MESSAGE
IRIS
IT'S OK, WE'LL HANG OUTSIDE OF SCHOOL! :')
LILI
FOR SURE!
TAP TAP TAP TAP TAP TAP
MATH 1S
PR3TTY COOL
BALZANO! PHONE!
CALCULUS IS ESSENTIAL FOR YOUR SUCCESS IN THE REAL WORLD.
ALRIGHT EVERYONE, I'M NOT GOING TO ASK AGAIN. PAY ATTENTION...

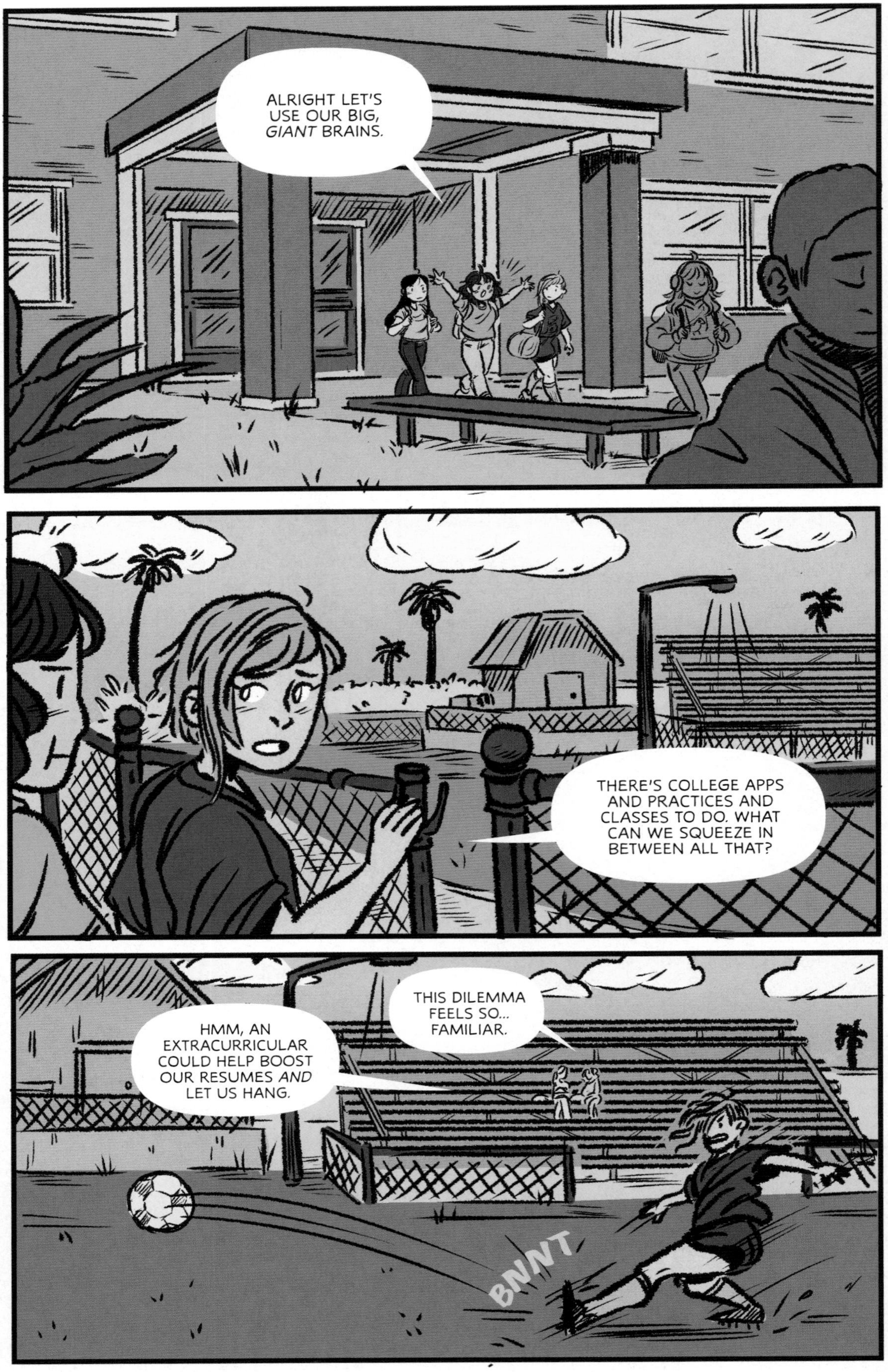
ALRIGHT LET'S USE OUR BIG, *GIANT* BRAINS.
THERE'S COLLEGE APPS AND PRACTICES AND CLASSES TO DO. WHAT CAN WE SQUEEZE IN BETWEEN ALL THAT?
HMM, AN EXTRACURRICULAR COULD HELP BOOST OUR RESUMES *AND* LET US HANG.
THIS DILEMMA FEELS SO... FAMILIAR.
BNNT

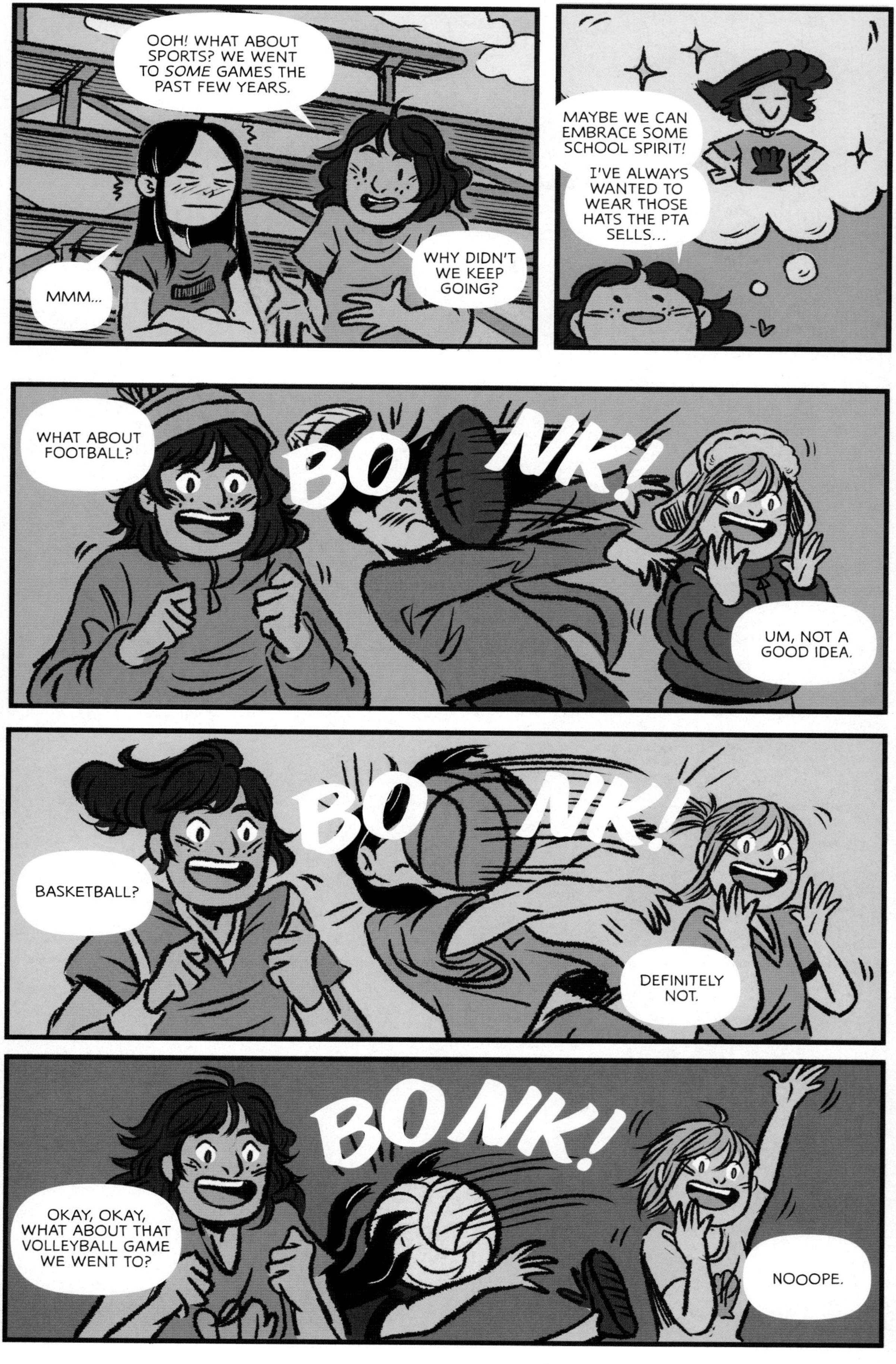
OOH! WHAT ABOUT SPORTS? WE WENT TO *SOME* GAMES THE PAST FEW YEARS.
MMM...
WHY DIDN'T WE KEEP GOING?
MAYBE WE CAN EMBRACE SOME SCHOOL SPIRIT!
I'VE ALWAYS WANTED TO WEAR THOSE HATS THE PTA SELLS...
WHAT ABOUT FOOTBALL?
BONK!
UM, NOT A GOOD IDEA.
BONK!
BASKETBALL?
DEFINITELY NOT.
BONK!
OKAY, OKAY, WHAT ABOUT THAT VOLLEYBALL GAME WE WENT TO?
NOOOPE.

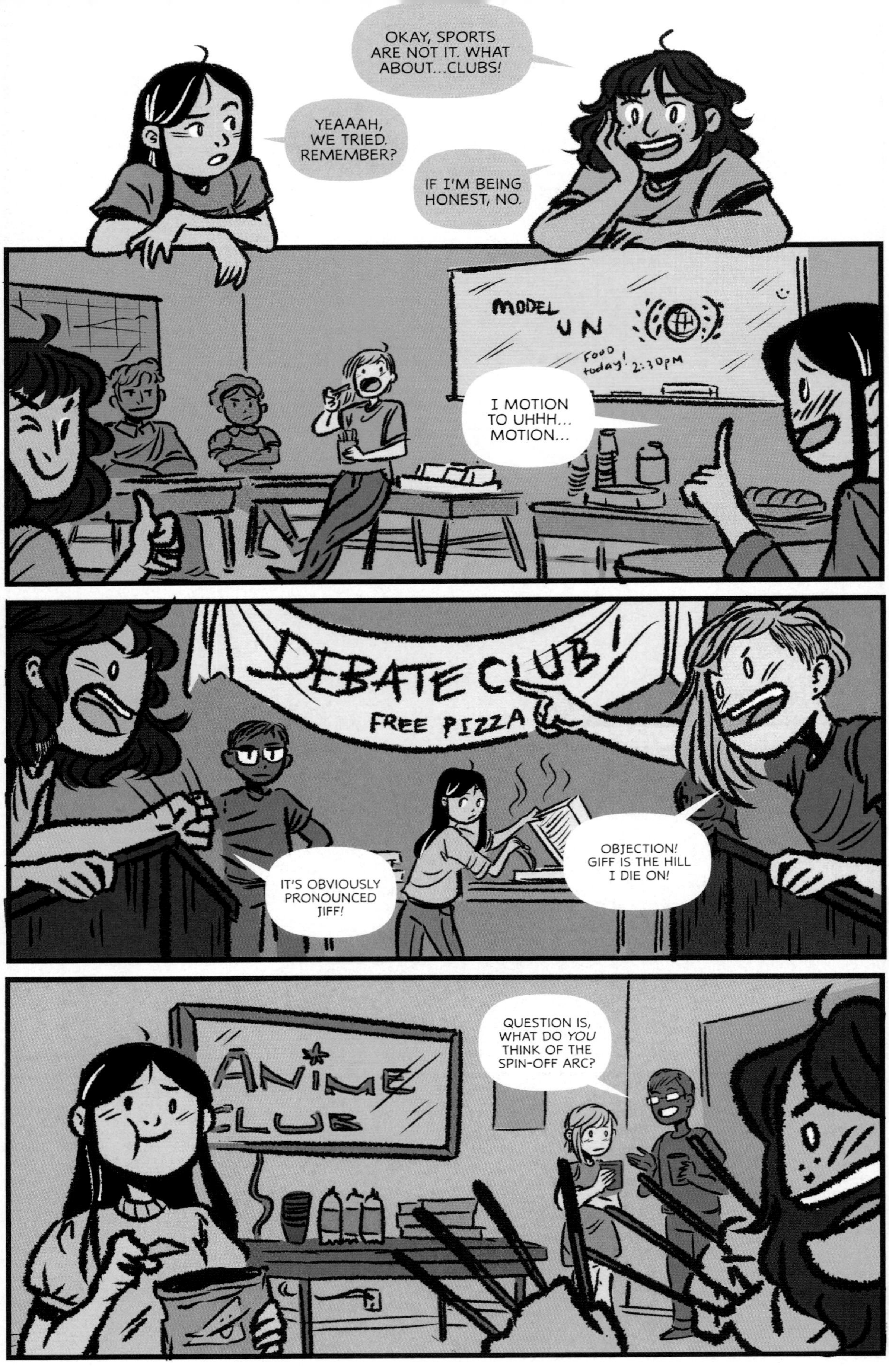

OKAY, SPORTS ARE NOT IT. WHAT ABOUT...CLUBS!
YEAAAH, WE TRIED. REMEMBER?
IF I'M BEING HONEST, NO.
MODEL UN
FOOD today! 2:30PM
I MOTION TO UHHH... MOTION...
DEBATE CLUB!
FREE PIZZA
IT'S OBVIOUSLY PRONOUNCED JIFF!
OBJECTION! GIFF IS THE HILL I DIE ON!
ANIME CLUB
QUESTION IS, WHAT DO *YOU* THINK OF THE SPIN-OFF ARC?

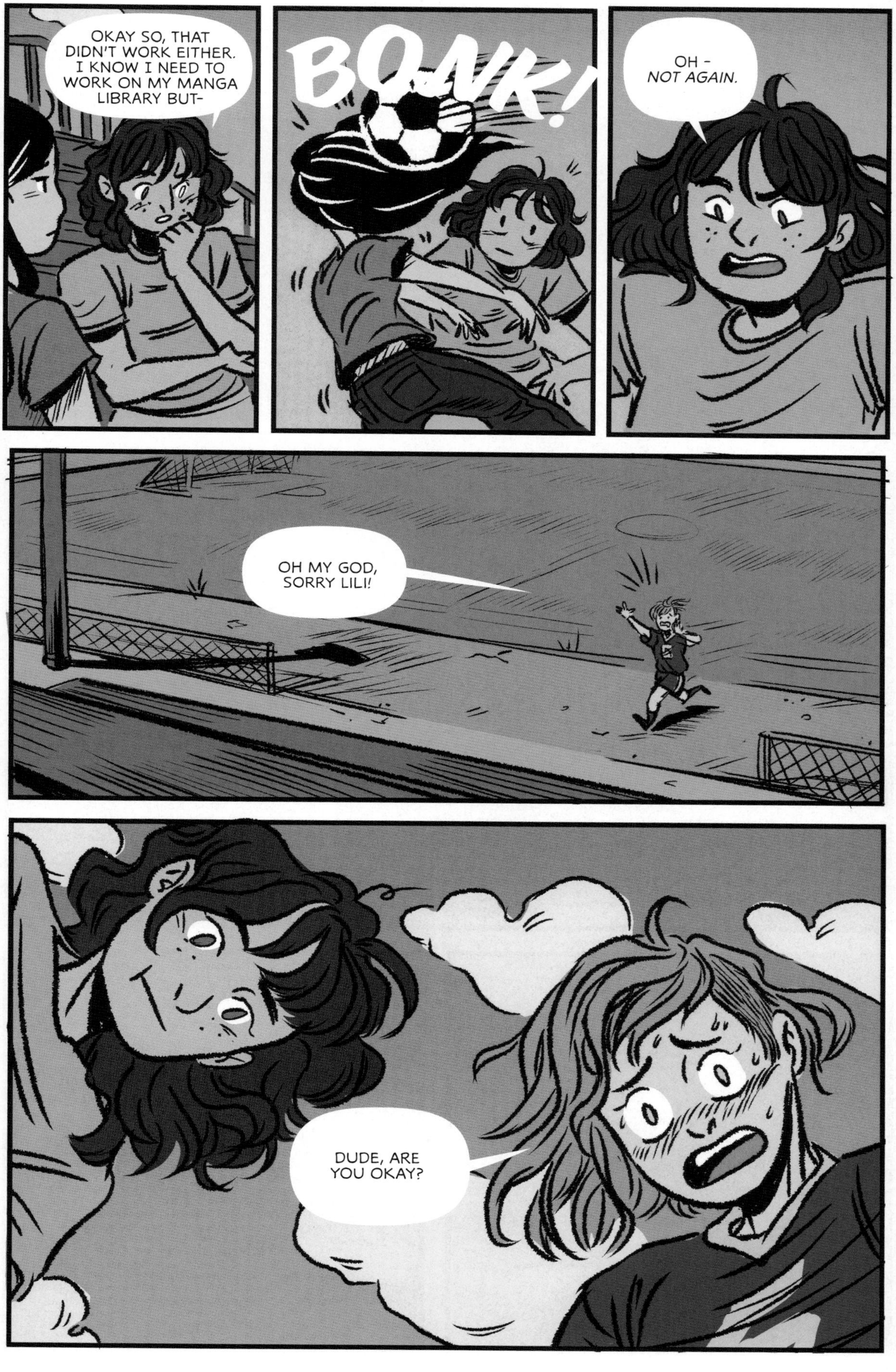
OKAY SO, THAT DIDN'T WORK EITHER. I KNOW I NEED TO WORK ON MY MANGA LIBRARY BUT-
BONK!
OH - NOT AGAIN.
OH MY GOD, SORRY LILI!
DUDE, ARE YOU OKAY?

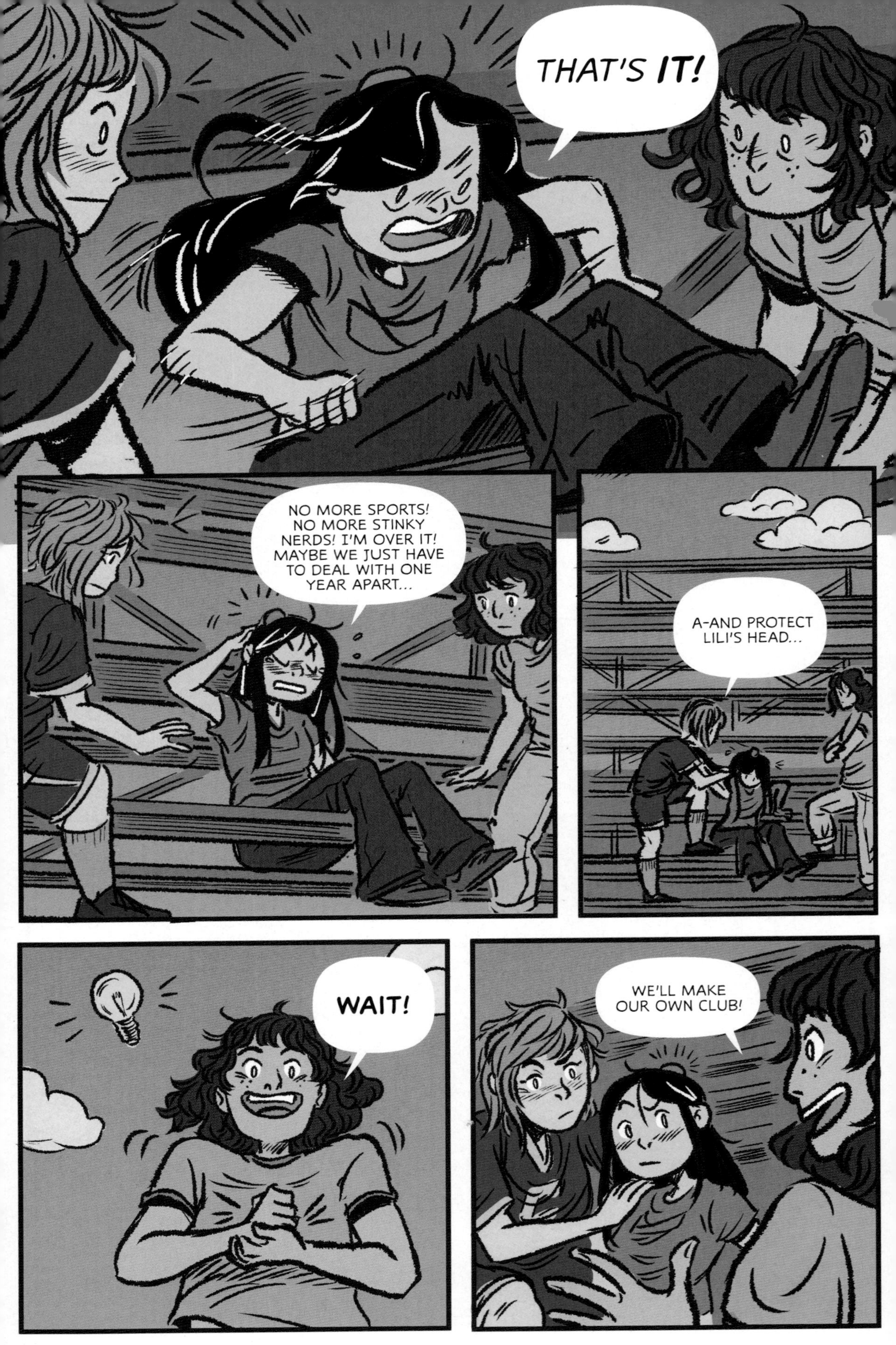
THAT'S IT!
NO MORE SPORTS! NO MORE STINKY NERDS! I'M OVER IT! MAYBE WE JUST HAVE TO DEAL WITH ONE YEAR APART...
A-AND PROTECT LILI'S HEAD...
WAIT!
WE'LL MAKE OUR OWN CLUB!

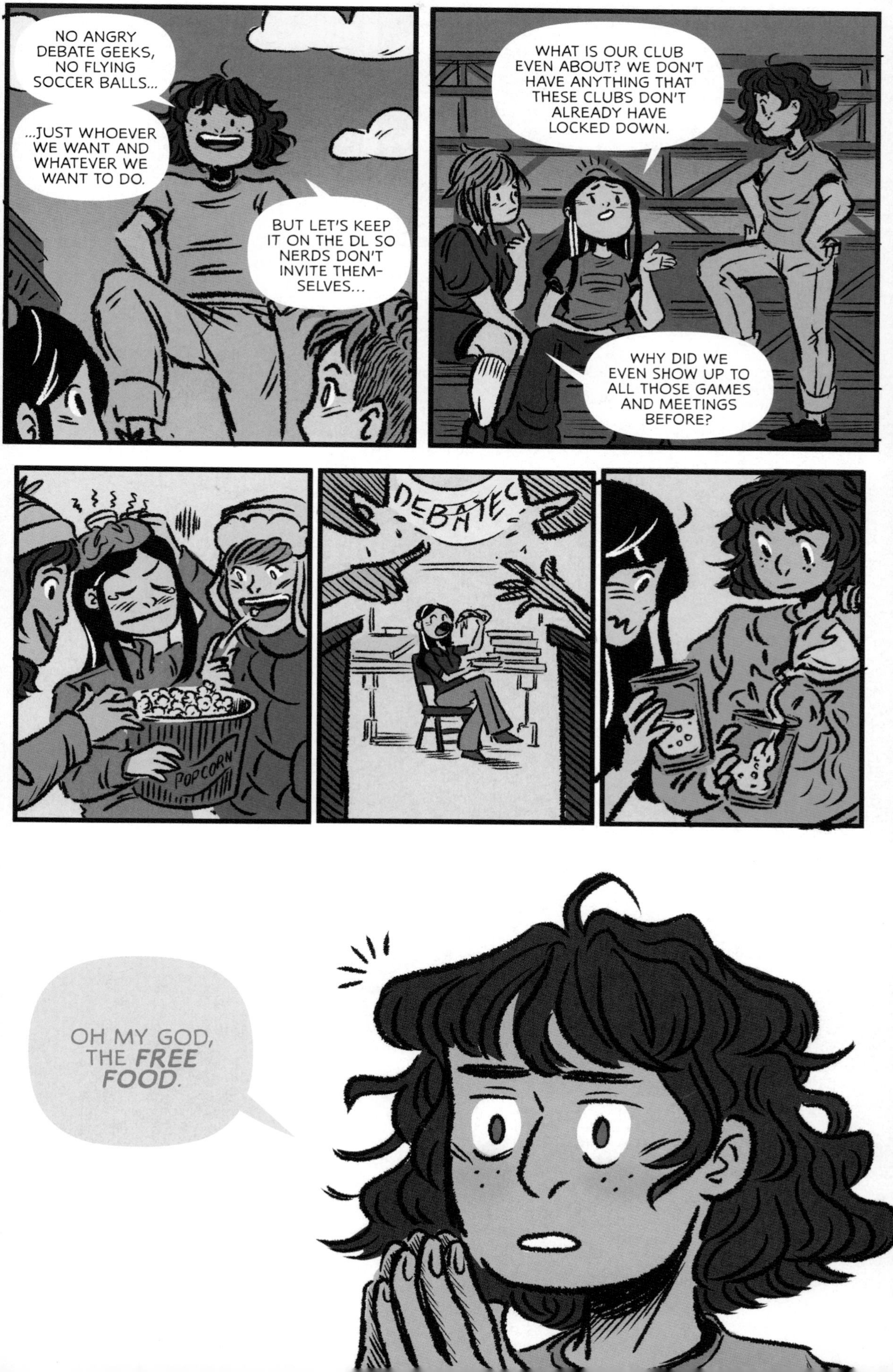
NO ANGRY DEBATE GEEKS, NO FLYING SOCCER BALLS...
...JUST WHOEVER WE WANT AND WHATEVER WE WANT TO DO.
BUT LET'S KEEP IT ON THE DL SO NERDS DON'T INVITE THEMSELVES...
WHAT IS OUR CLUB EVEN ABOUT? WE DON'T HAVE ANYTHING THAT THESE CLUBS DON'T ALREADY HAVE LOCKED DOWN.
WHY DID WE EVEN SHOW UP TO ALL THOSE GAMES AND MEETINGS BEFORE?
POPCORN
DEBATEC
OH MY GOD, THE *FREE FOOD*.

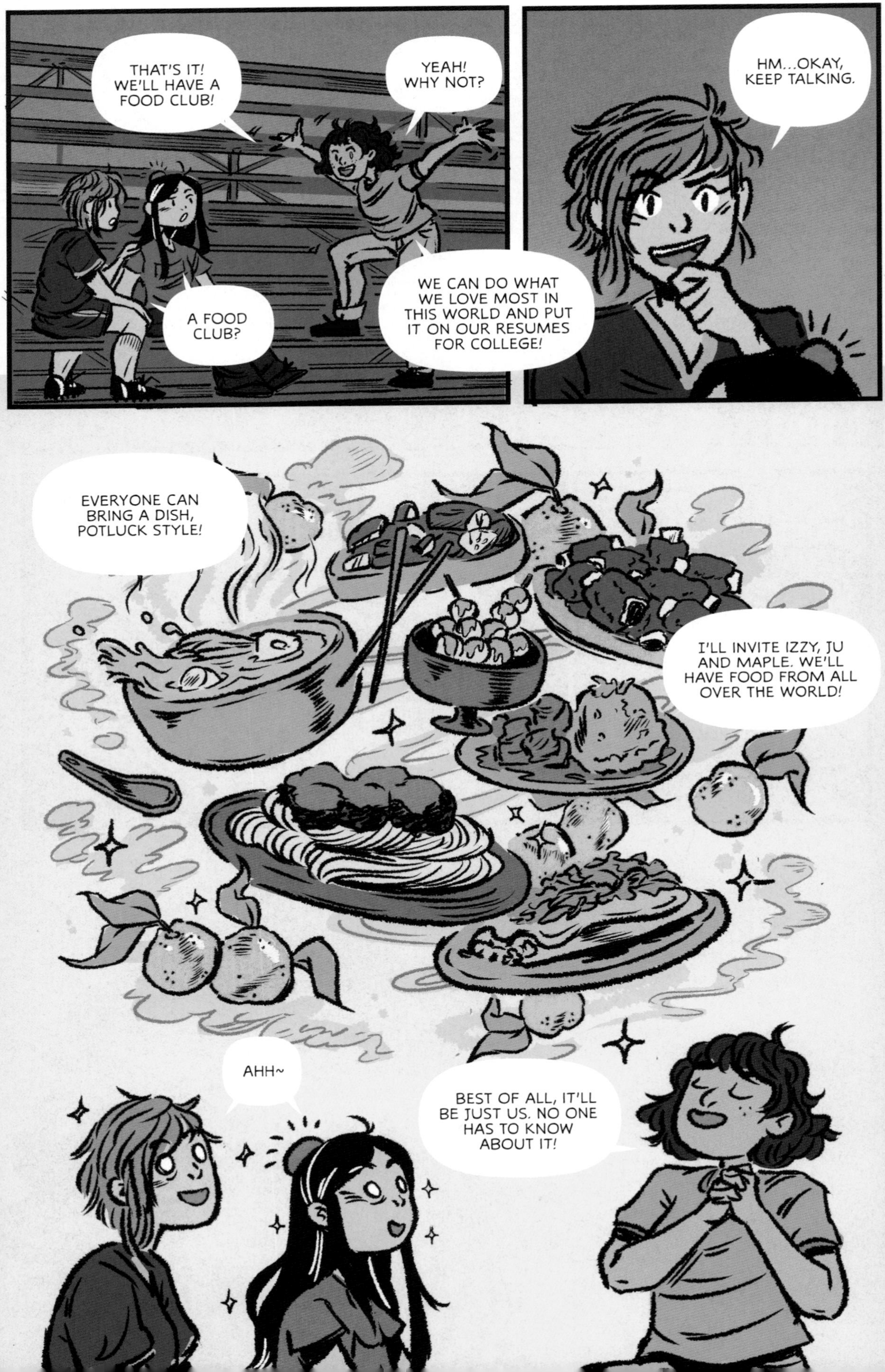
THAT'S IT! WE'LL HAVE A FOOD CLUB!
YEAH! WHY NOT?
A FOOD CLUB?
WE CAN DO WHAT WE LOVE MOST IN THIS WORLD AND PUT IT ON OUR RESUMES FOR COLLEGE!
HM...OKAY, KEEP TALKING.
EVERYONE CAN BRING A DISH, POTLUCK STYLE!
I'LL INVITE IZZY, JU AND MAPLE. WE'LL HAVE FOOD FROM ALL OVER THE WORLD!
AHH~
BEST OF ALL, IT'LL BE JUST US. NO ONE HAS TO KNOW ABOUT IT!

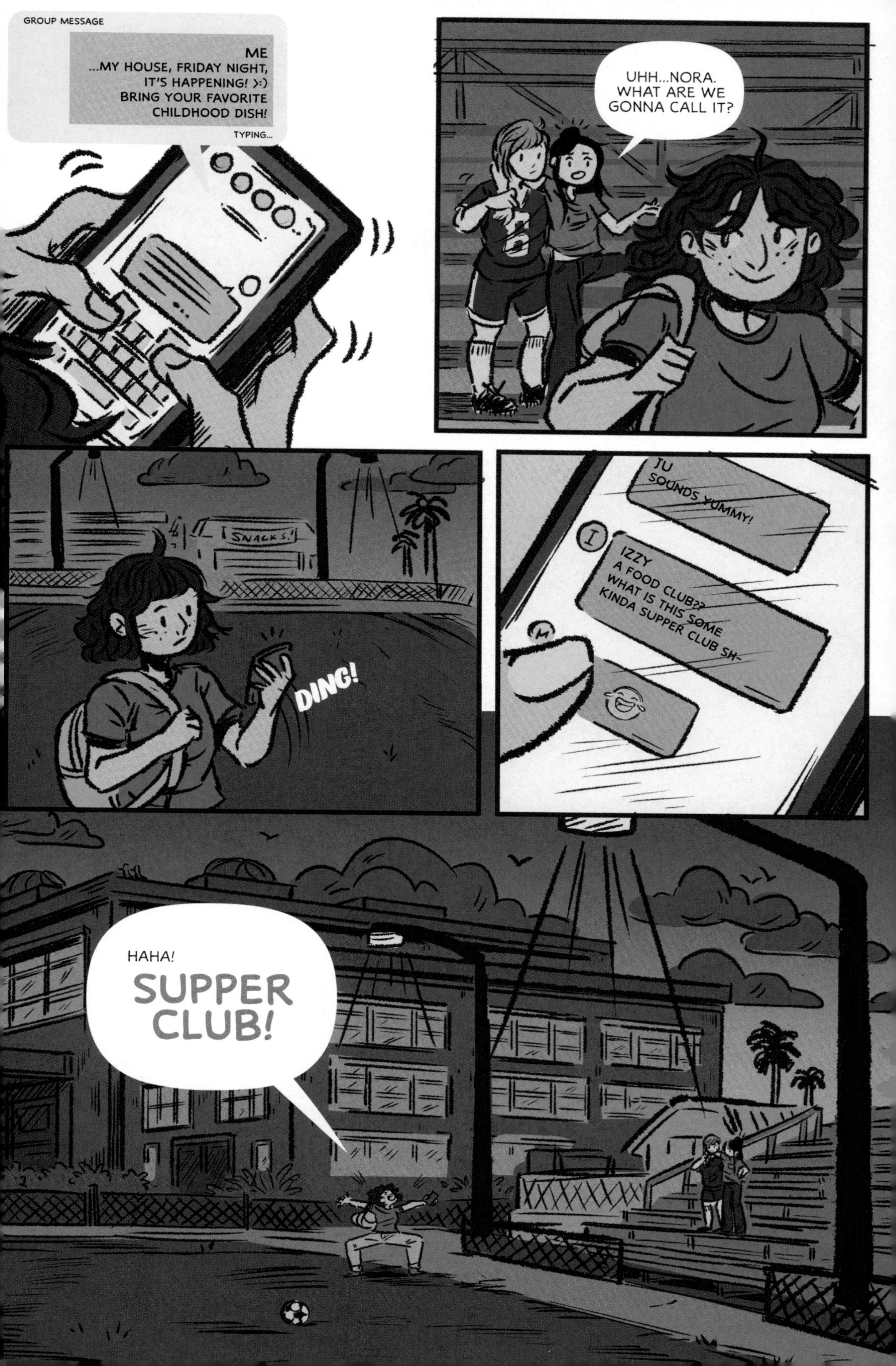

GROUP MESSAGE
ME
...MY HOUSE, FRIDAY NIGHT, IT'S HAPPENING! >:)
BRING YOUR FAVORITE CHILDHOOD DISH!
TYPING...
UHH...NORA. WHAT ARE WE GONNA CALL IT?
SNACKS.
DING!
JU
SOUNDS YUMMY!
IZZY
A FOOD CLUB??
WHAT IS THIS SOME KINDA SUPPER CLUB SH-
HAHA!
SUPPER CLUB!

Chapter Two
rainbow cookies

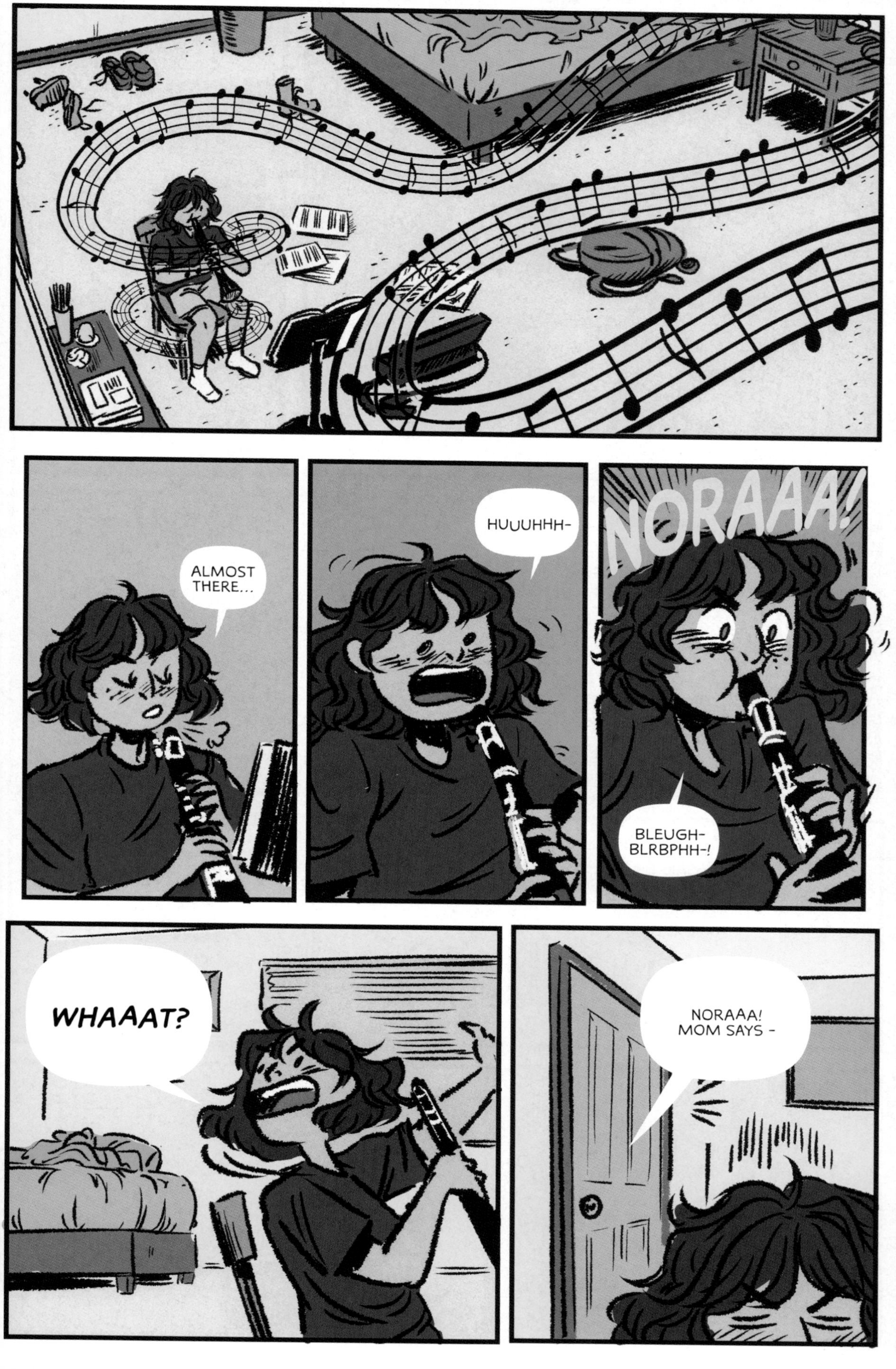
ALMOST THERE...
HUUUHHH-
NORAAA!
BLEUGH-BLRBPHH-!
WHAAAT?
NORAAA! MOM SAYS -

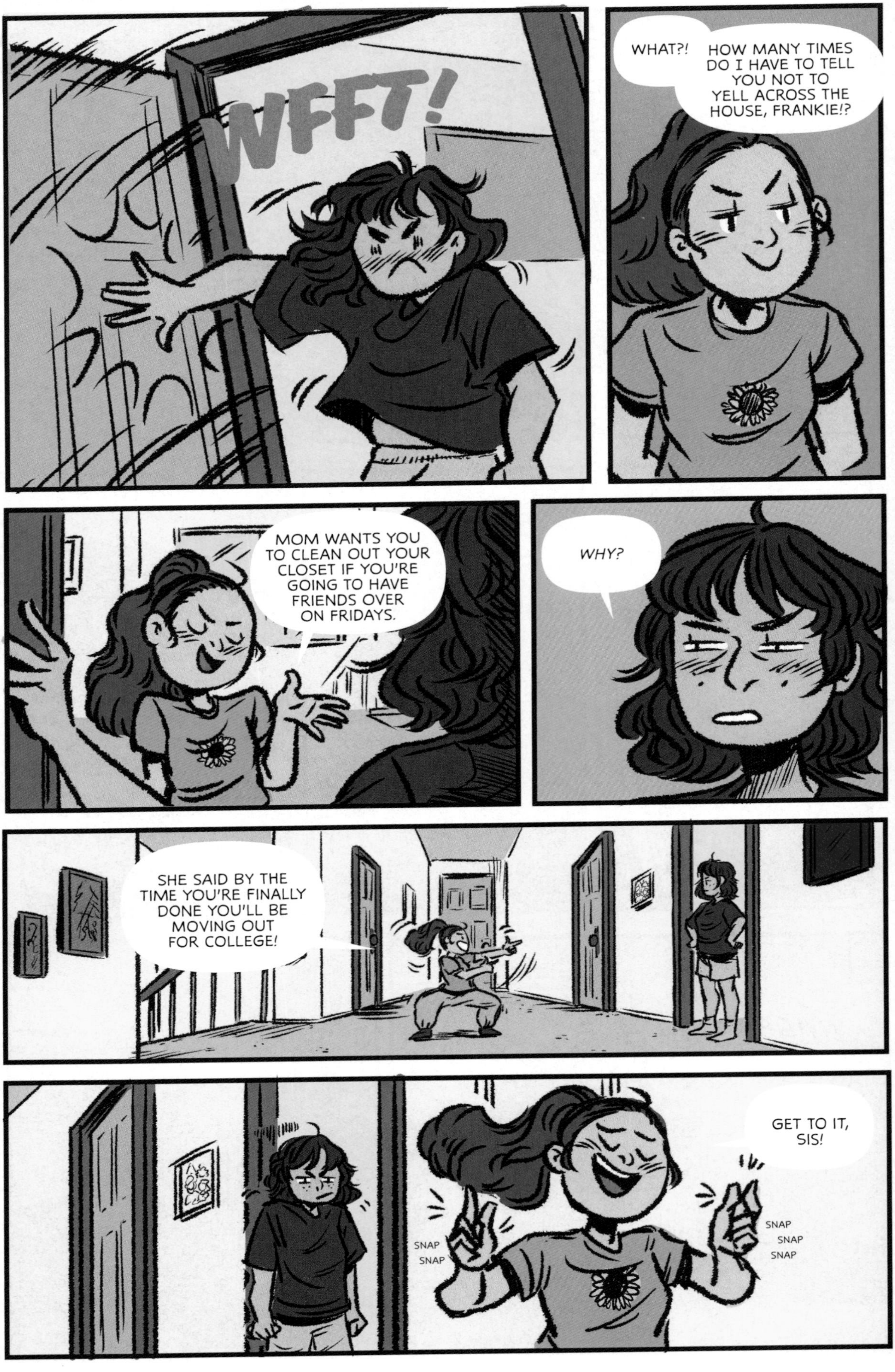
WFFT!
WHAT?!
HOW MANY TIMES DO I HAVE TO TELL YOU NOT TO YELL ACROSS THE HOUSE, FRANKIE!?
MOM WANTS YOU TO CLEAN OUT YOUR CLOSET IF YOU'RE GOING TO HAVE FRIENDS OVER ON FRIDAYS.
WHY?
SHE SAID BY THE TIME YOU'RE FINALLY DONE YOU'LL BE MOVING OUT FOR COLLEGE!
SNAP
SNAP
GET TO IT, SIS!
SNAP
SNAP
SNAP

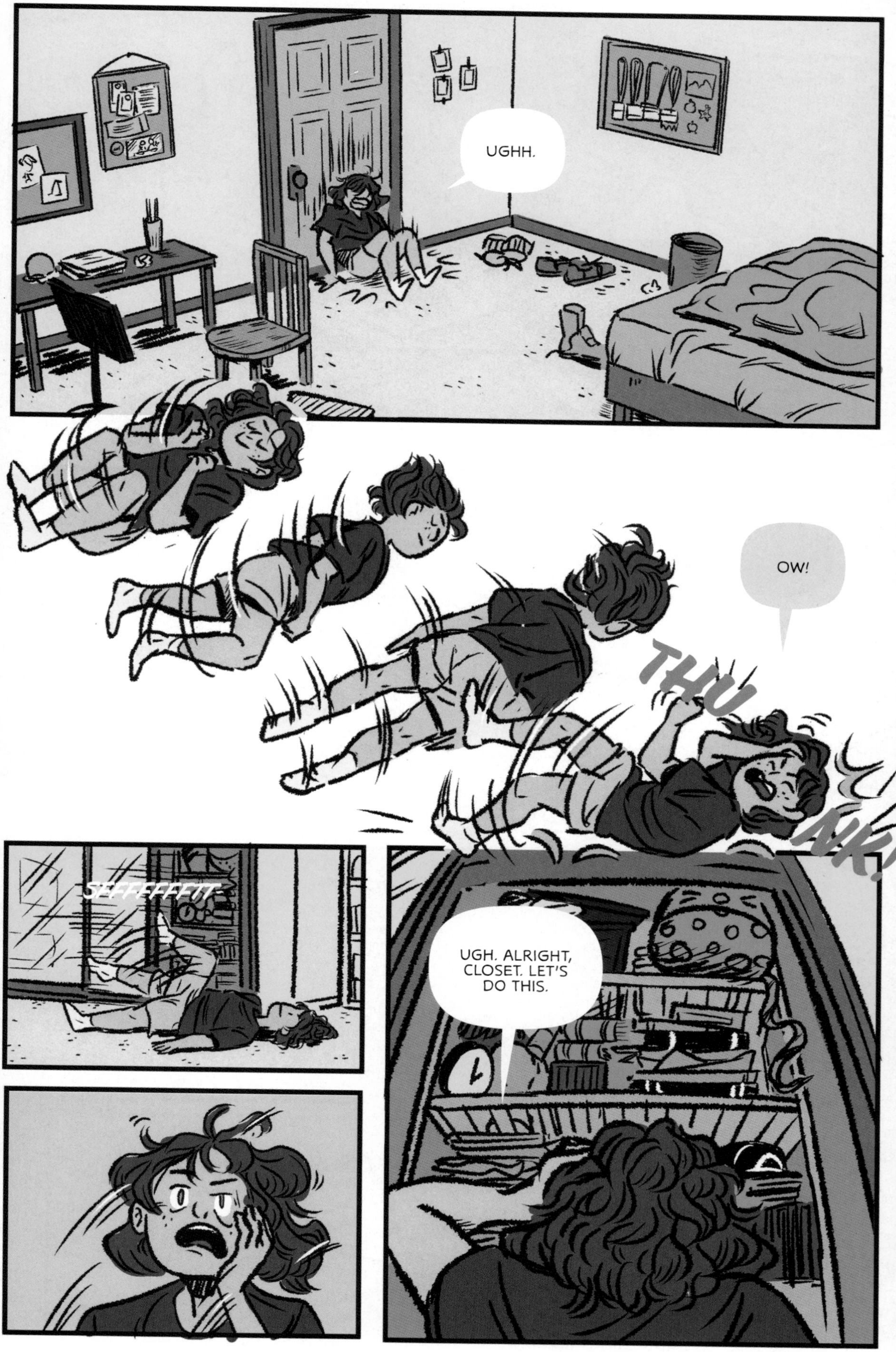
UGHH.
OW!
THUNK!
SFFFFFFFTT-
UGH. ALRIGHT, CLOSET. LET'S DO THIS.

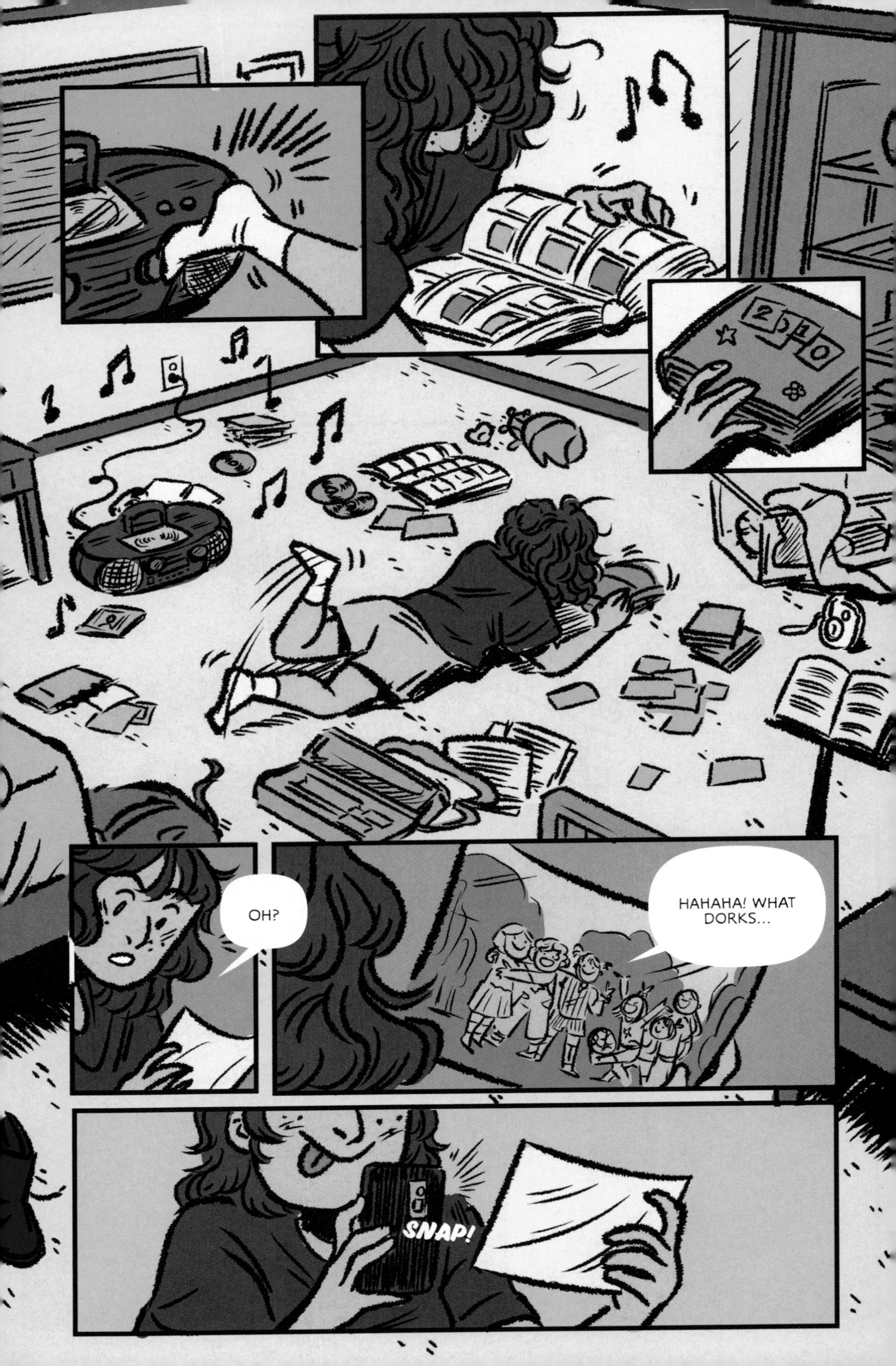
2010
OH?
HAHAHA! WHAT DORKS...
SNAP!

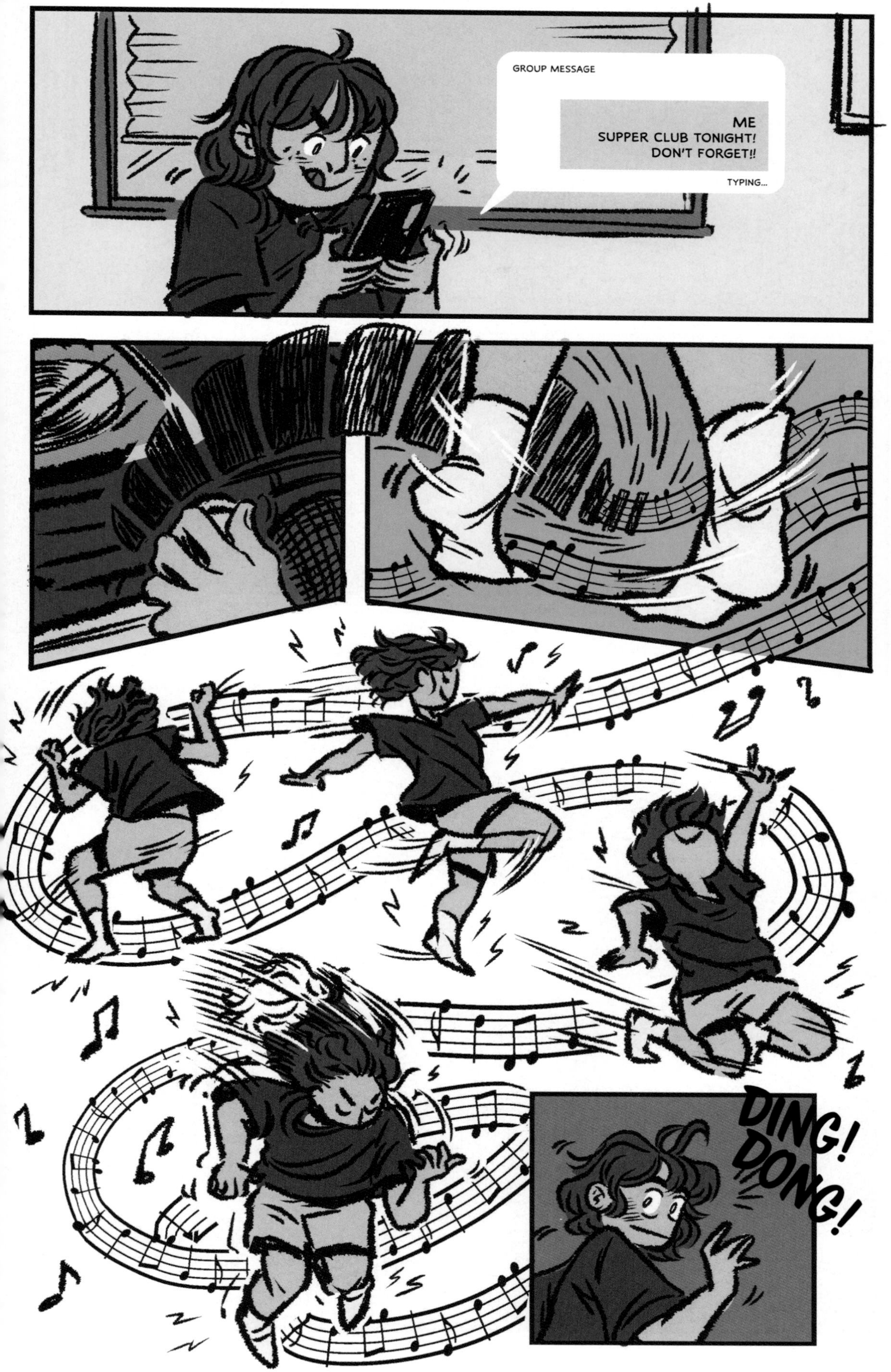
GROUP MESSAGE
ME
SUPPER CLUB TONIGHT!
DON'T FORGET!!
TYPING...
DING! DONG!

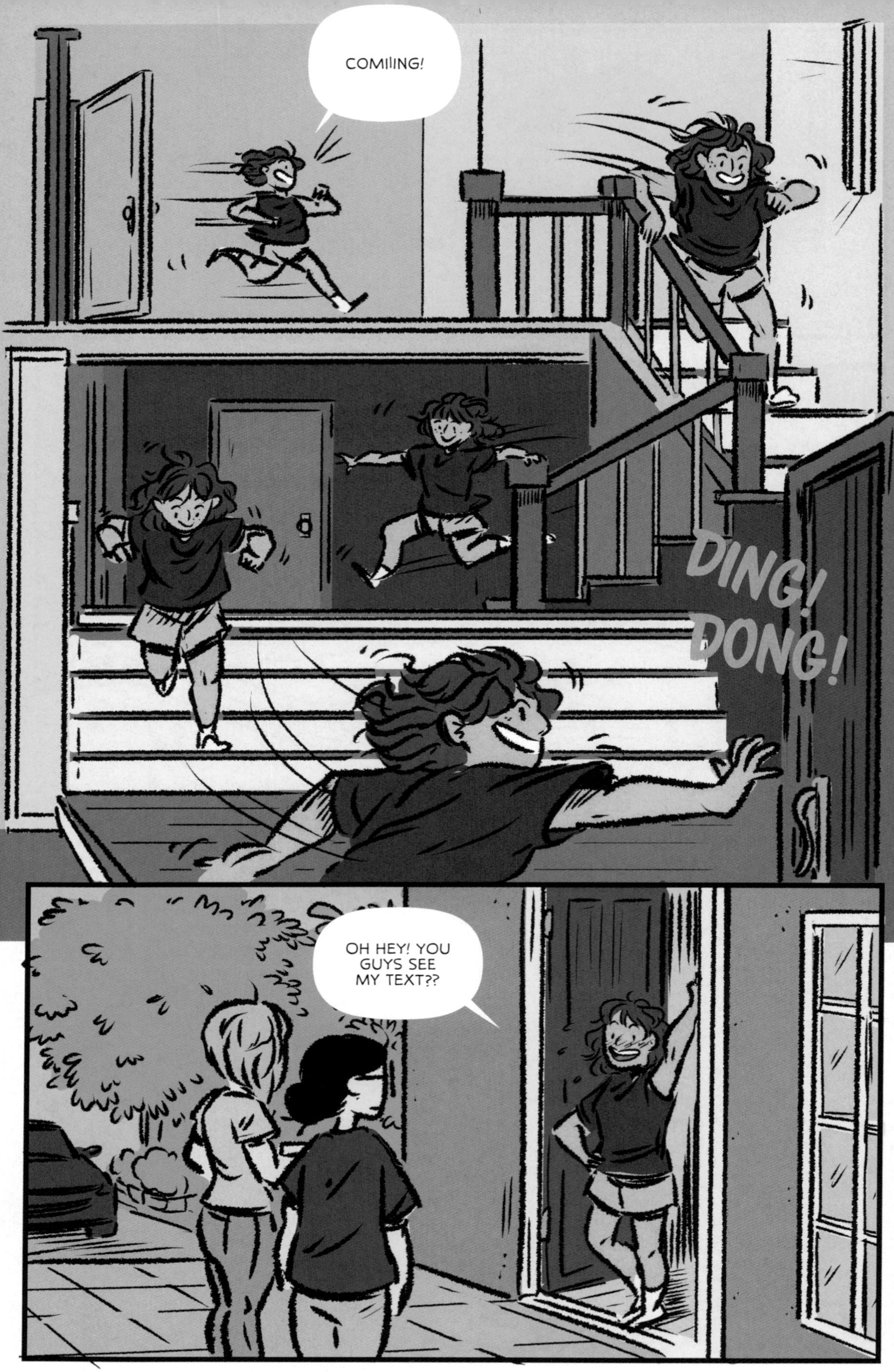
COMIIING!
DING! DONG!
OH HEY! YOU GUYS SEE MY TEXT??

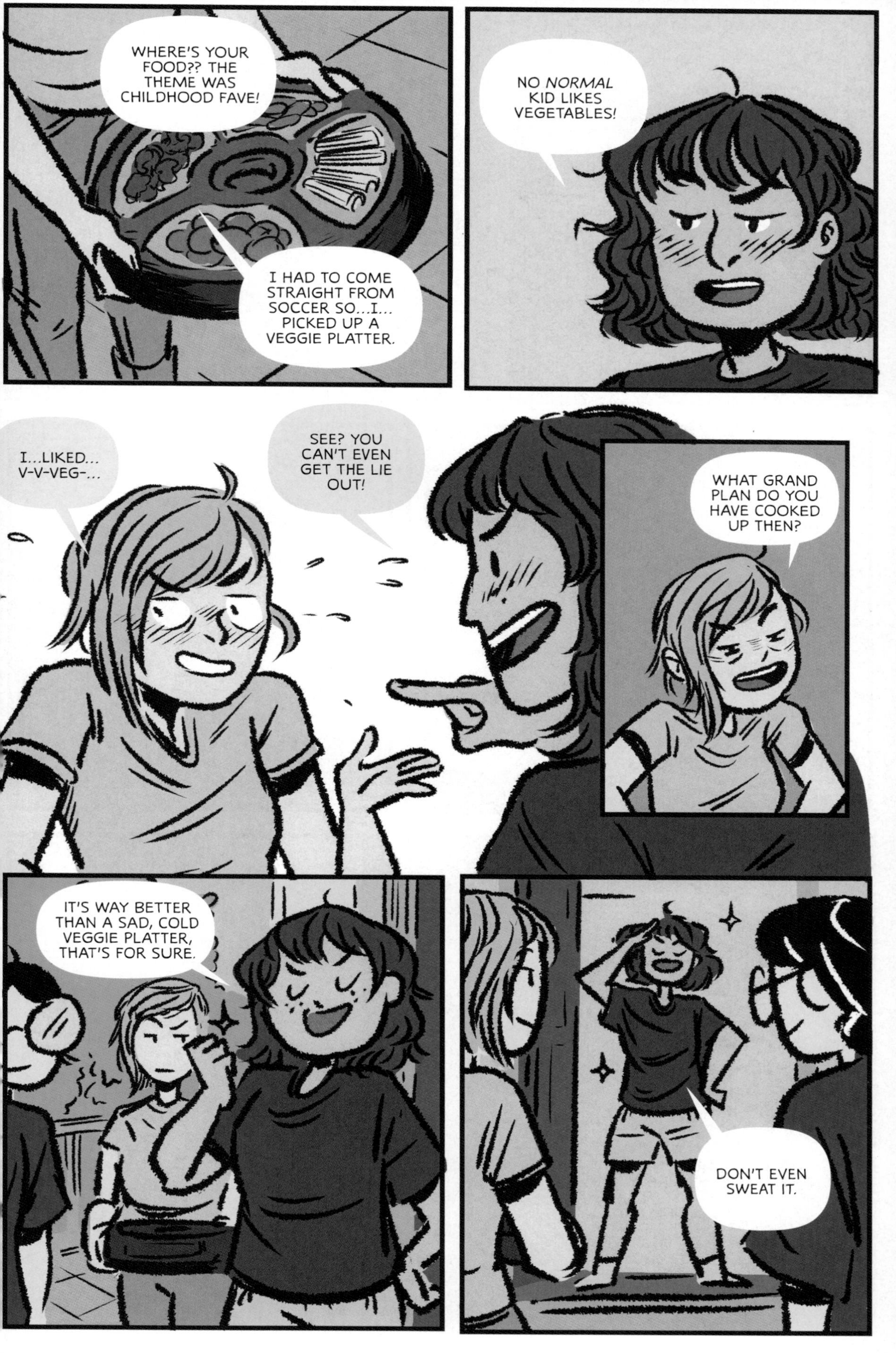
WHERE'S YOUR FOOD?? THE THEME WAS CHILDHOOD FAVE!
I HAD TO COME STRAIGHT FROM SOCCER SO...I... PICKED UP A VEGGIE PLATTER.
NO *NORMAL* KID LIKES VEGETABLES!
I...LIKED... V-V-VEG-...
SEE? YOU CAN'T EVEN GET THE LIE OUT!
WHAT GRAND PLAN DO YOU HAVE COOKED UP THEN?
IT'S WAY BETTER THAN A SAD, COLD VEGGIE PLATTER, THAT'S FOR SURE.
DON'T EVEN SWEAT IT.

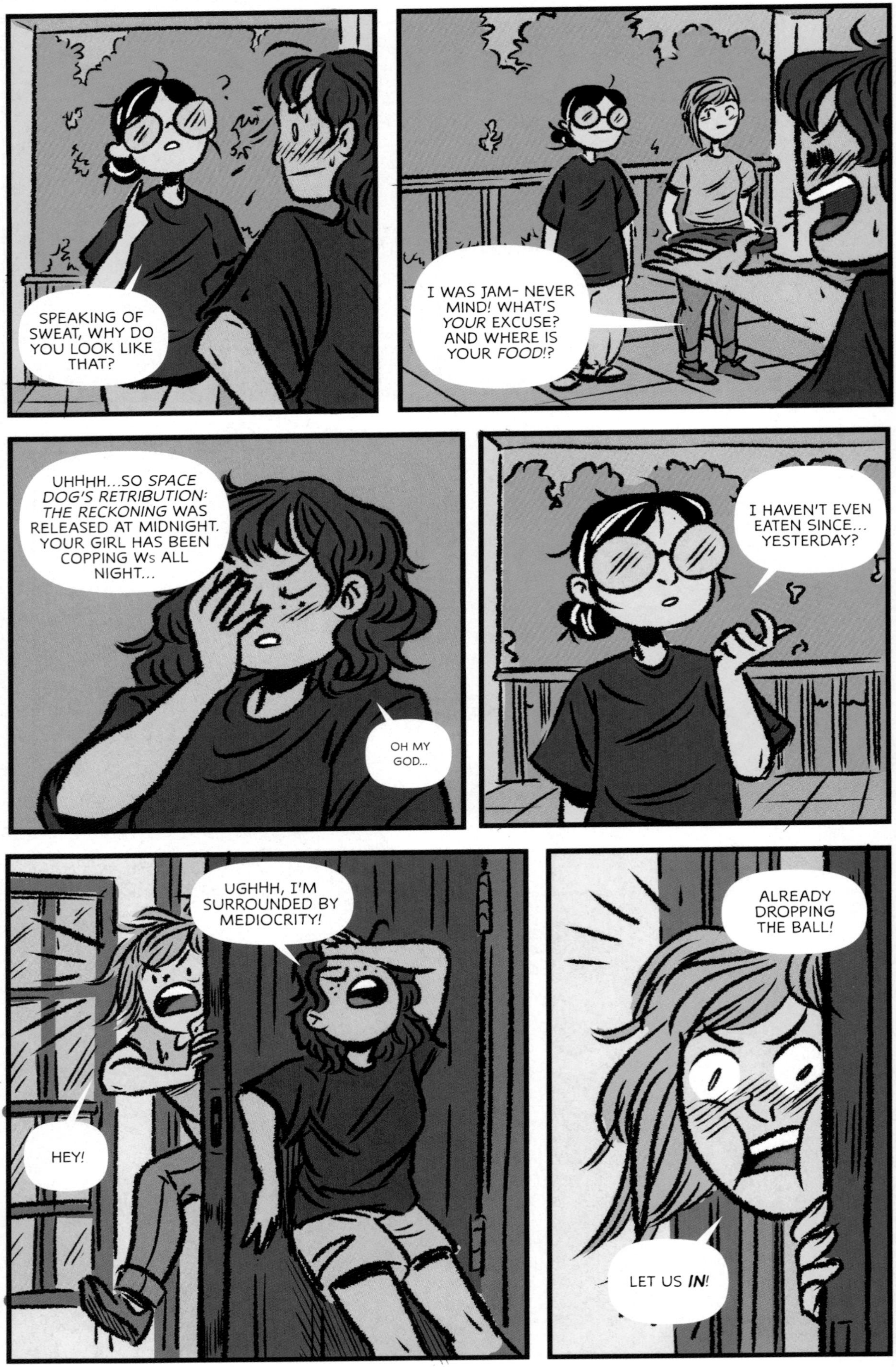
SPEAKING OF SWEAT, WHY DO YOU LOOK LIKE THAT?
I WAS JAM- NEVER MIND! WHAT'S *YOUR* EXCUSE? AND WHERE IS YOUR *FOOD!*?
UHHHH...SO *SPACE DOG'S RETRIBUTION: THE RECKONING* WAS RELEASED AT MIDNIGHT. YOUR GIRL HAS BEEN COPPING Ws ALL NIGHT...
OH MY GOD...
I HAVEN'T EVEN EATEN SINCE... YESTERDAY?
UGHHH, I'M SURROUNDED BY MEDIOCRITY!
HEY!
ALREADY DROPPING THE BALL!
LET US ***IN***!

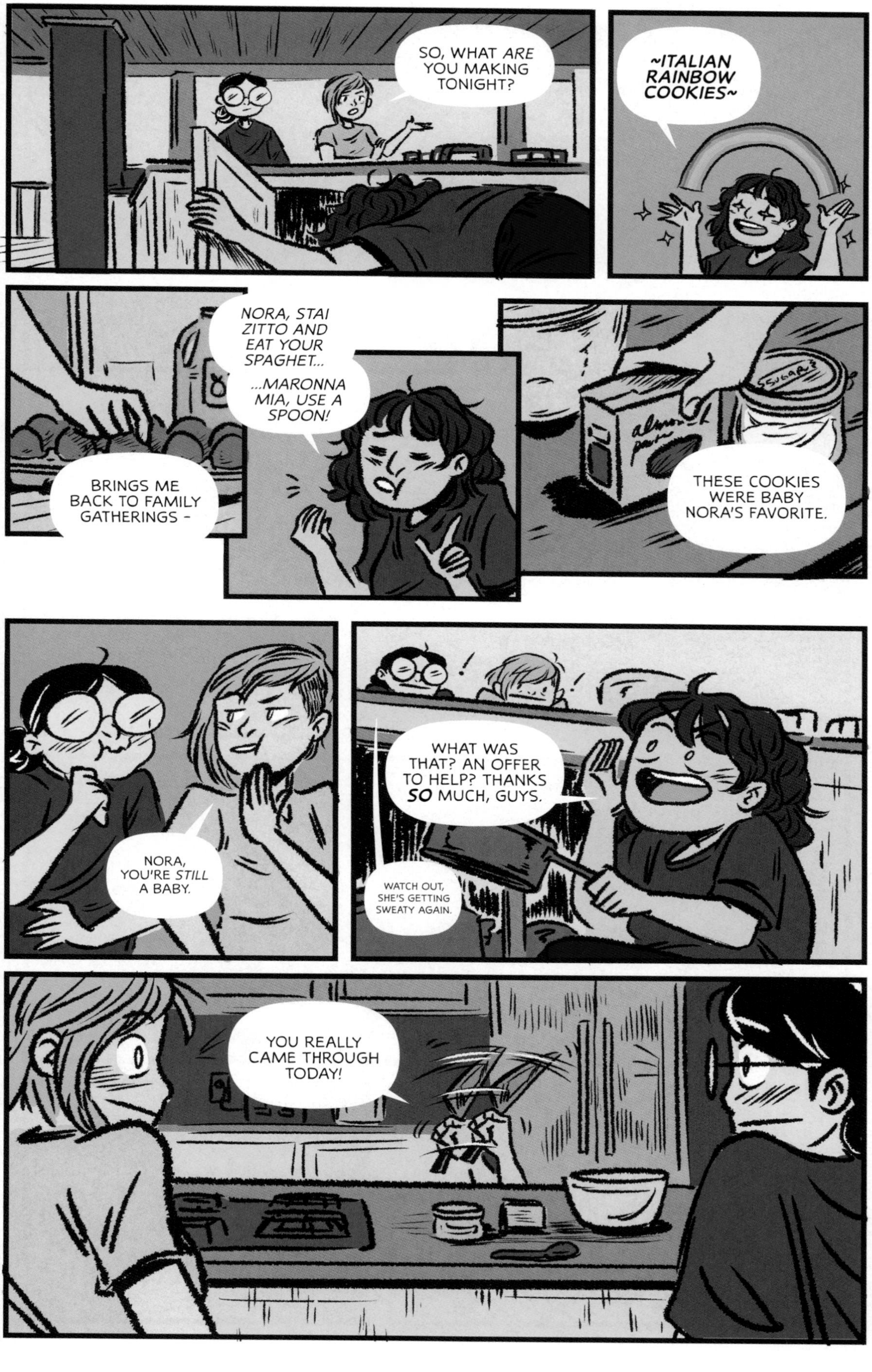
SO, WHAT *ARE* YOU MAKING TONIGHT?
~ITALIAN RAINBOW COOKIES~
NORA, STAI ZITTO AND EAT YOUR SPAGHET...
...MARONNA MIA, USE A SPOON!
BRINGS ME BACK TO FAMILY GATHERINGS -
SSUGAR??
almond paste
THESE COOKIES WERE BABY NORA'S FAVORITE.
NORA, YOU'RE *STILL* A BABY.
WHAT WAS THAT? AN OFFER TO HELP? THANKS ***SO*** MUCH, GUYS.
WATCH OUT, SHE'S GETTING SWEATY AGAIN.
YOU REALLY CAME THROUGH TODAY!

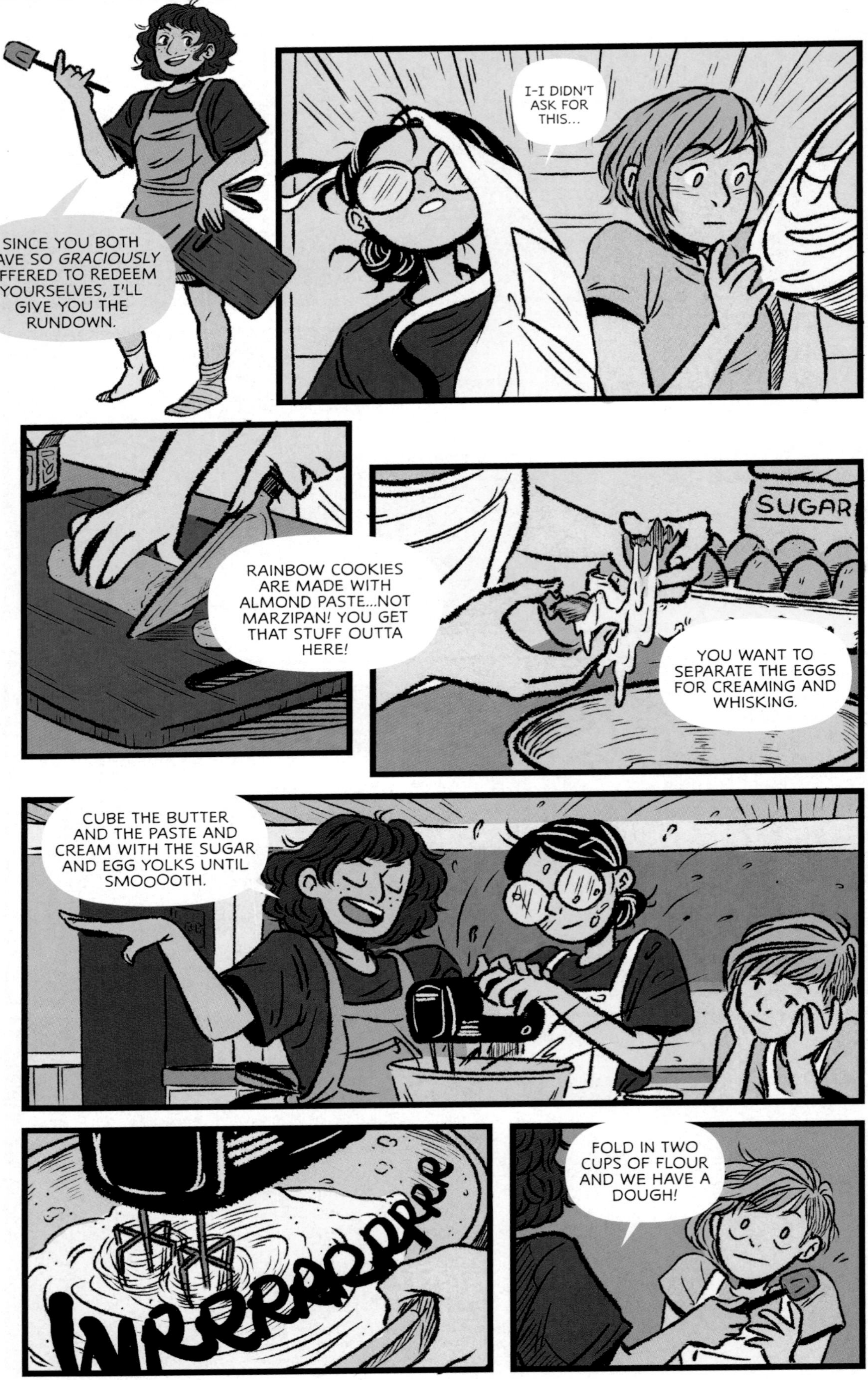
SINCE YOU BOTH HAVE SO *GRACIOUSLY* OFFERED TO REDEEM YOURSELVES, I'LL GIVE YOU THE RUNDOWN.
I-I DIDN'T ASK FOR THIS...
RAINBOW COOKIES ARE MADE WITH ALMOND PASTE...NOT MARZIPAN! YOU GET THAT STUFF OUTTA HERE!
SUGAR
YOU WANT TO SEPARATE THE EGGS FOR CREAMING AND WHISKING.
CUBE THE BUTTER AND THE PASTE AND CREAM WITH THE SUGAR AND EGG YOLKS UNTIL SMOOOOTH.
WRRRRRRRRR
FOLD IN TWO CUPS OF FLOUR AND WE HAVE A DOUGH!

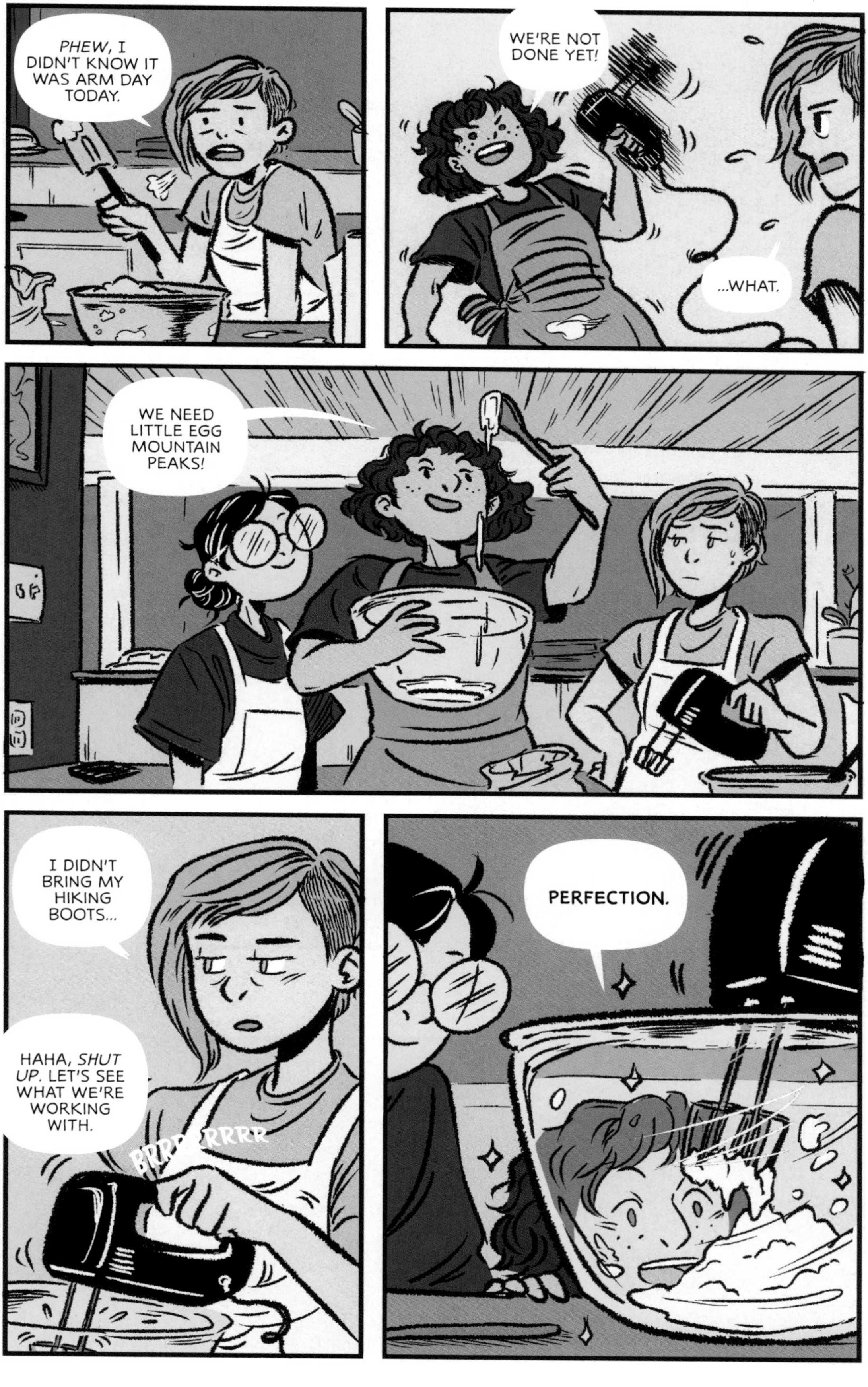
PHEW, I DIDN'T KNOW IT WAS ARM DAY TODAY.
WE'RE NOT DONE YET!
...WHAT.
WE NEED LITTLE EGG MOUNTAIN PEAKS!
I DIDN'T BRING MY HIKING BOOTS...
HAHA, *SHUT UP*. LET'S SEE WHAT WE'RE WORKING WITH.
BRRRRRRR
PERFECTION.

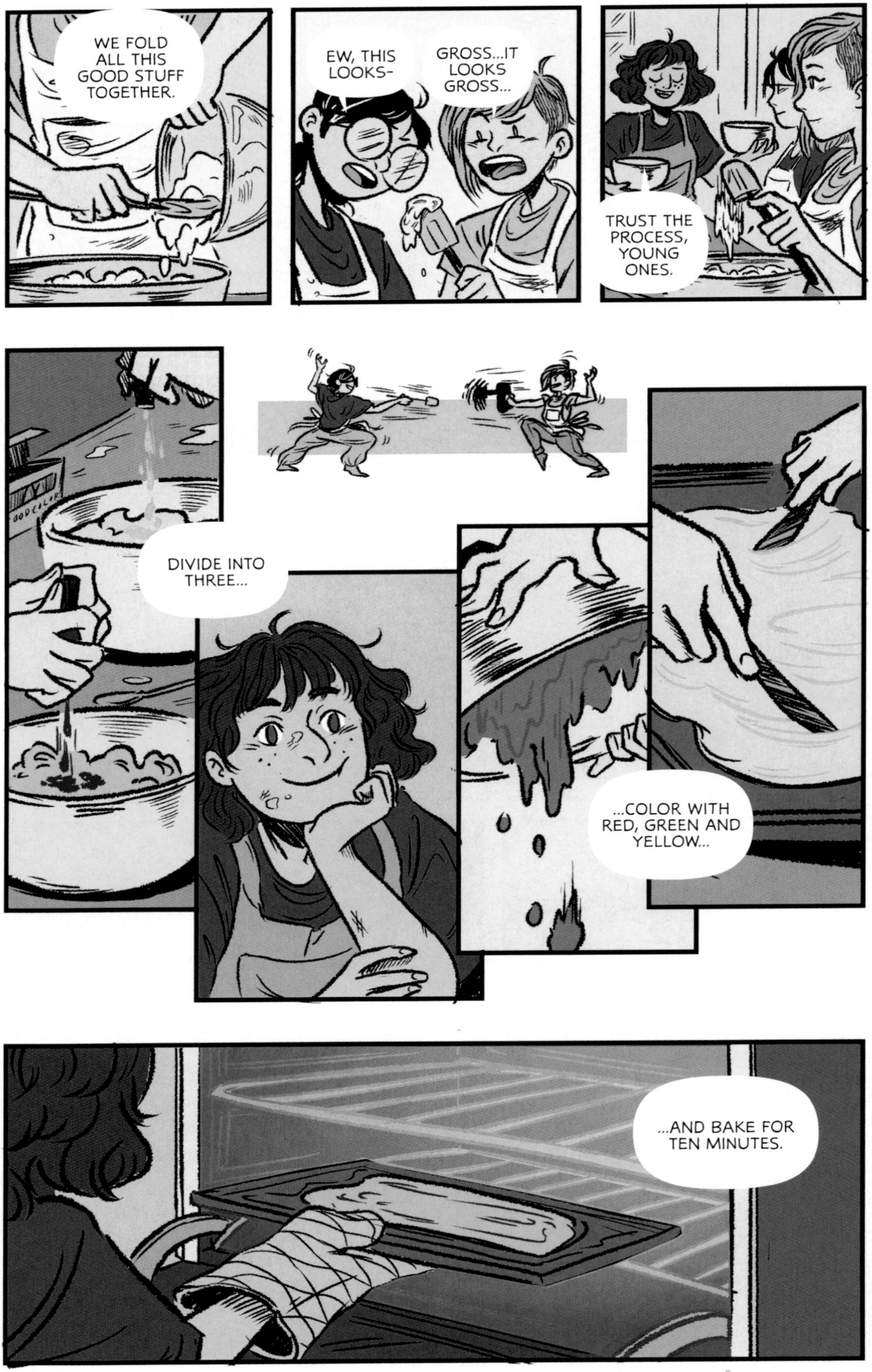
WE FOLD ALL THIS GOOD STUFF TOGETHER.
EW, THIS LOOKS-
GROSS...IT LOOKS GROSS...
TRUST THE PROCESS, YOUNG ONES.
DIVIDE INTO THREE...
...COLOR WITH RED, GREEN AND YELLOW...
...AND BAKE FOR TEN MINUTES.

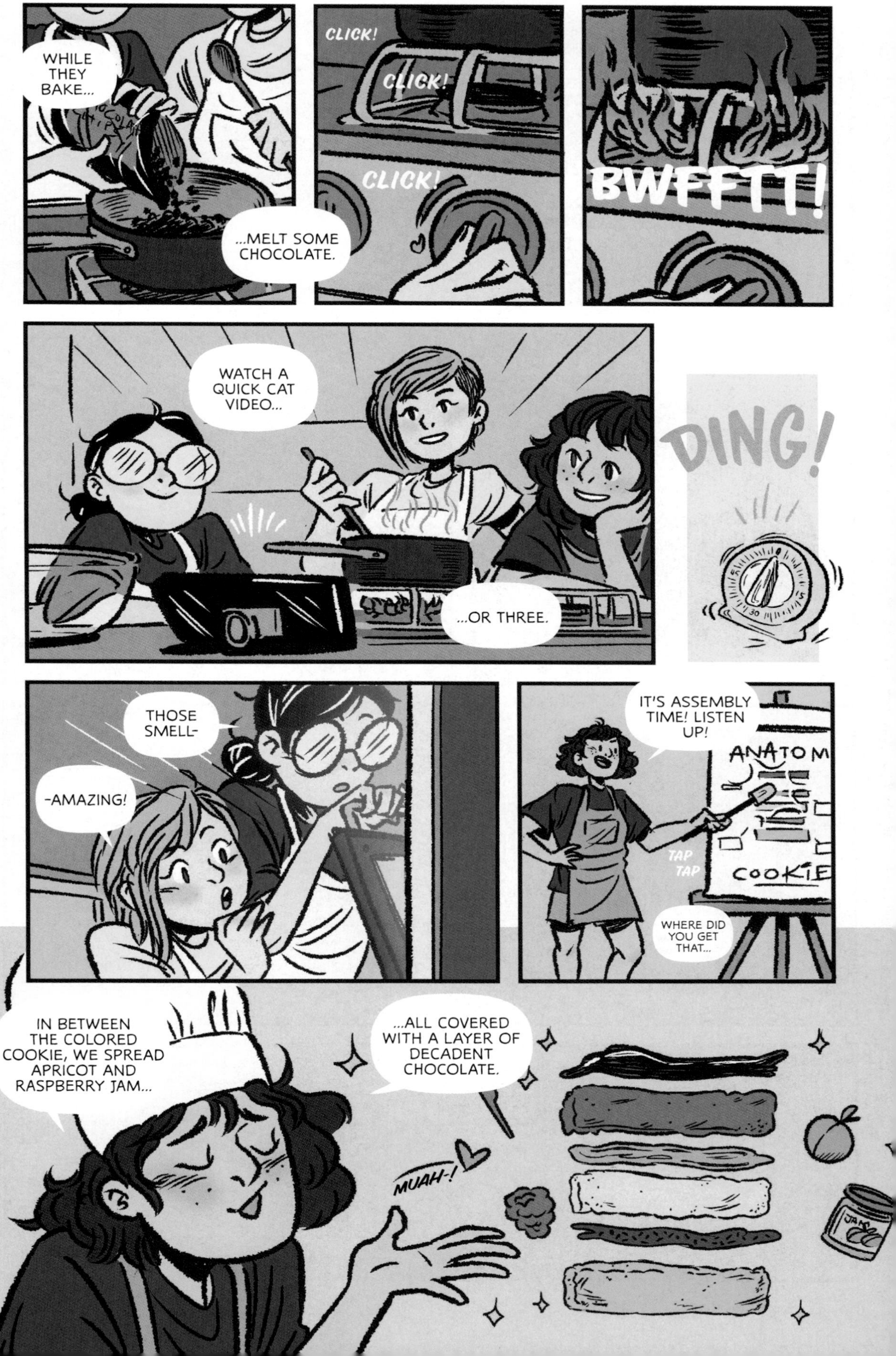
WHILE THEY BAKE...
CLICK!
CLICK!
CLICK!
...MELT SOME CHOCOLATE.
BWFFTT!
WATCH A QUICK CAT VIDEO...
...OR THREE.
DING!
THOSE SMELL-
-AMAZING!
IT'S ASSEMBLY TIME! LISTEN UP!
ANATOM
COOKIE
TAP TAP
WHERE DID YOU GET THAT...
IN BETWEEN THE COLORED COOKIE, WE SPREAD APRICOT AND RASPBERRY JAM...
...ALL COVERED WITH A LAYER OF DECADENT CHOCOLATE.
MUAH-!
JAM

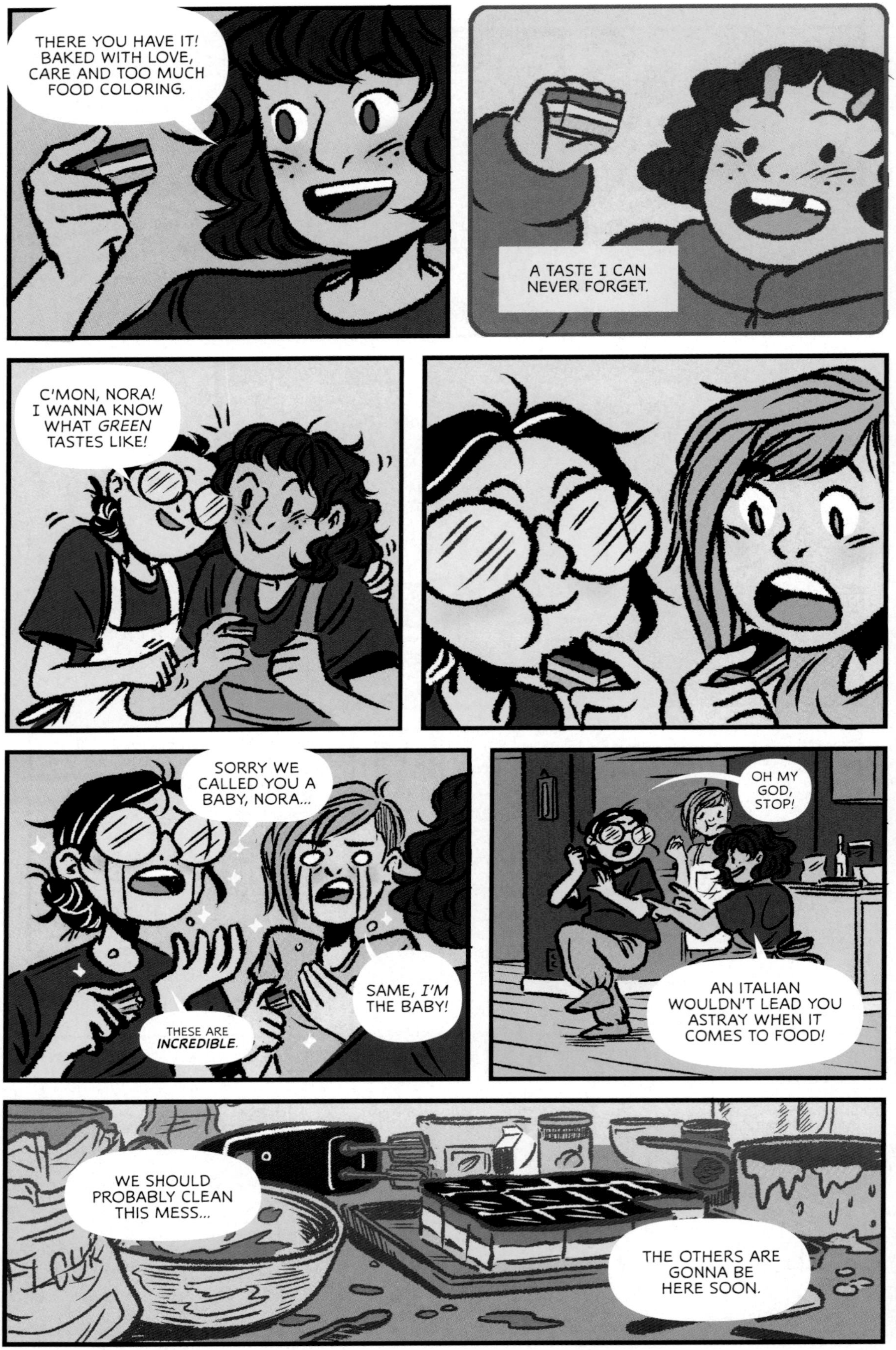
THERE YOU HAVE IT! BAKED WITH LOVE, CARE AND TOO MUCH FOOD COLORING.
A TASTE I CAN NEVER FORGET.
C'MON, NORA! I WANNA KNOW WHAT *GREEN* TASTES LIKE!
SORRY WE CALLED YOU A BABY, NORA...
THESE ARE ***INCREDIBLE***.
SAME, *I'M* THE BABY!
OH MY GOD, STOP!
AN ITALIAN WOULDN'T LEAD YOU ASTRAY WHEN IT COMES TO FOOD!
WE SHOULD PROBABLY CLEAN THIS MESS...
THE OTHERS ARE GONNA BE HERE SOON.

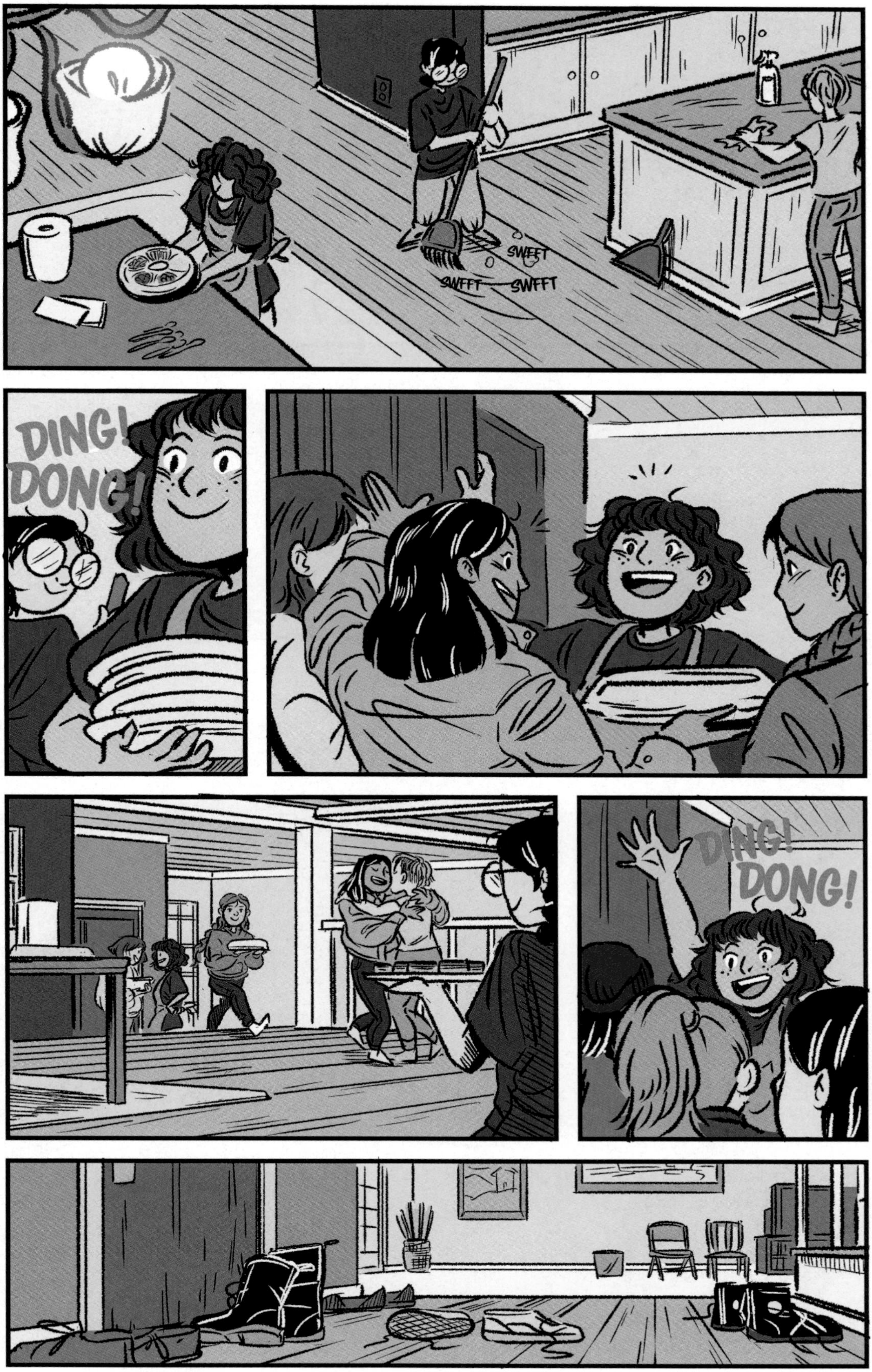
SWFFT
SWFFT
SWFFT
DING! DONG!
DING! DONG!

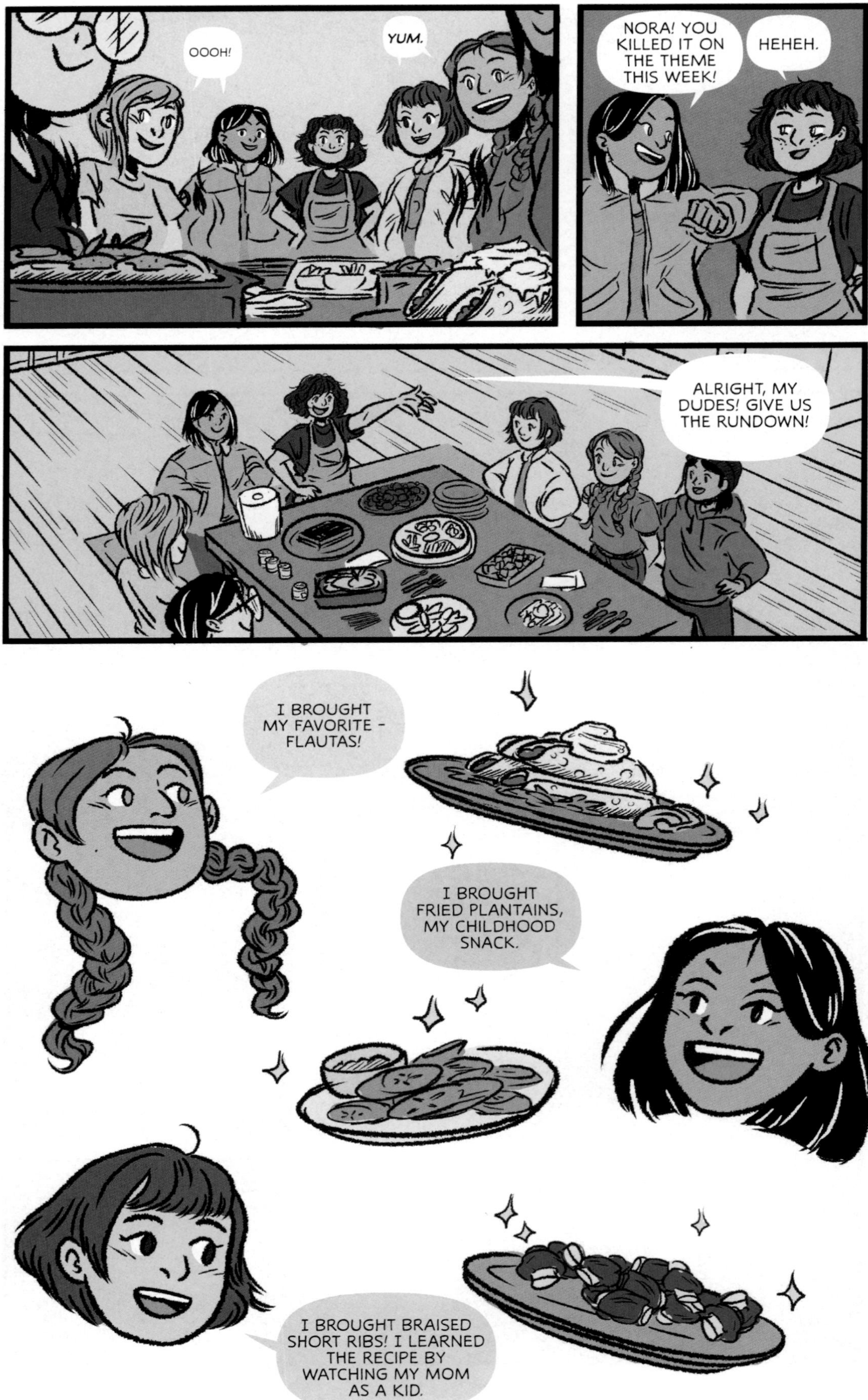
OOOH!
YUM.
NORA! YOU KILLED IT ON THE THEME THIS WEEK!
HEHEH.
ALRIGHT, MY DUDES! GIVE US THE RUNDOWN!
I BROUGHT MY FAVORITE - FLAUTAS!
I BROUGHT FRIED PLANTAINS, MY CHILDHOOD SNACK.
I BROUGHT BRAISED SHORT RIBS! I LEARNED THE RECIPE BY WATCHING MY MOM AS A KID.

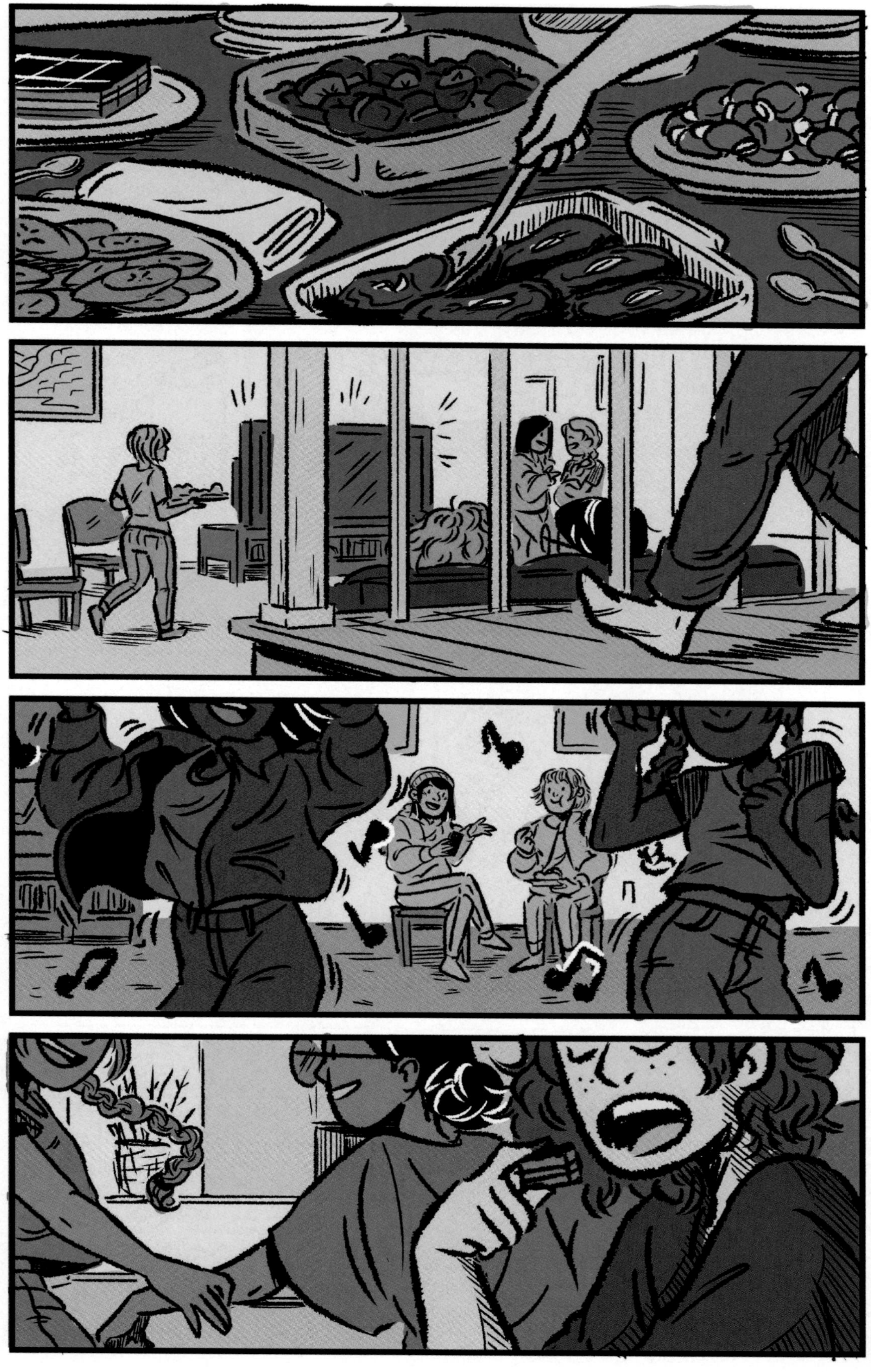

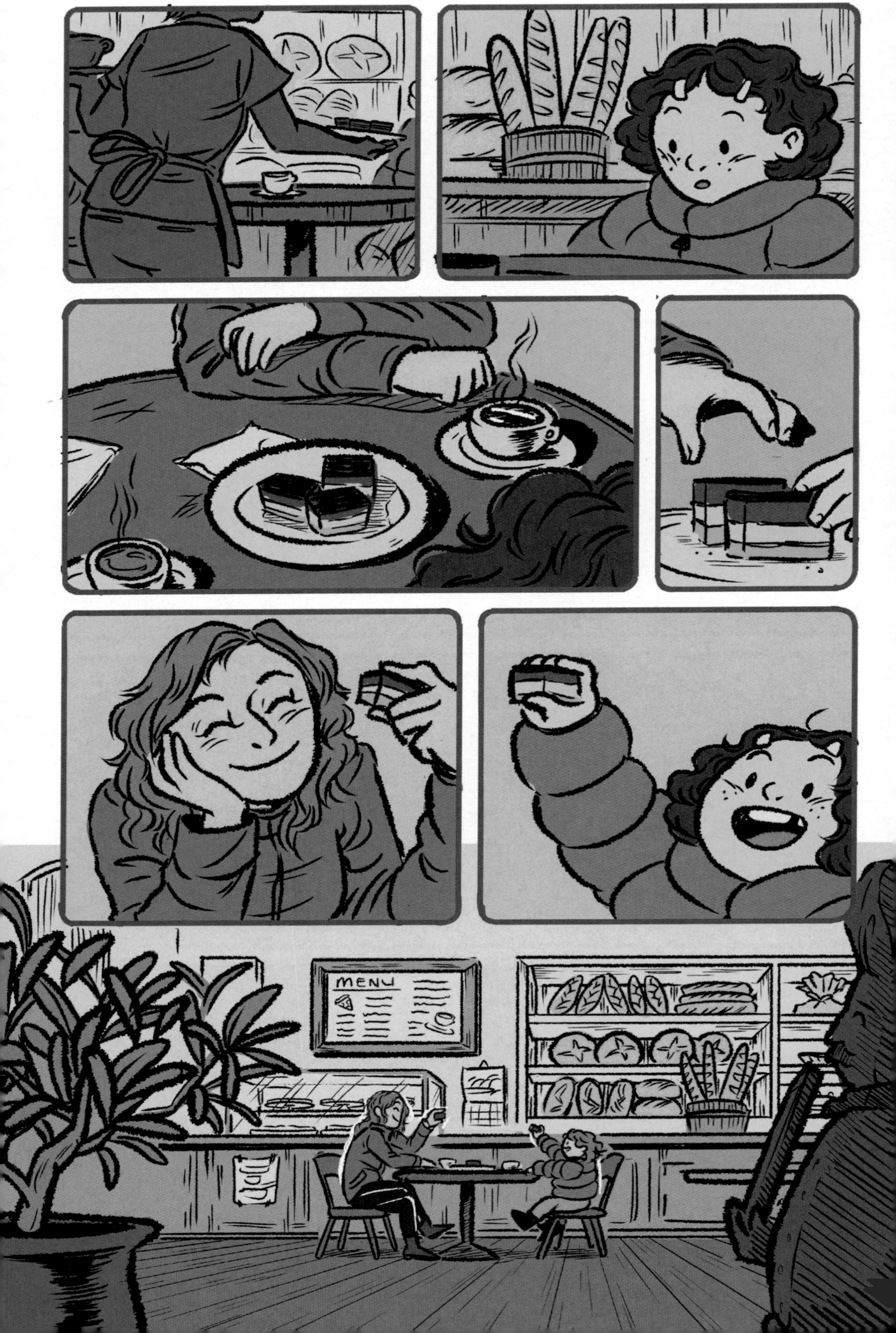
MENU

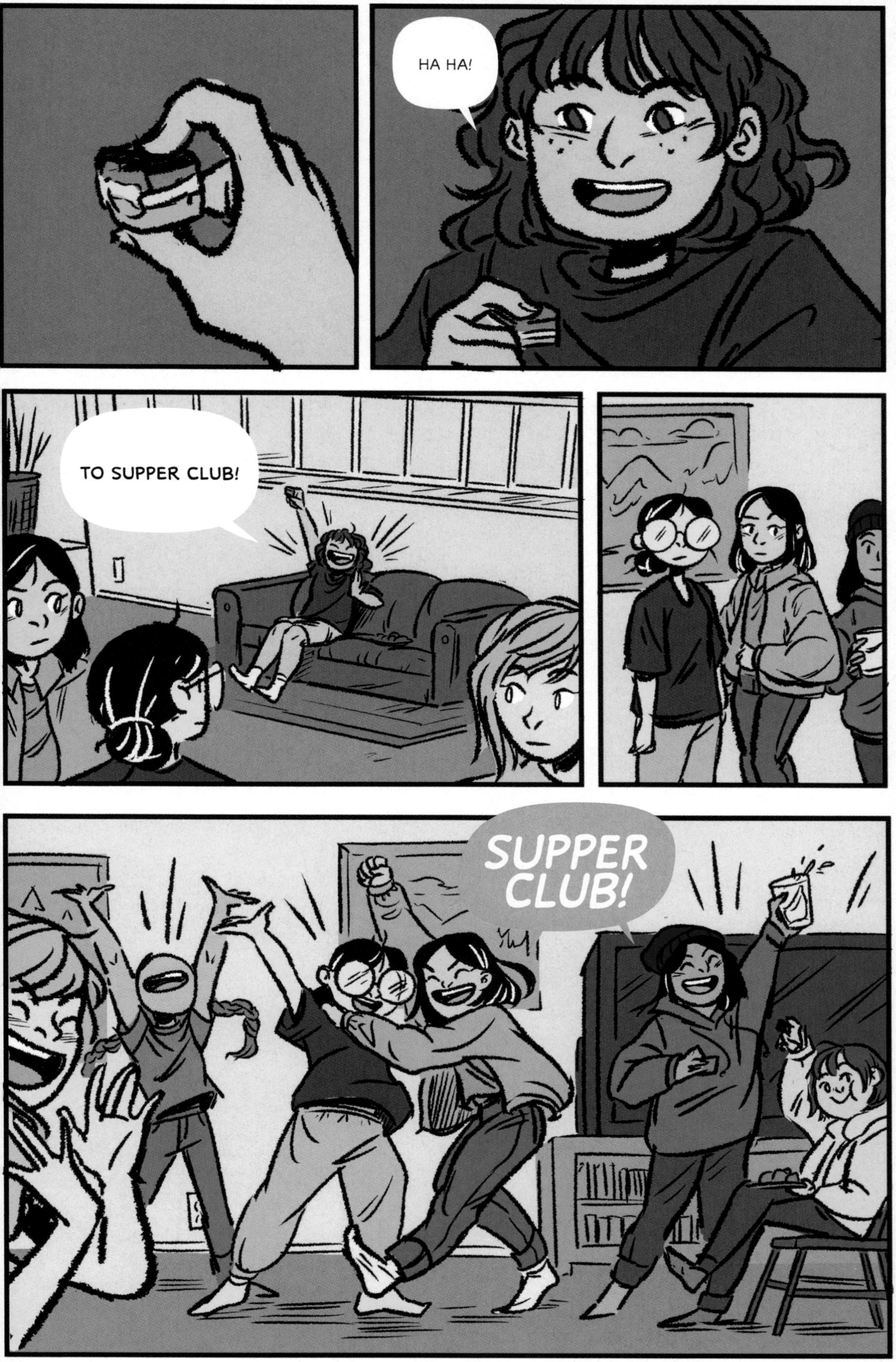
HA HA!
TO SUPPER CLUB!
SUPPER CLUB!

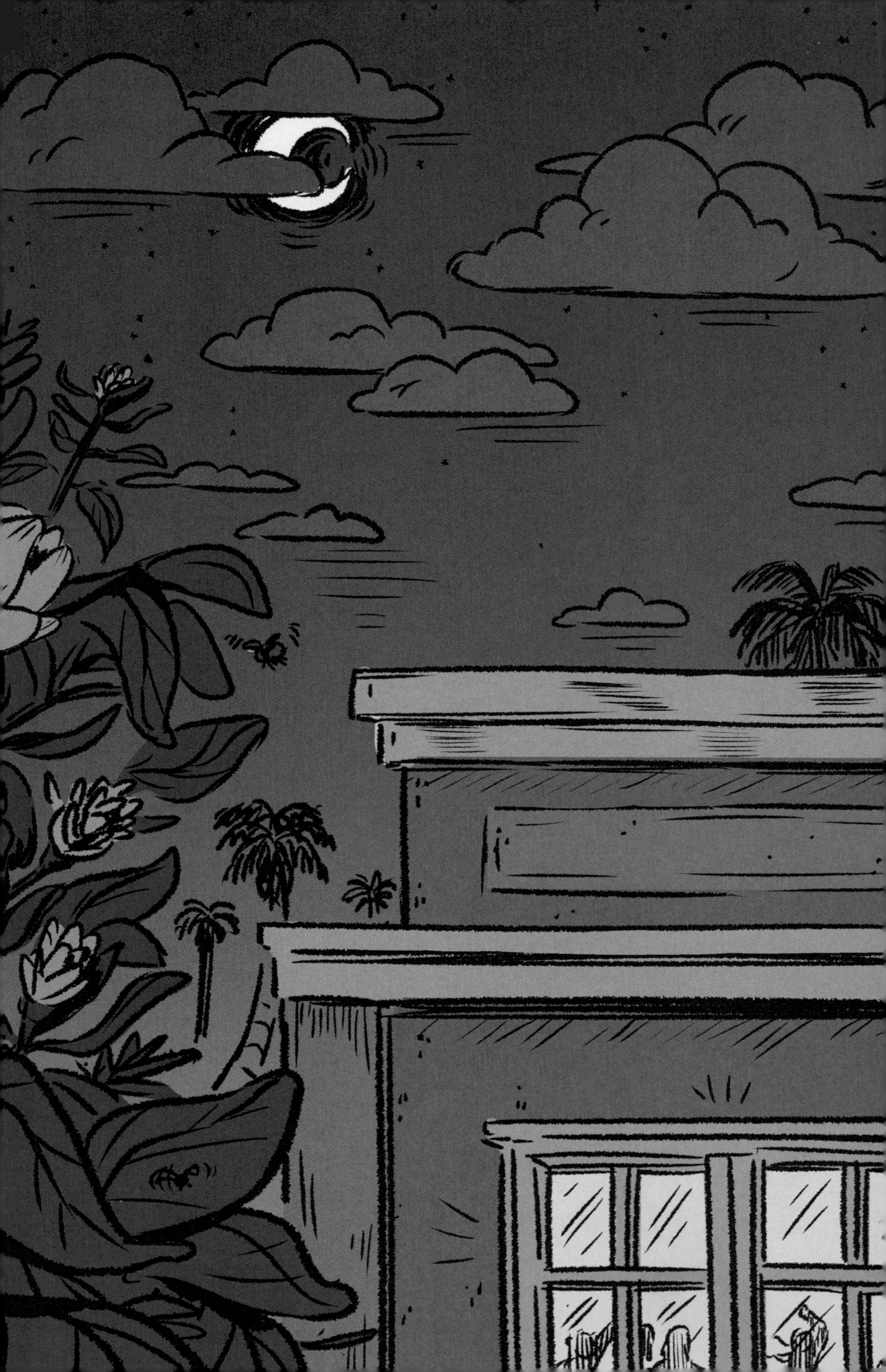

Chapter Three
tofu scramble

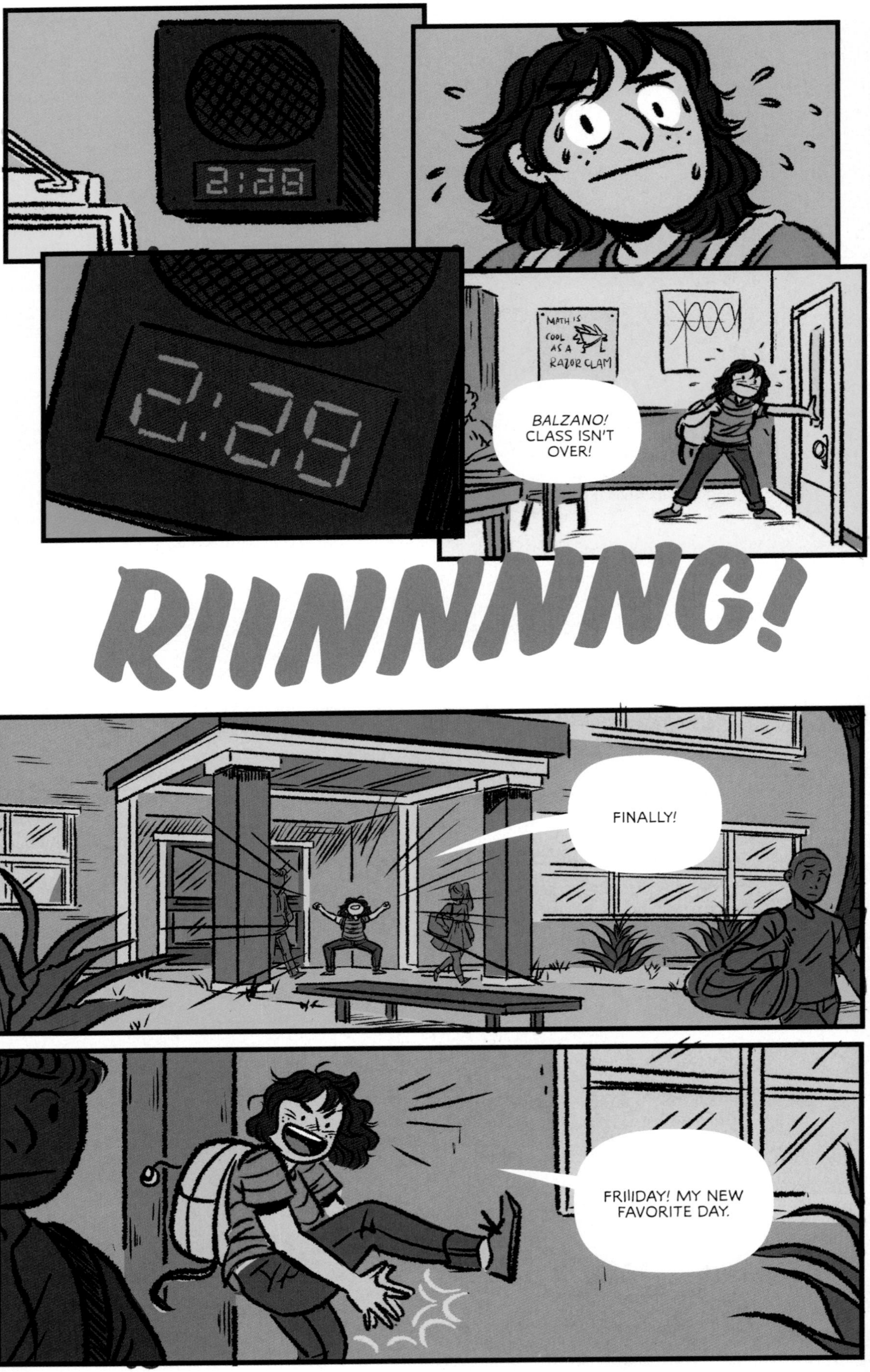
2:28
2:29
MATH IS COOL AS A RAZOR CLAM
BALZANO! CLASS ISN'T OVER!
RIINNNG!
FINALLY!
FRIIIDAY! MY NEW FAVORITE DAY.

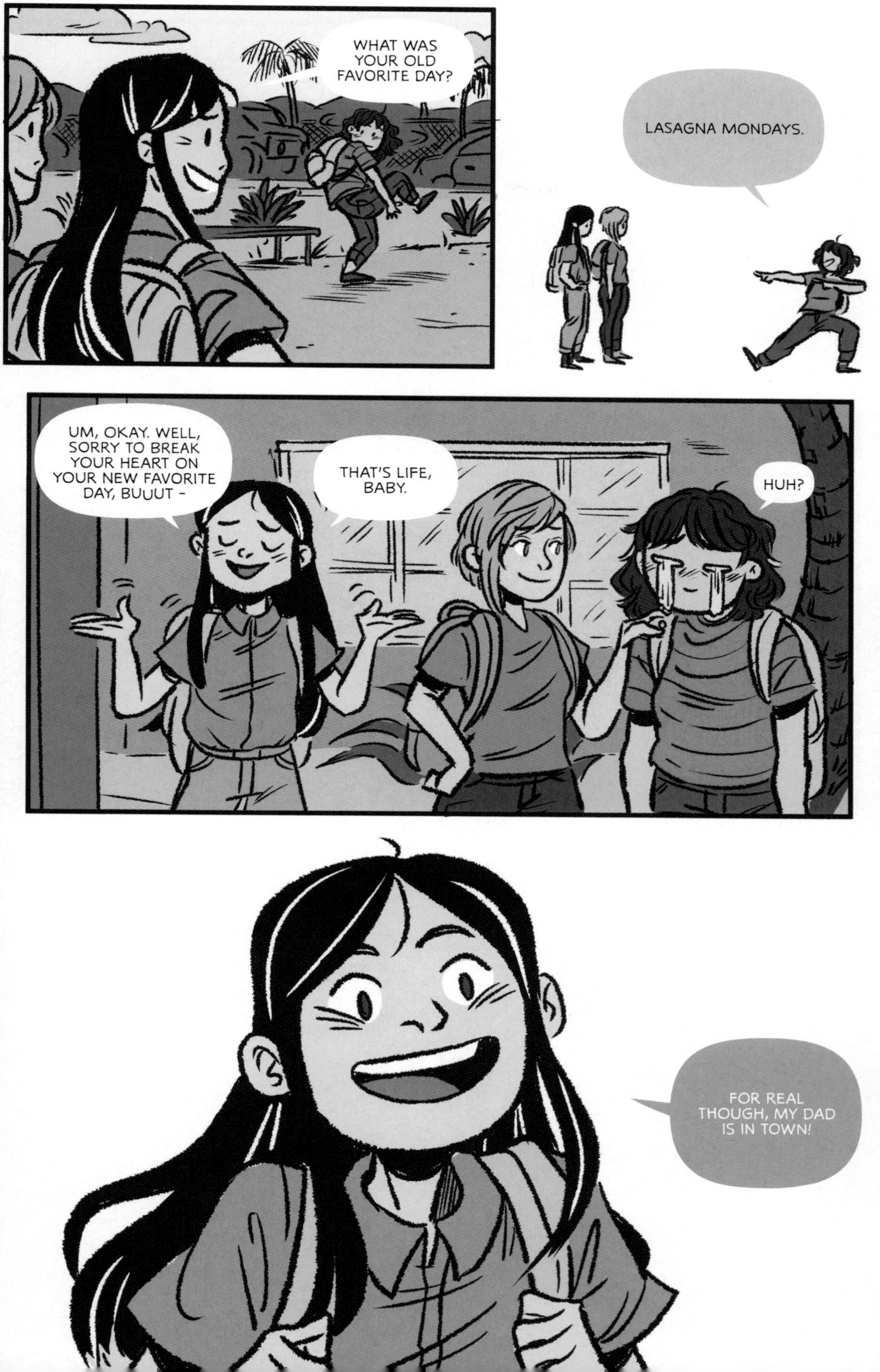
WHAT WAS YOUR OLD FAVORITE DAY?
LASAGNA MONDAYS.
UM, OKAY. WELL, SORRY TO BREAK YOUR HEART ON YOUR NEW FAVORITE DAY, BUUUT -
THAT'S LIFE, BABY.
HUH?
FOR REAL THOUGH, MY DAD IS IN TOWN!

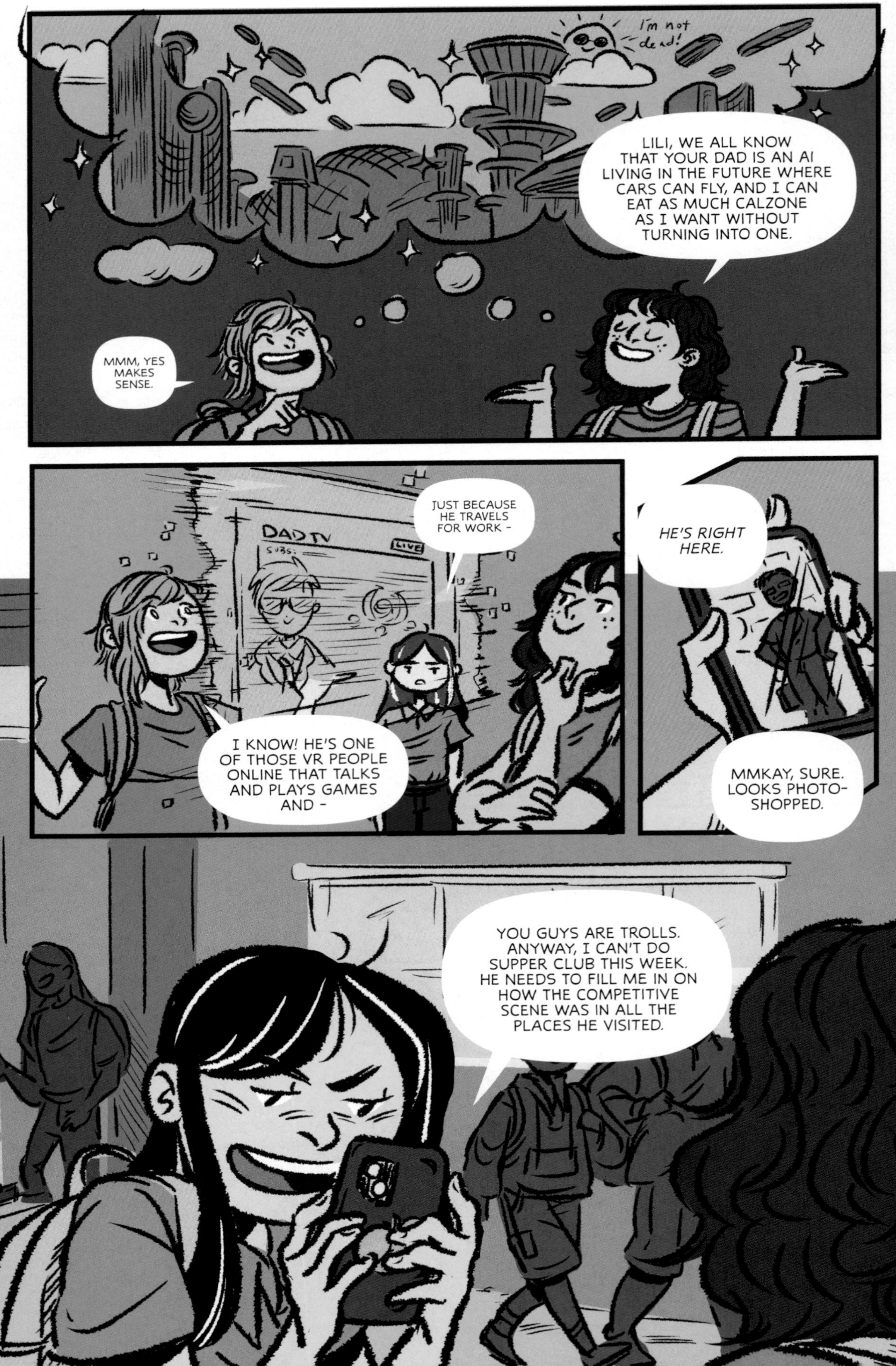
I'm not dead!
LILI, WE ALL KNOW THAT YOUR DAD IS AN AI LIVING IN THE FUTURE WHERE CARS CAN FLY, AND I CAN EAT AS MUCH CALZONE AS I WANT WITHOUT TURNING INTO ONE.
MMM, YES MAKES SENSE.
DAD TV
SUBS:
LIVE
JUST BECAUSE HE TRAVELS FOR WORK -
I KNOW! HE'S ONE OF THOSE VR PEOPLE ONLINE THAT TALKS AND PLAYS GAMES AND -
HE'S RIGHT HERE.
MMKAY, SURE. LOOKS PHOTO-SHOPPED.
YOU GUYS ARE TROLLS. ANYWAY, I CAN'T DO SUPPER CLUB THIS WEEK. HE NEEDS TO FILL ME IN ON HOW THE COMPETITIVE SCENE WAS IN ALL THE PLACES HE VISITED.

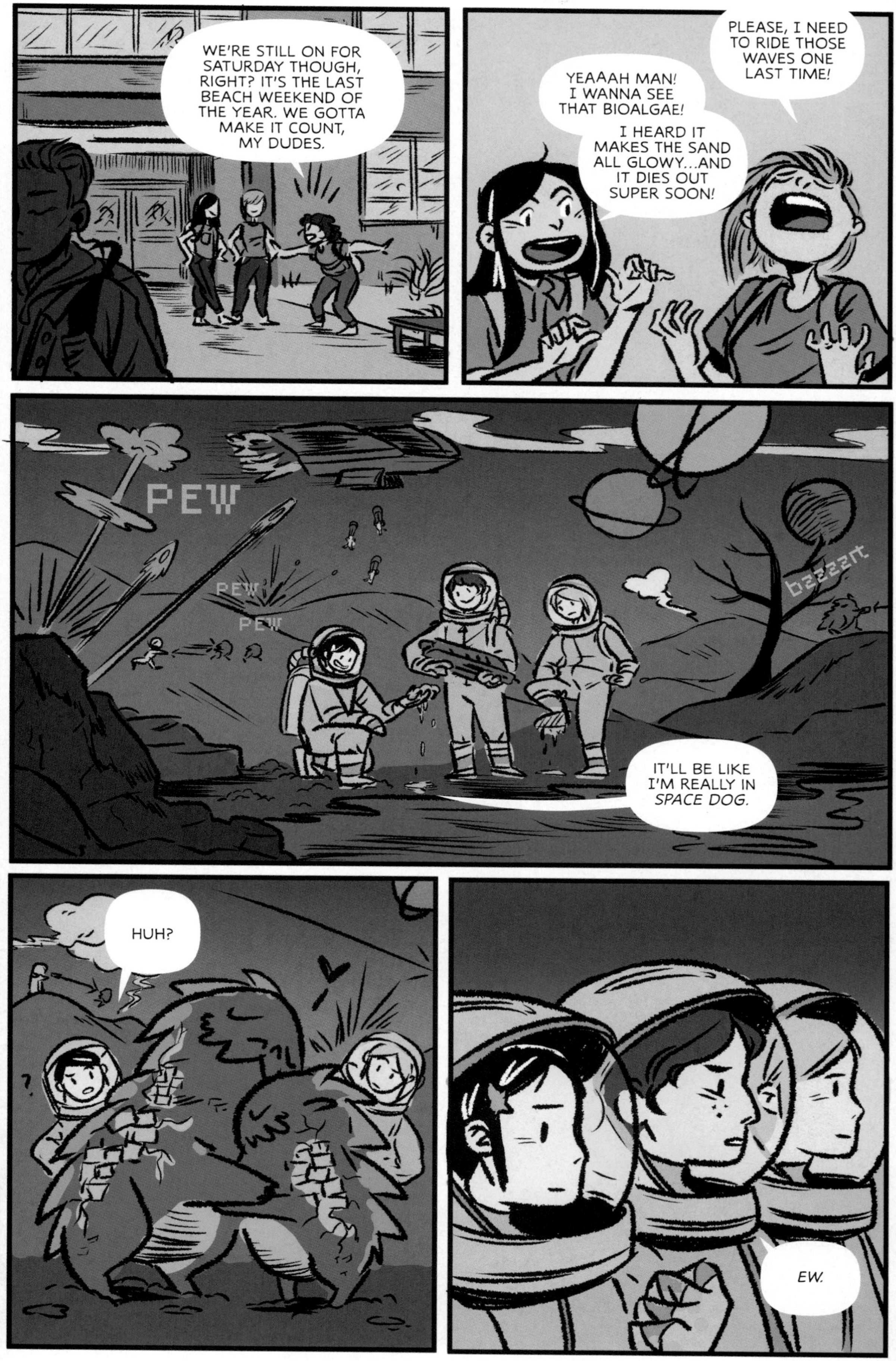
WE'RE STILL ON FOR SATURDAY THOUGH, RIGHT? IT'S THE LAST BEACH WEEKEND OF THE YEAR. WE GOTTA MAKE IT COUNT, MY DUDES.
YEAAAH MAN! I WANNA SEE THAT BIOALGAE!
I HEARD IT MAKES THE SAND ALL GLOWY...AND IT DIES OUT SUPER SOON!
PLEASE, I NEED TO RIDE THOSE WAVES ONE LAST TIME!
PEW
PEW
PEW
bzzzzt
IT'LL BE LIKE I'M REALLY IN *SPACE DOG.*
HUH?
EW.

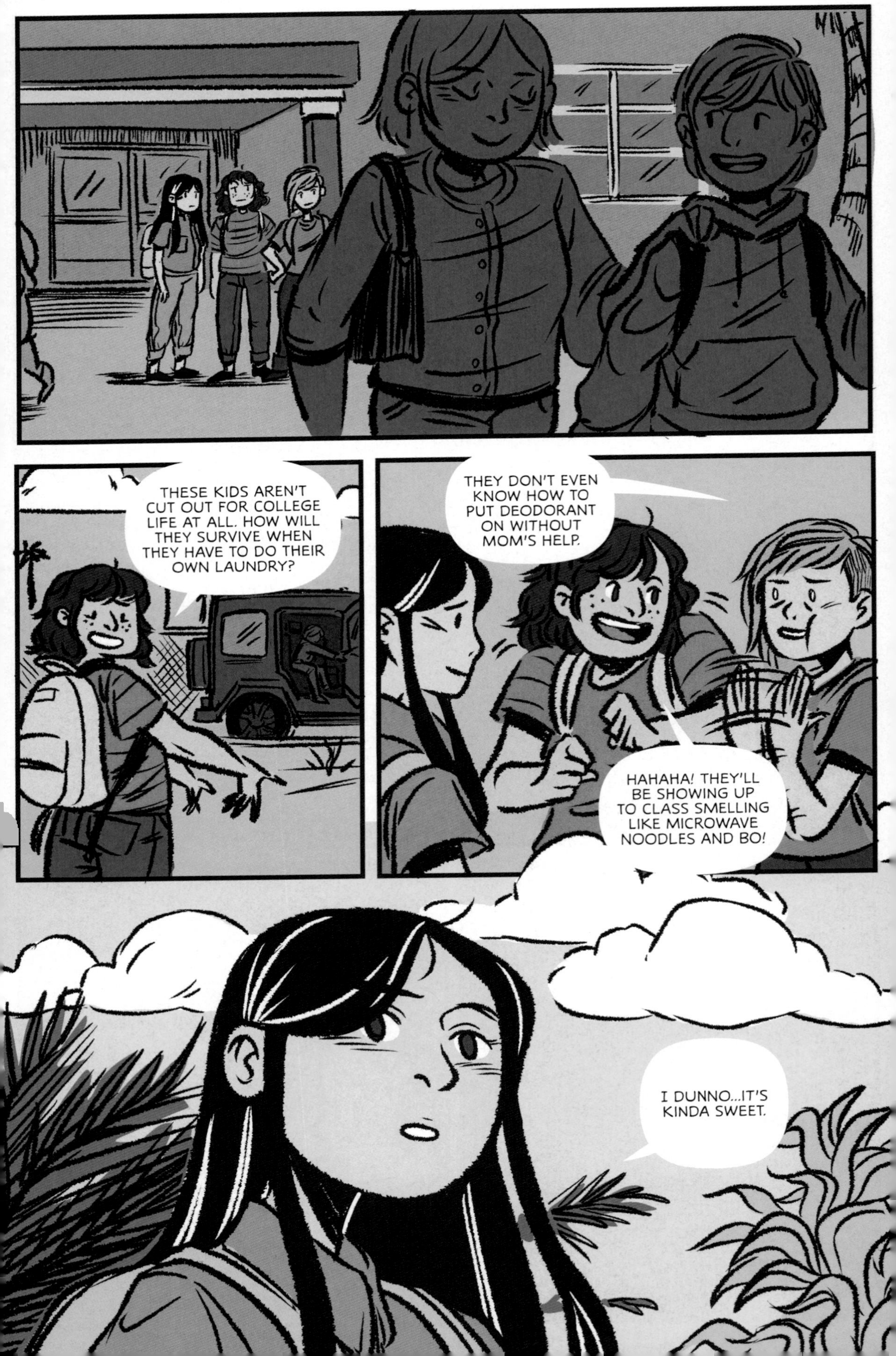
THESE KIDS AREN'T CUT OUT FOR COLLEGE LIFE AT ALL. HOW WILL THEY SURVIVE WHEN THEY HAVE TO DO THEIR OWN LAUNDRY?
THEY DON'T EVEN KNOW HOW TO PUT DEODORANT ON WITHOUT MOM'S HELP.
HAHAHA! THEY'LL BE SHOWING UP TO CLASS SMELLING LIKE MICROWAVE NOODLES AND BO!
I DUNNO...IT'S KINDA SWEET.

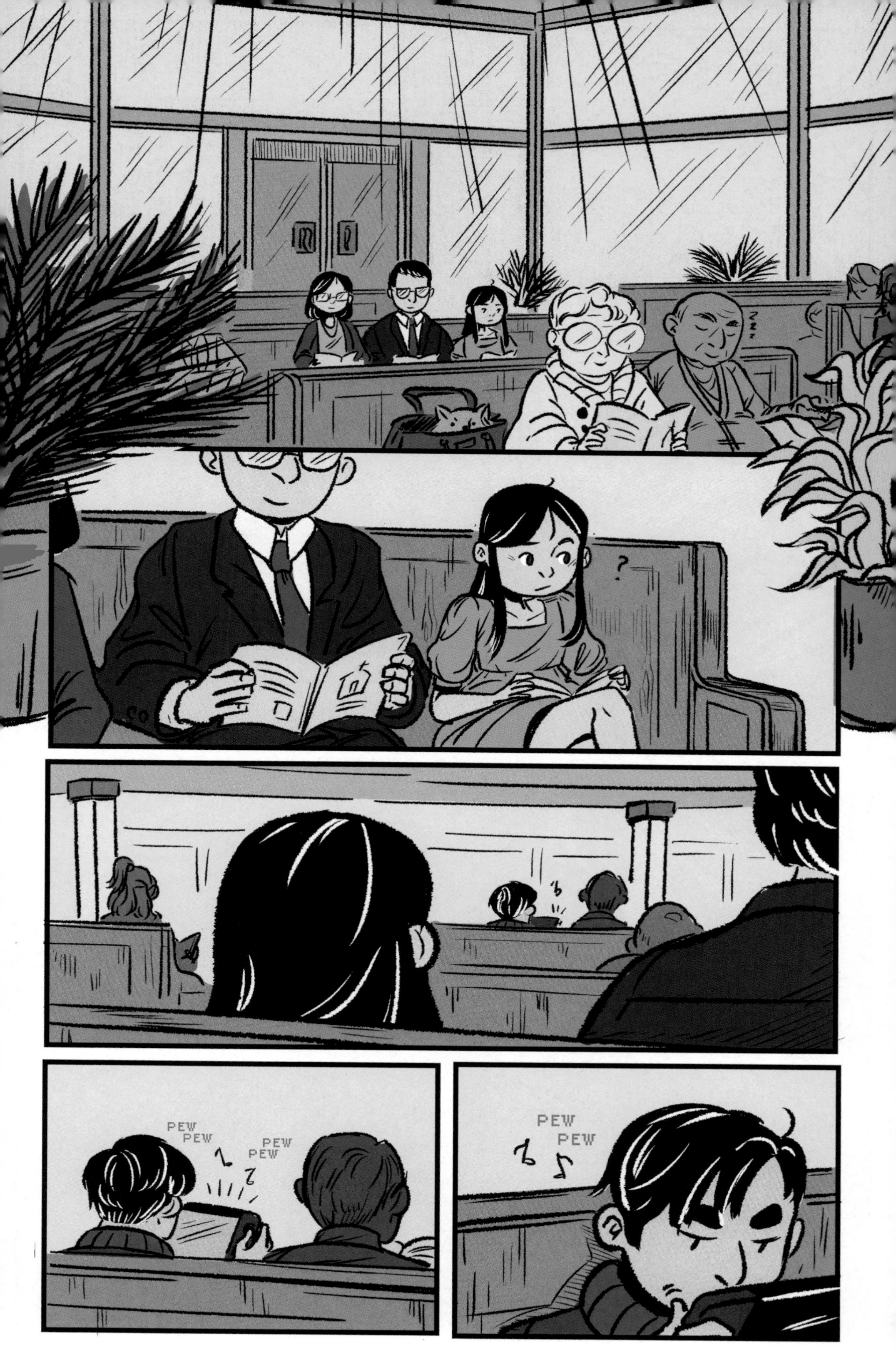
?
PEW
PEW
PEW
PEW
PEW
PEW

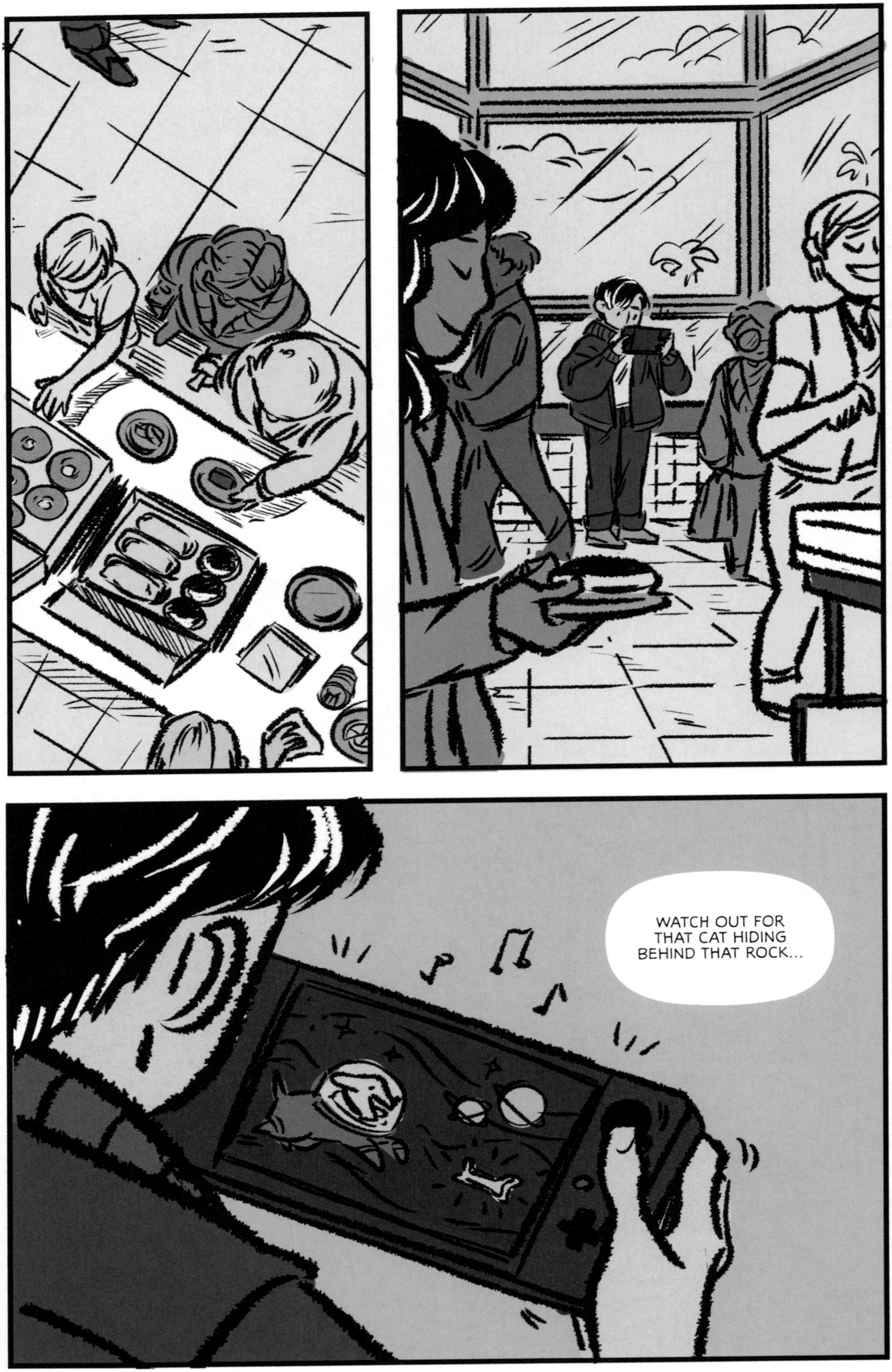
WATCH OUT FOR THAT CAT HIDING BEHIND THAT ROCK...

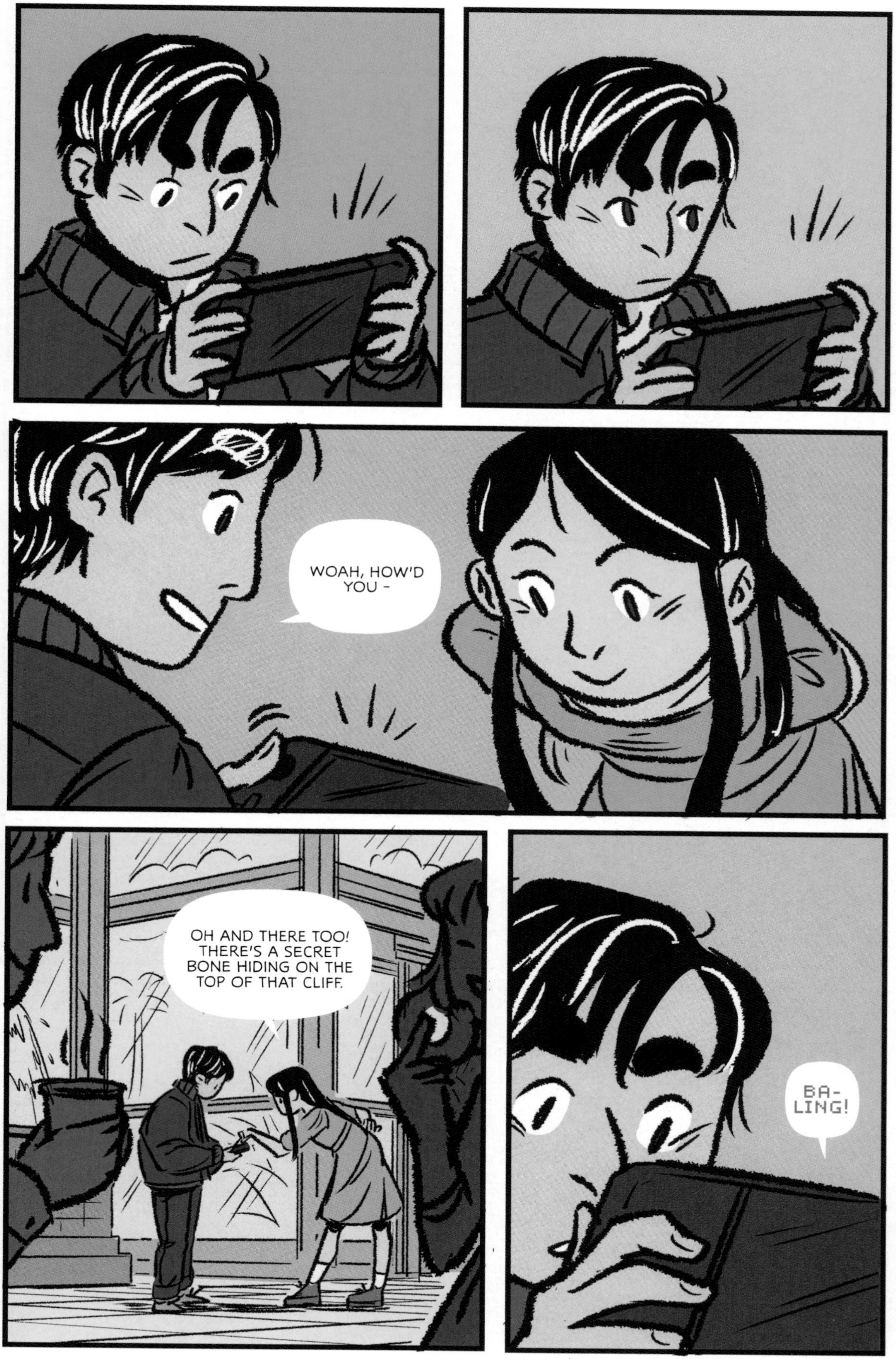
WOAH, HOW'D YOU -
OH AND THERE TOO! THERE'S A SECRET BONE HIDING ON THE TOP OF THAT CLIFF.
BA-LING!

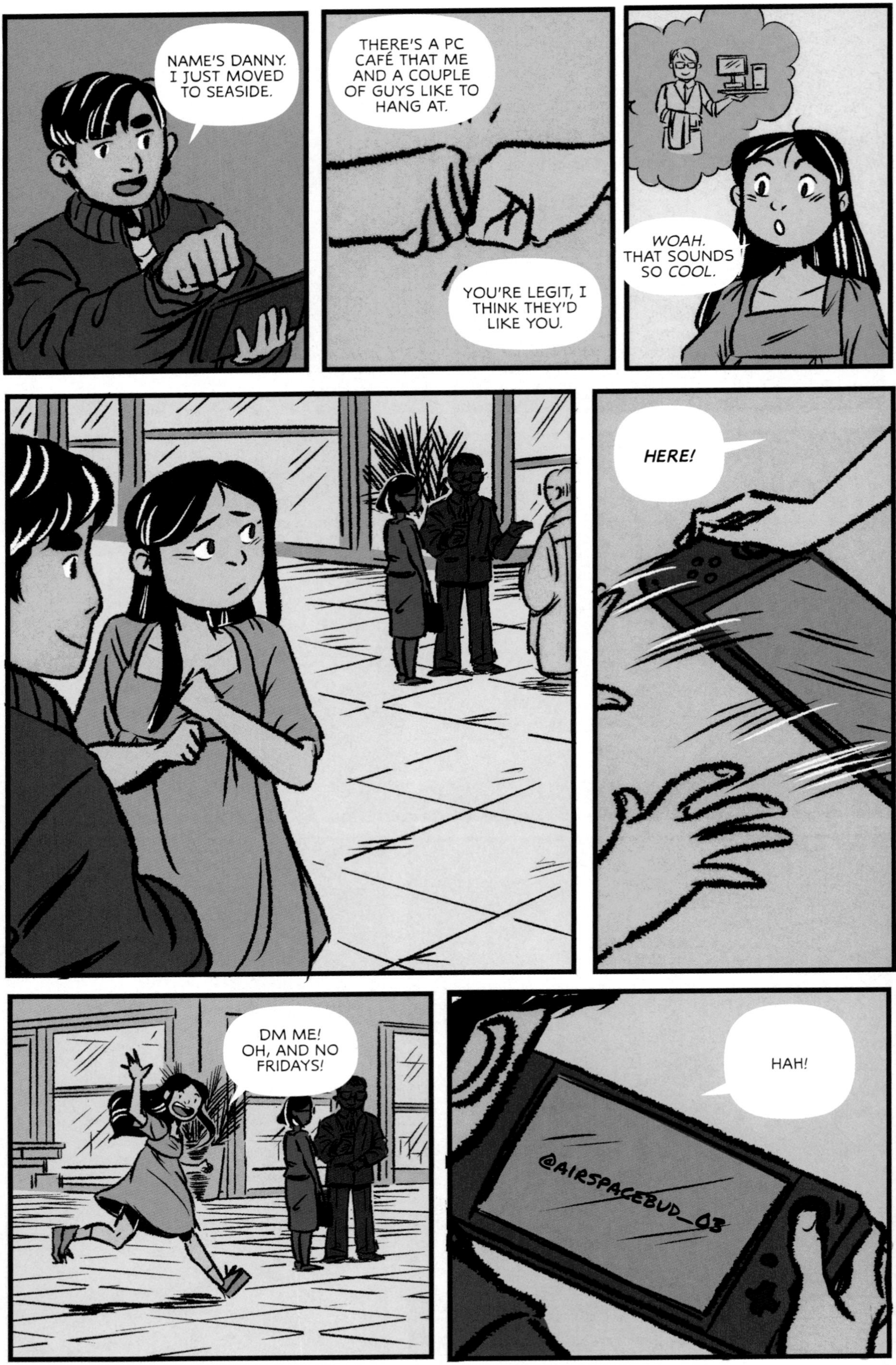
NAME'S DANNY. I JUST MOVED TO SEASIDE.
THERE'S A PC CAFÉ THAT ME AND A COUPLE OF GUYS LIKE TO HANG AT.
YOU'RE LEGIT, I THINK THEY'D LIKE YOU.
WOAH. THAT SOUNDS SO COOL.
HERE!
DM ME! OH, AND NO FRIDAYS!
HAH!
@AIRSPACEBUD_03

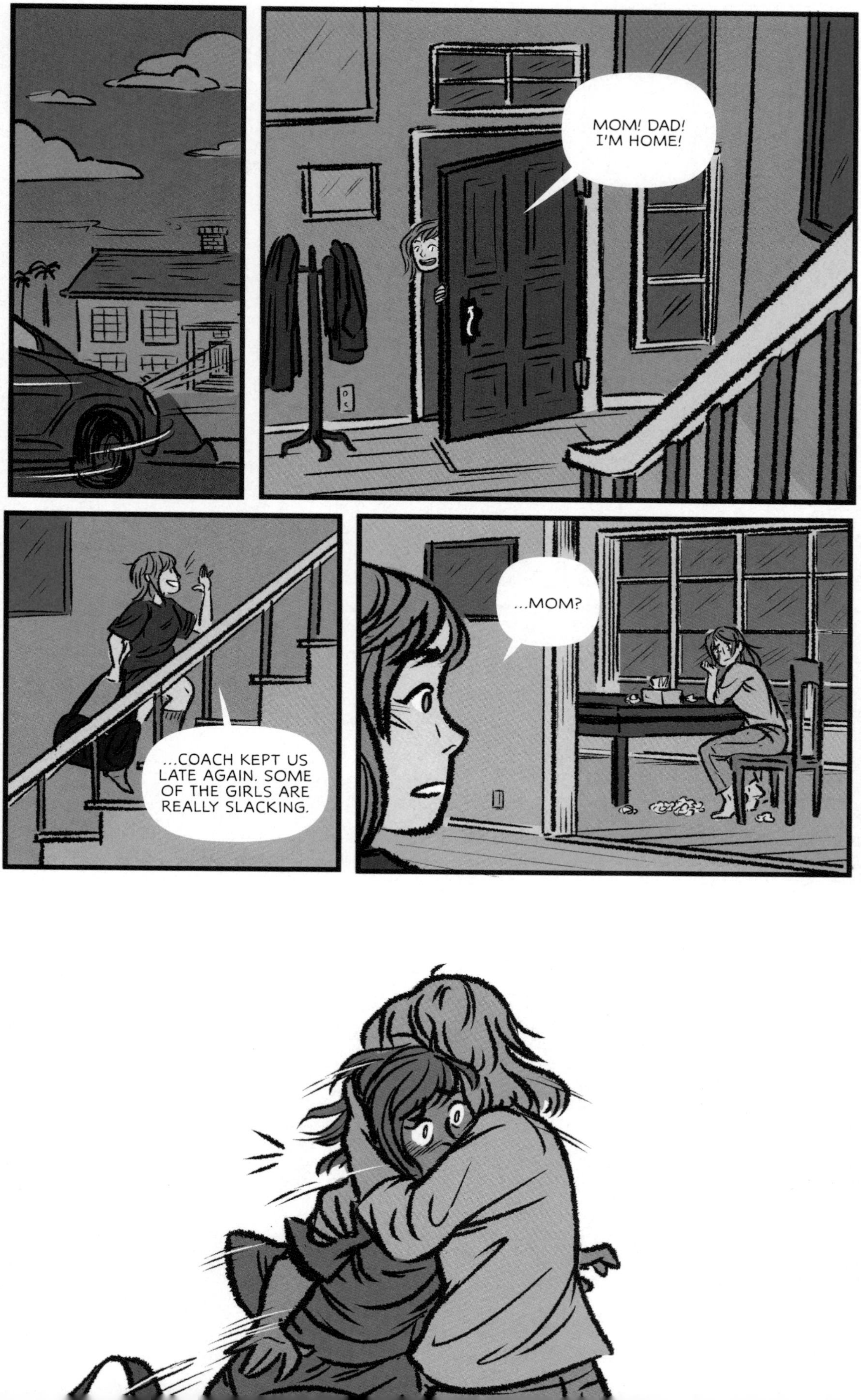
MOM! DAD! I'M HOME!
...COACH KEPT US LATE AGAIN. SOME OF THE GIRLS ARE REALLY SLACKING.
...MOM?

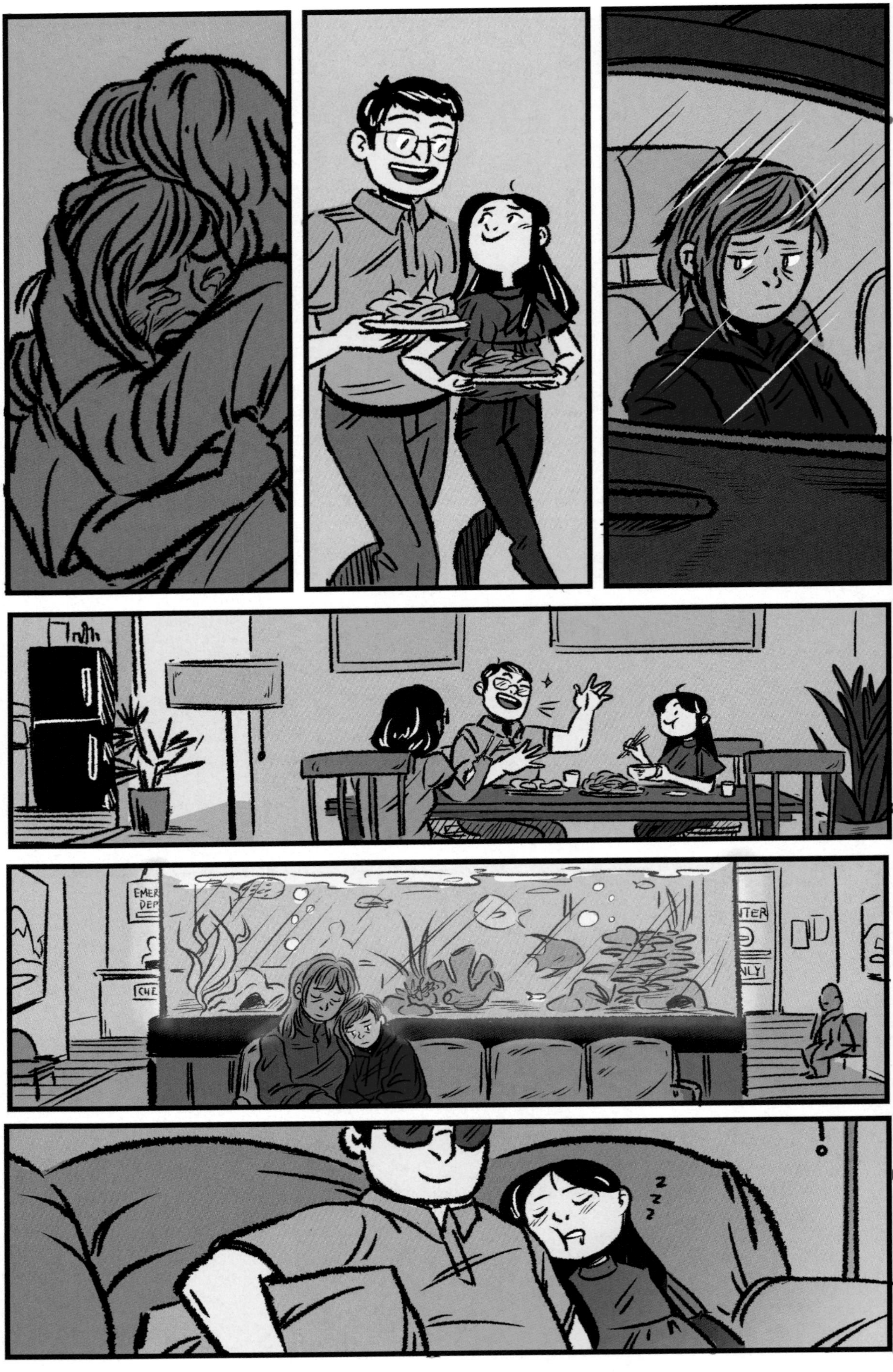
EMER
DEP
CHE
NTER
NLY
Z
Z
Z

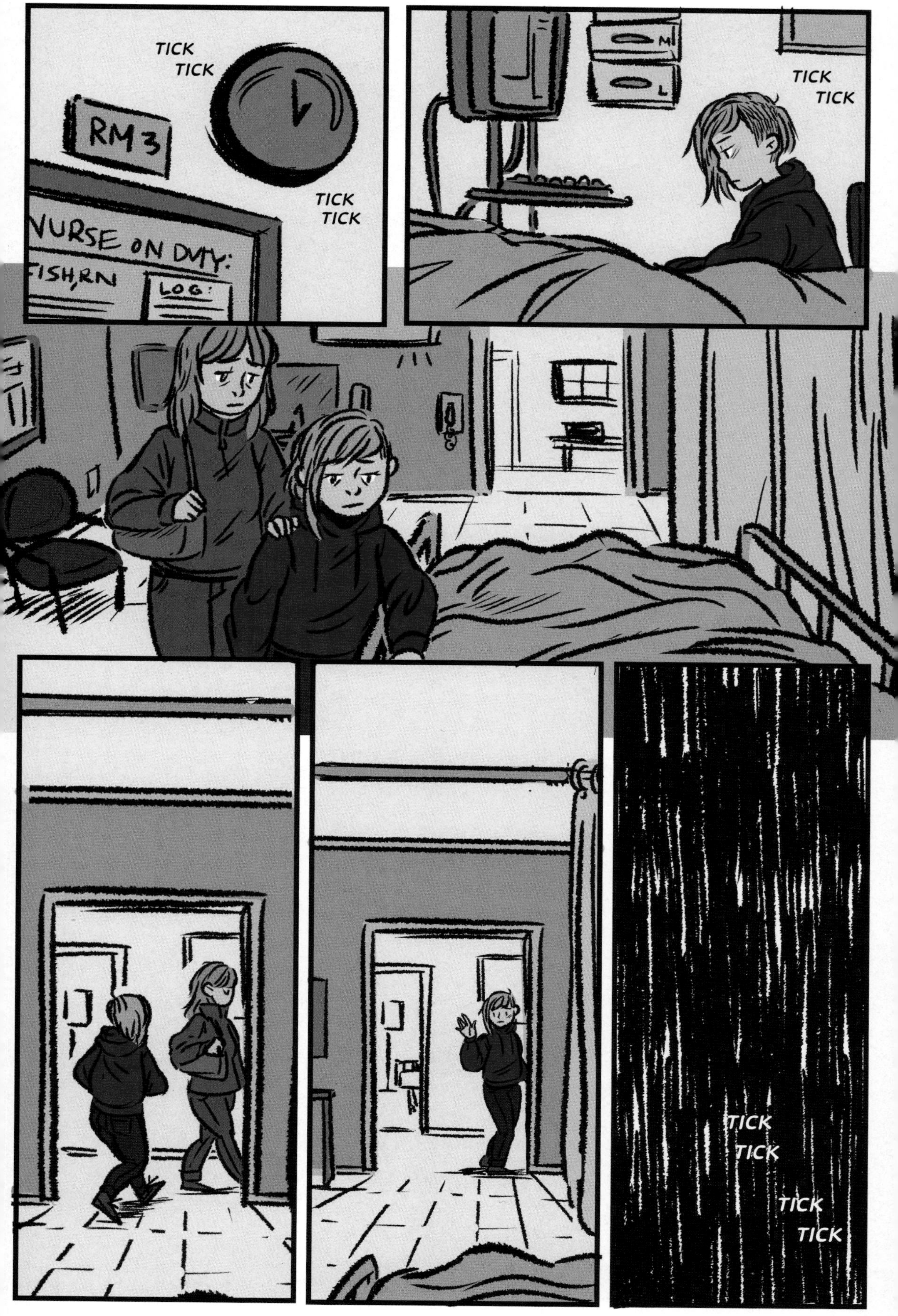
TICK
TICK
RM 3
NURSE ON DUTY:
FISH, RN
LOG:
TICK
TICK
TICK
TICK
TICK
TICK
TICK
TICK

Chapter Four
mom's banana bread

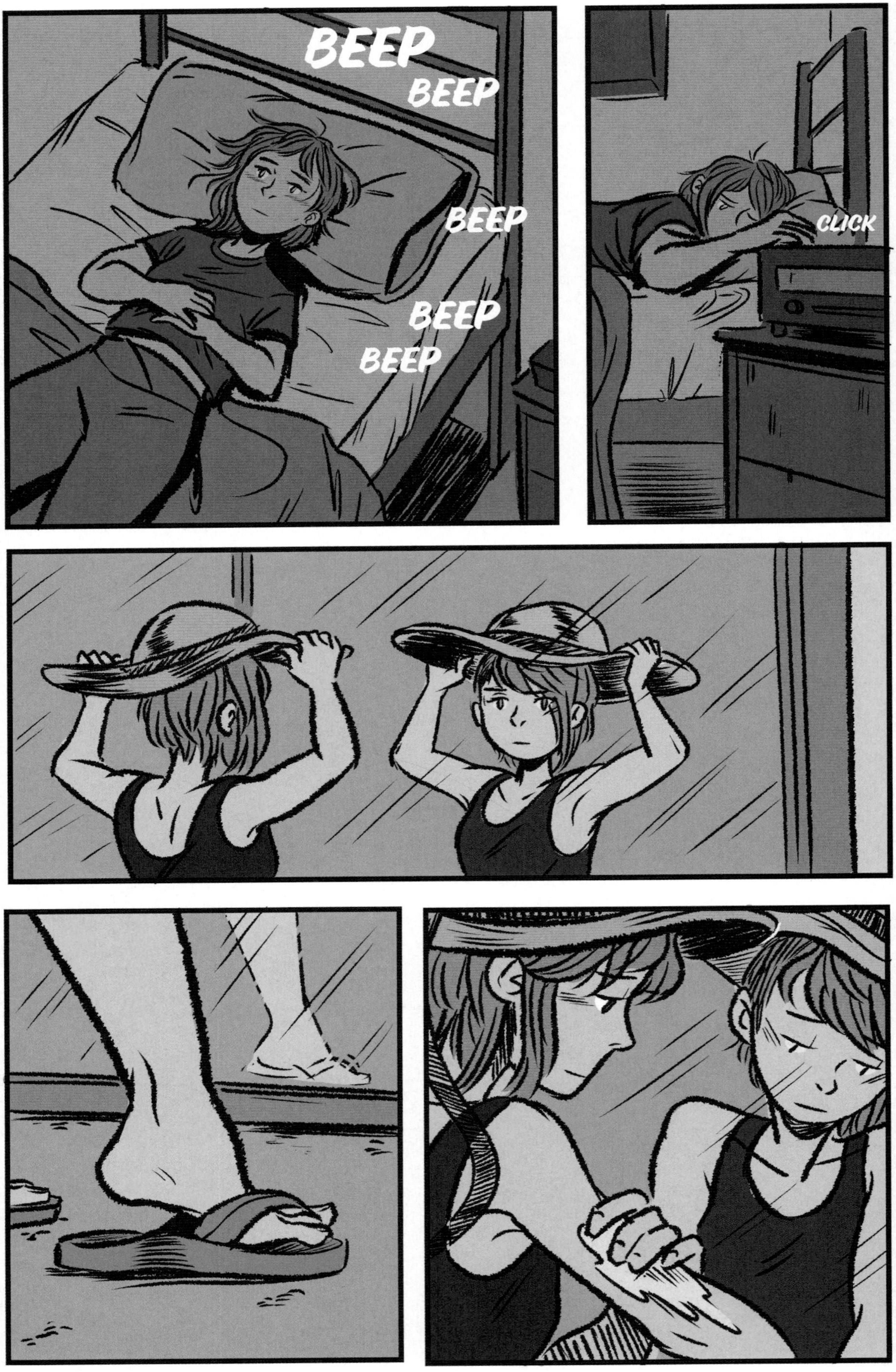
BEEP
BEEP
BEEP
BEEP
BEEP
CLICK

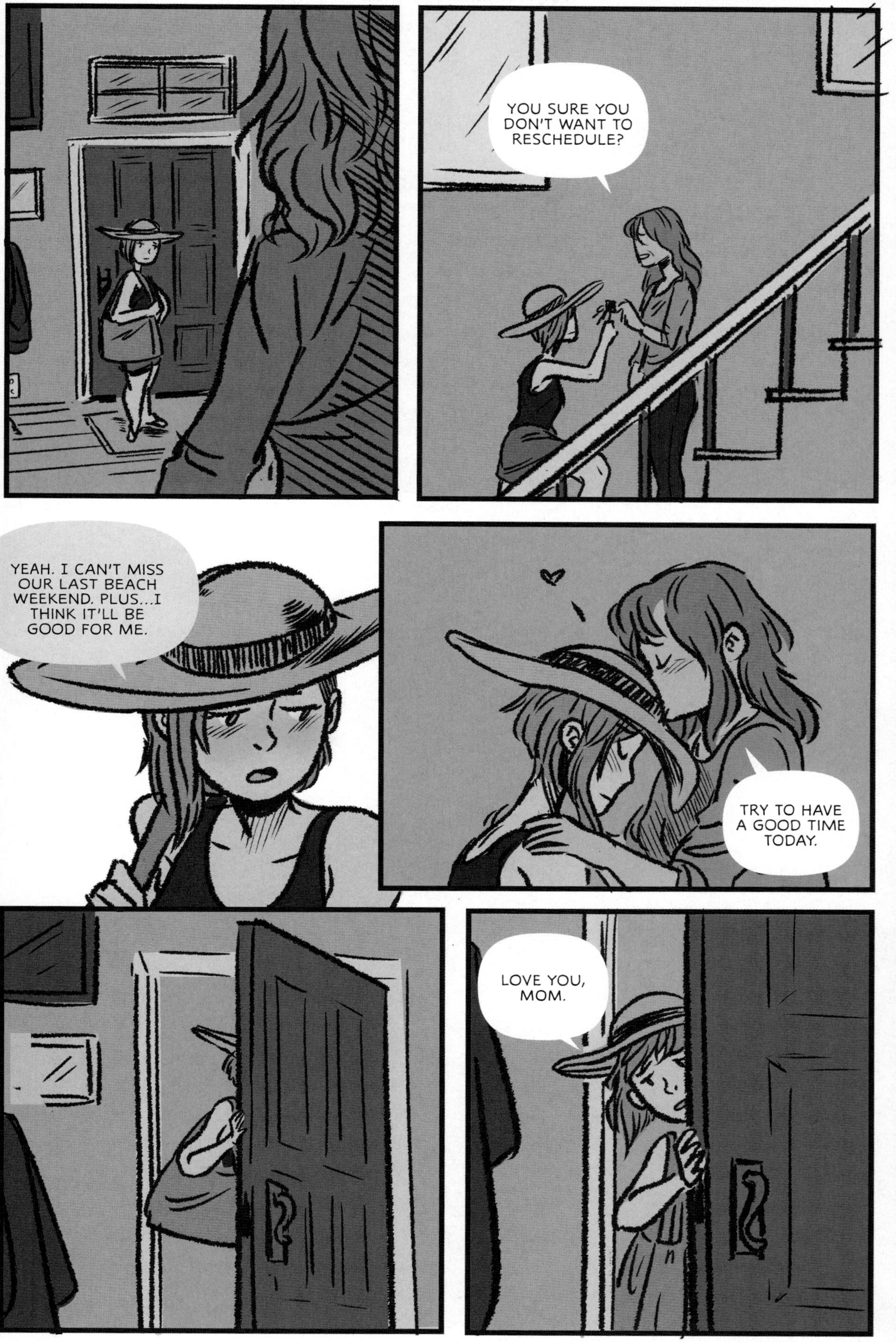
YOU SURE YOU DON'T WANT TO RESCHEDULE?
YEAH. I CAN'T MISS OUR LAST BEACH WEEKEND. PLUS...I THINK IT'LL BE GOOD FOR ME.
TRY TO HAVE A GOOD TIME TODAY.
LOVE YOU, MOM.

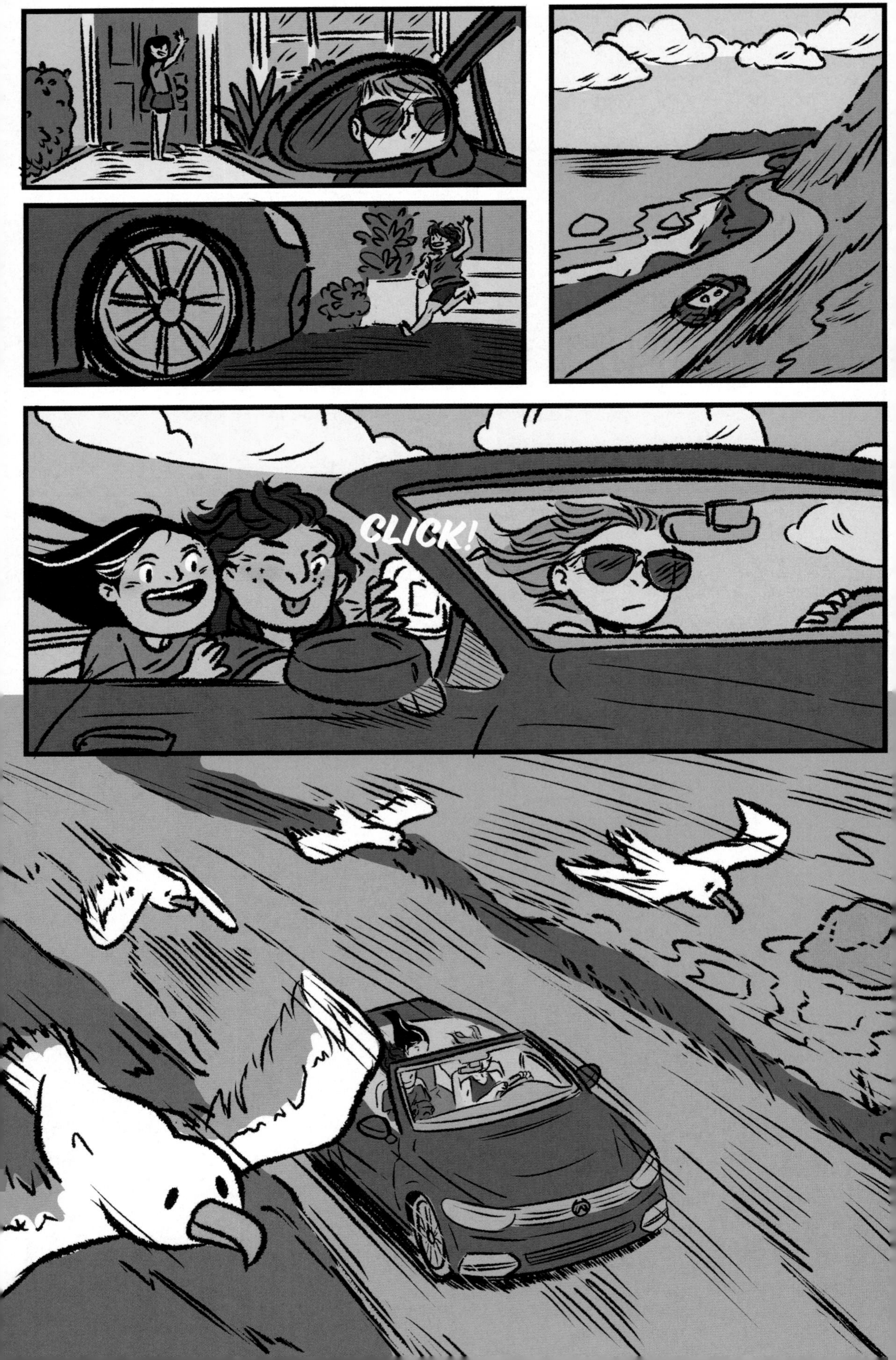
CLICK!

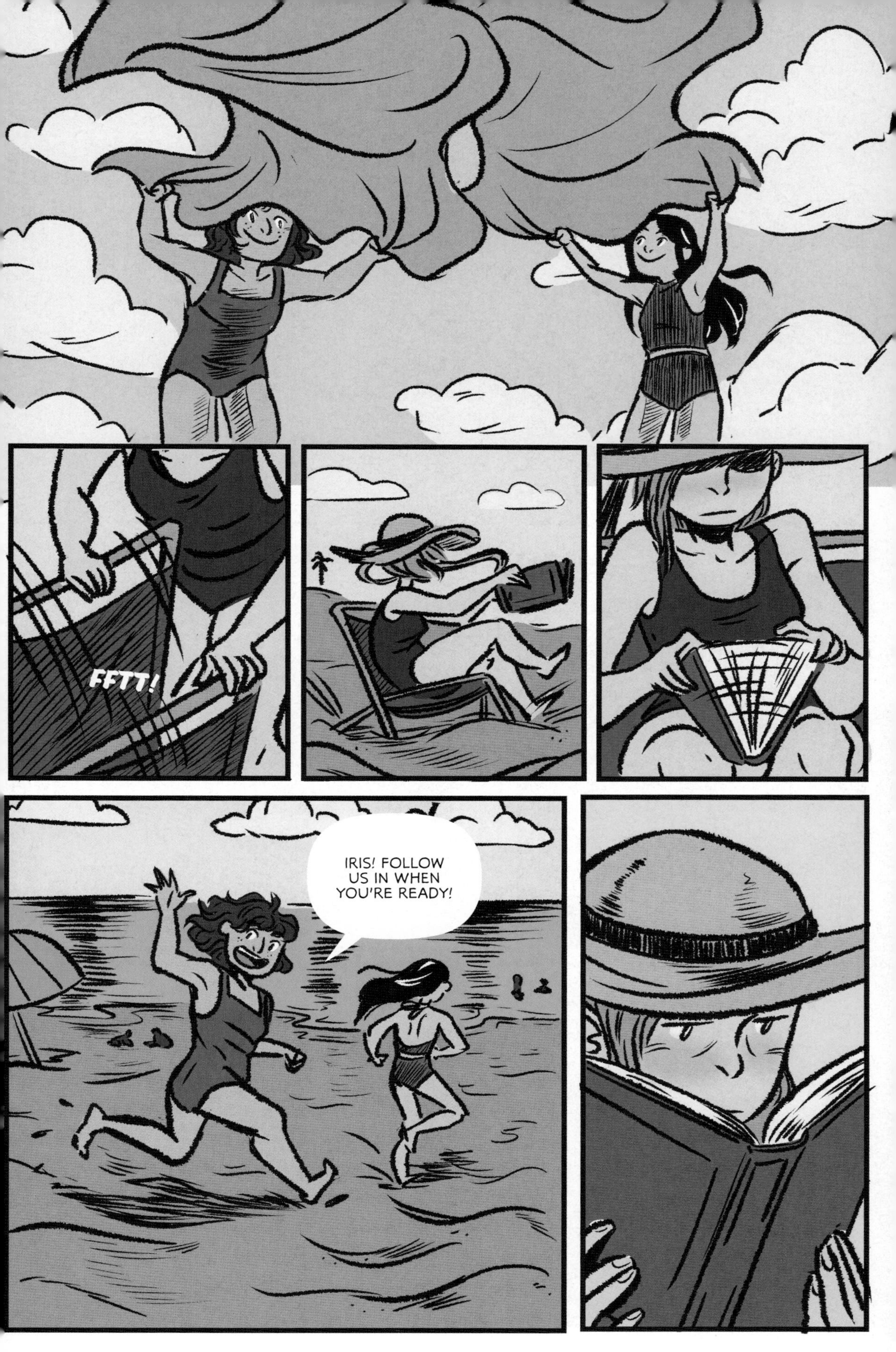
FFTT!
IRIS! FOLLOW US IN WHEN YOU'RE READY!

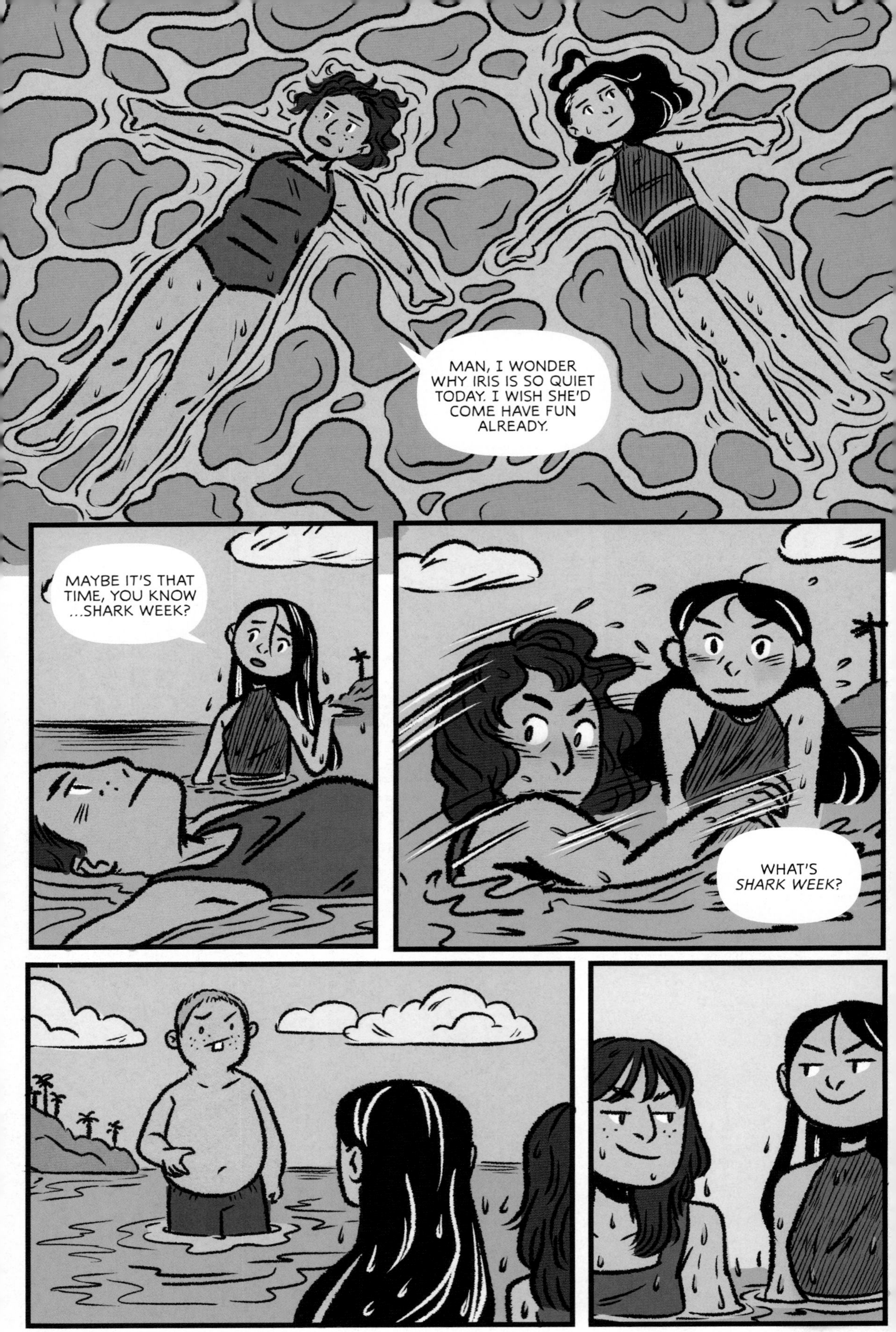
MAN, I WONDER WHY IRIS IS SO QUIET TODAY. I WISH SHE'D COME HAVE FUN ALREADY.
MAYBE IT'S THAT TIME, YOU KNOW ...SHARK WEEK?
WHAT'S *SHARK WEEK?*

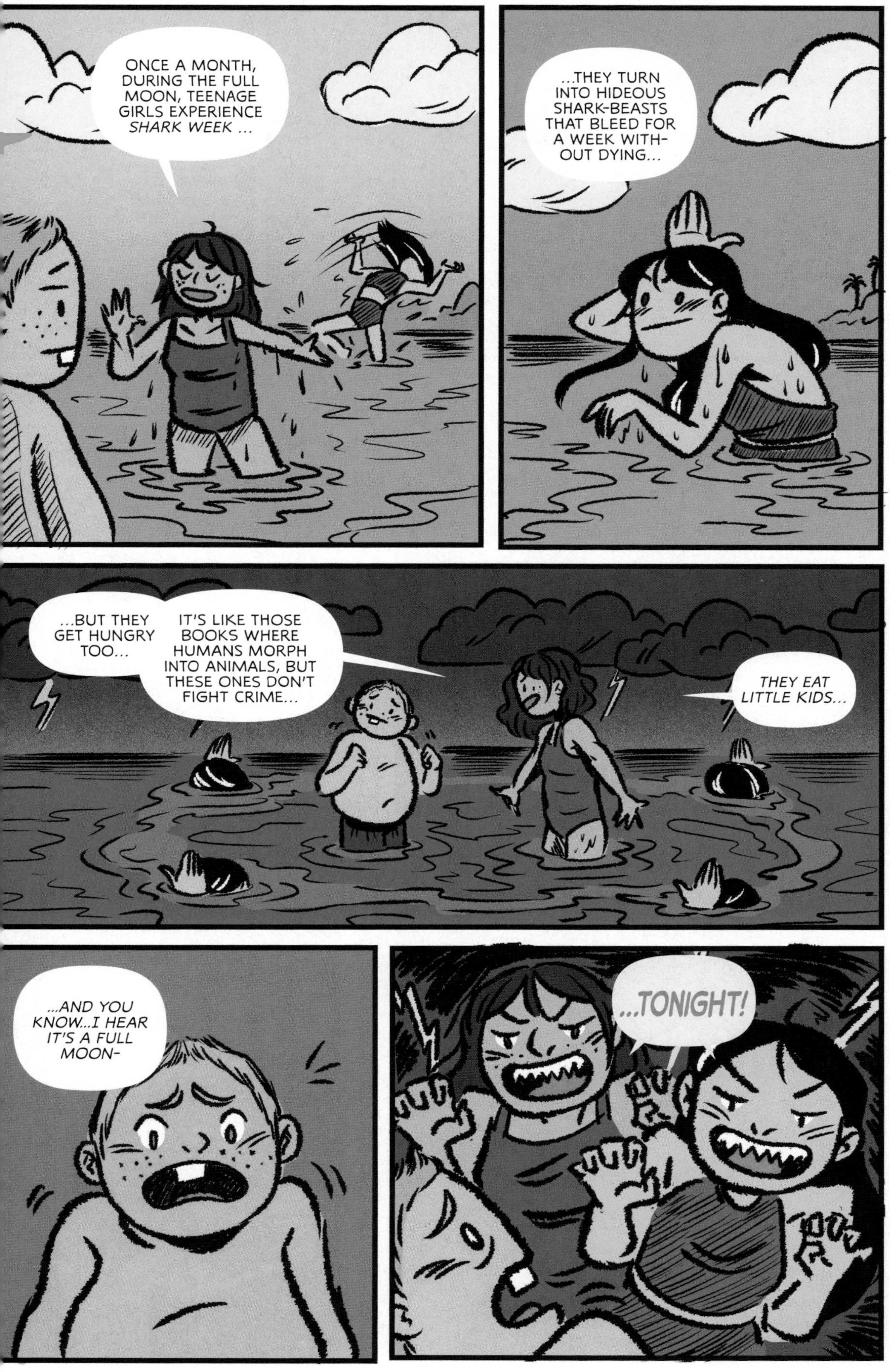

ONCE A MONTH, DURING THE FULL MOON, TEENAGE GIRLS EXPERIENCE *SHARK WEEK* ...
...THEY TURN INTO HIDEOUS SHARK-BEASTS THAT BLEED FOR A WEEK WITH-OUT DYING...
...BUT THEY GET HUNGRY TOO...
IT'S LIKE THOSE BOOKS WHERE HUMANS MORPH INTO ANIMALS, BUT THESE ONES DON'T FIGHT CRIME...
THEY EAT LITTLE KIDS...
...AND YOU KNOW...I HEAR IT'S A FULL MOON-
...TONIGHT!

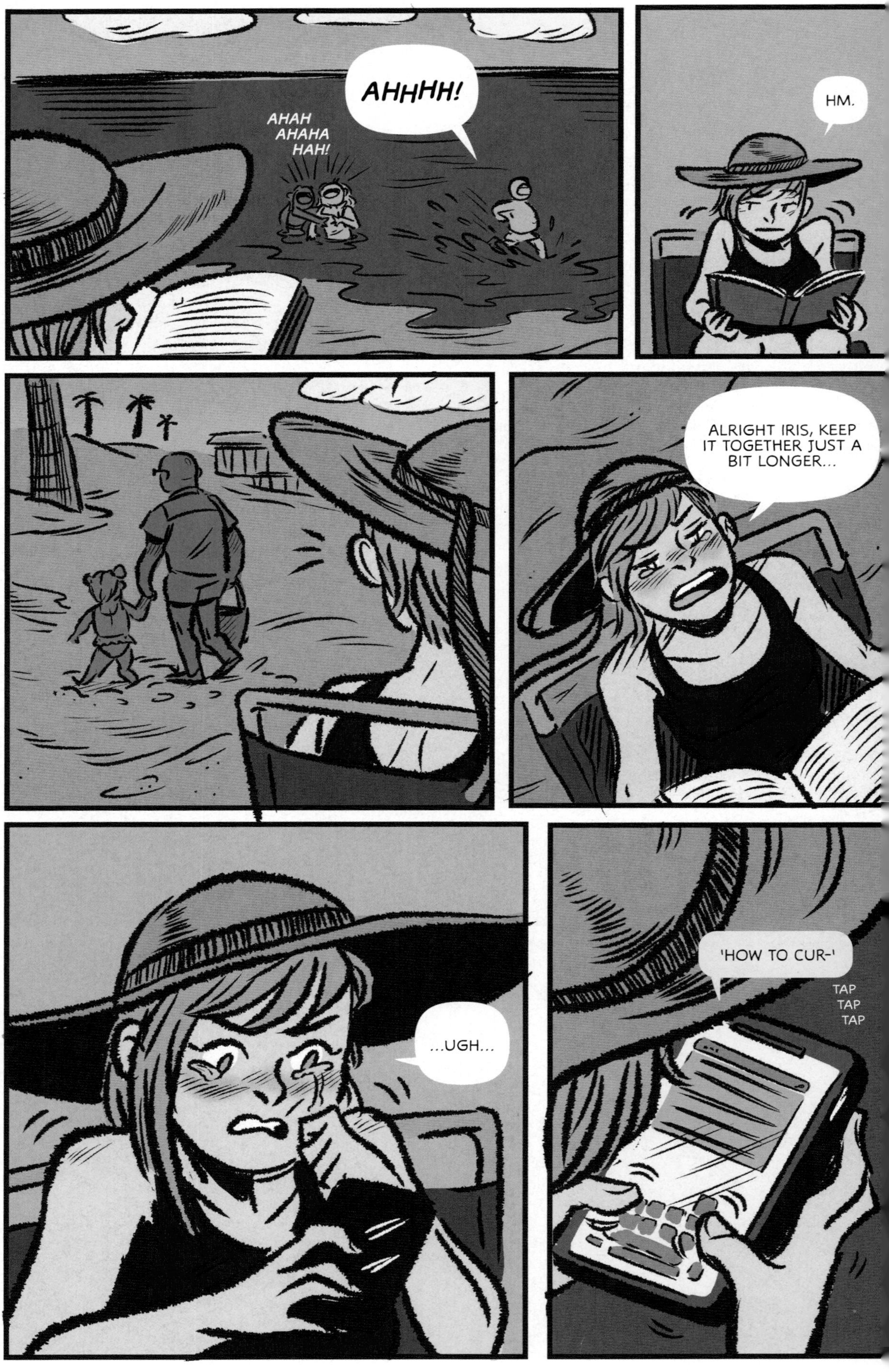
AHAH AHAHA HAH!
AHHHH!
HM.
ALRIGHT IRIS, KEEP IT TOGETHER JUST A BIT LONGER...
...UGH...
'HOW TO CUR-'
TAP TAP TAP

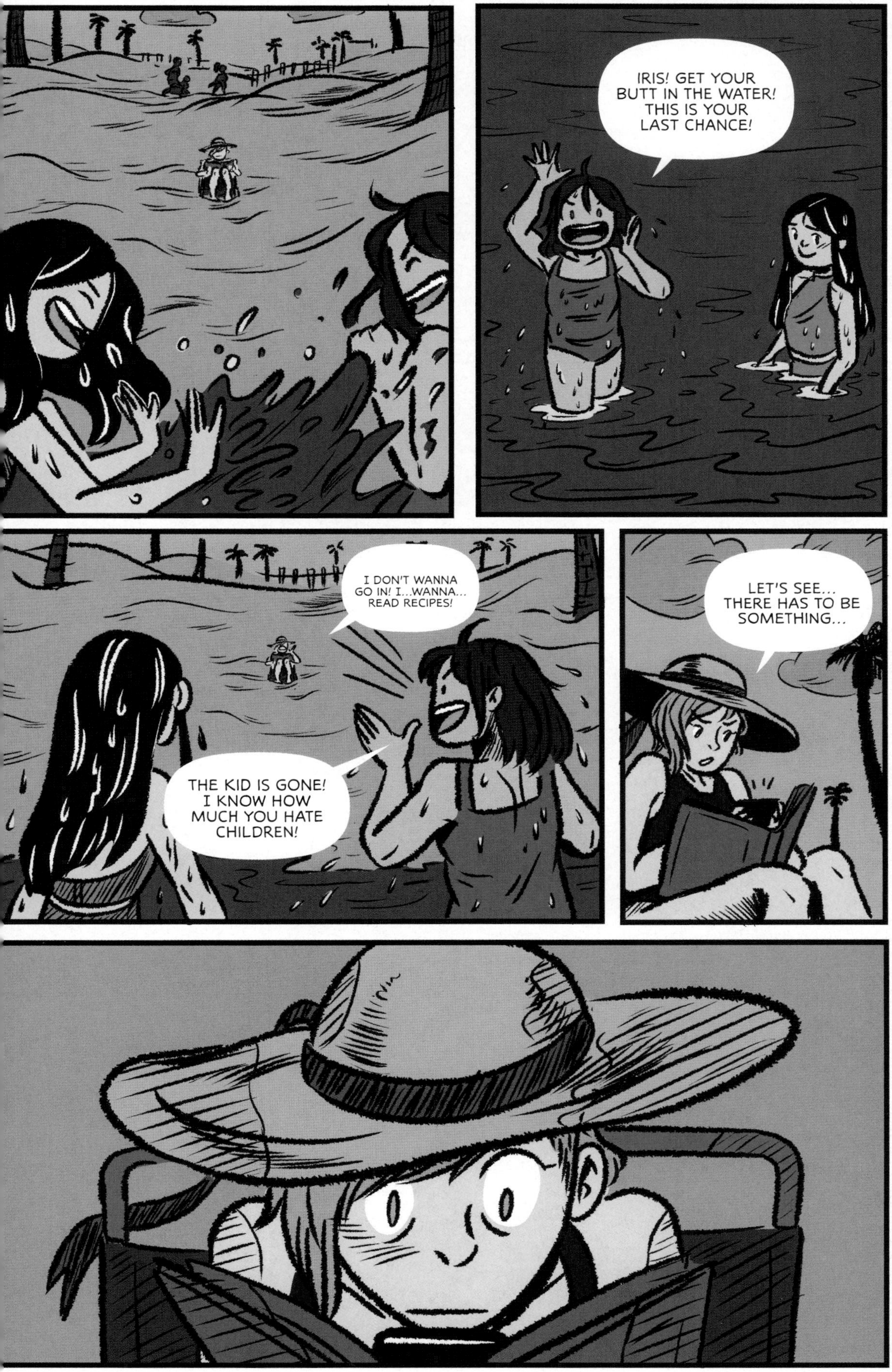
IRIS! GET YOUR BUTT IN THE WATER! THIS IS YOUR LAST CHANCE!
I DON'T WANNA GO IN! I...WANNA... READ RECIPES!
THE KID IS GONE! I KNOW HOW MUCH YOU HATE CHILDREN!
LET'S SEE... THERE HAS TO BE SOMETHING...

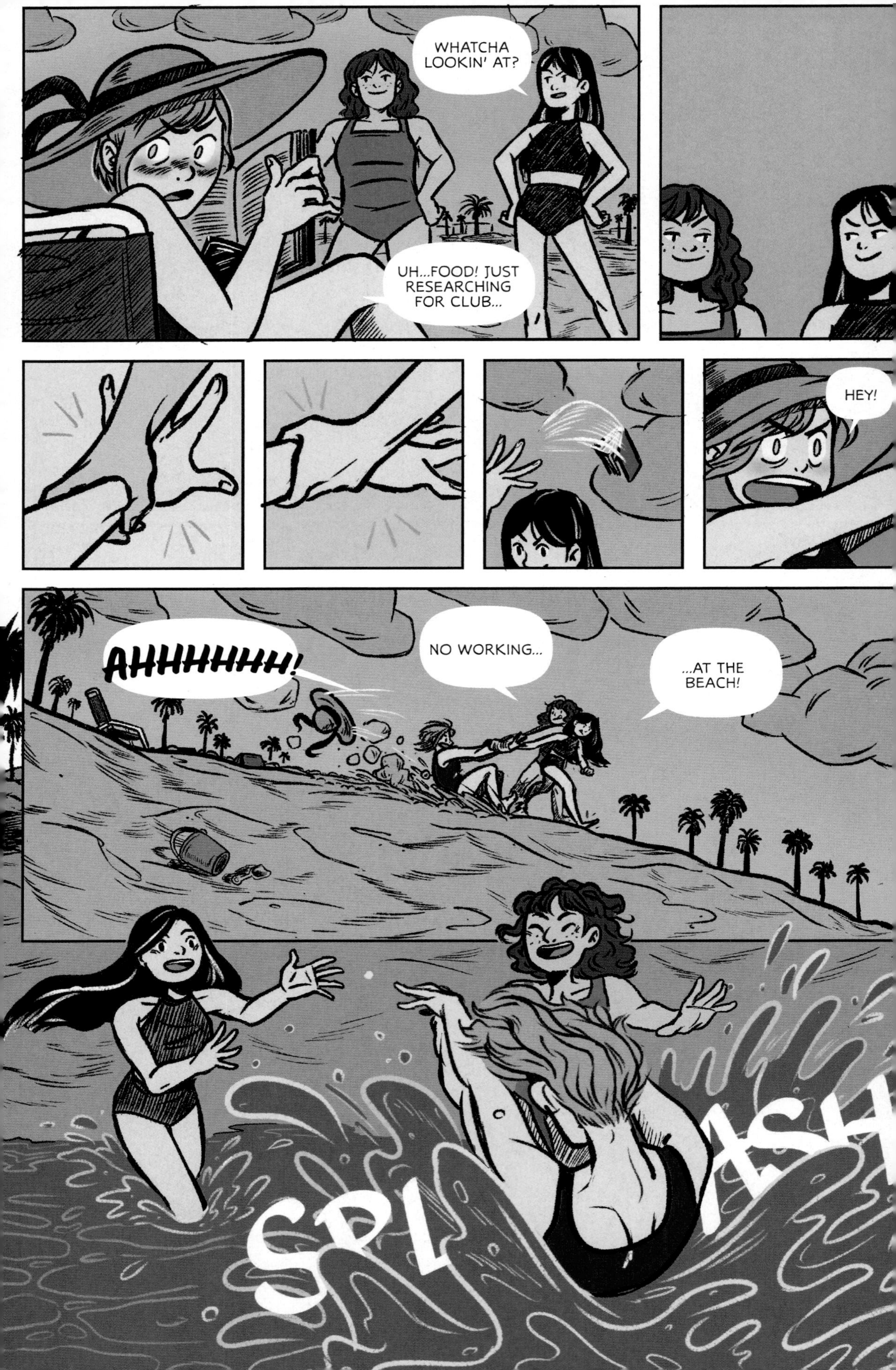

WHATCHA LOOKIN' AT?
UH...FOOD! JUST RESEARCHING FOR CLUB...
HEY!
AHHHHHHH!
NO WORKING...
...AT THE BEACH!
SPLASH

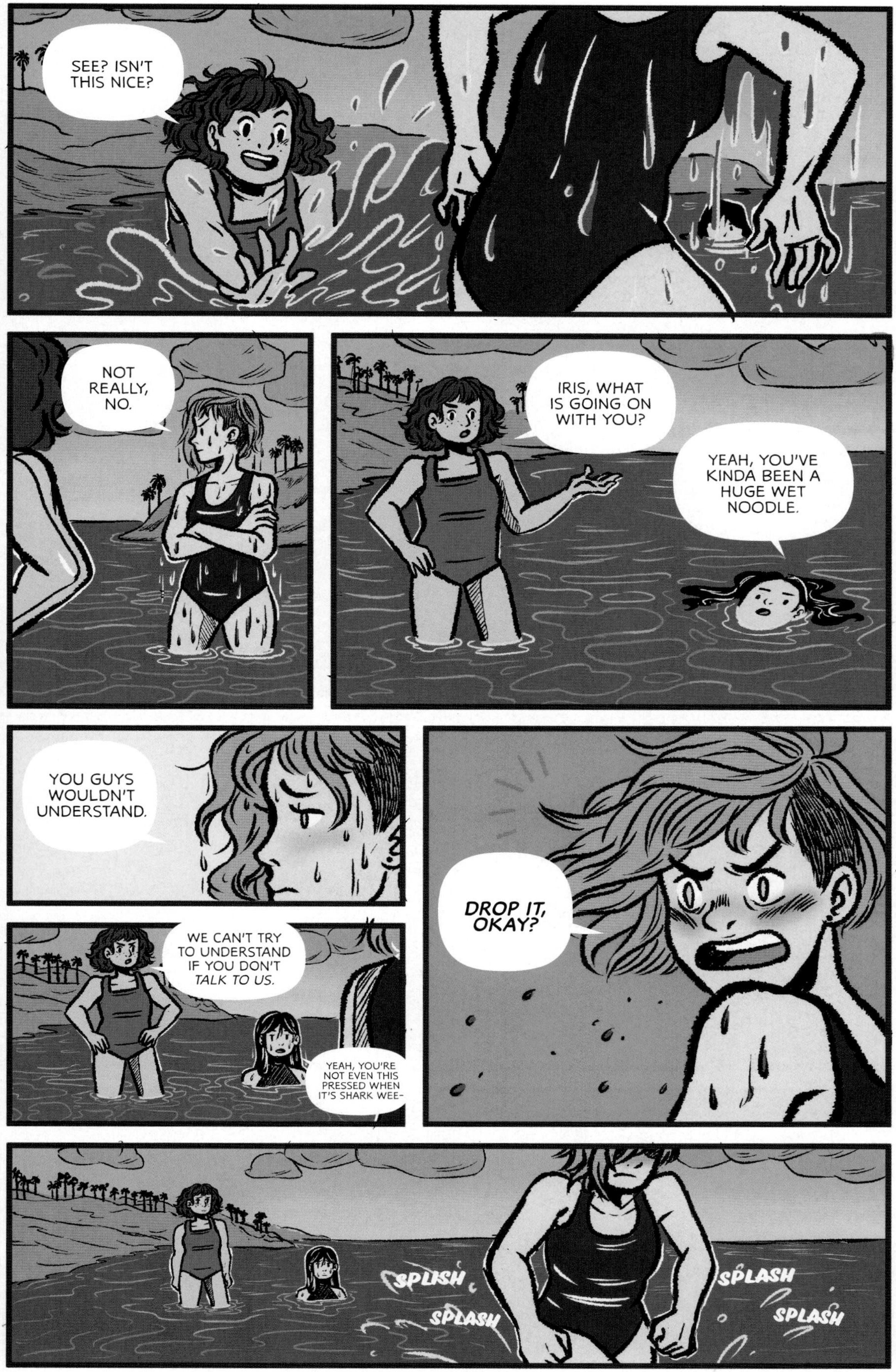
SEE? ISN'T THIS NICE?
NOT REALLY, NO.
IRIS, WHAT IS GOING ON WITH YOU?
YEAH, YOU'VE KINDA BEEN A HUGE WET NOODLE.
YOU GUYS WOULDN'T UNDERSTAND.
WE CAN'T TRY TO UNDERSTAND IF YOU DON'T *TALK TO US.*
YEAH, YOU'RE NOT EVEN THIS PRESSED WHEN IT'S SHARK WEE-
DROP IT, OKAY?
SPLISH
SPLASH
SPLASH
SPLASH

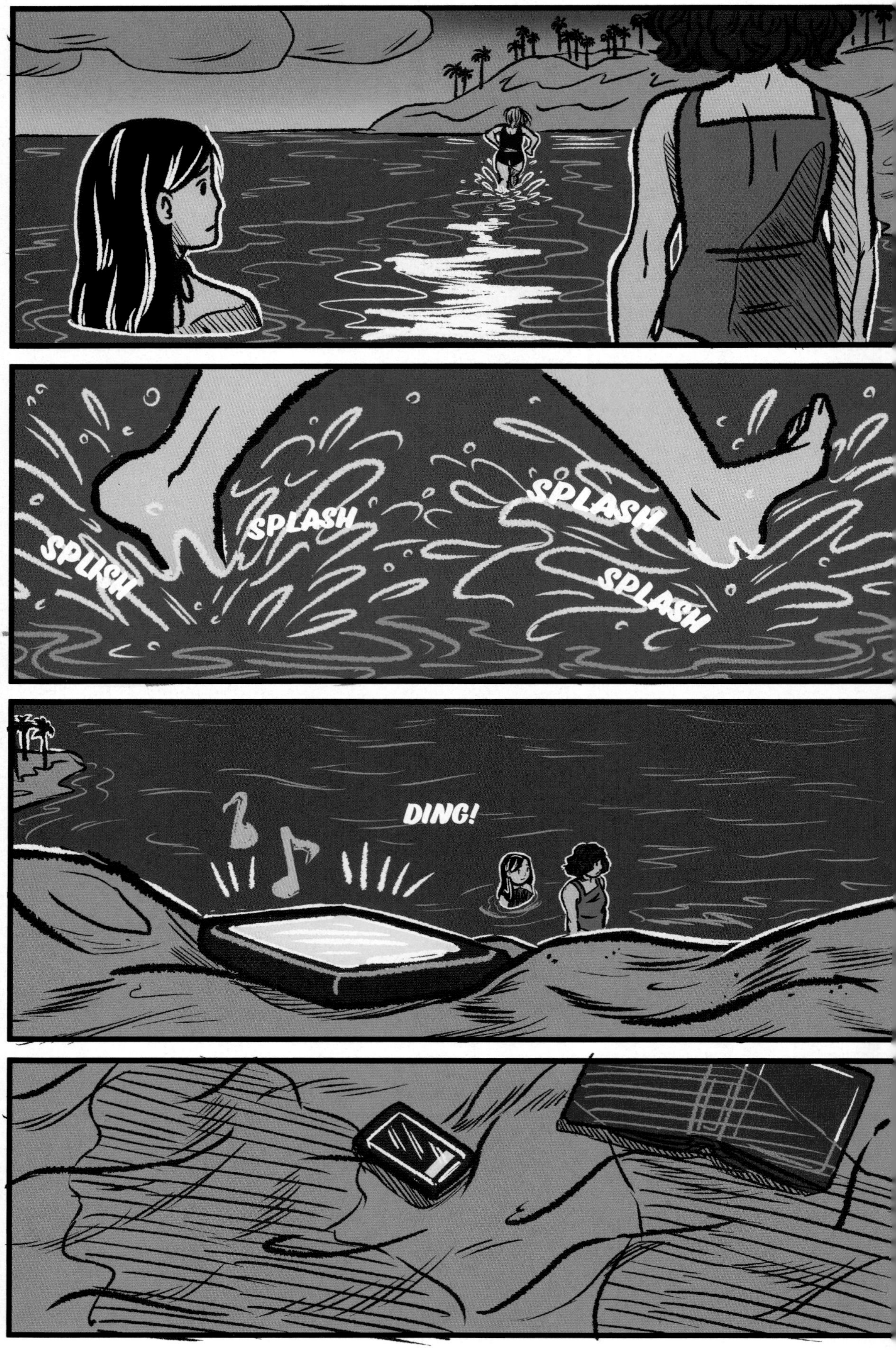
SPLISH
SPLASH
SPLASH
SPLASH
DING!

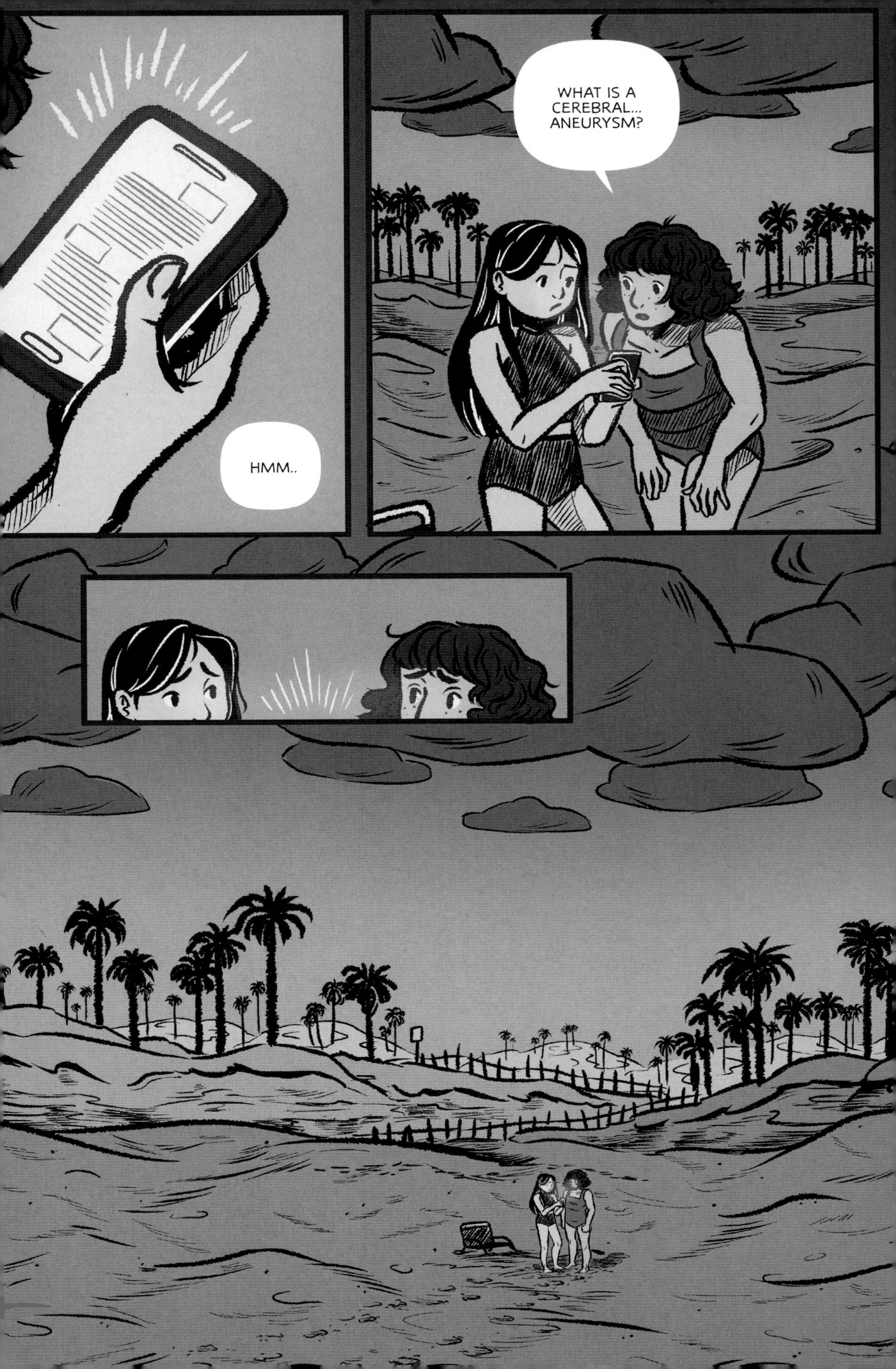
HMM..
WHAT IS A CEREBRAL... ANEURYSM?

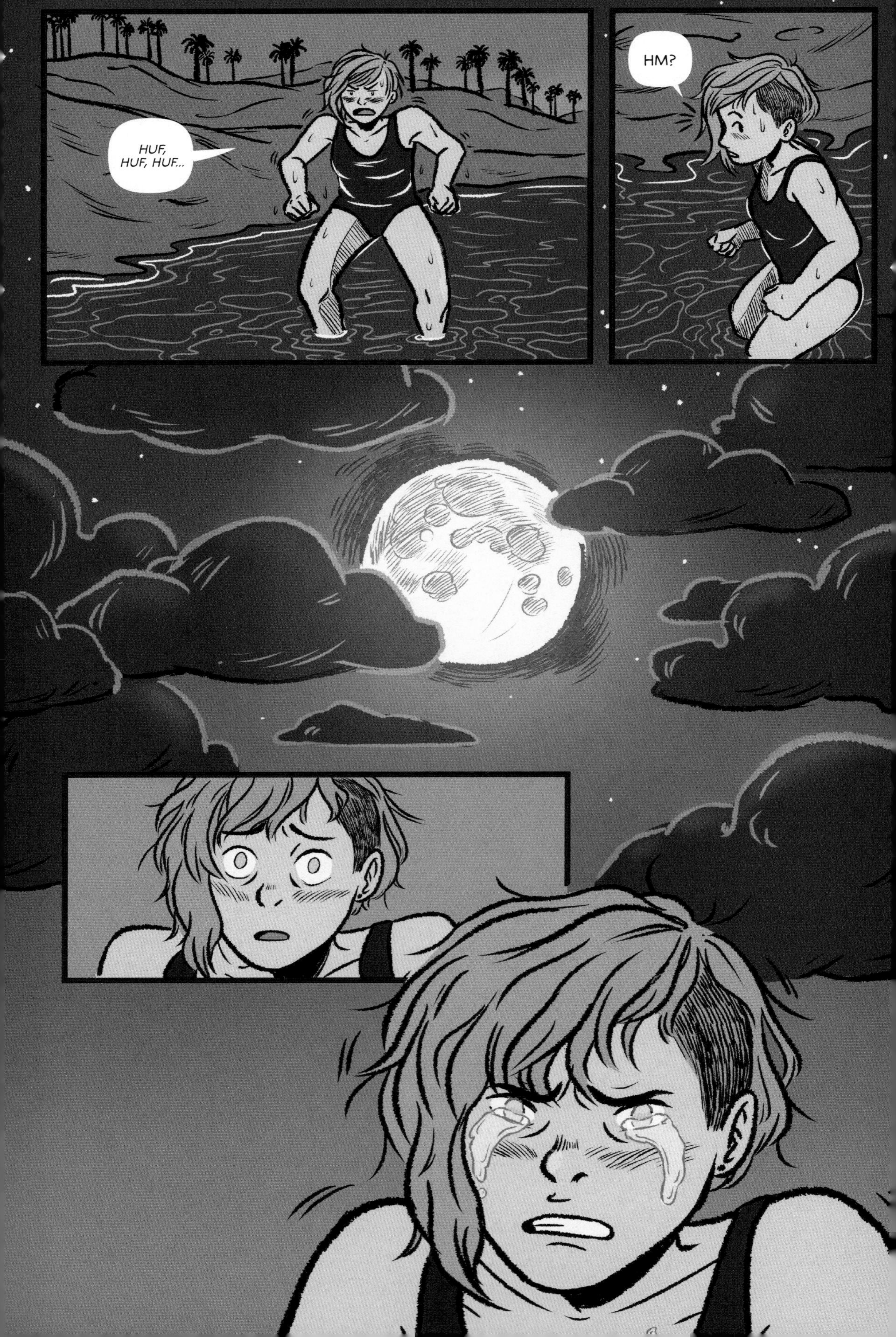
HUF, HUF, HUF...
HM?

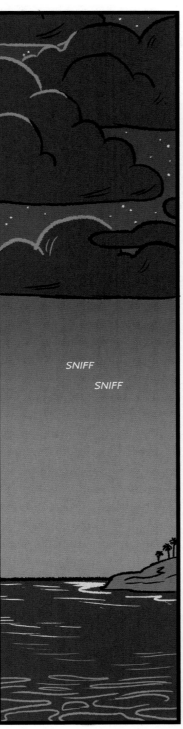

SNIFF

SNIFF

SNIFF

SNIFF

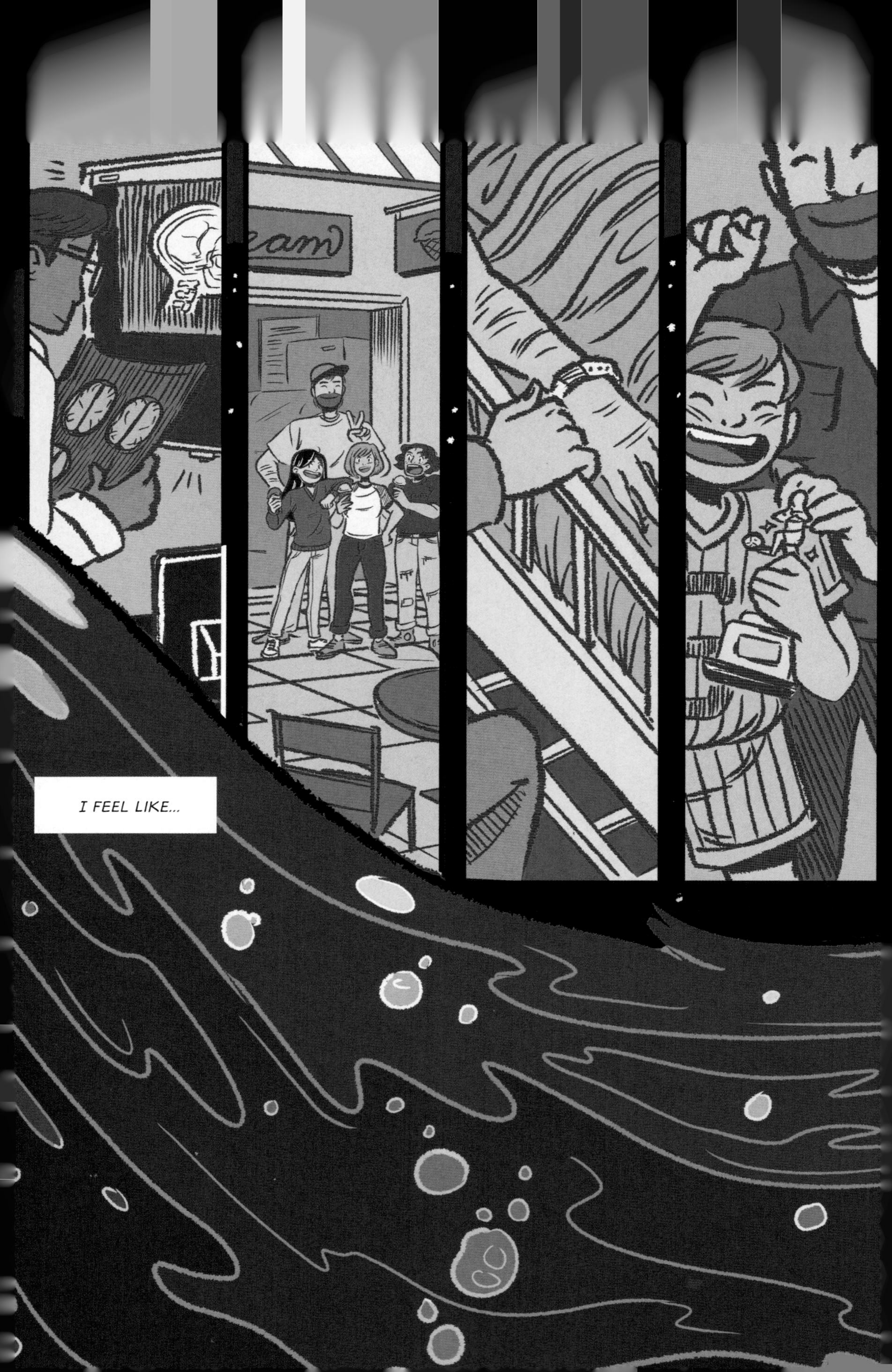
I FEEL LIKE...

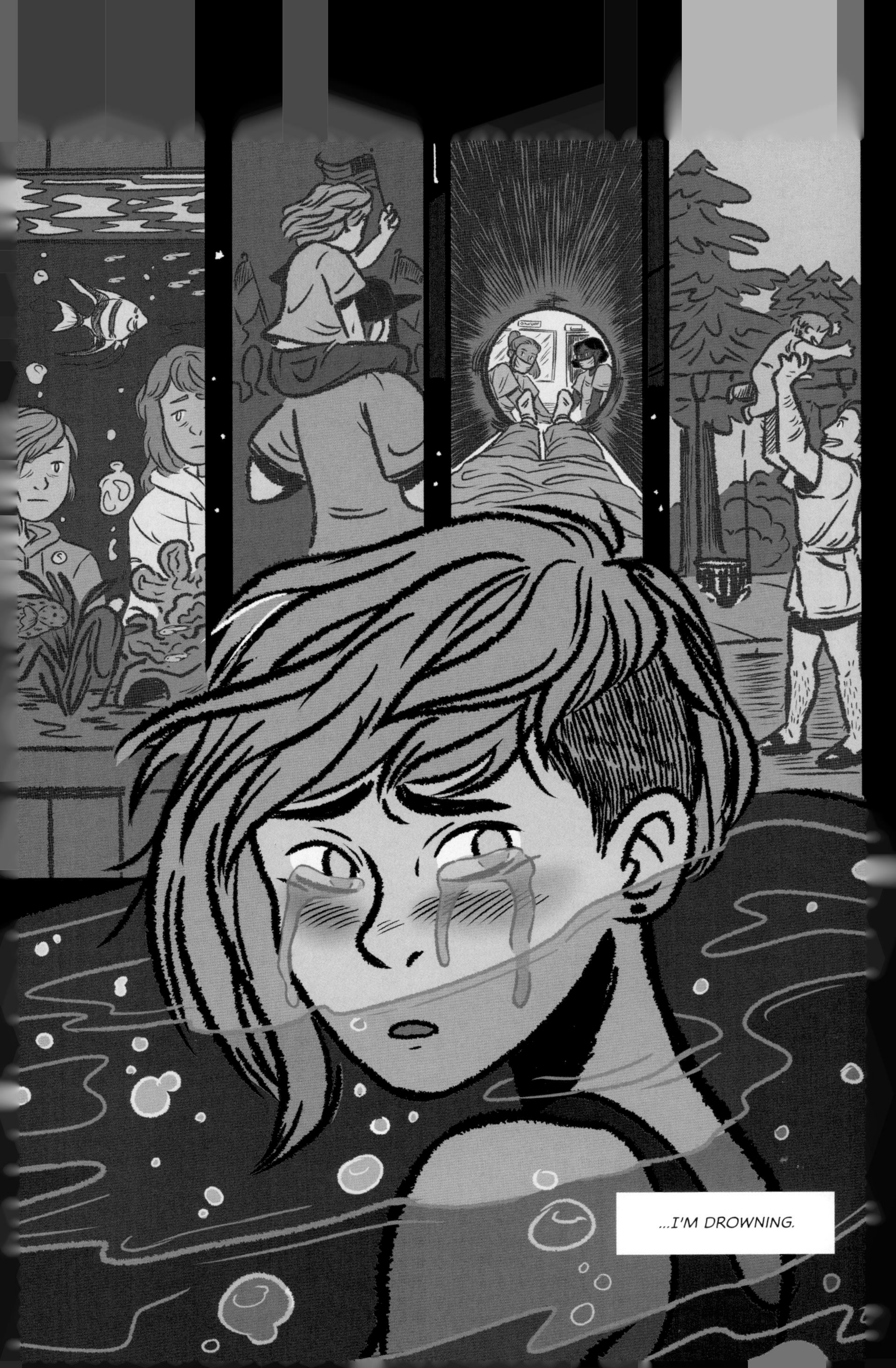
...I'M DROWNING.

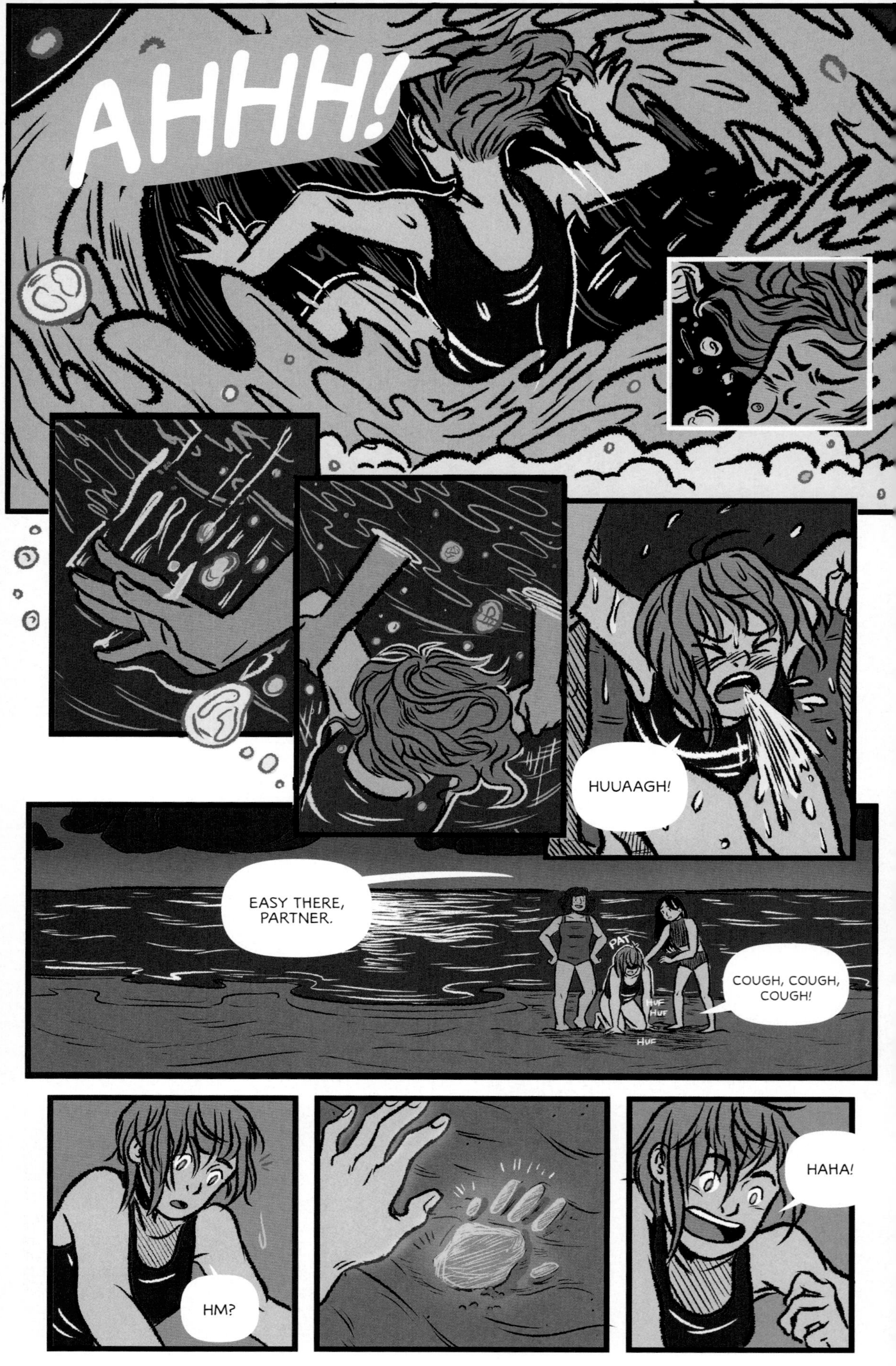
AHHH!
HUUAAGH!
EASY THERE, PARTNER.
PAT
COUGH, COUGH, COUGH!
HUF HUF
HUF
HM?
HAHA!

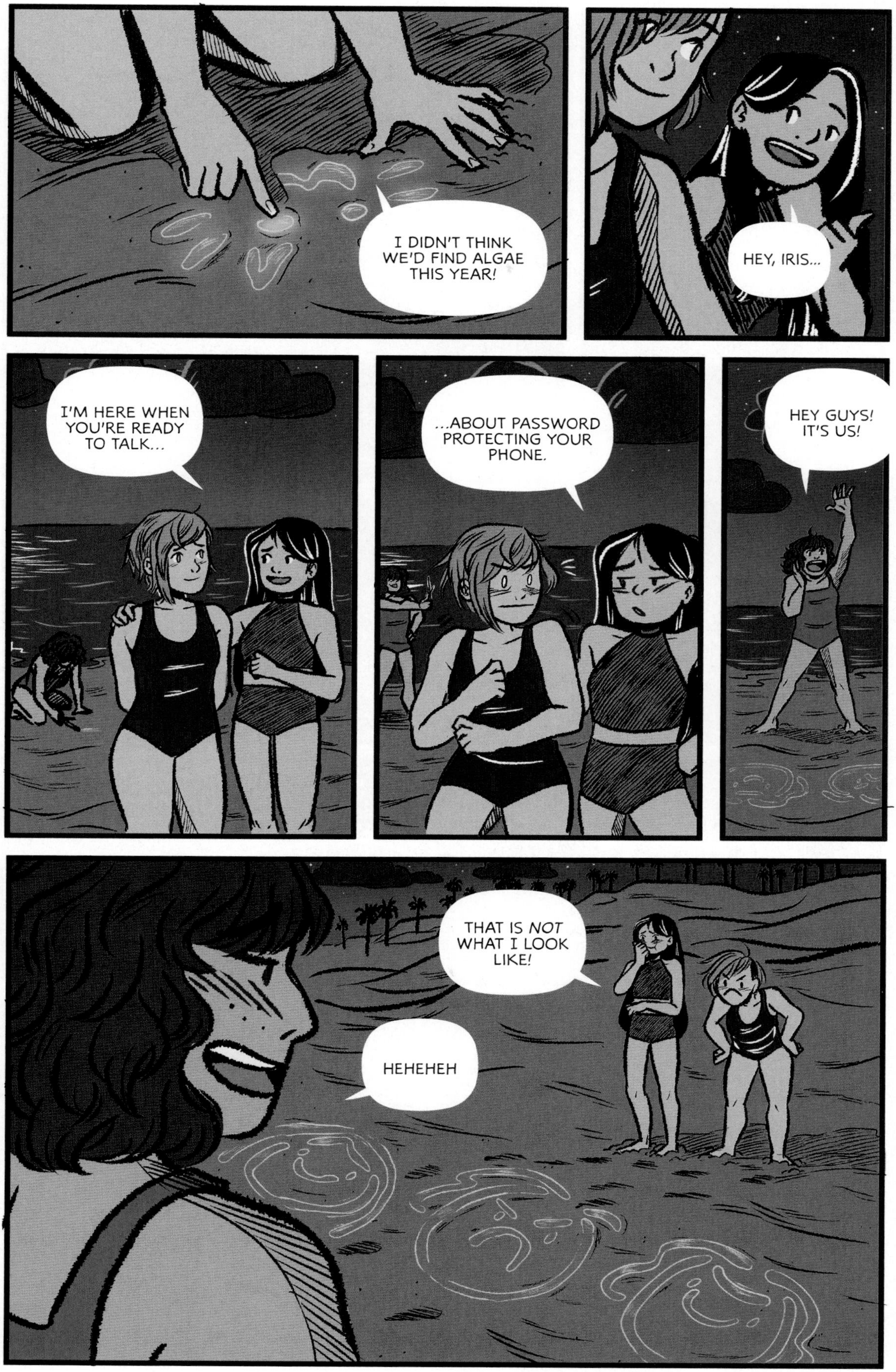

I DIDN'T THINK WE'D FIND ALGAE THIS YEAR!
HEY, IRIS...
I'M HERE WHEN YOU'RE READY TO TALK...
...ABOUT PASSWORD PROTECTING YOUR PHONE.
HEY GUYS! IT'S US!
THAT IS NOT WHAT I LOOK LIKE!
HEHEHEH

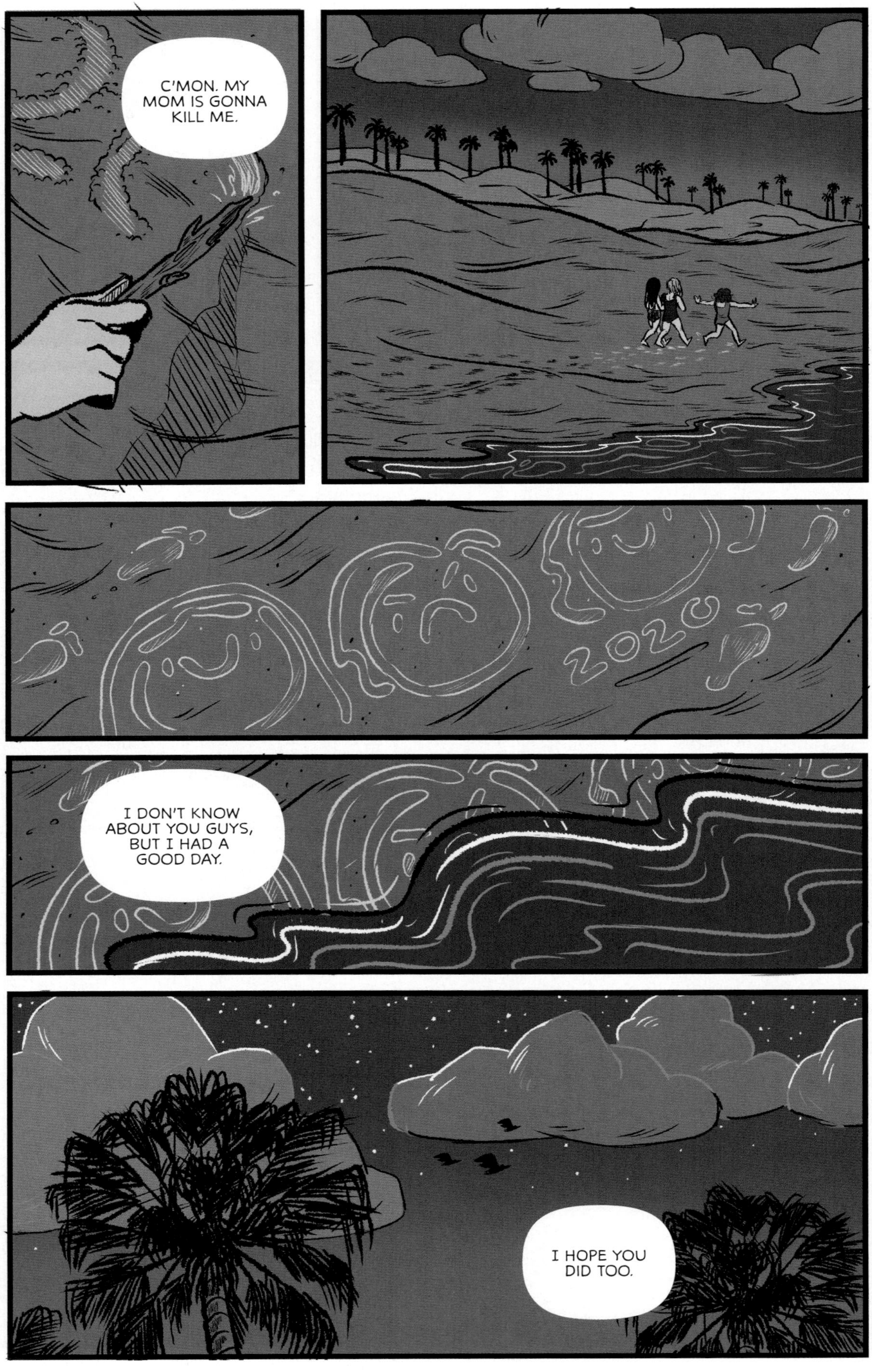
C'MON. MY MOM IS GONNA KILL ME.
2020
I DON'T KNOW ABOUT YOU GUYS, BUT I HAD A GOOD DAY.
I HOPE YOU DID TOO.

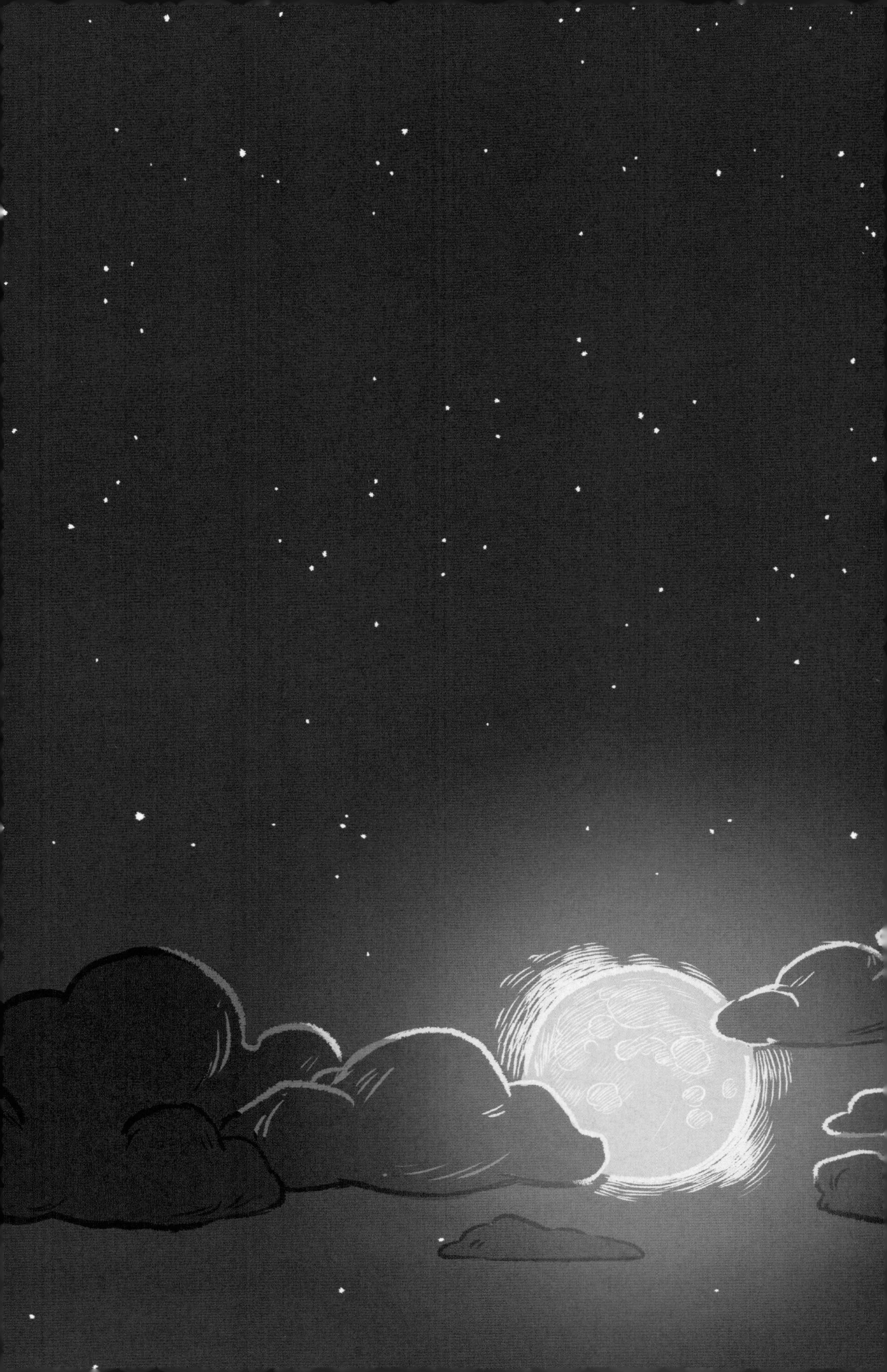

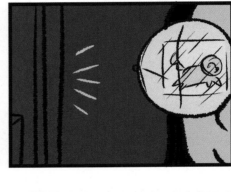

STUDY GUIDE

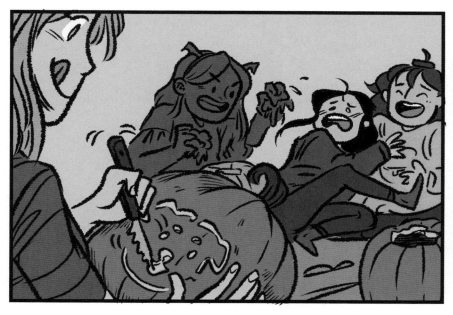

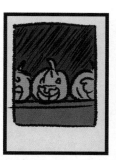

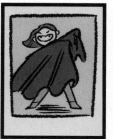

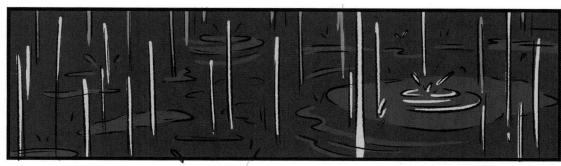

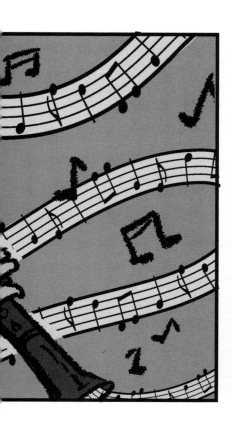

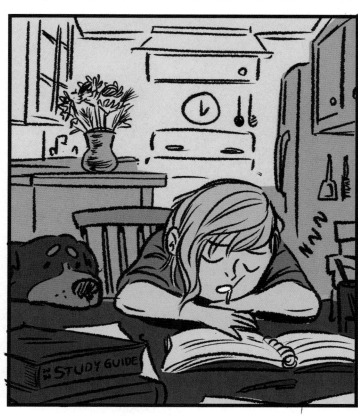

Chapter Five
lasagna

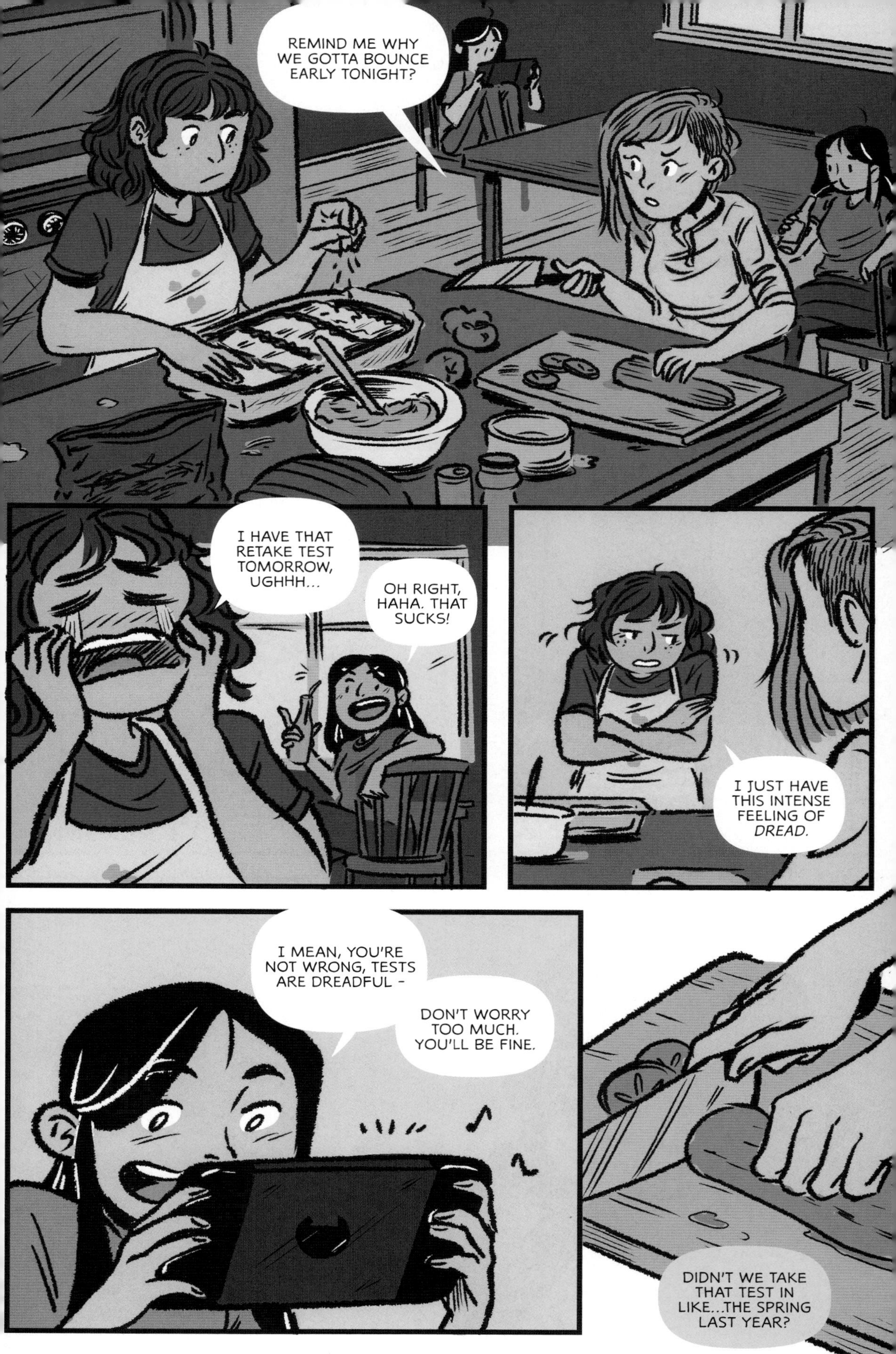
REMIND ME WHY WE GOTTA BOUNCE EARLY TONIGHT?
I HAVE THAT RETAKE TEST TOMORROW, UGHHH...
OH RIGHT, HAHA. THAT SUCKS!
I JUST HAVE THIS INTENSE FEELING OF *DREAD.*
I MEAN, YOU'RE NOT WRONG, TESTS ARE DREADFUL -
DON'T WORRY TOO MUCH. YOU'LL BE FINE.
DIDN'T WE TAKE THAT TEST IN LIKE...THE SPRING LAST YEAR?

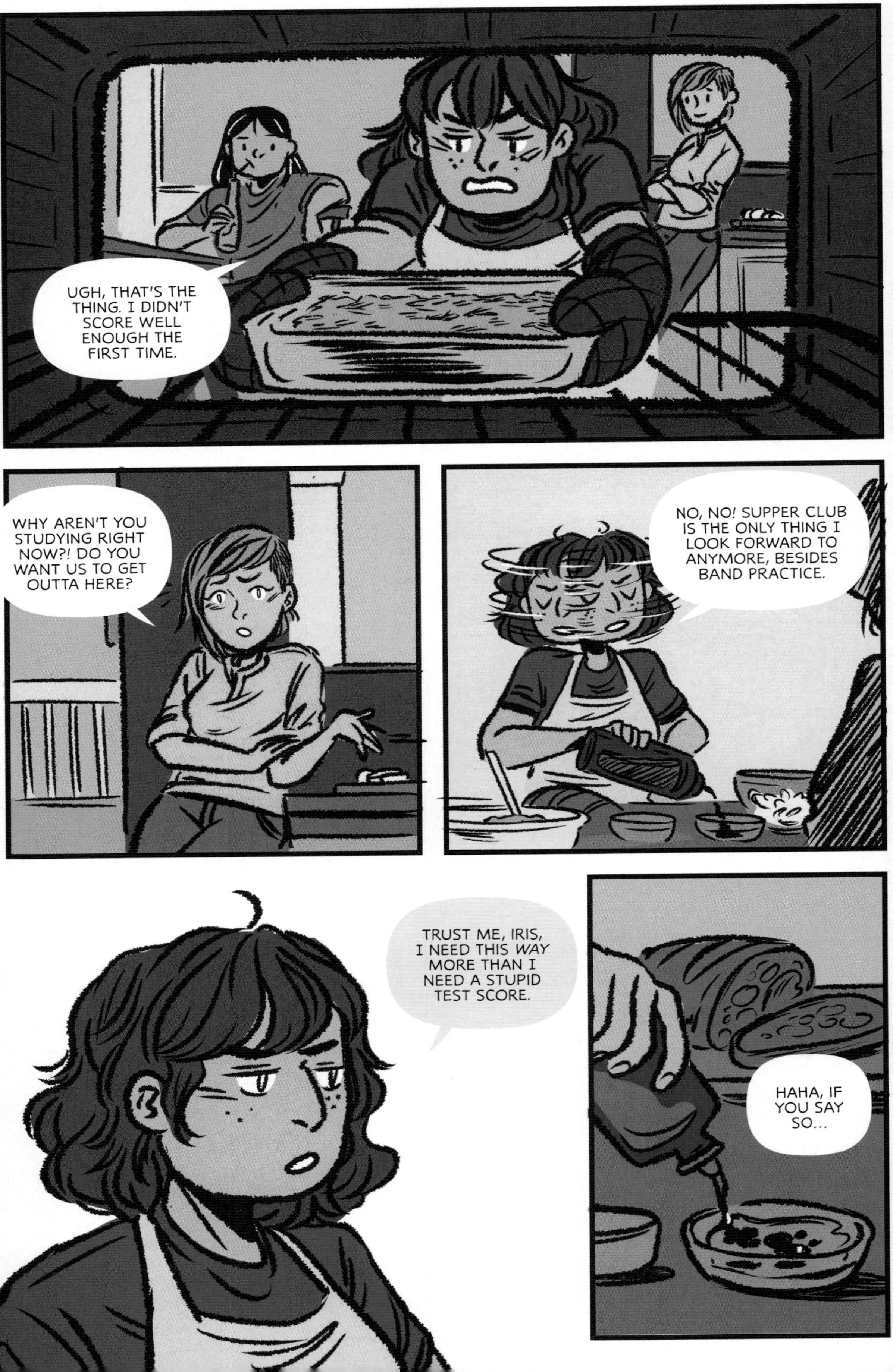
UGH, THAT'S THE THING. I DIDN'T SCORE WELL ENOUGH THE FIRST TIME.
WHY AREN'T YOU STUDYING RIGHT NOW?! DO YOU WANT US TO GET OUTTA HERE?
NO, NO! SUPPER CLUB IS THE ONLY THING I LOOK FORWARD TO ANYMORE, BESIDES BAND PRACTICE.
TRUST ME, IRIS, I NEED THIS *WAY* MORE THAN I NEED A STUPID TEST SCORE.
HAHA, IF YOU SAY SO...

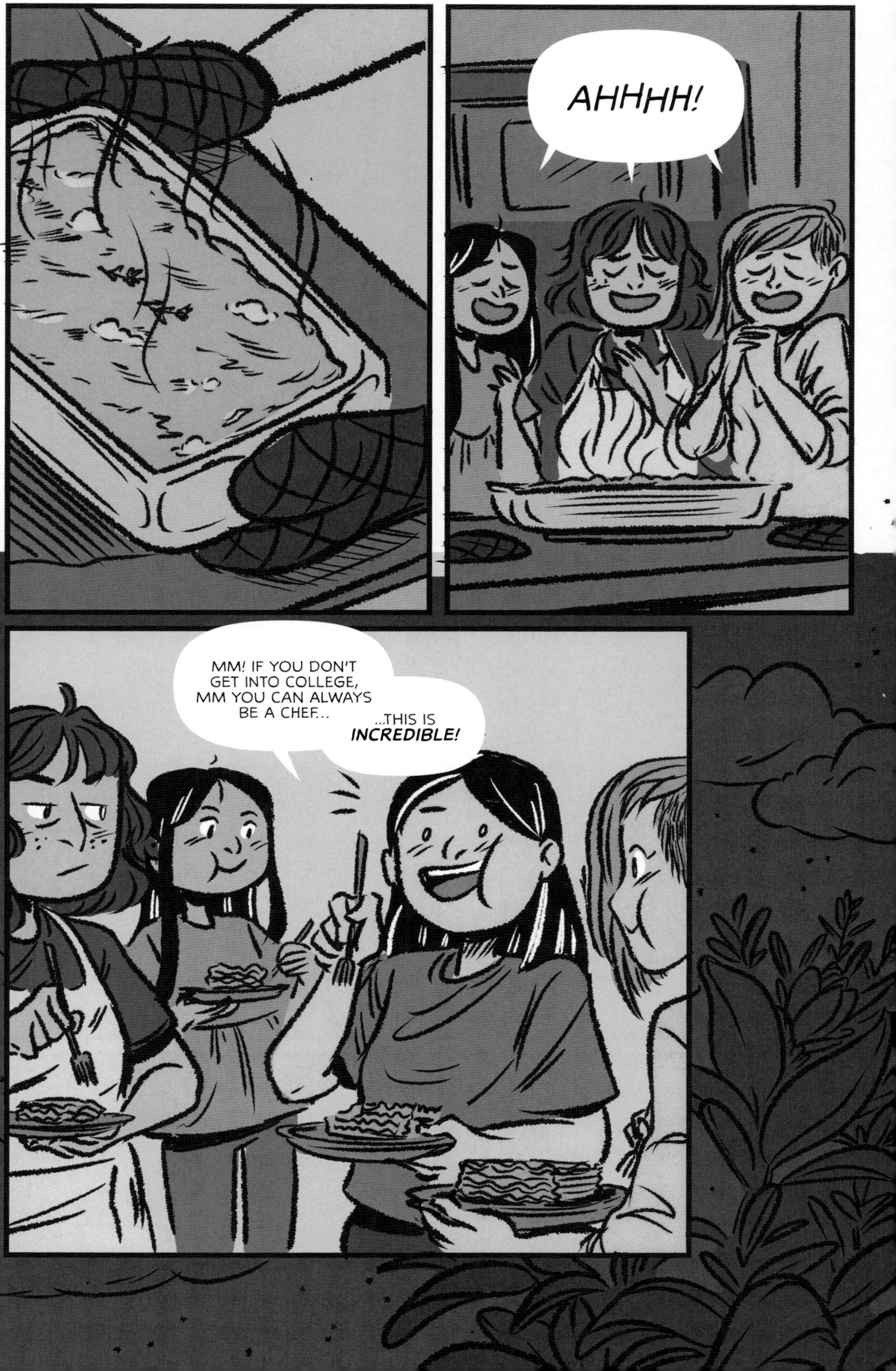
AHHHH!
MM! IF YOU DON'T GET INTO COLLEGE, MM YOU CAN ALWAYS BE A CHEF...
...THIS IS *INCREDIBLE!*

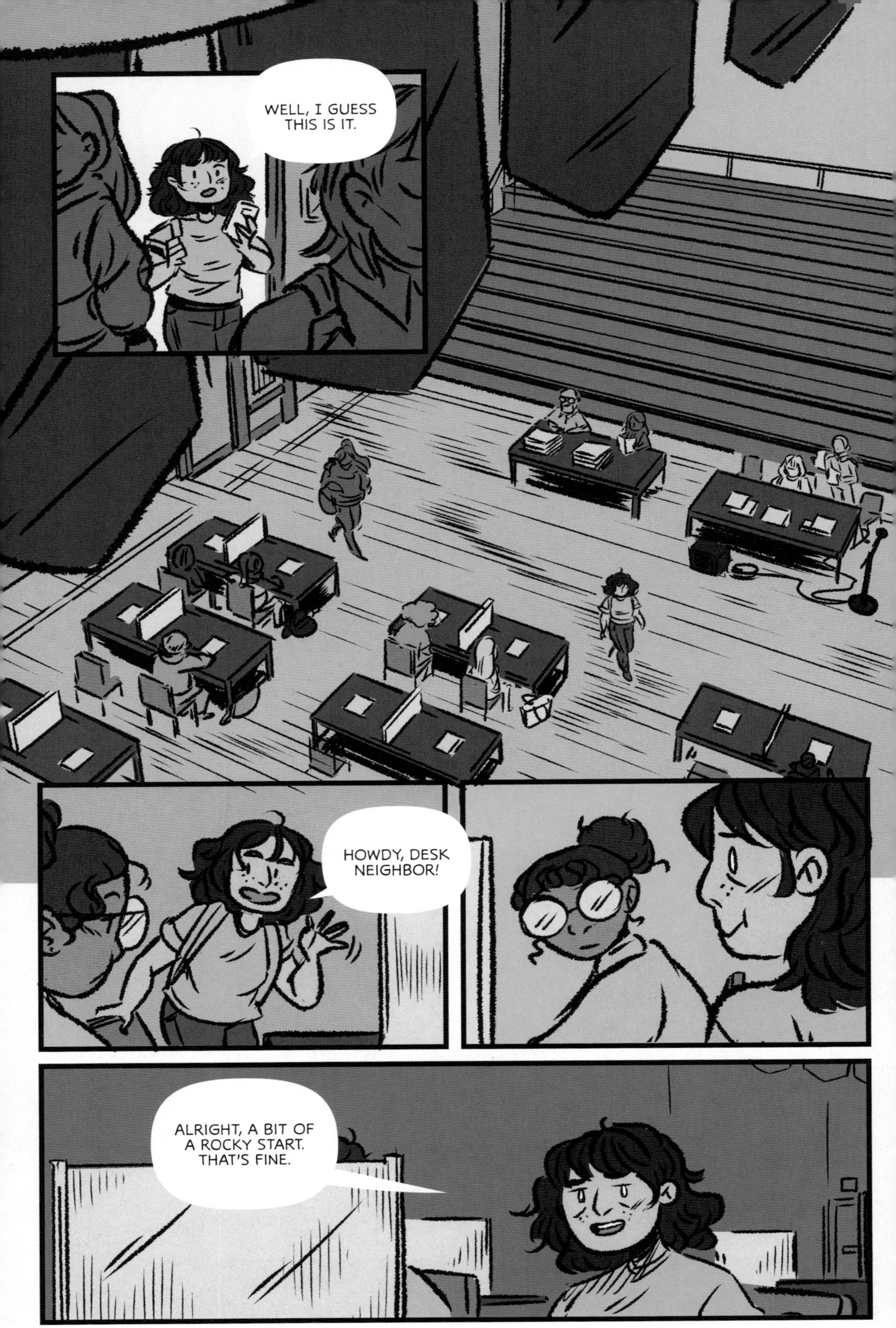
WELL, I GUESS THIS IS IT.
HOWDY, DESK NEIGHBOR!
ALRIGHT, A BIT OF A ROCKY START. THAT'S FINE.

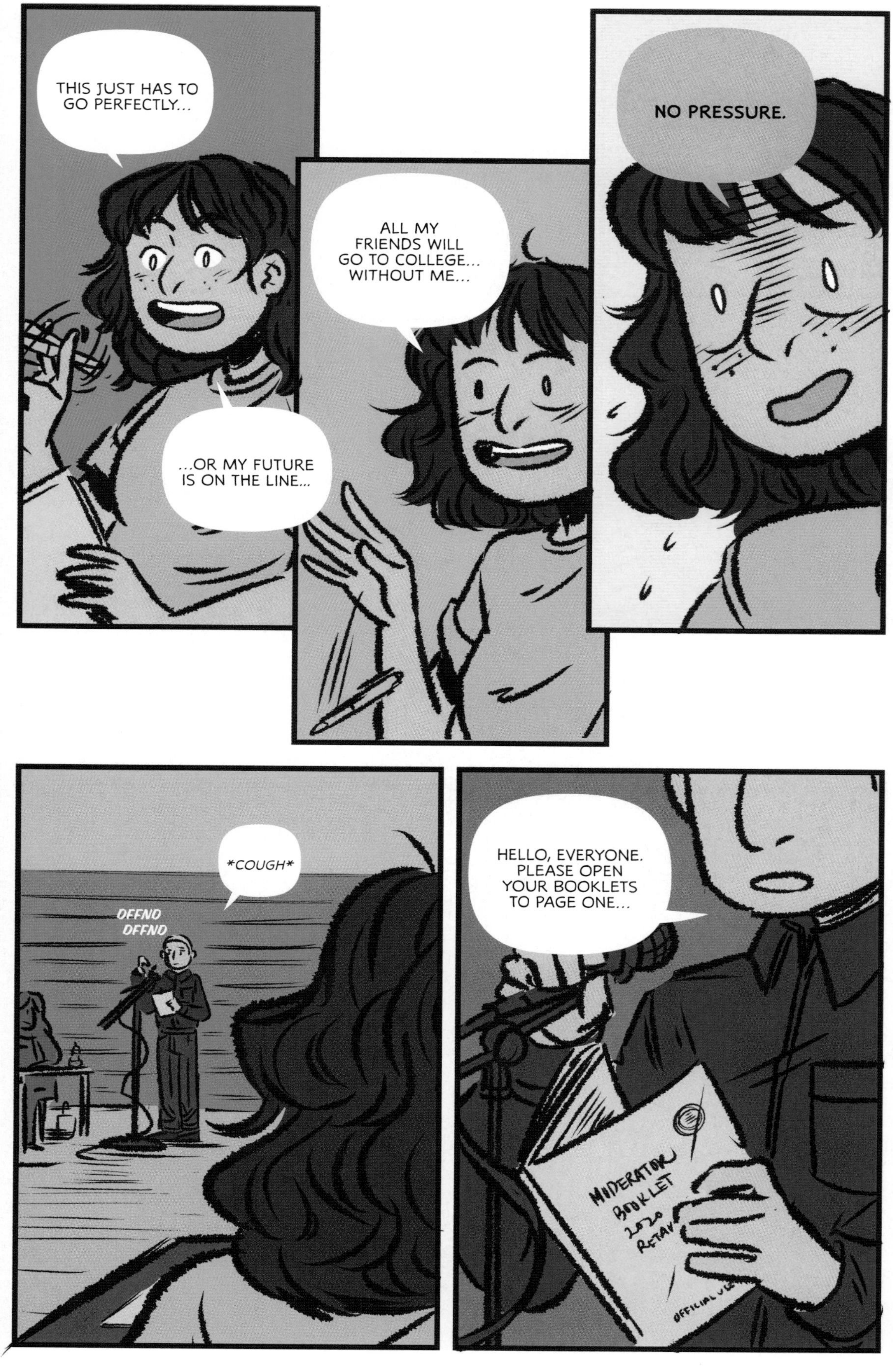
THIS JUST HAS TO GO PERFECTLY...
...OR MY FUTURE IS ON THE LINE...
ALL MY FRIENDS WILL GO TO COLLEGE... WITHOUT ME...
NO PRESSURE.
DFFND DFFND
COUGH
HELLO, EVERYONE. PLEASE OPEN YOUR BOOKLETS TO PAGE ONE...
MODERATOR BOOKLET 2020 RETAKE
OFFICIAL USE

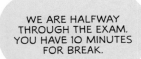

WE ARE HALFWAY THROUGH THE EXAM. YOU HAVE 10 MINUTES FOR BREAK.

~GURGLE~

OH BLESS, I WAS GETTING SO HUNGRY.

WAIT UP... *HALFWAY?*

OH CRAAAP.

EXCUSE ME! BOOKLETS *DOWN!*

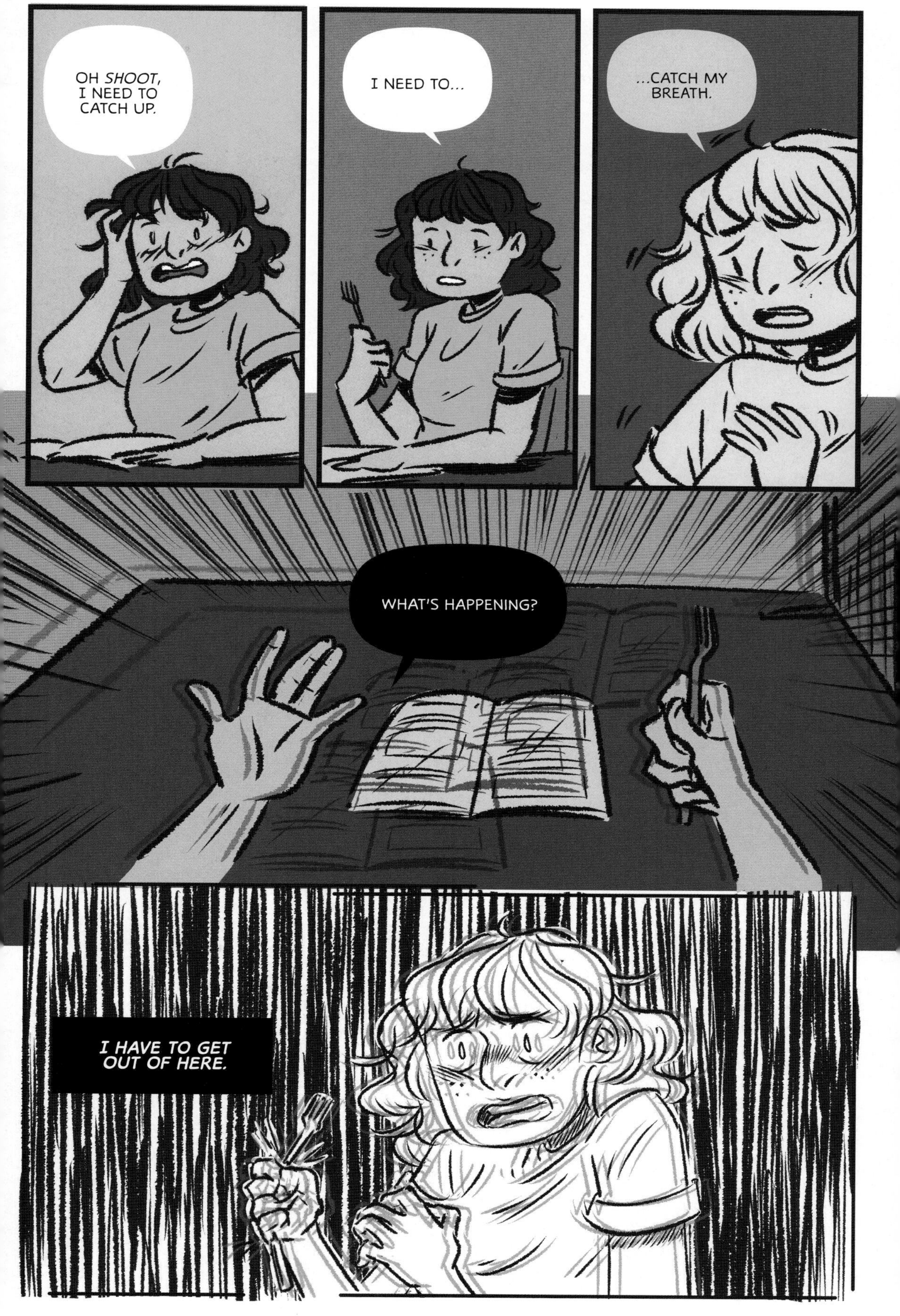

OH *SHOOT*, I NEED TO CATCH UP.
I NEED TO...
...CATCH MY BREATH.
WHAT'S HAPPENING?
I HAVE TO GET OUT OF HERE.

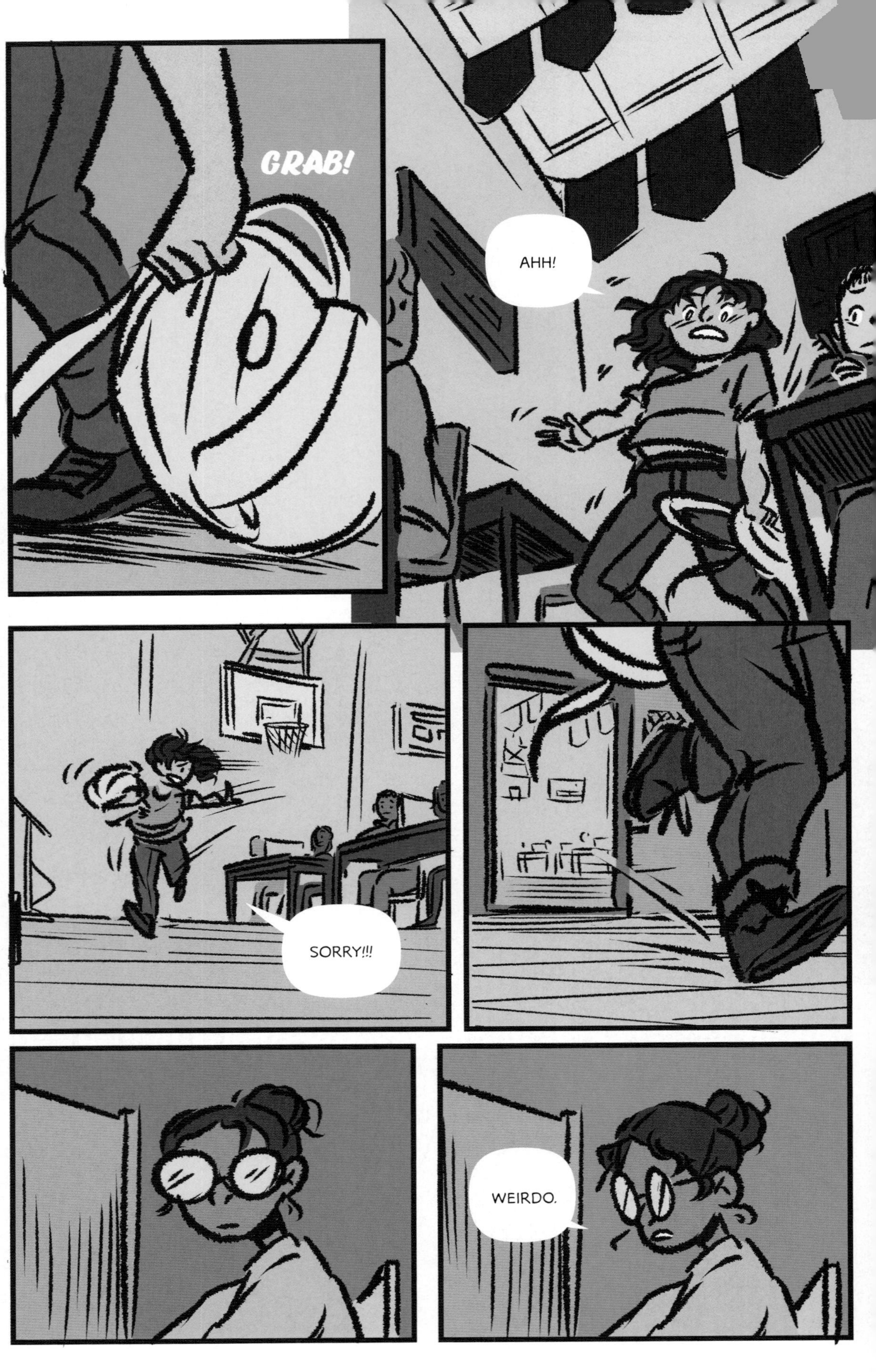
GRAB!
AHH!
SORRY!!!
WEIRDO.

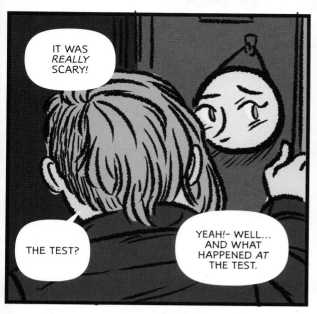

IT WAS *REALLY* SCARY!

THE TEST?

YEAH!- WELL... AND WHAT HAPPENED *AT* THE TEST.

SLAM!

IT SOUNDS STUPID BUT...I FELT LIKE I WAS GOING TO DIE.

NORA, YOU SAY THAT YOU'RE 'DYING' WHEN YOU HAVEN'T EATEN IN LIKE...TWO HOURS.

YEAH, 'CAUSE IT'S *TRUE,* BUT -

TESTS ARE REALLY INTIMIDATING. I WOULDN'T WORRY TOO MUCH ABOUT IT.

I DUNNO. THIS WAS... DIFFERENT.

I TOTALLY LOST CONTROL.

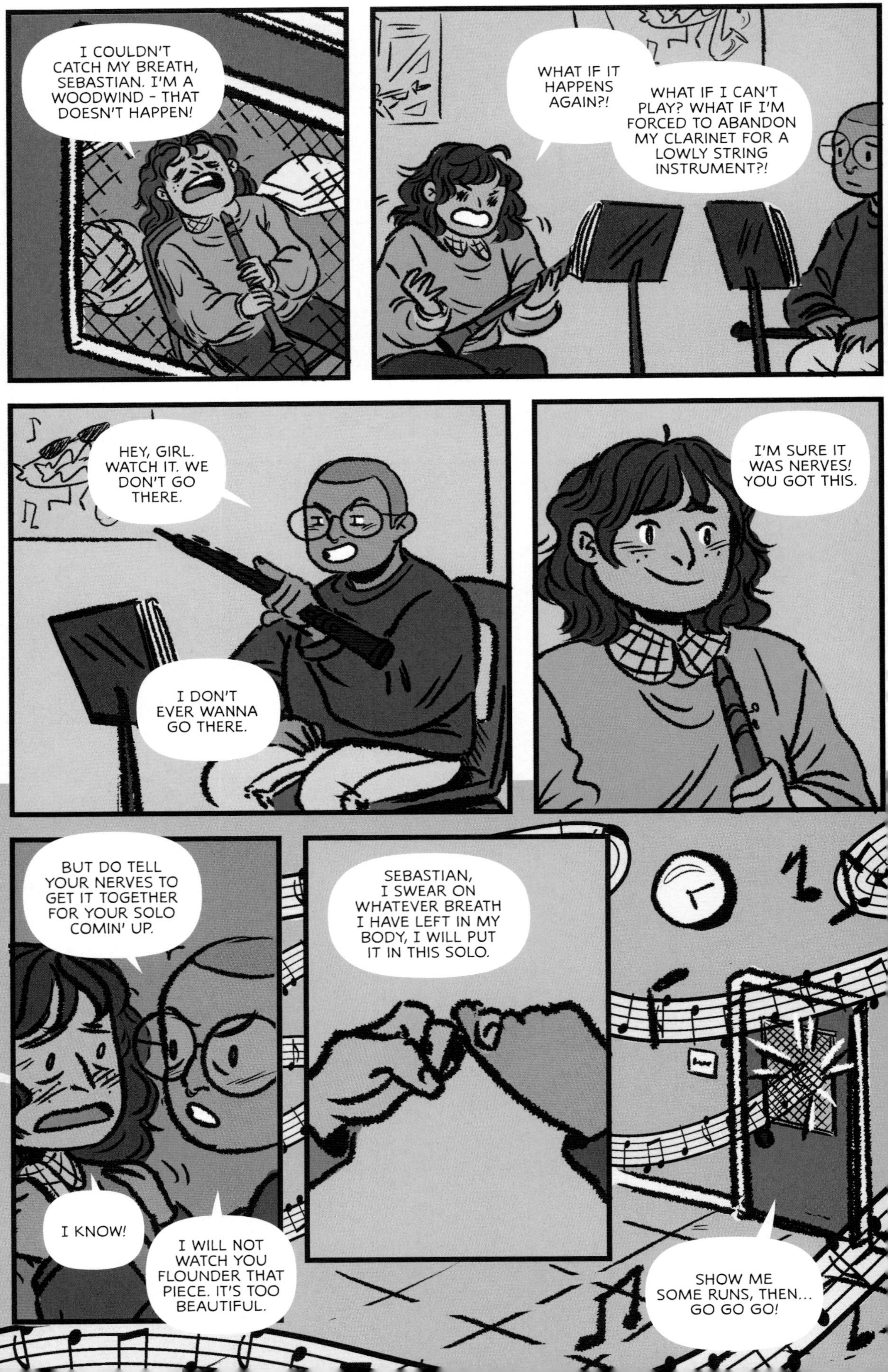

I COULDN'T CATCH MY BREATH, SEBASTIAN. I'M A WOODWIND - THAT DOESN'T HAPPEN!
WHAT IF IT HAPPENS AGAIN?!
WHAT IF I CAN'T PLAY? WHAT IF I'M FORCED TO ABANDON MY CLARINET FOR A LOWLY STRING INSTRUMENT?!
HEY, GIRL. WATCH IT. WE DON'T GO THERE.
I DON'T EVER WANNA GO THERE.
I'M SURE IT WAS NERVES! YOU GOT THIS.
BUT DO TELL YOUR NERVES TO GET IT TOGETHER FOR YOUR SOLO COMIN' UP.
I KNOW!
I WILL NOT WATCH YOU FLOUNDER THAT PIECE. IT'S TOO BEAUTIFUL.
SEBASTIAN, I SWEAR ON WHATEVER BREATH I HAVE LEFT IN MY BODY, I WILL PUT IT IN THIS SOLO.
SHOW ME SOME RUNS, THEN... GO GO GO!

Chapter Six
vegan brownies

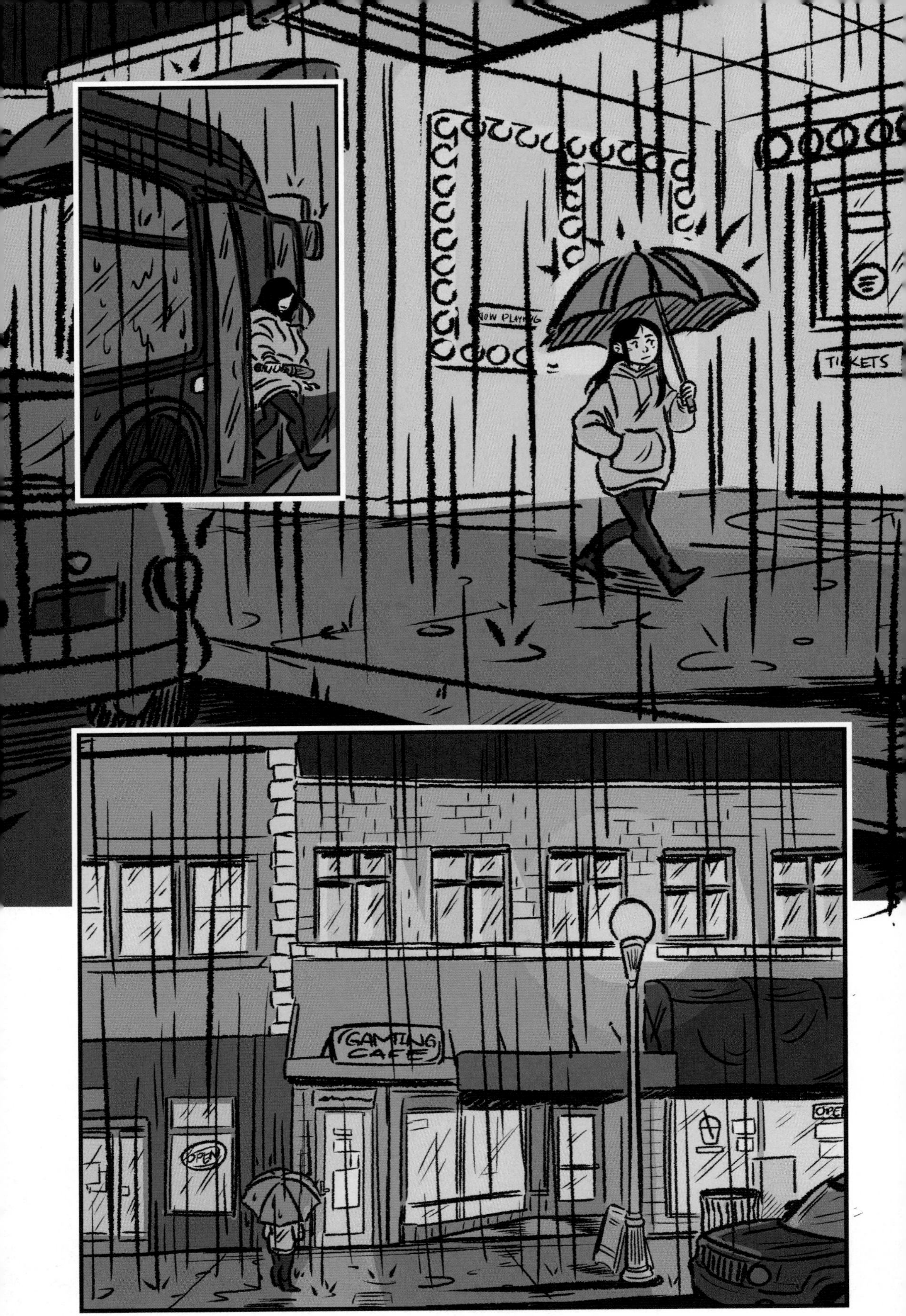
NOW PLAYING
TICKETS
GAMING CAFE
OPEN
OPEN

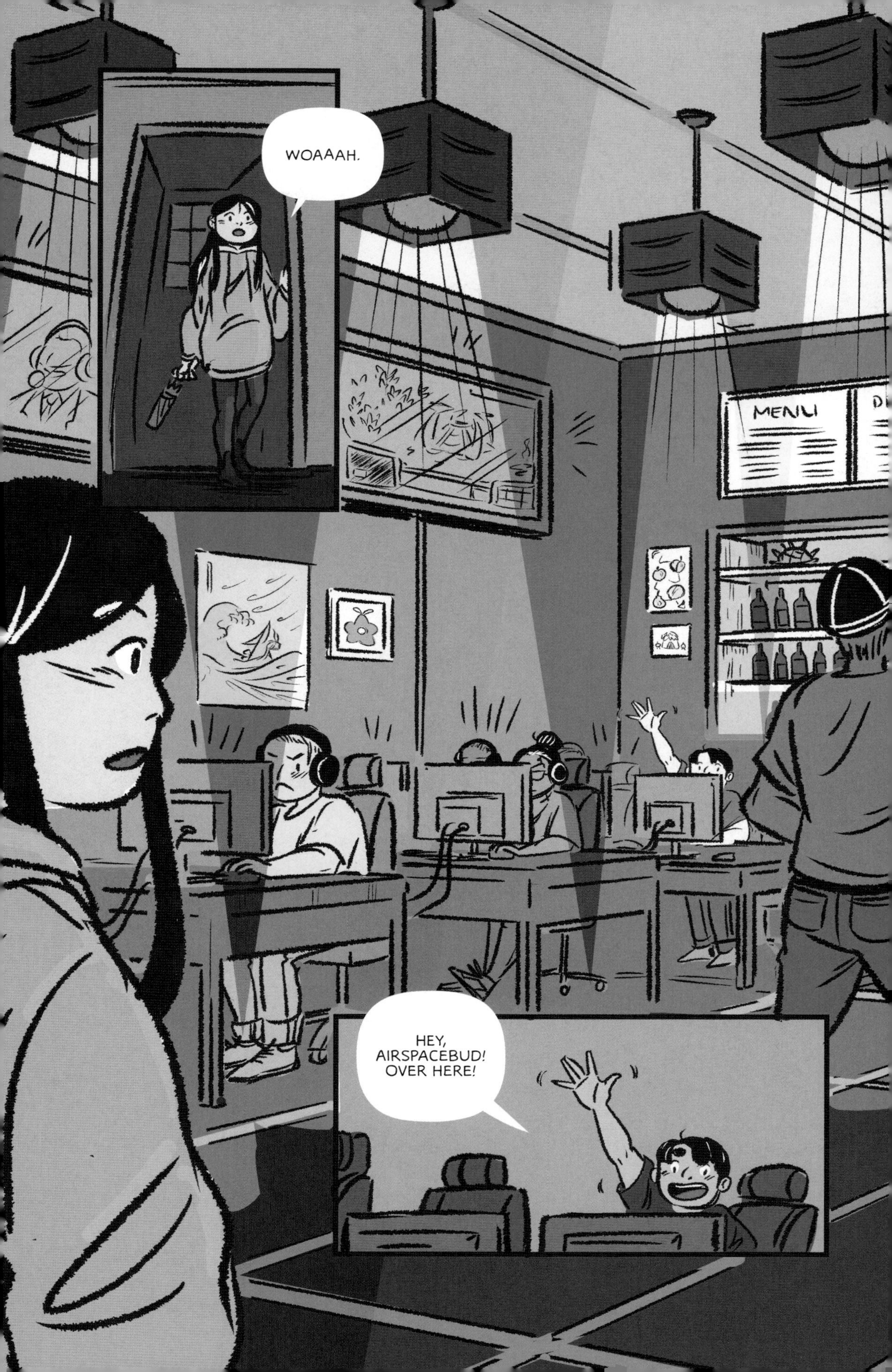
WOAAAH.
MENU
HEY, AIRSPACEBUD! OVER HERE!

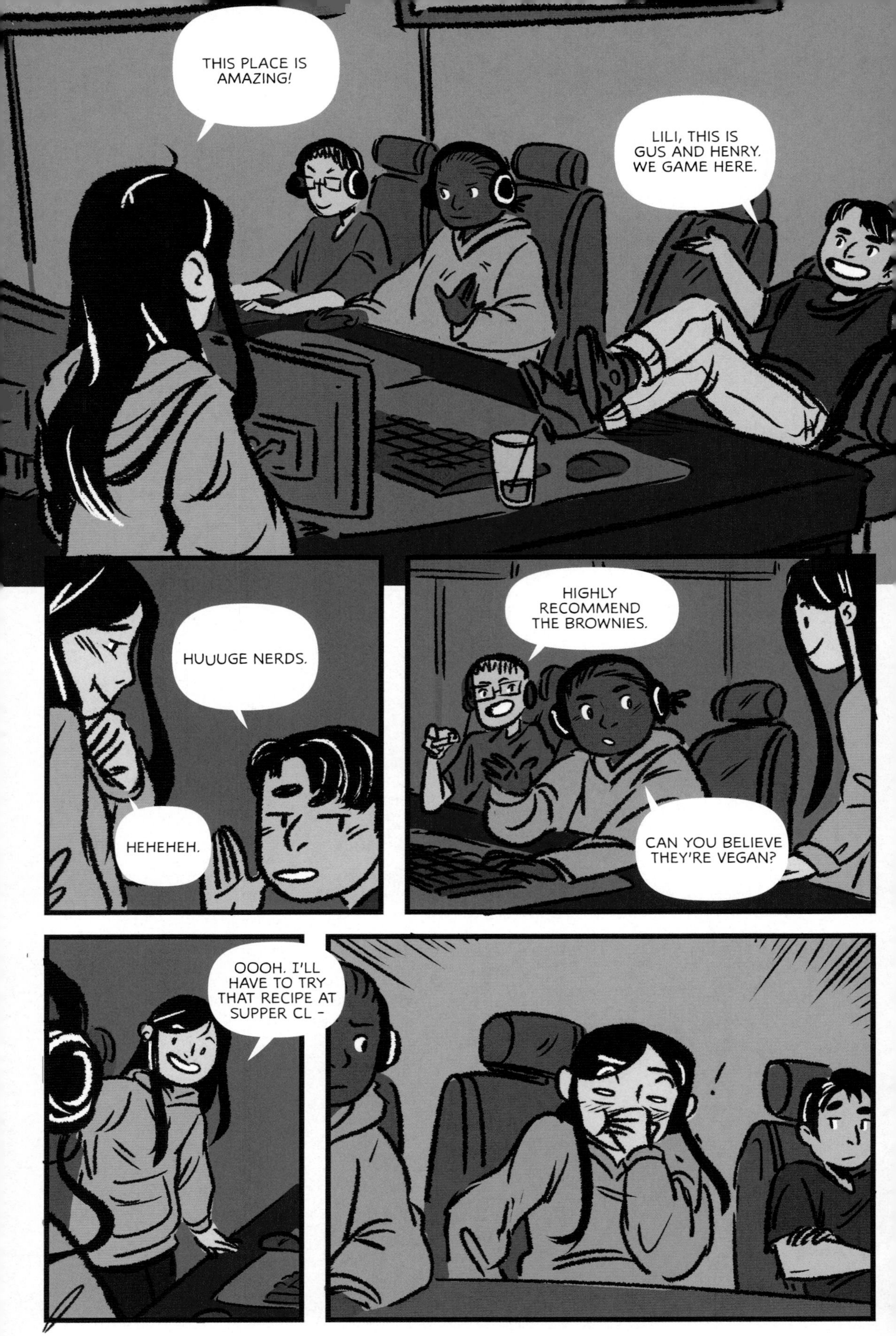
THIS PLACE IS AMAZING!
LILI, THIS IS GUS AND HENRY. WE GAME HERE.
HUUUGE NERDS.
HEHEHEH.
HIGHLY RECOMMEND THE BROWNIES.
CAN YOU BELIEVE THEY'RE VEGAN?
OOOH. I'LL HAVE TO TRY THAT RECIPE AT SUPPER CL -

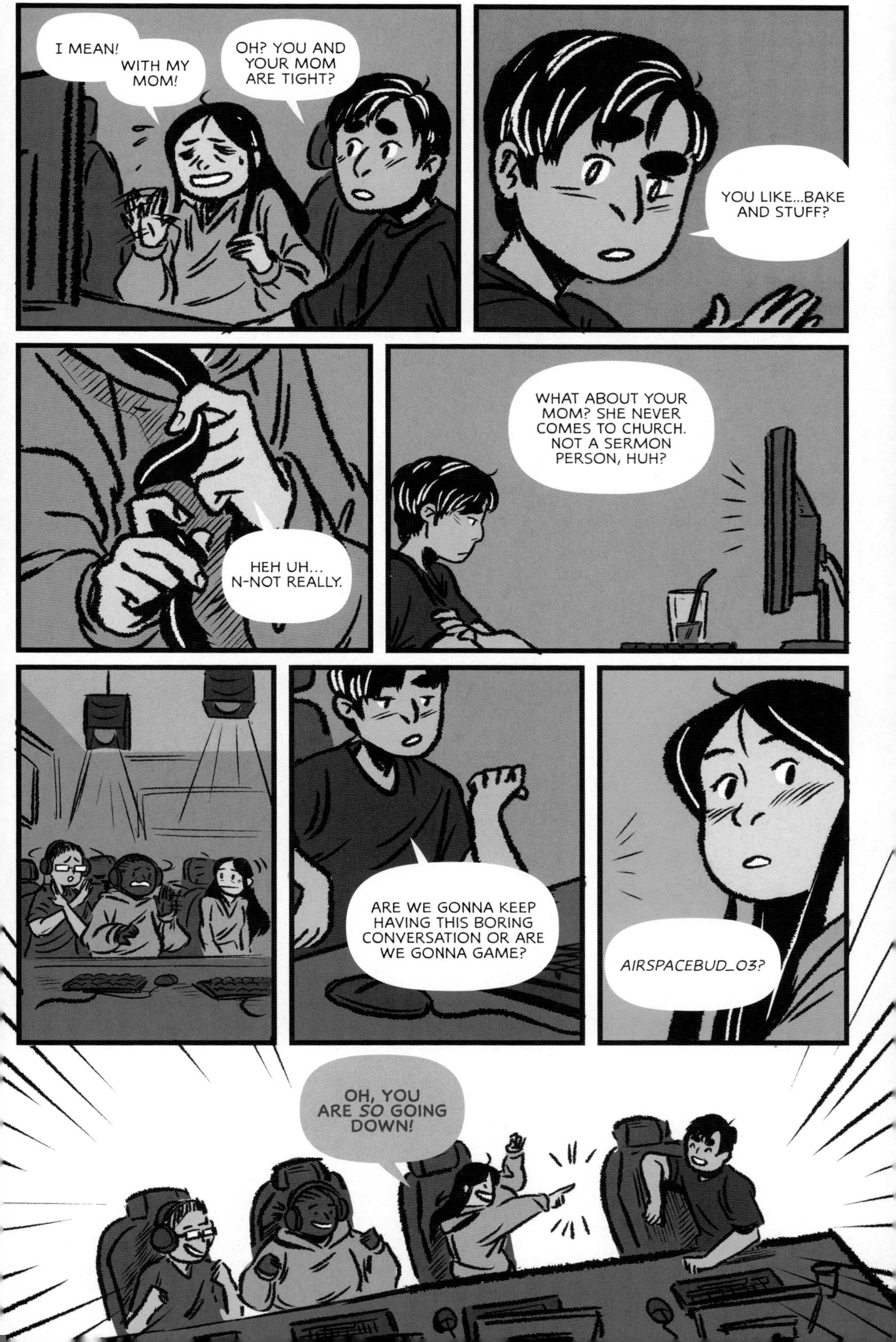
I MEAN!
WITH MY MOM!
OH? YOU AND YOUR MOM ARE TIGHT?
YOU LIKE...BAKE AND STUFF?
HEH UH... N-NOT REALLY.
WHAT ABOUT YOUR MOM? SHE NEVER COMES TO CHURCH. NOT A SERMON PERSON, HUH?
ARE WE GONNA KEEP HAVING THIS BORING CONVERSATION OR ARE WE GONNA GAME?
AIRSPACEBUD_03?
OH, YOU ARE *SO* GOING DOWN!

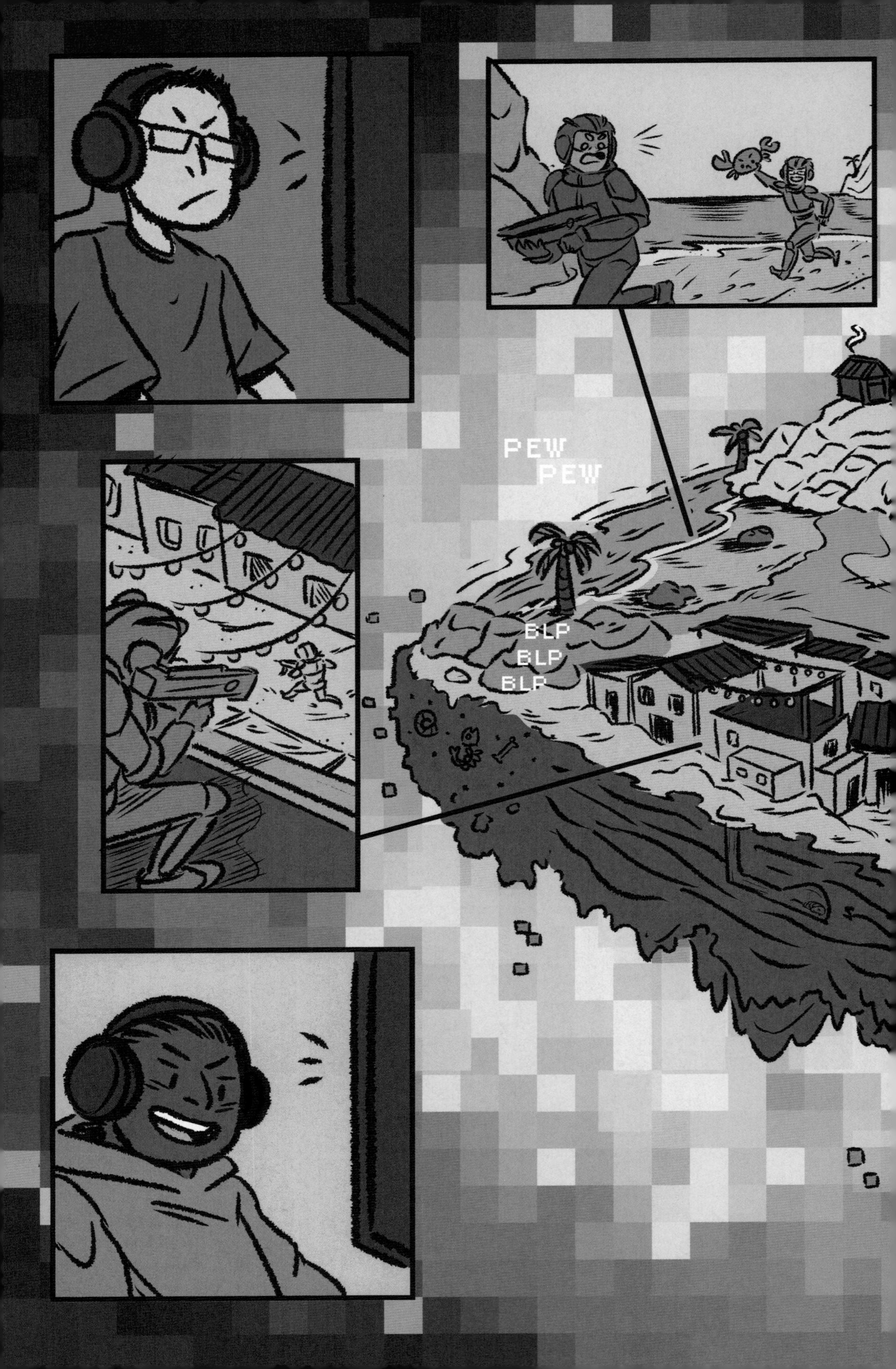
PEW
PEW
BLP
BLP
BLP

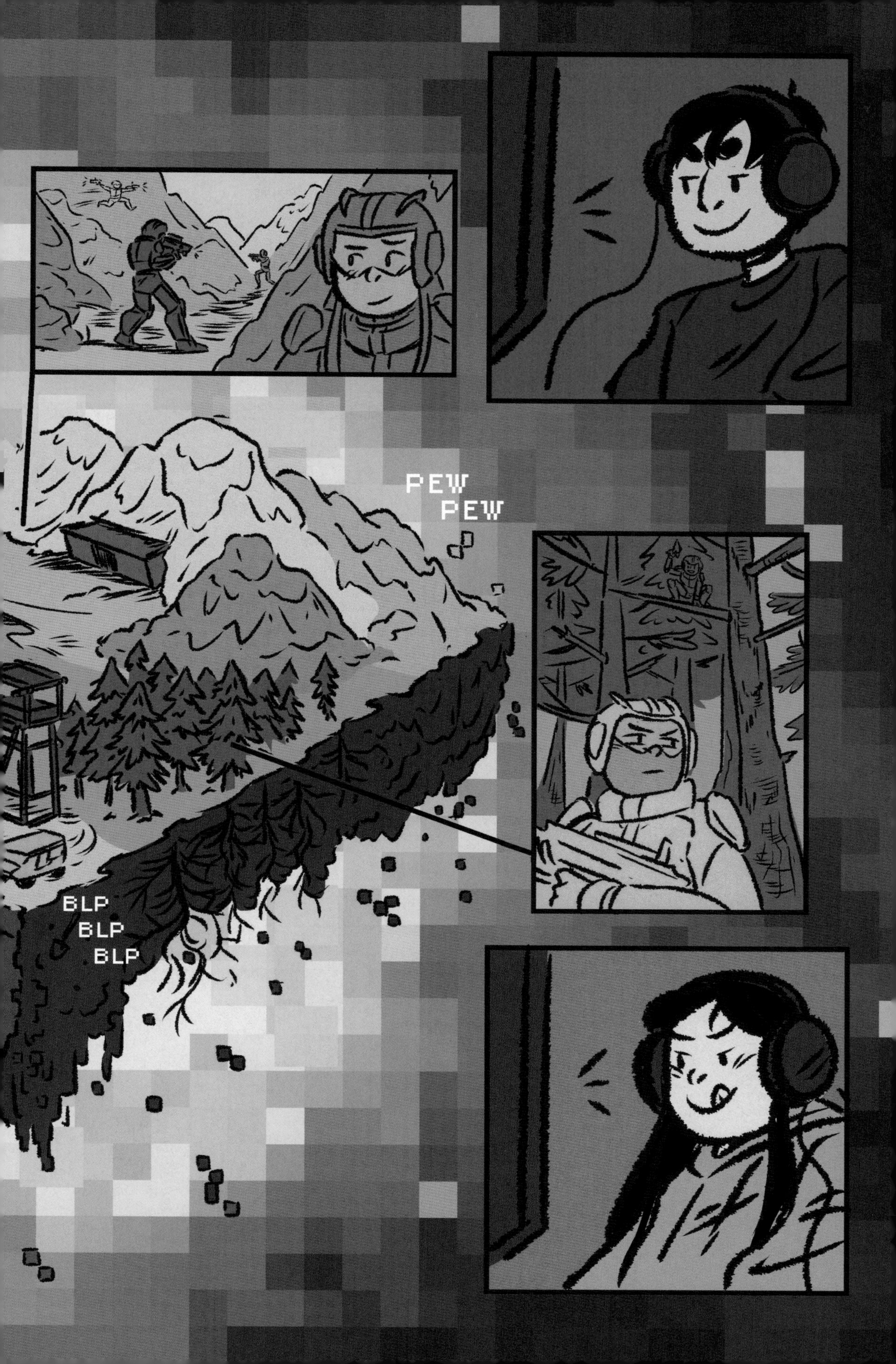
PEW
PEW
BLP
BLP
BLP

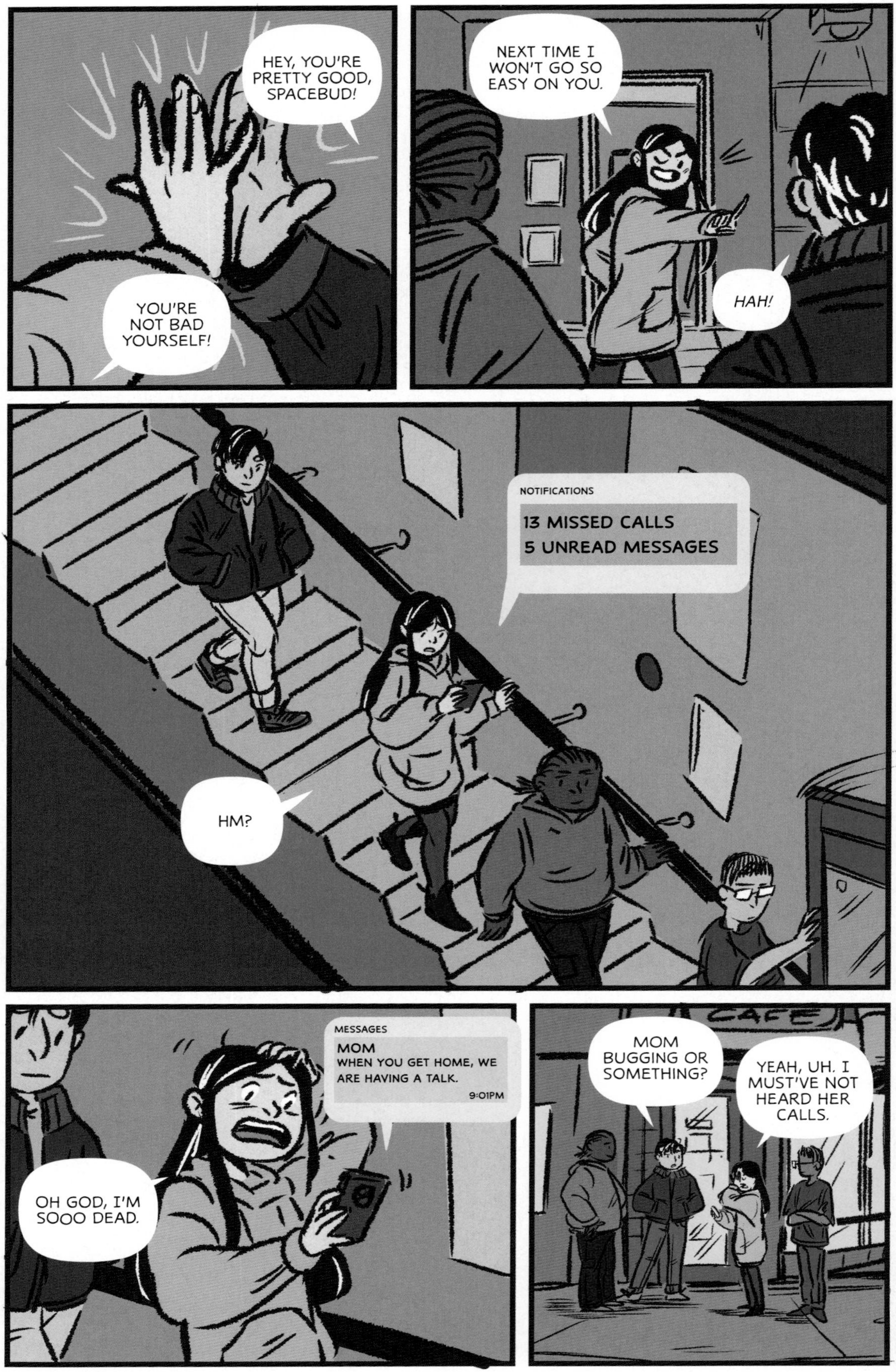
HEY, YOU'RE PRETTY GOOD, SPACEBUD!
YOU'RE NOT BAD YOURSELF!
NEXT TIME I WON'T GO SO EASY ON YOU.
HAH!
NOTIFICATIONS
13 MISSED CALLS
5 UNREAD MESSAGES
HM?
MESSAGES
MOM
WHEN YOU GET HOME, WE ARE HAVING A TALK.
9:01PM
OH GOD, I'M SOOO DEAD.
CAFE
MOM BUGGING OR SOMETHING?
YEAH, UH. I MUST'VE NOT HEARD HER CALLS.

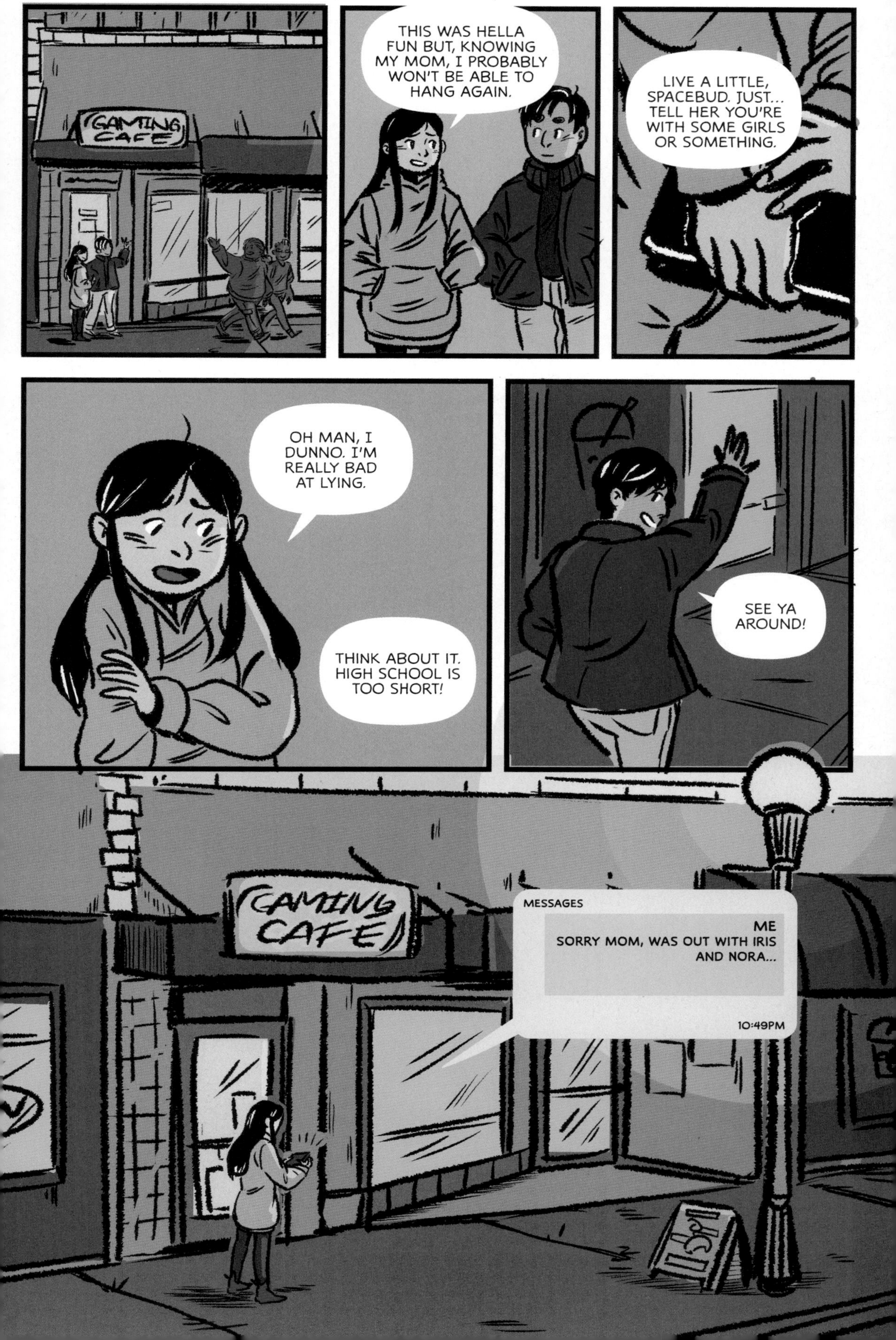
GAMING CAFE
THIS WAS HELLA FUN BUT, KNOWING MY MOM, I PROBABLY WON'T BE ABLE TO HANG AGAIN.
LIVE A LITTLE, SPACEBUD. JUST... TELL HER YOU'RE WITH SOME GIRLS OR SOMETHING.
OH MAN, I DUNNO. I'M REALLY BAD AT LYING.
THINK ABOUT IT. HIGH SCHOOL IS TOO SHORT!
SEE YA AROUND!
GAMING CAFE
MESSAGES
ME
SORRY MOM, WAS OUT WITH IRIS AND NORA...
10:49PM

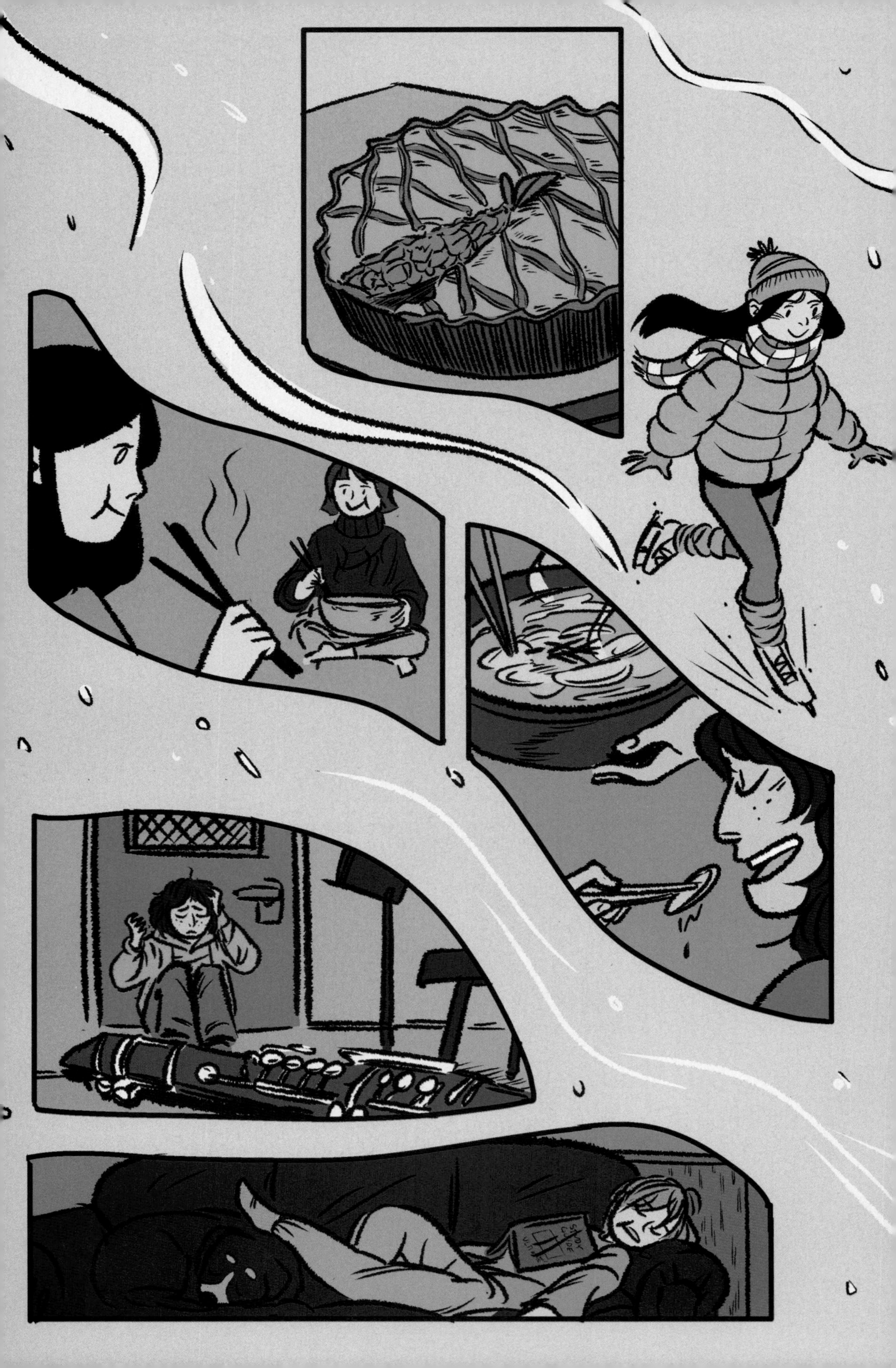
STUDY GUIDE

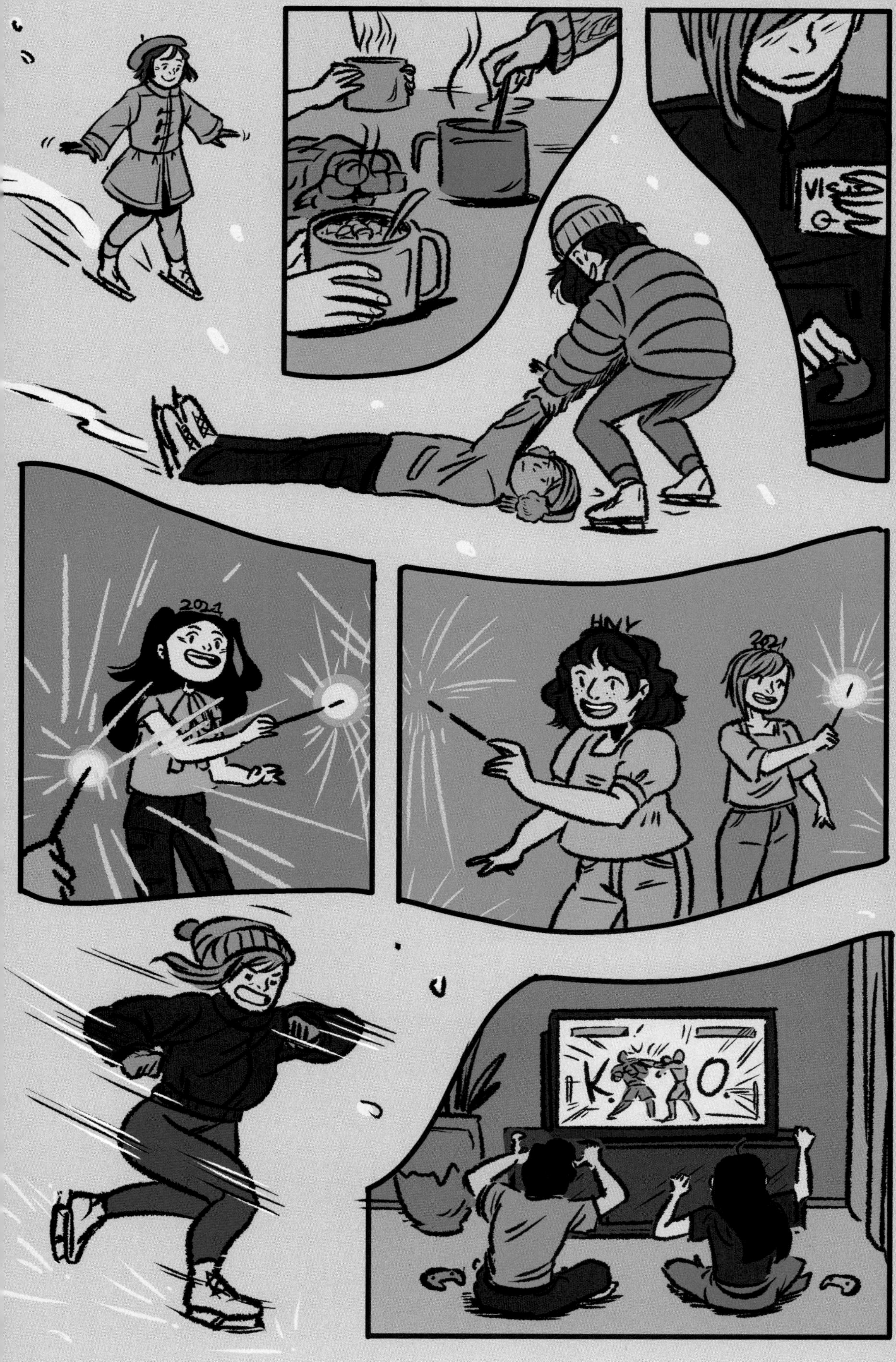
2021
HNY
2021
K.O.

Chapter Seven
nian nian you yu

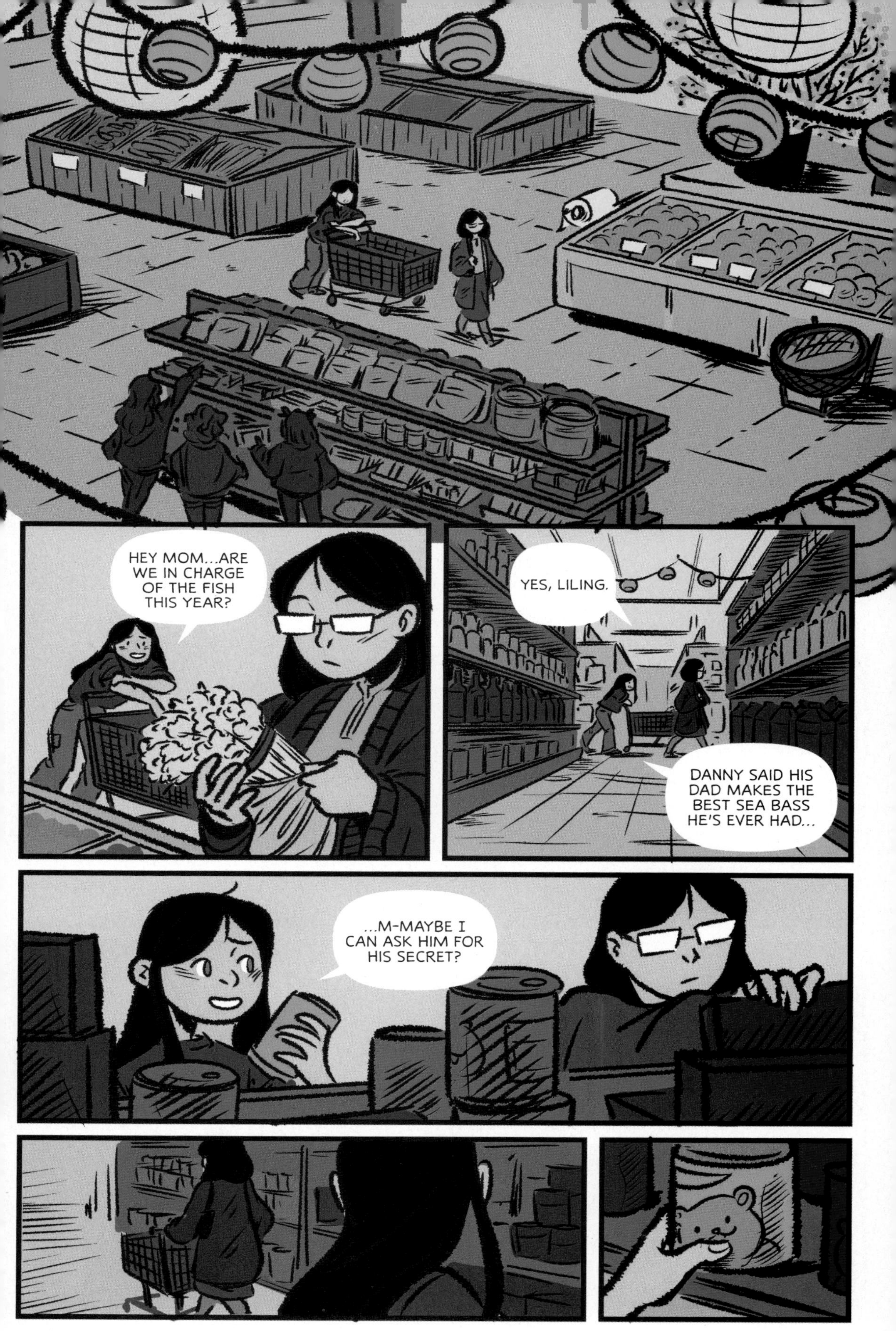
HEY MOM...ARE WE IN CHARGE OF THE FISH THIS YEAR?
YES, LILING.
DANNY SAID HIS DAD MAKES THE BEST SEA BASS HE'S EVER HAD...
...M-MAYBE I CAN ASK HIM FOR HIS SECRET?

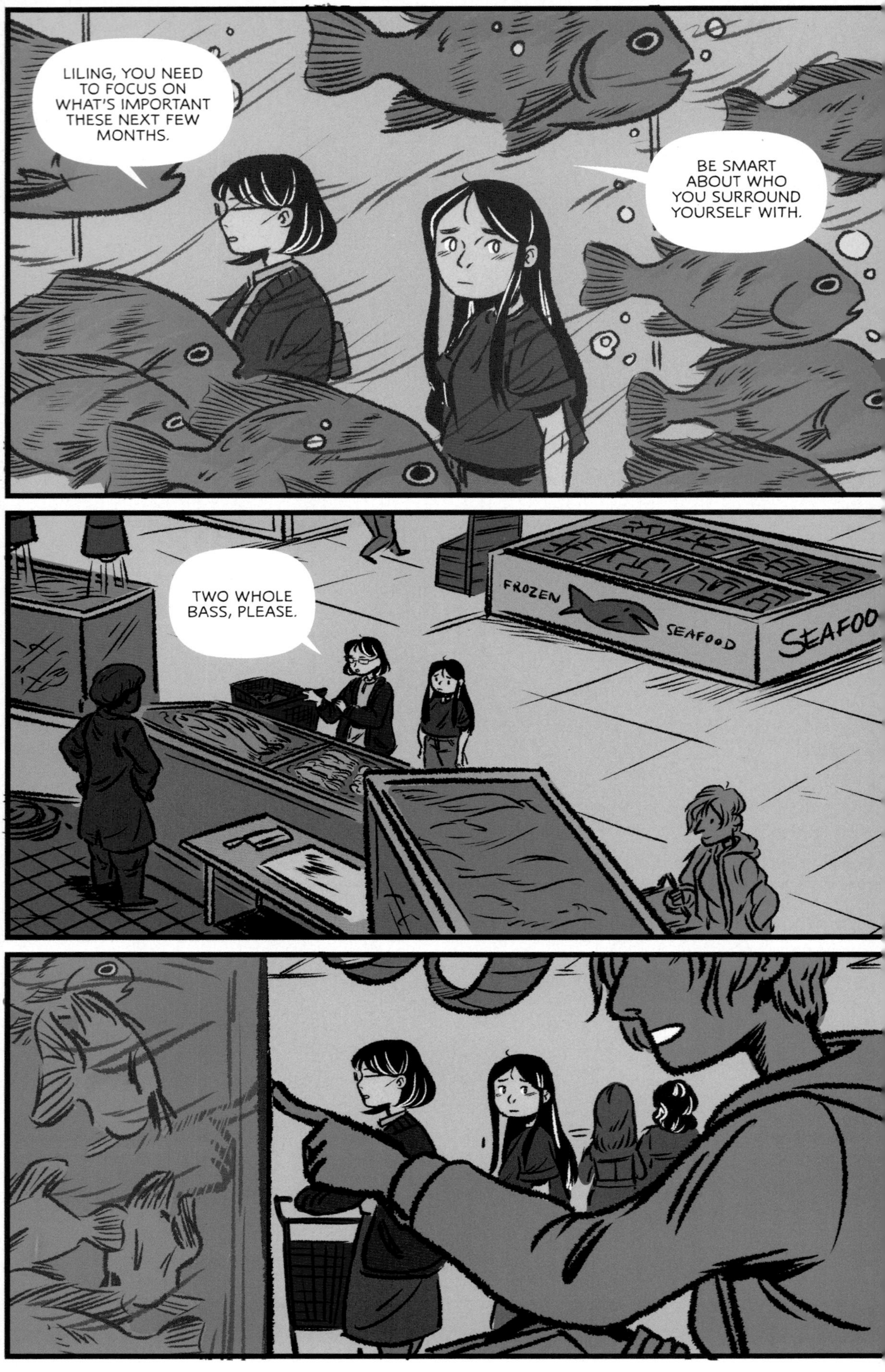
LILING, YOU NEED TO FOCUS ON WHAT'S IMPORTANT THESE NEXT FEW MONTHS.
BE SMART ABOUT WHO YOU SURROUND YOURSELF WITH.
TWO WHOLE BASS, PLEASE.
FROZEN
SEAFOOD
SEAFOO

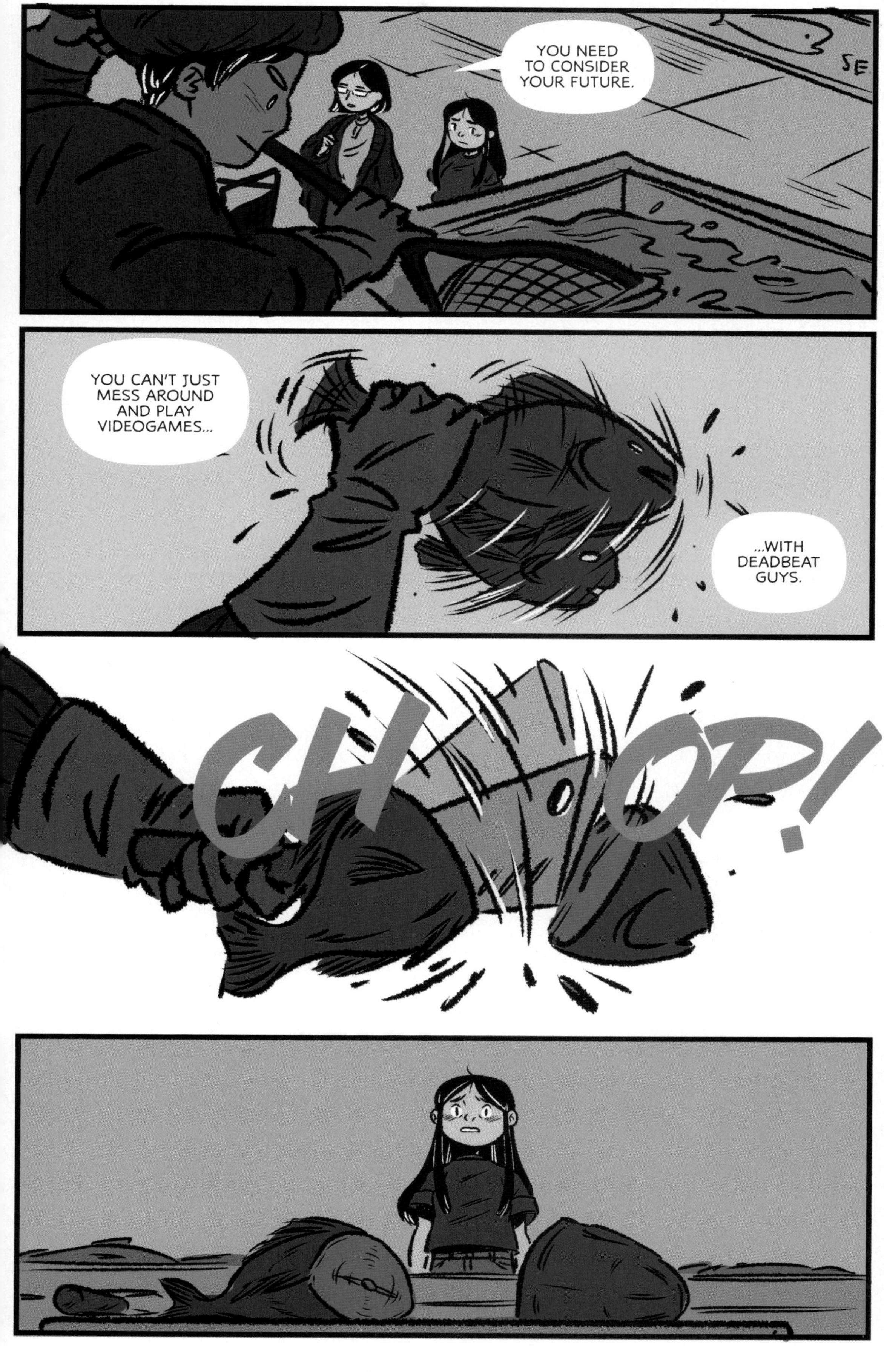
SE
YOU NEED TO CONSIDER YOUR FUTURE.
YOU CAN'T JUST MESS AROUND AND PLAY VIDEOGAMES...
...WITH DEADBEAT GUYS.
CHOP!

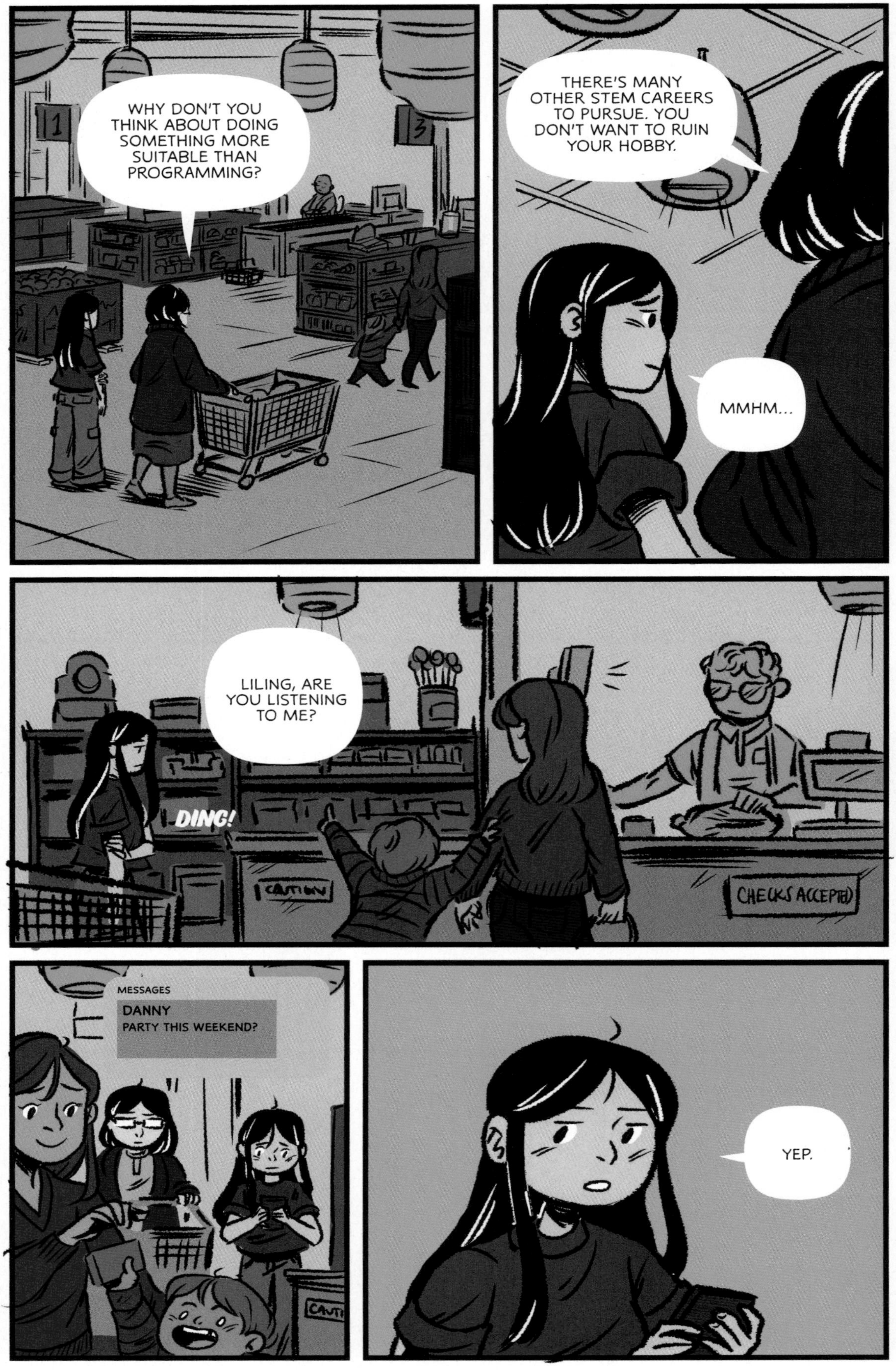
1
3
WHY DON'T YOU THINK ABOUT DOING SOMETHING MORE SUITABLE THAN PROGRAMMING?
THERE'S MANY OTHER STEM CAREERS TO PURSUE. YOU DON'T WANT TO RUIN YOUR HOBBY.
MMHM...
LILING, ARE YOU LISTENING TO ME?
DING!
CAUTION
CHECKS ACCEPTED
MESSAGES
DANNY
PARTY THIS WEEKEND?
YEP.

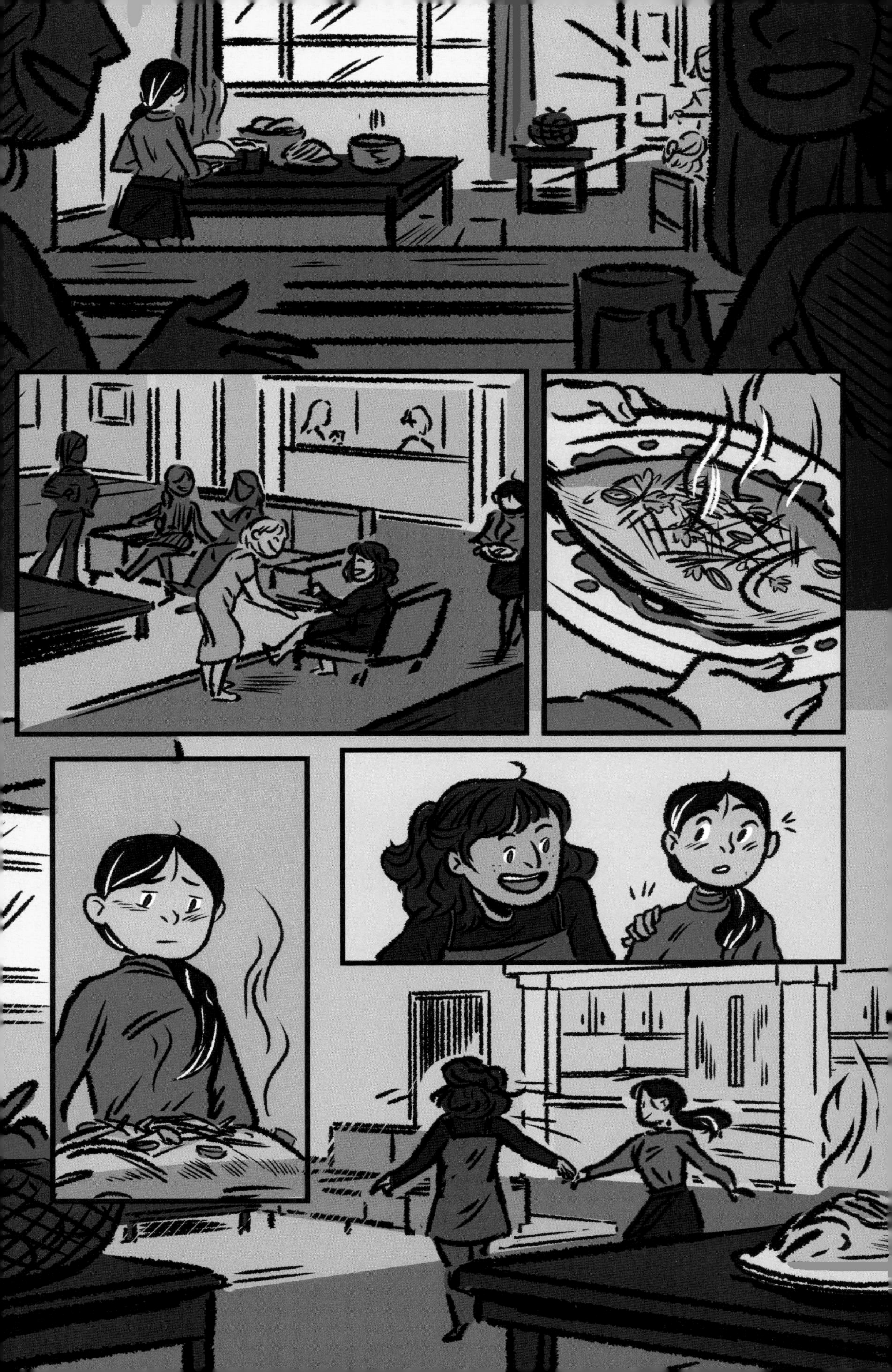

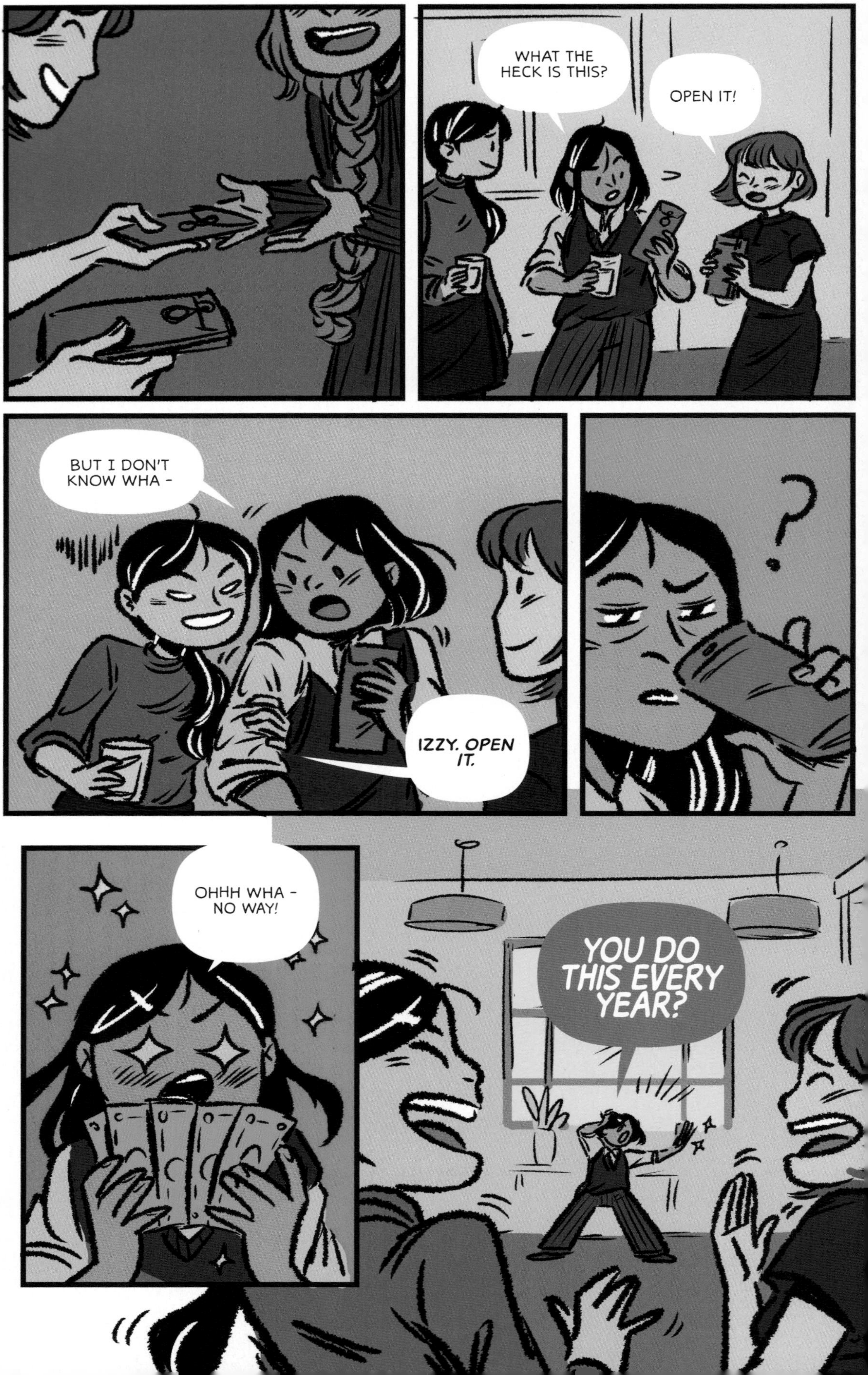
WHAT THE HECK IS THIS?
OPEN IT!
BUT I DON'T KNOW WHA -
IZZY. OPEN IT.
?
OHHH WHA - NO WAY!
YOU DO THIS EVERY YEAR?

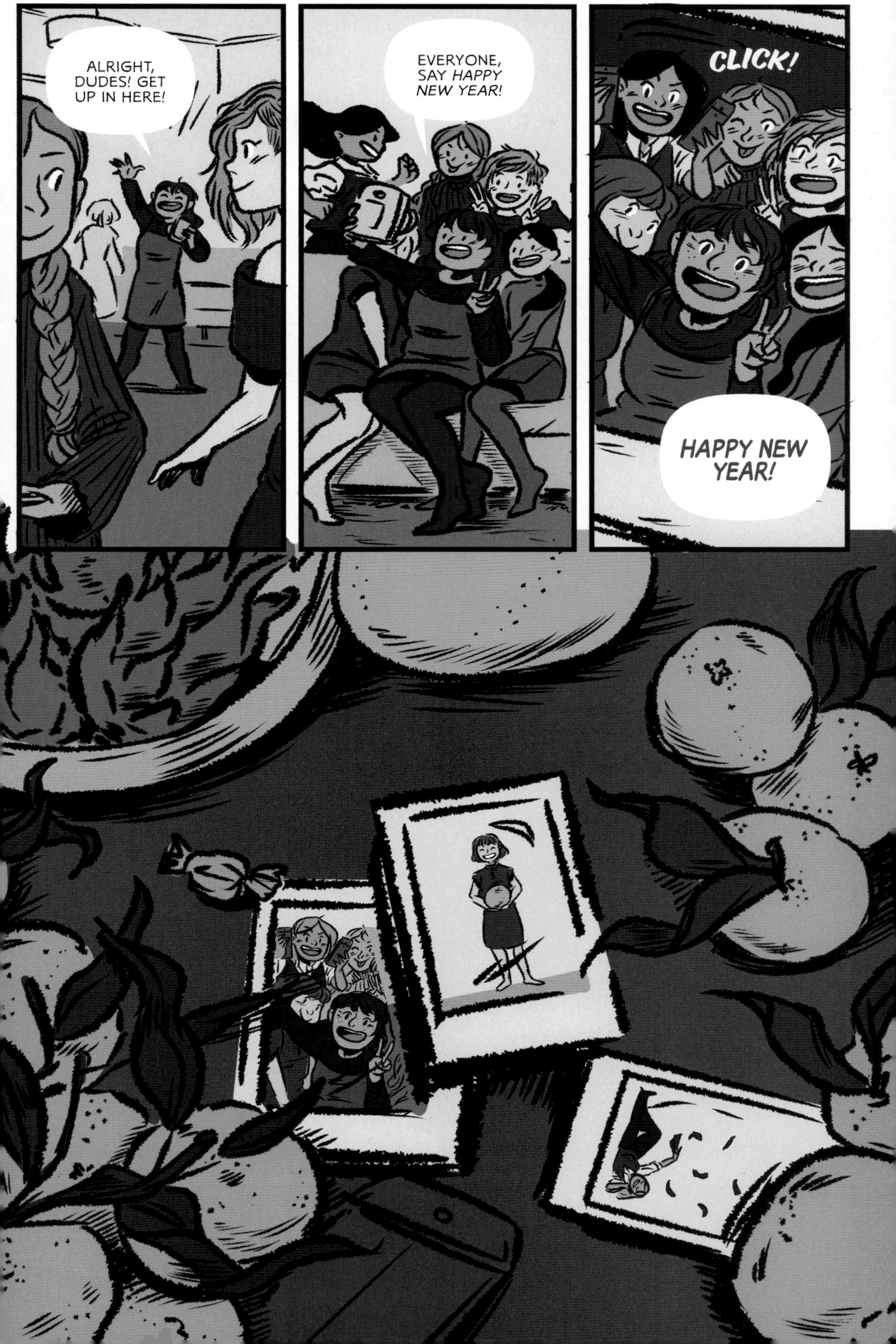
ALRIGHT, DUDES! GET UP IN HERE!
EVERYONE, SAY *HAPPY NEW YEAR!*
CLICK!
HAPPY NEW YEAR!

Chapter Eight
mac & cheese

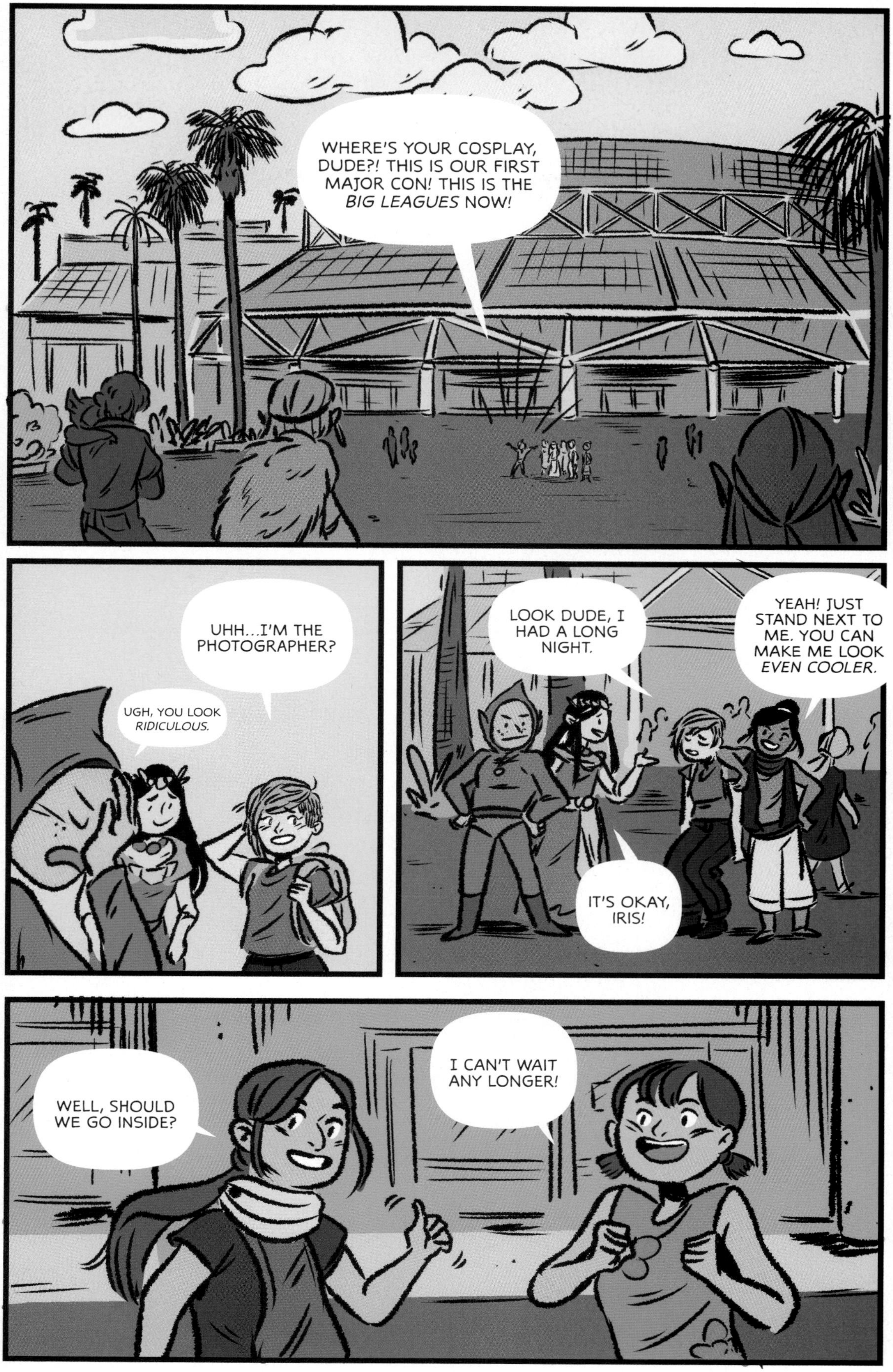
WHERE'S YOUR COSPLAY, DUDE?! THIS IS OUR FIRST MAJOR CON! THIS IS THE *BIG LEAGUES* NOW!
UHH...I'M THE PHOTOGRAPHER?
UGH, YOU LOOK *RIDICULOUS.*
LOOK DUDE, I HAD A LONG NIGHT.
YEAH! JUST STAND NEXT TO ME. YOU CAN MAKE ME LOOK *EVEN COOLER.*
IT'S OKAY, IRIS!
WELL, SHOULD WE GO INSIDE?
I CAN'T WAIT ANY LONGER!

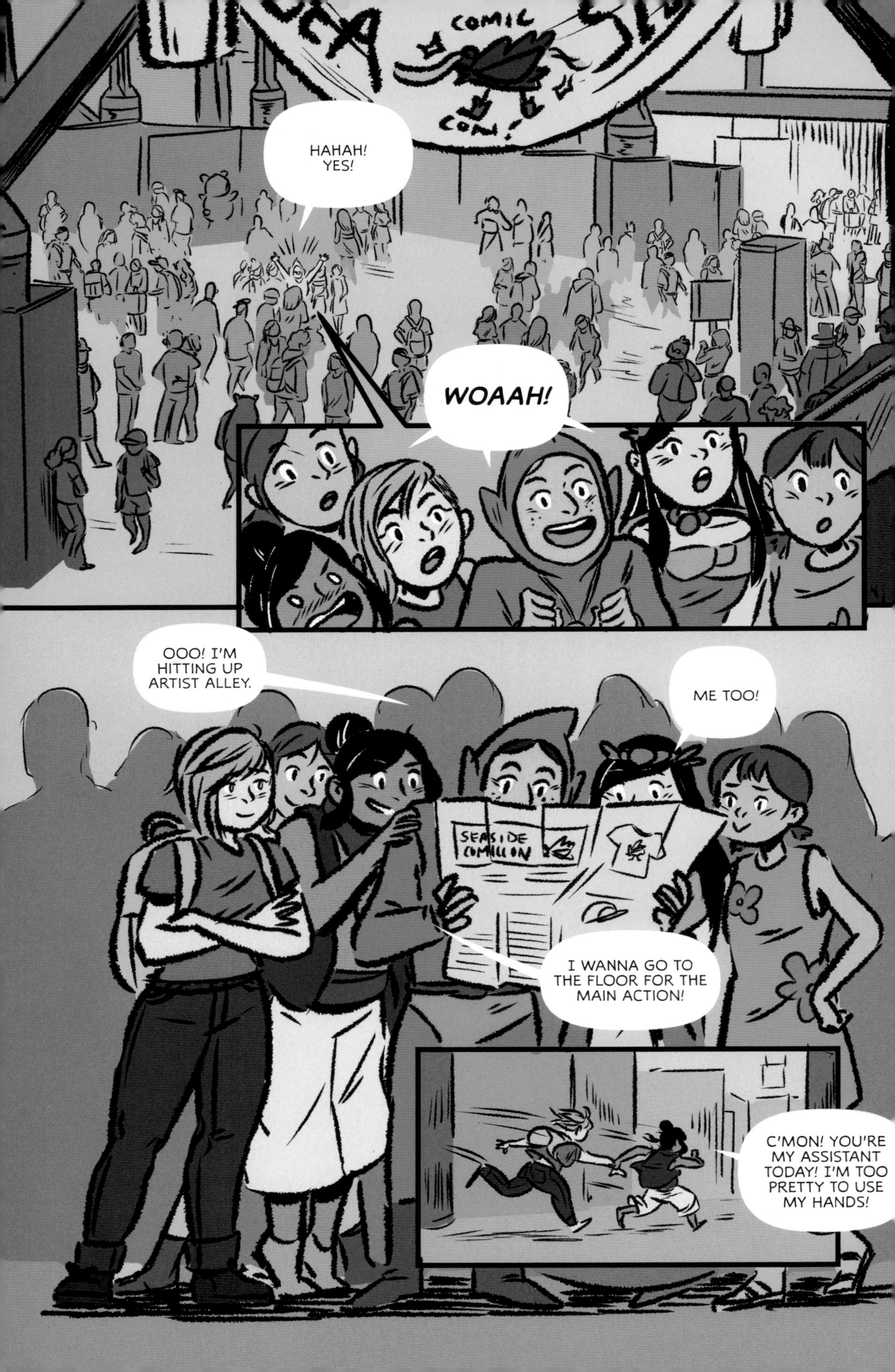
COMIC
CON!
HAHAH! YES!
WOAAH!
OOO! I'M HITTING UP ARTIST ALLEY.
ME TOO!
SEASIDE COMIC CON
I WANNA GO TO THE FLOOR FOR THE MAIN ACTION!
C'MON! YOU'RE MY ASSISTANT TODAY! I'M TOO PRETTY TO USE MY HANDS!

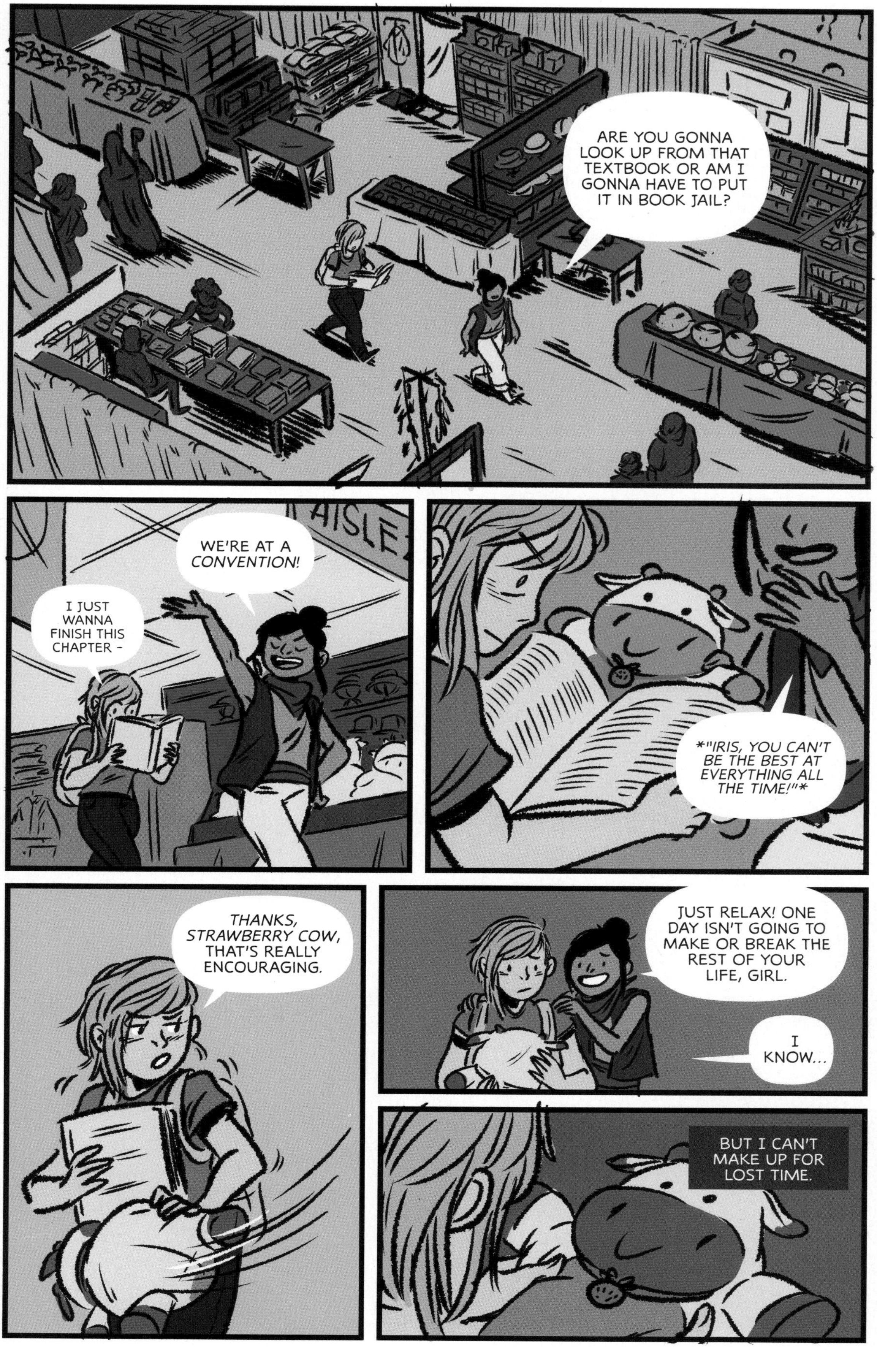
ARE YOU GONNA LOOK UP FROM THAT TEXTBOOK OR AM I GONNA HAVE TO PUT IT IN BOOK JAIL?
AISLE
WE'RE AT A *CONVENTION!*
I JUST WANNA FINISH THIS CHAPTER -
"IRIS, YOU CAN'T BE THE BEST AT EVERYTHING ALL THE TIME!"
THANKS, STRAWBERRY COW, THAT'S REALLY ENCOURAGING.
JUST RELAX! ONE DAY ISN'T GOING TO MAKE OR BREAK THE REST OF YOUR LIFE, GIRL.
I KNOW...
BUT I CAN'T MAKE UP FOR LOST TIME.

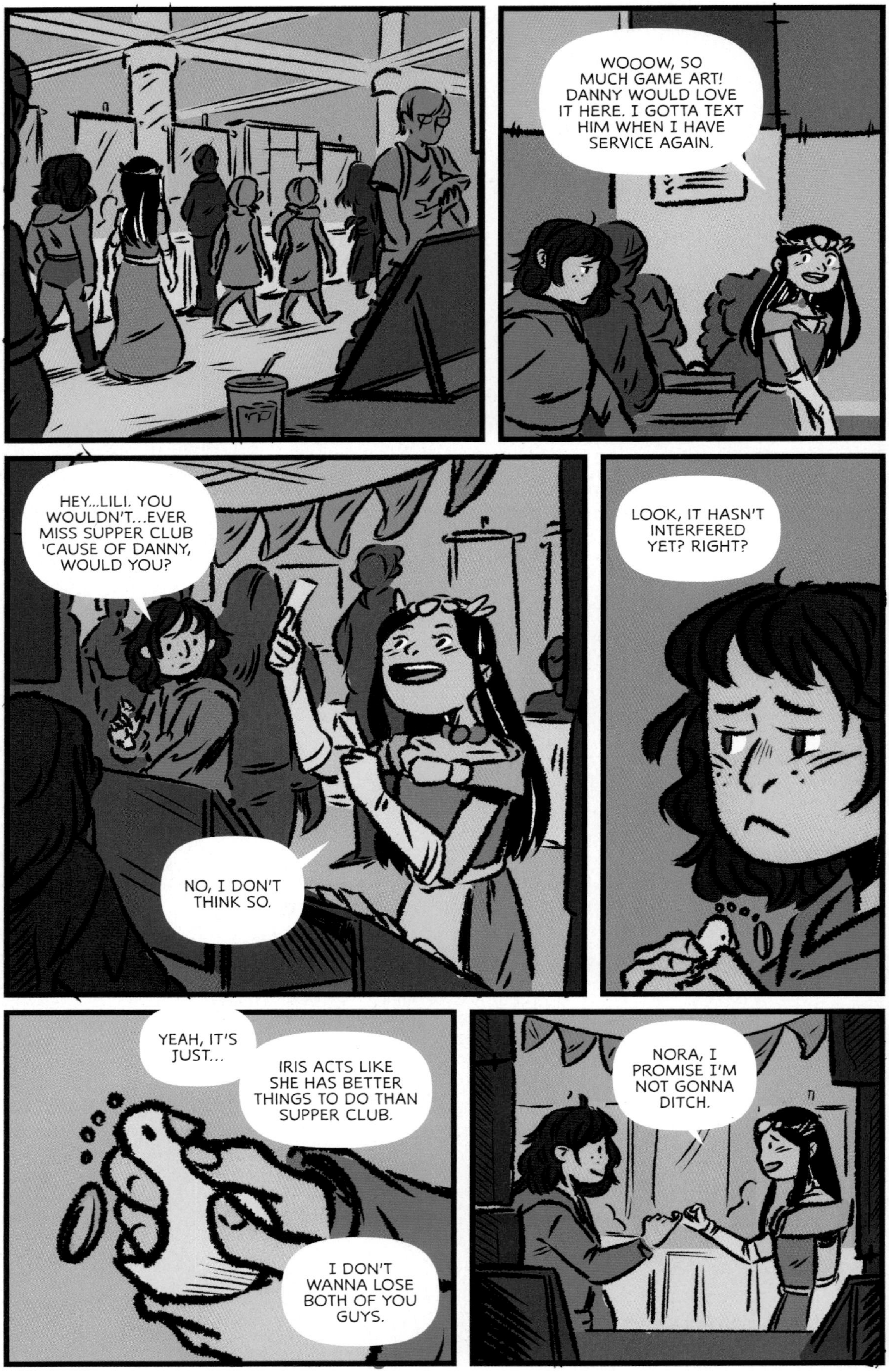
WOOOW, SO MUCH GAME ART! DANNY WOULD LOVE IT HERE. I GOTTA TEXT HIM WHEN I HAVE SERVICE AGAIN.
HEY...LILI. YOU WOULDN'T...EVER MISS SUPPER CLUB 'CAUSE OF DANNY, WOULD YOU?
NO, I DON'T THINK SO.
LOOK, IT HASN'T INTERFERED YET? RIGHT?
YEAH, IT'S JUST...
IRIS ACTS LIKE SHE HAS BETTER THINGS TO DO THAN SUPPER CLUB.
I DON'T WANNA LOSE BOTH OF YOU GUYS.
NORA, I PROMISE I'M NOT GONNA DITCH.

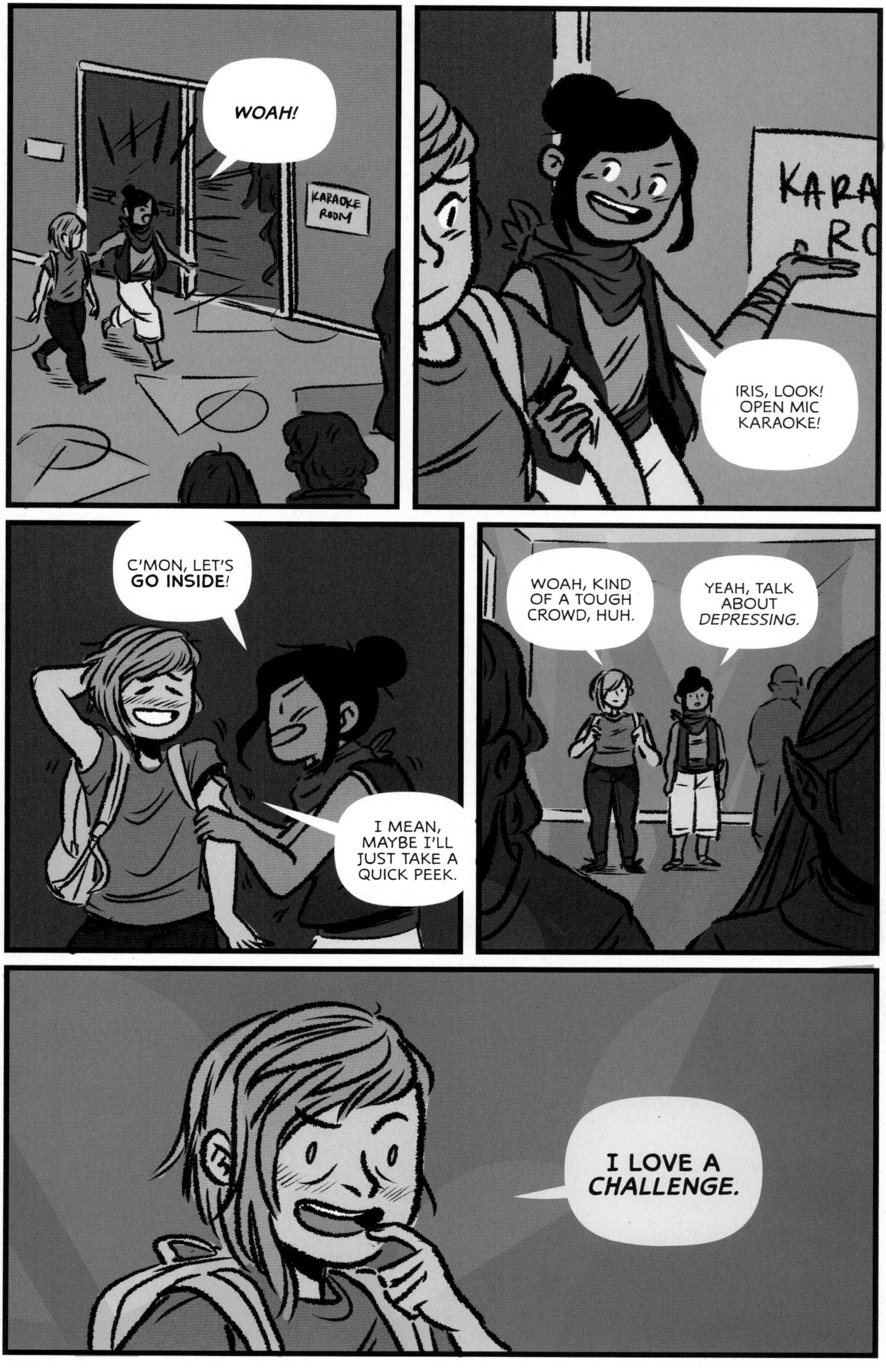
WOAH!
KARAOKE ROOM
IRIS, LOOK! OPEN MIC KARAOKE!
KARA RO
C'MON, LET'S GO INSIDE!
I MEAN, MAYBE I'LL JUST TAKE A QUICK PEEK.
WOAH, KIND OF A TOUGH CROWD, HUH.
YEAH, TALK ABOUT DEPRESSING.
I LOVE A CHALLENGE.

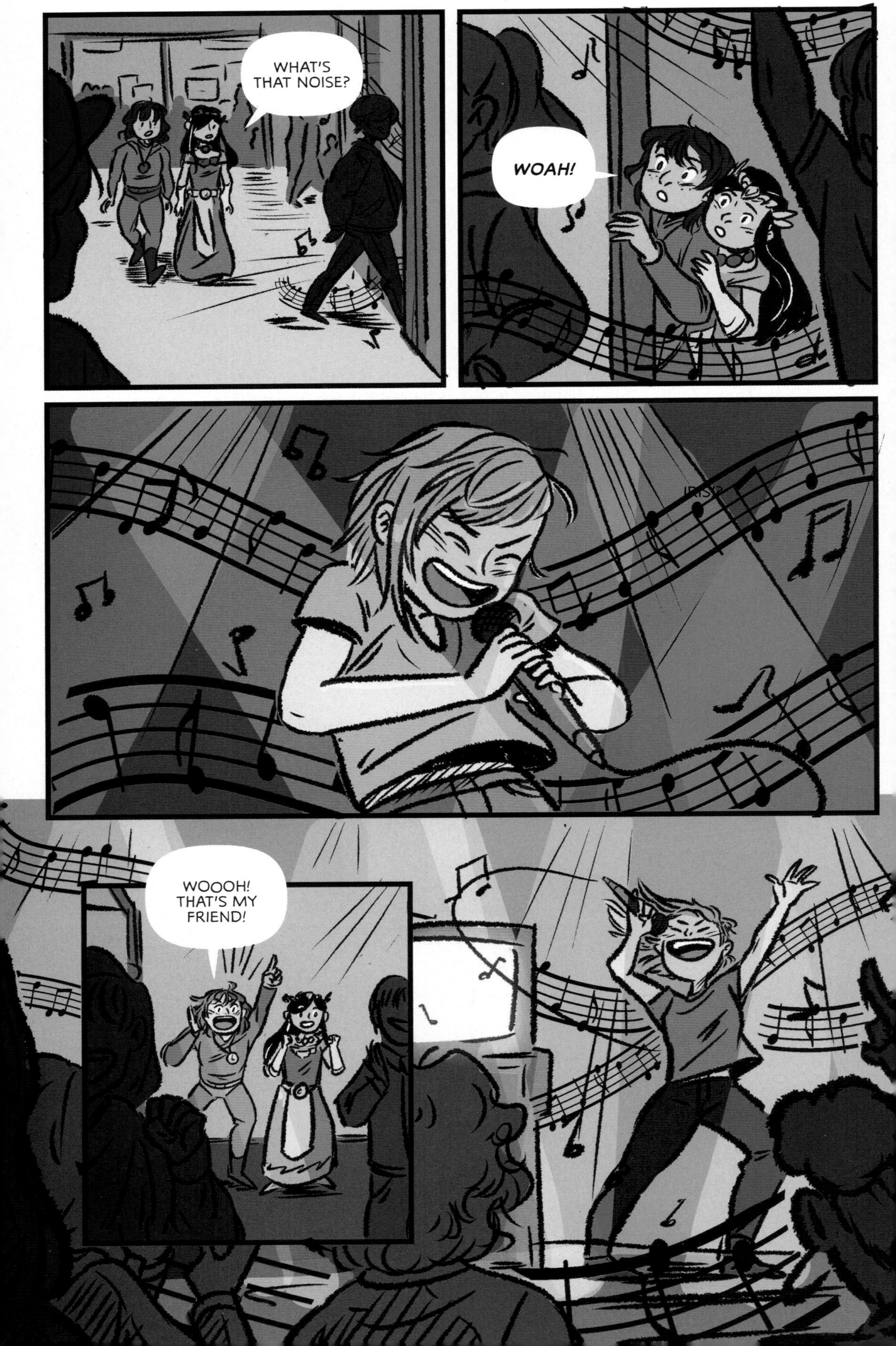
WHAT'S THAT NOISE?
WOAH!
IRIS?
WOOOH! THAT'S MY FRIEND!

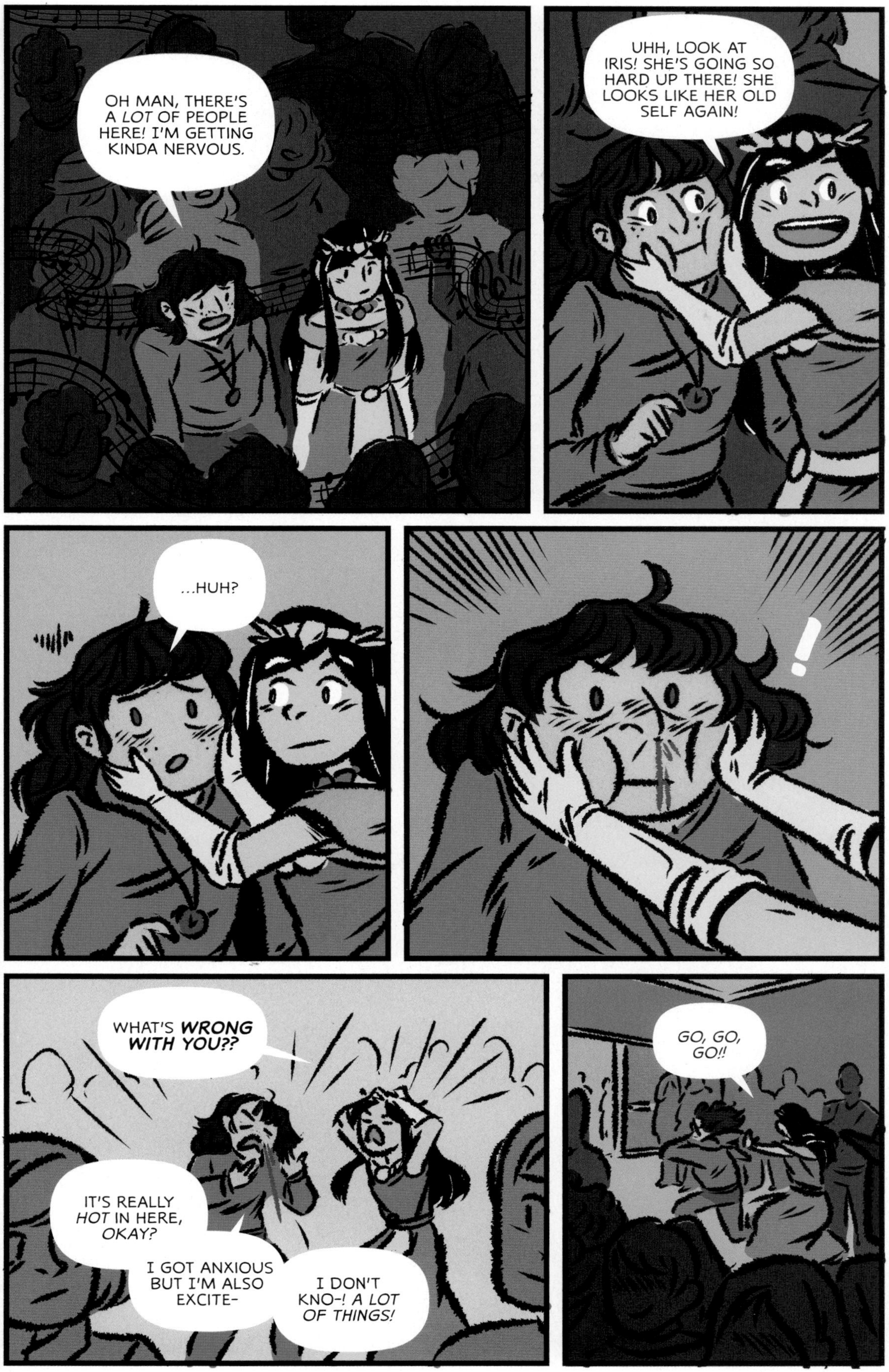
OH MAN, THERE'S A *LOT* OF PEOPLE HERE! I'M GETTING KINDA NERVOUS.
UHH, LOOK AT IRIS! SHE'S GOING SO HARD UP THERE! SHE LOOKS LIKE HER OLD SELF AGAIN!
...HUH?
!
WHAT'S ***WRONG WITH YOU??***
IT'S REALLY *HOT* IN HERE, *OKAY?*
I GOT ANXIOUS BUT I'M ALSO EXCITE-
I DON'T KNO-! *A LOT OF THINGS!*
GO, GO, GO!!

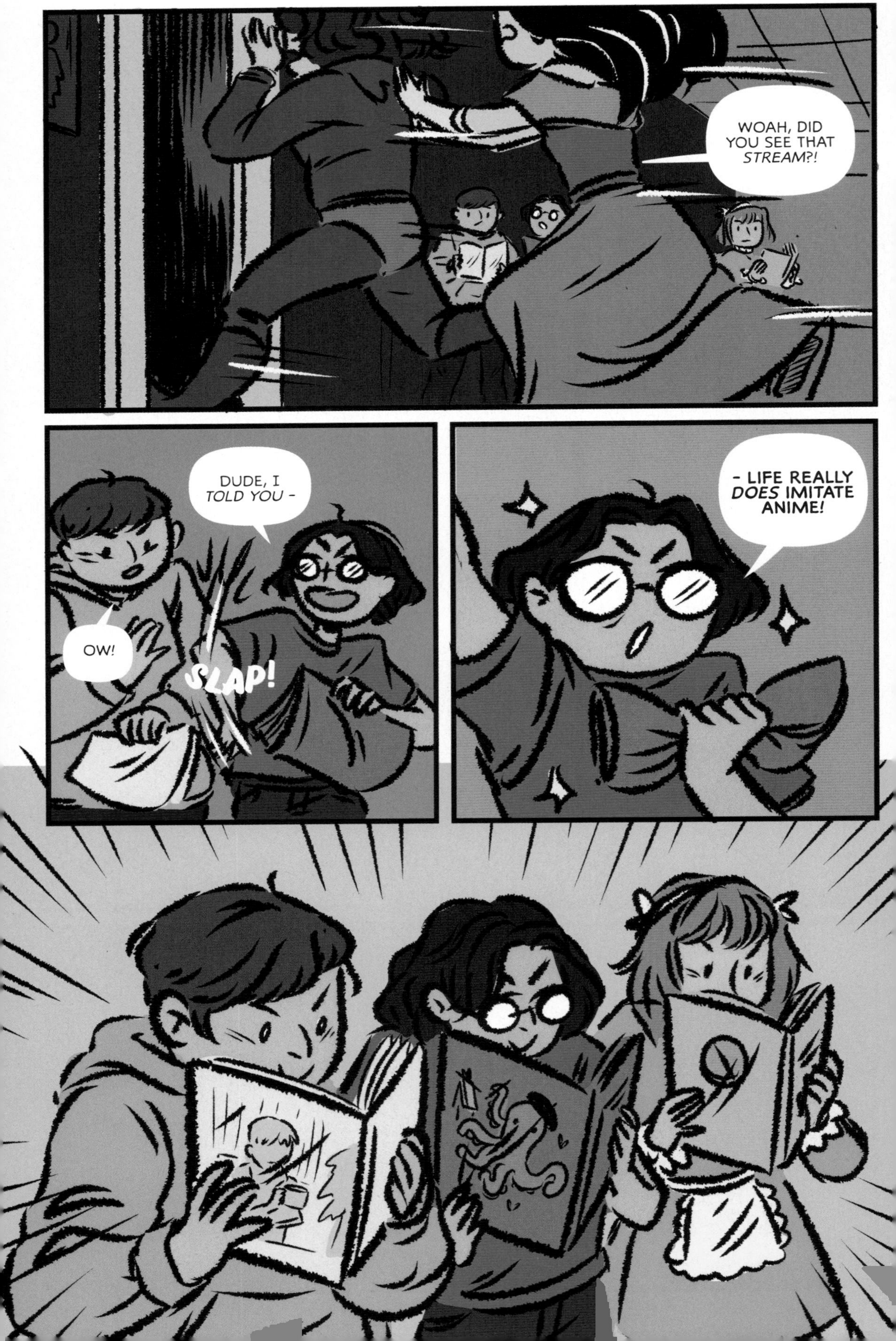
WOAH, DID YOU SEE THAT *STREAM*?!
DUDE, I *TOLD YOU* -
OW!
SLAP!
- LIFE REALLY *DOES* IMITATE ANIME!

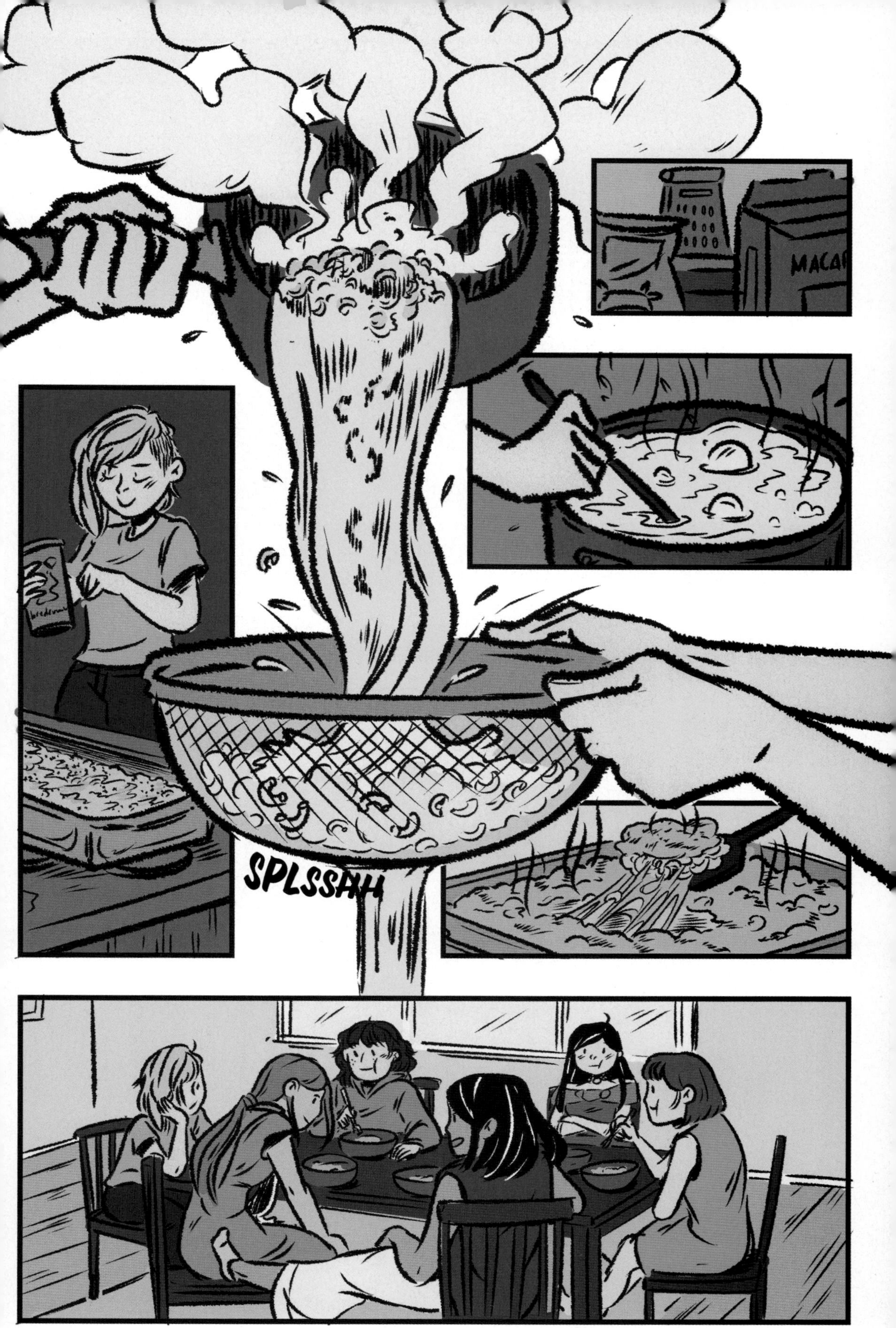
SPLSSHH

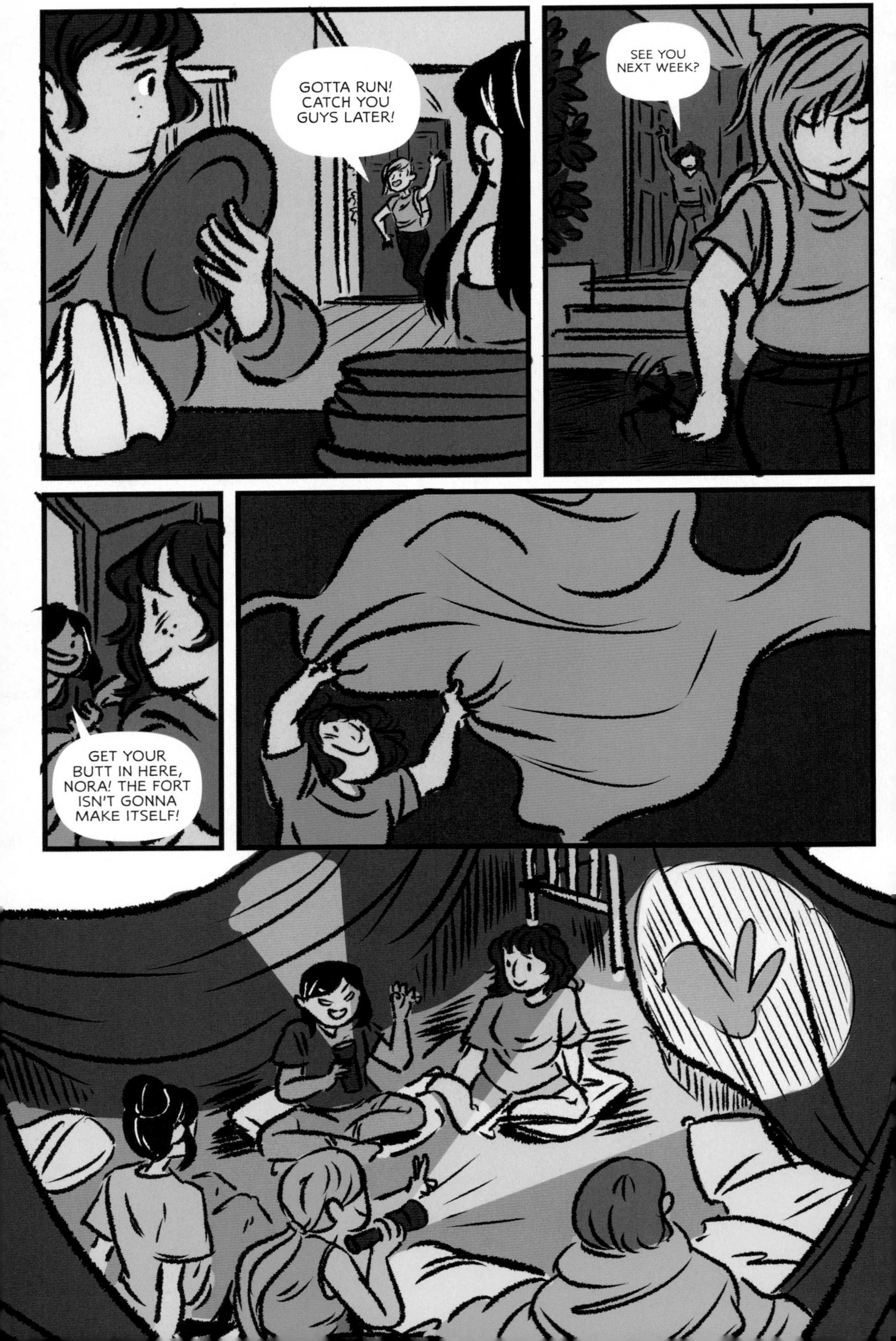
GOTTA RUN! CATCH YOU GUYS LATER!
SEE YOU NEXT WEEK?
GET YOUR BUTT IN HERE, NORA! THE FORT ISN'T GONNA MAKE ITSELF!

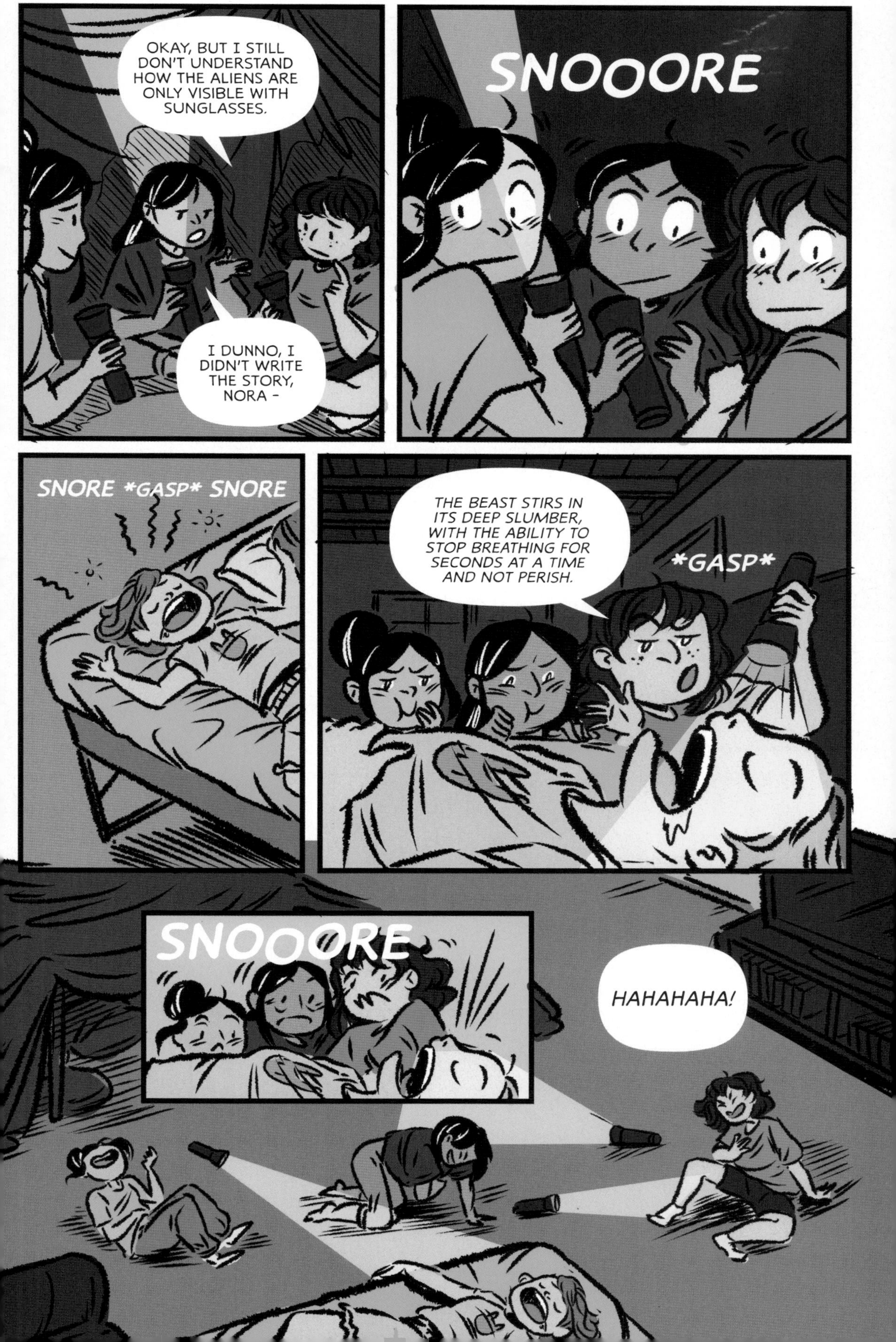
OKAY, BUT I STILL DON'T UNDERSTAND HOW THE ALIENS ARE ONLY VISIBLE WITH SUNGLASSES.
I DUNNO, I DIDN'T WRITE THE STORY, NORA -
SNOOORE
SNORE *GASP* SNORE
THE BEAST STIRS IN ITS DEEP SLUMBER, WITH THE ABILITY TO STOP BREATHING FOR SECONDS AT A TIME AND NOT PERISH.
GASP
SNOOORE
HAHAHAHA!

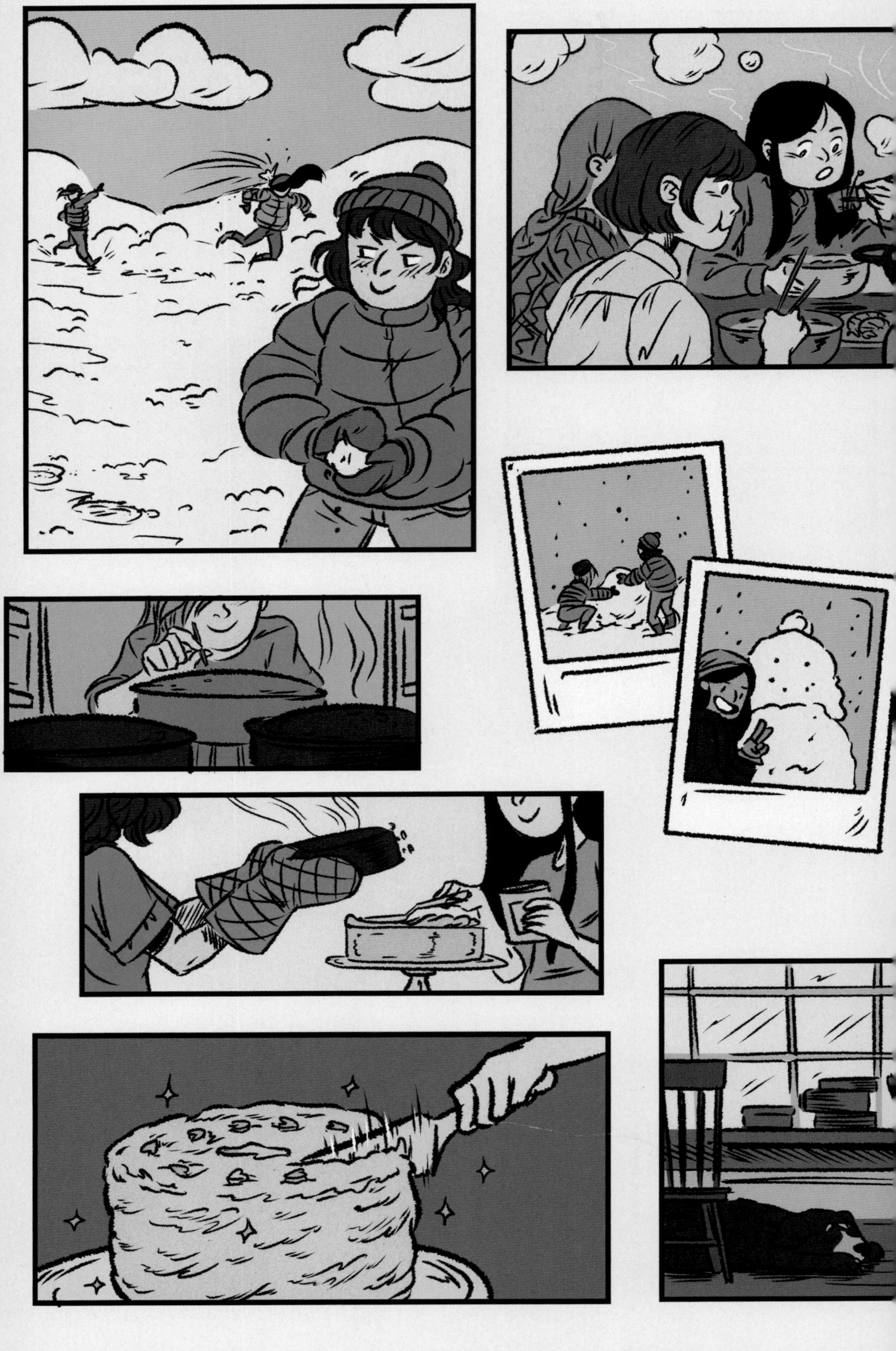

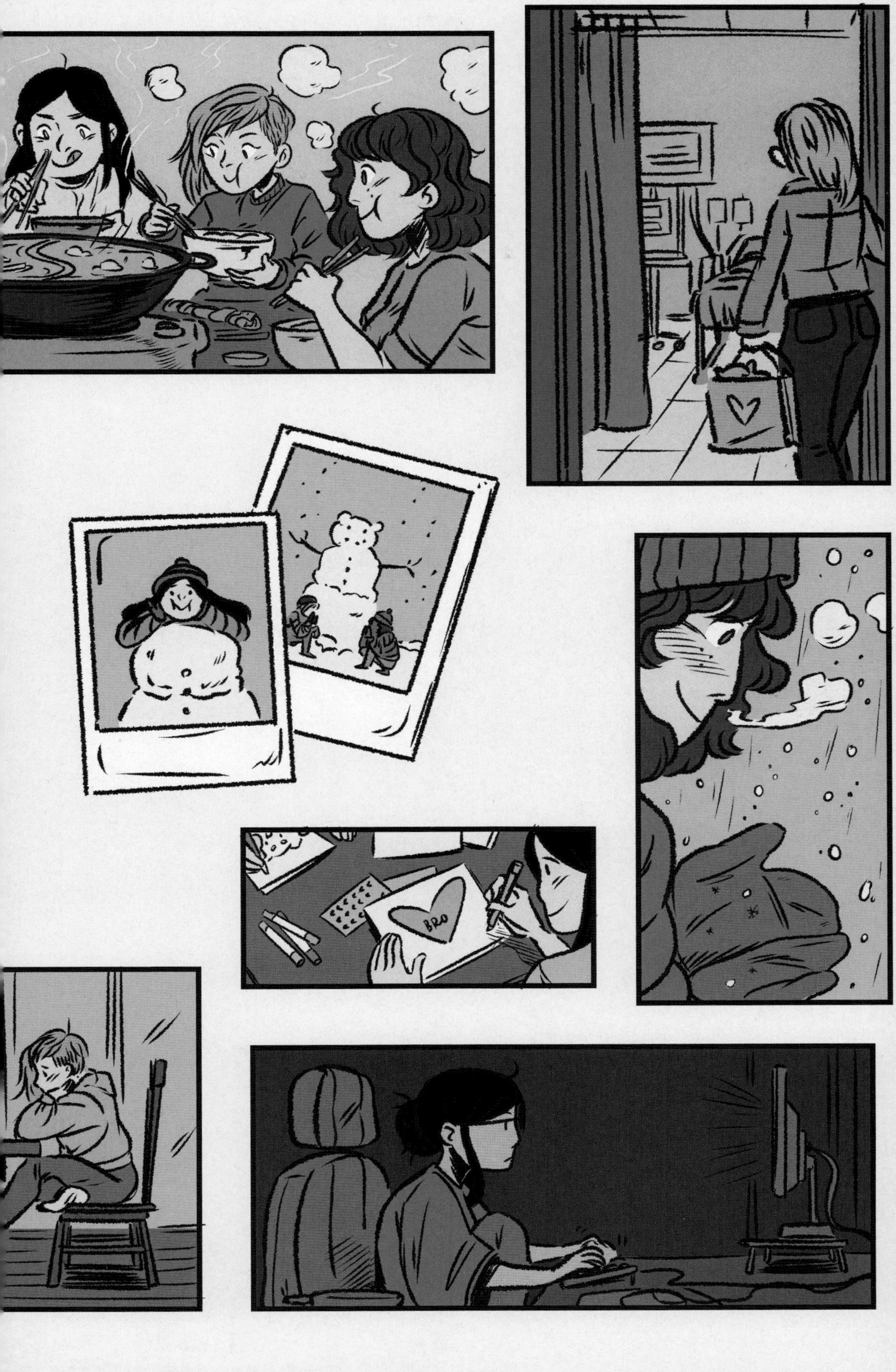
BRO

Chapter Nine
mofongo

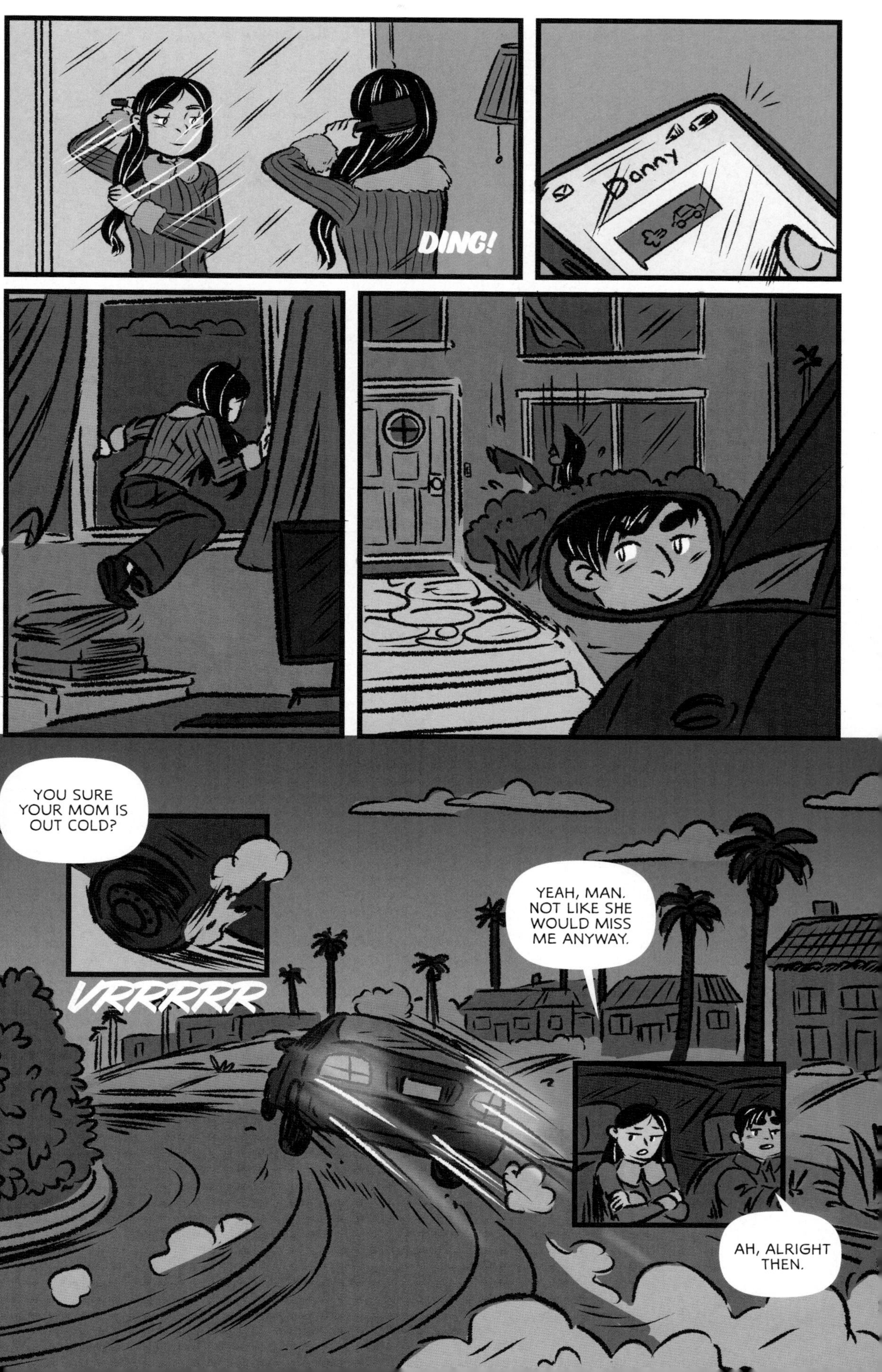
DING!
Danny
YOU SURE YOUR MOM IS OUT COLD?
VRRRRR
YEAH, MAN. NOT LIKE SHE WOULD MISS ME ANYWAY.
AH, ALRIGHT THEN.

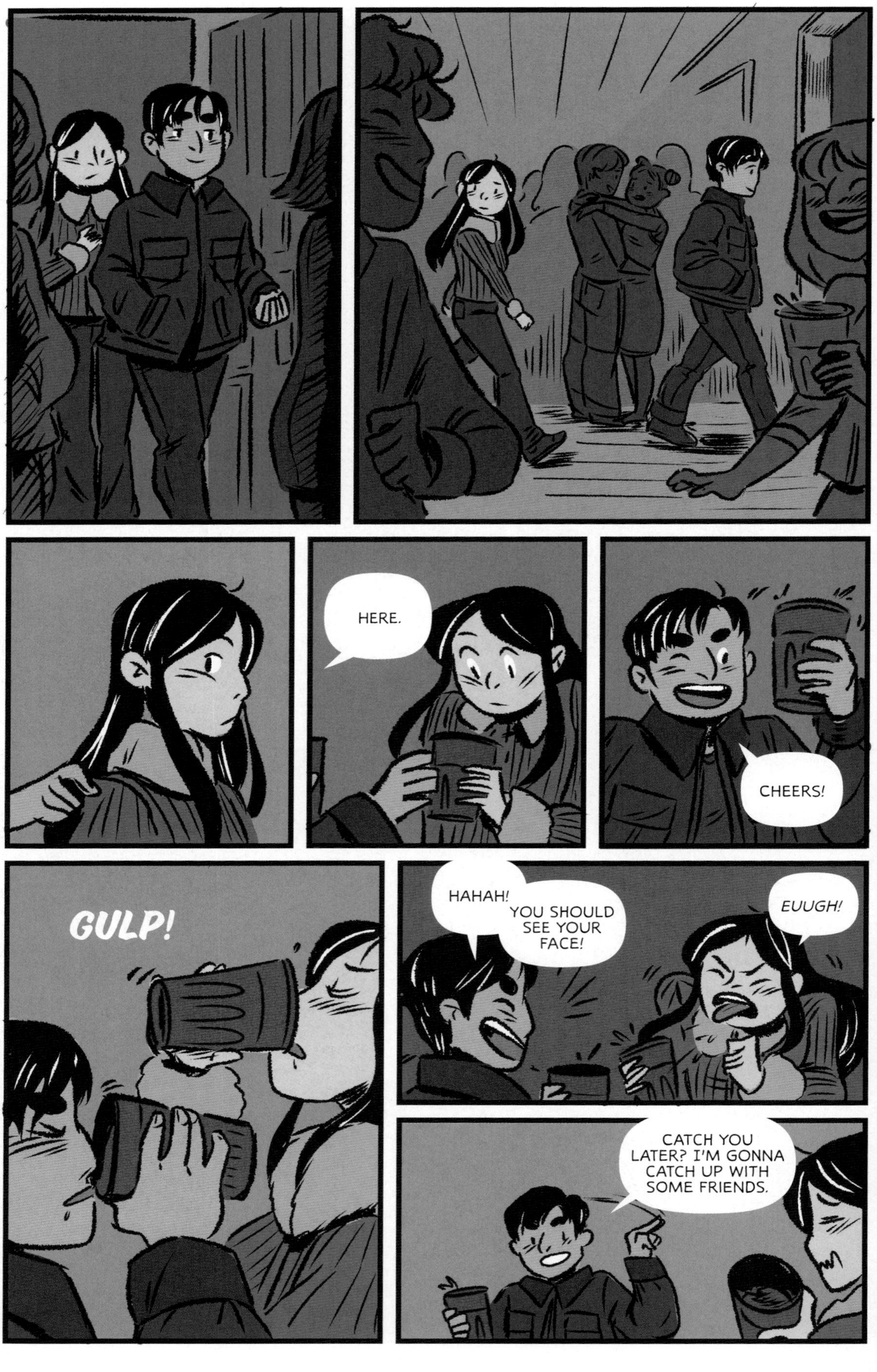
HERE.
CHEERS!
GULP!
HAHAH!
YOU SHOULD SEE YOUR FACE!
EUUGH!
CATCH YOU LATER? I'M GONNA CATCH UP WITH SOME FRIENDS.

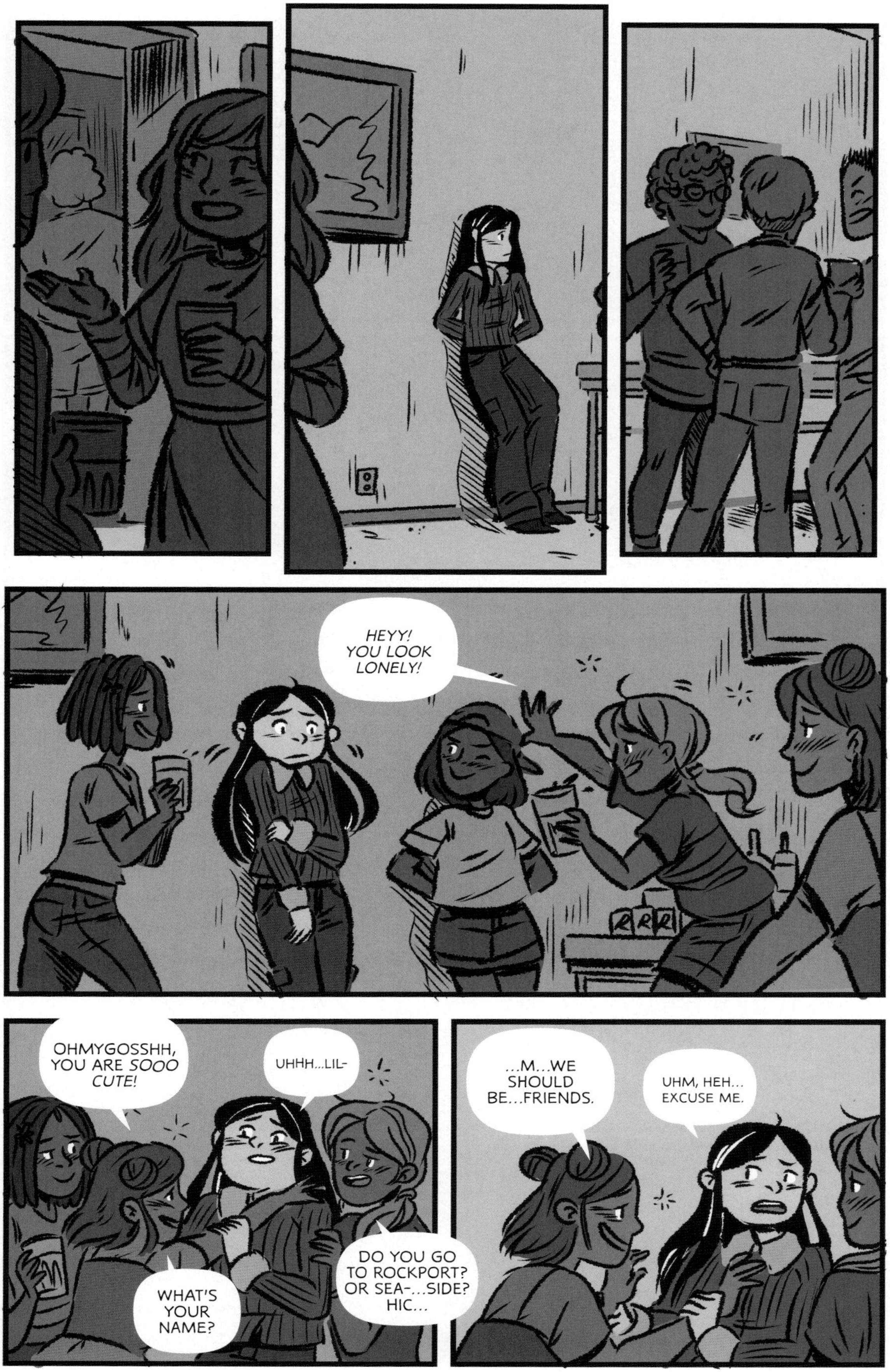
HEYY! YOU LOOK LONELY!
OHMYGOSSHH, YOU ARE *SOOO* CUTE!
UHHH...LIL-
WHAT'S YOUR NAME?
DO YOU GO TO ROCKPORT? OR SEA-...SIDE? HIC...
...M...WE SHOULD BE...FRIENDS.
UHM, HEH... EXCUSE ME.

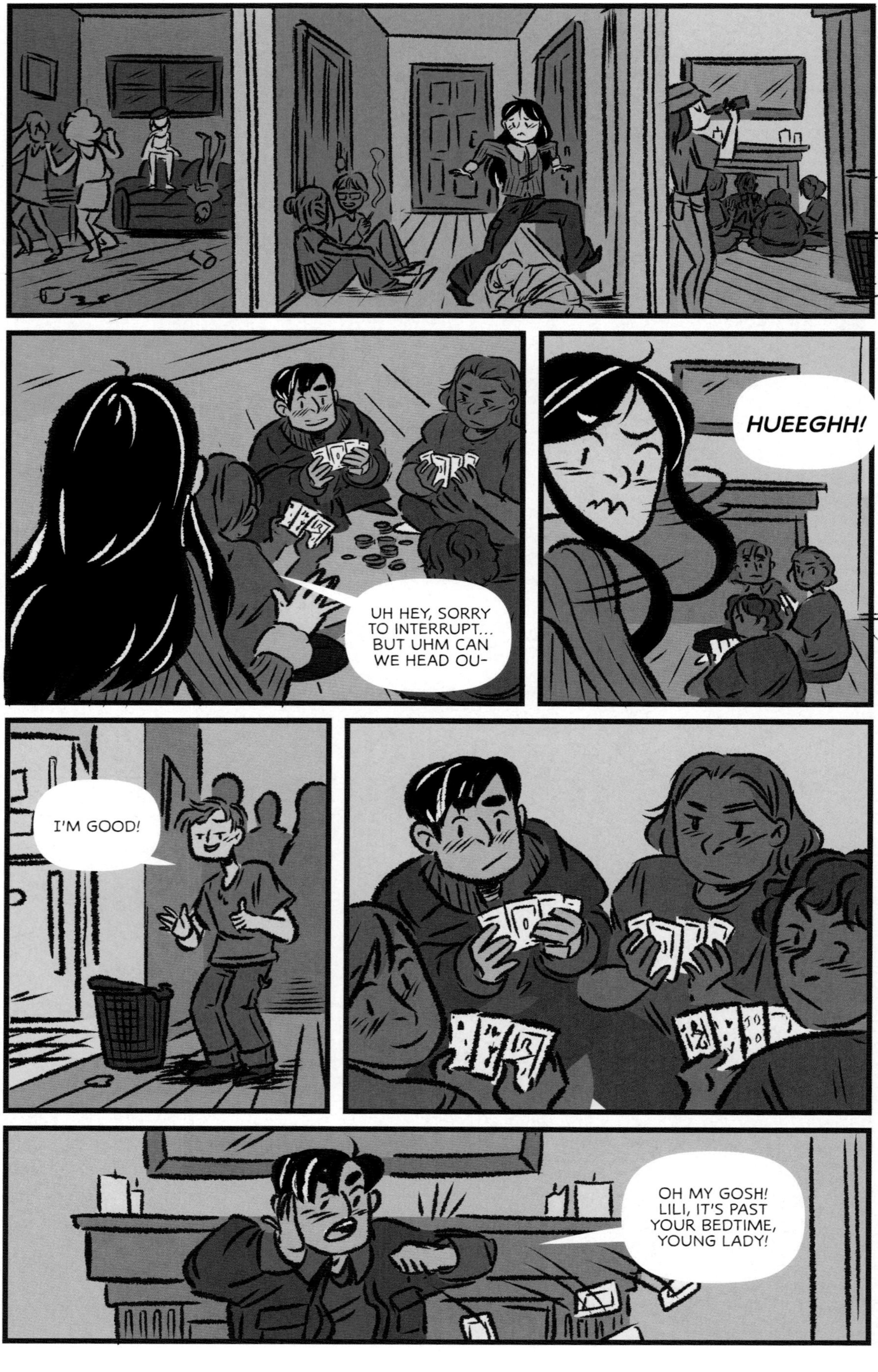
UH HEY, SORRY TO INTERRUPT... BUT UHM CAN WE HEAD OU-
HUEEGHH!
I'M GOOD!
OH MY GOSH! LILI, IT'S PAST YOUR BEDTIME, YOUNG LADY!

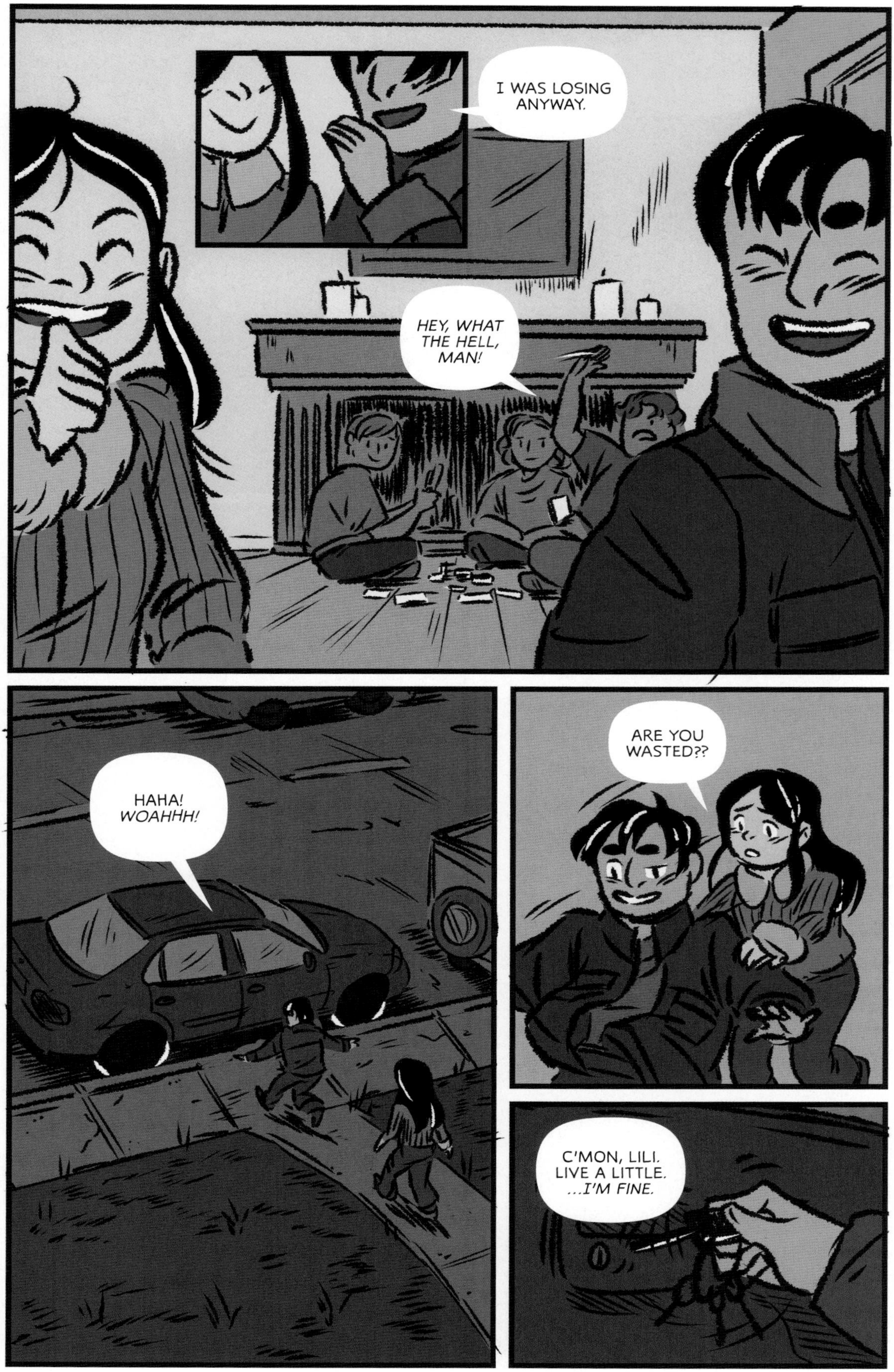
I WAS LOSING ANYWAY.
HEY, WHAT THE HELL, MAN!
HAHA! WOAHHH!
ARE YOU WASTED??
C'MON, LILI. LIVE A LITTLE. ...I'M FINE.

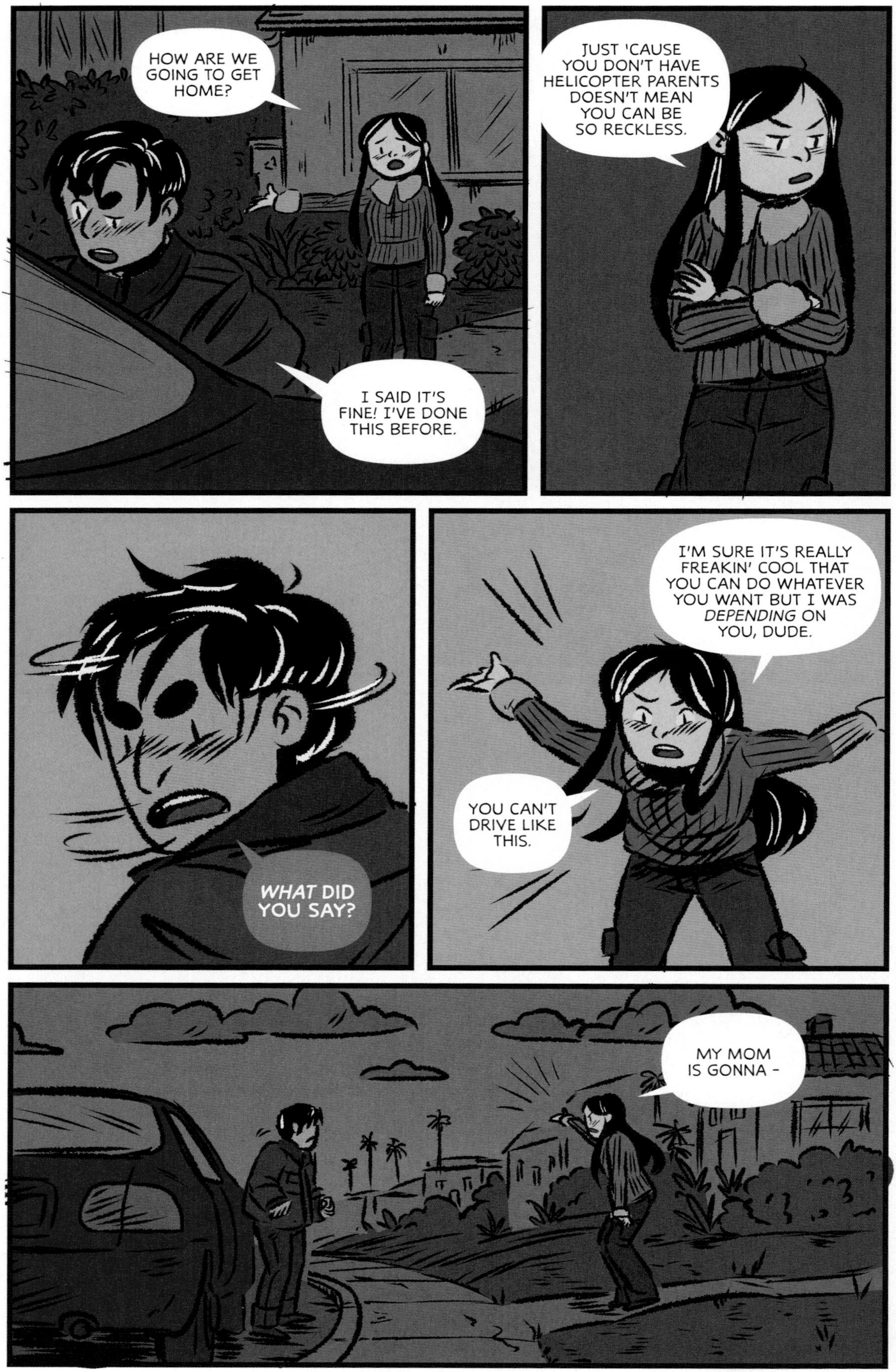
HOW ARE WE GOING TO GET HOME?
I SAID IT'S FINE! I'VE DONE THIS BEFORE.
JUST 'CAUSE YOU DON'T HAVE HELICOPTER PARENTS DOESN'T MEAN YOU CAN BE SO RECKLESS.
I'M SURE IT'S REALLY FREAKIN' COOL THAT YOU CAN DO WHATEVER YOU WANT BUT I WAS *DEPENDING* ON YOU, DUDE.
YOU CAN'T DRIVE LIKE THIS.
WHAT DID YOU SAY?
MY MOM IS GONNA -

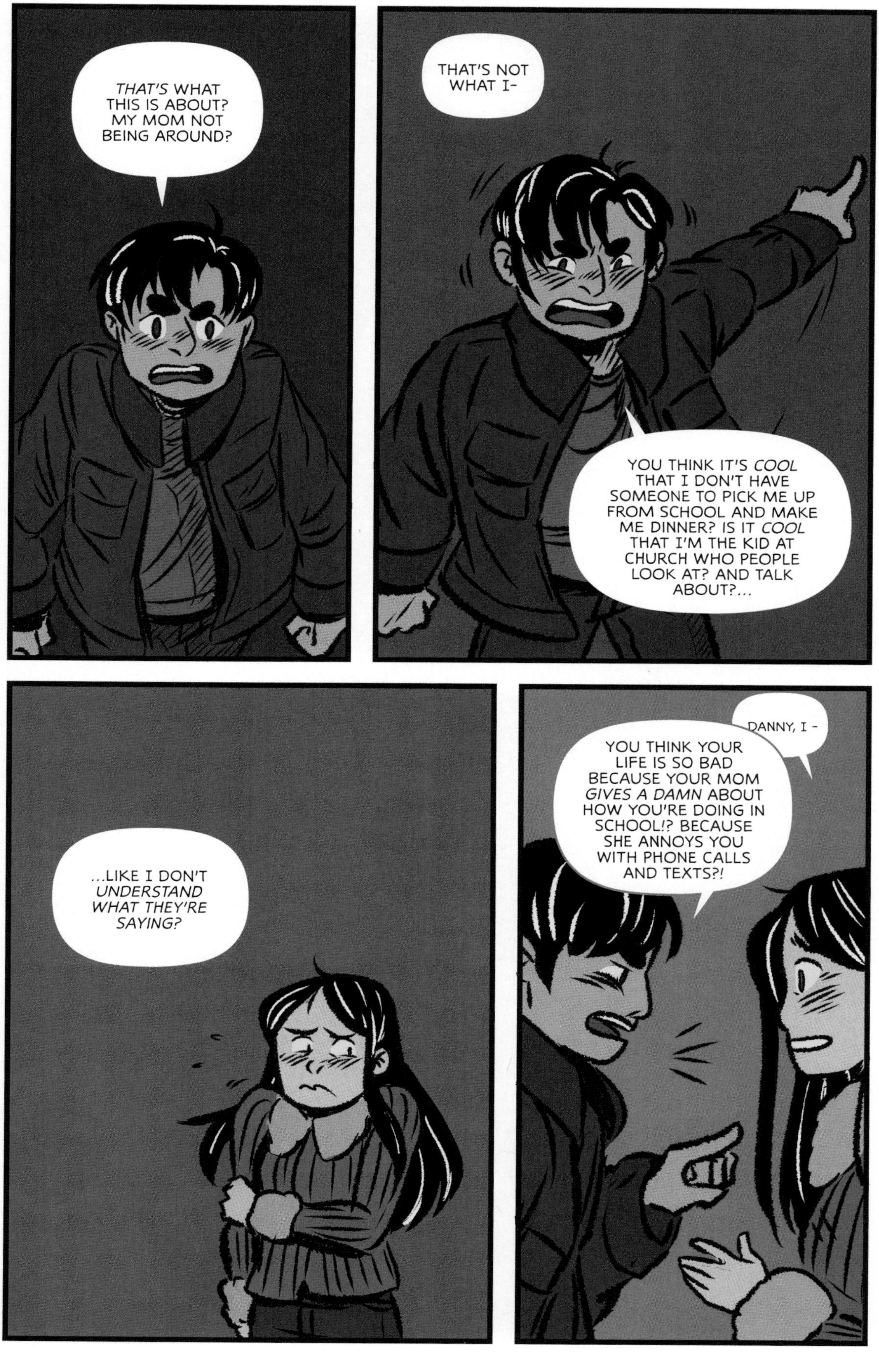
THAT'S WHAT THIS IS ABOUT? MY MOM NOT BEING AROUND?
THAT'S NOT WHAT I-
YOU THINK IT'S COOL THAT I DON'T HAVE SOMEONE TO PICK ME UP FROM SCHOOL AND MAKE ME DINNER? IS IT COOL THAT I'M THE KID AT CHURCH WHO PEOPLE LOOK AT? AND TALK ABOUT?...
...LIKE I DON'T UNDERSTAND WHAT THEY'RE SAYING?
DANNY, I -
YOU THINK YOUR LIFE IS SO BAD BECAUSE YOUR MOM GIVES A DAMN ABOUT HOW YOU'RE DOING IN SCHOOL!? BECAUSE SHE ANNOYS YOU WITH PHONE CALLS AND TEXTS?!

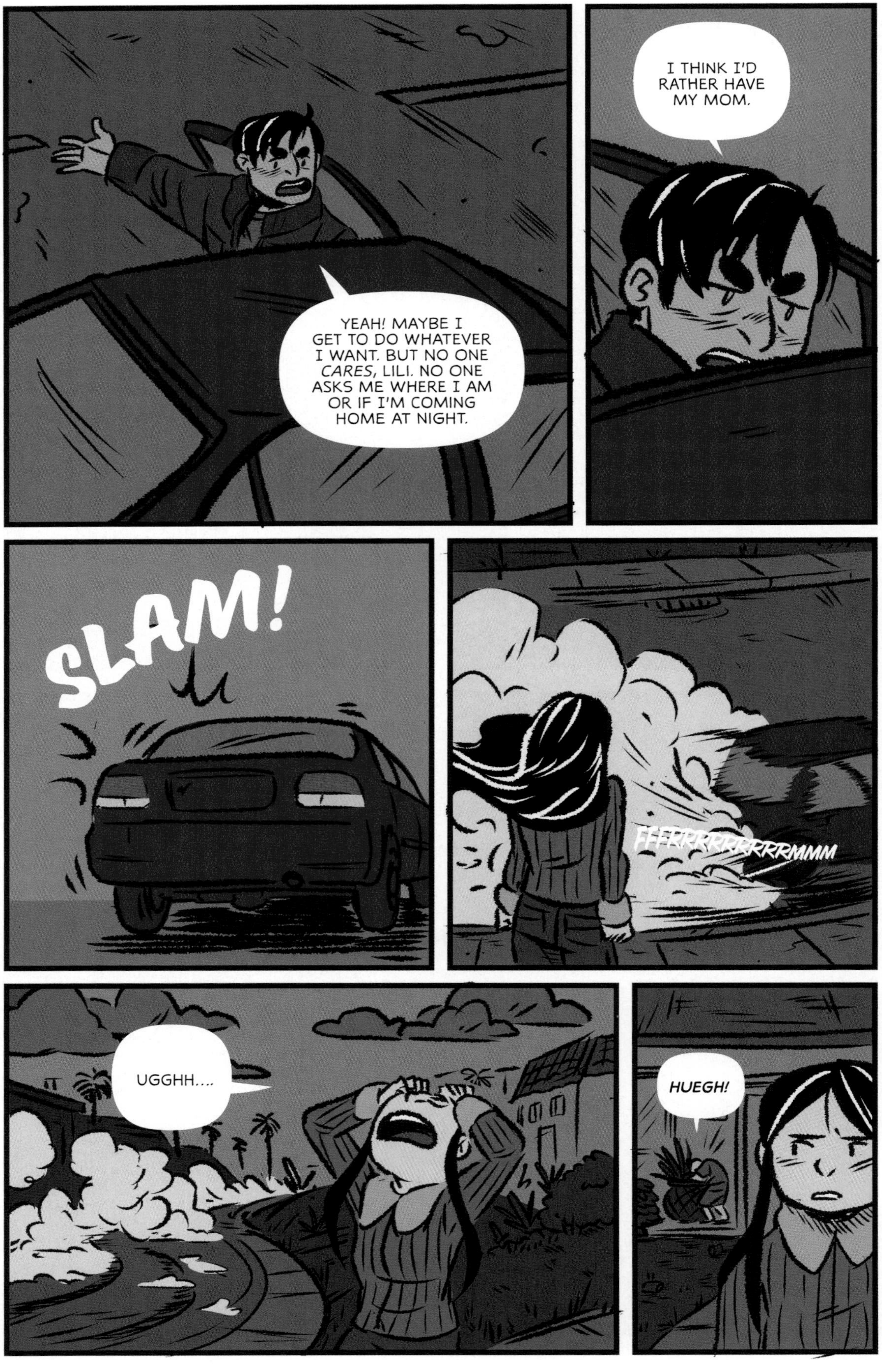
YEAH! MAYBE I GET TO DO WHATEVER I WANT. BUT NO ONE *CARES*, LILI. NO ONE ASKS ME WHERE I AM OR IF I'M COMING HOME AT NIGHT.
I THINK I'D RATHER HAVE MY MOM.
SLAM!
FFFRRRRRRRRRRRMMM
UGGHH....
HUEGH!

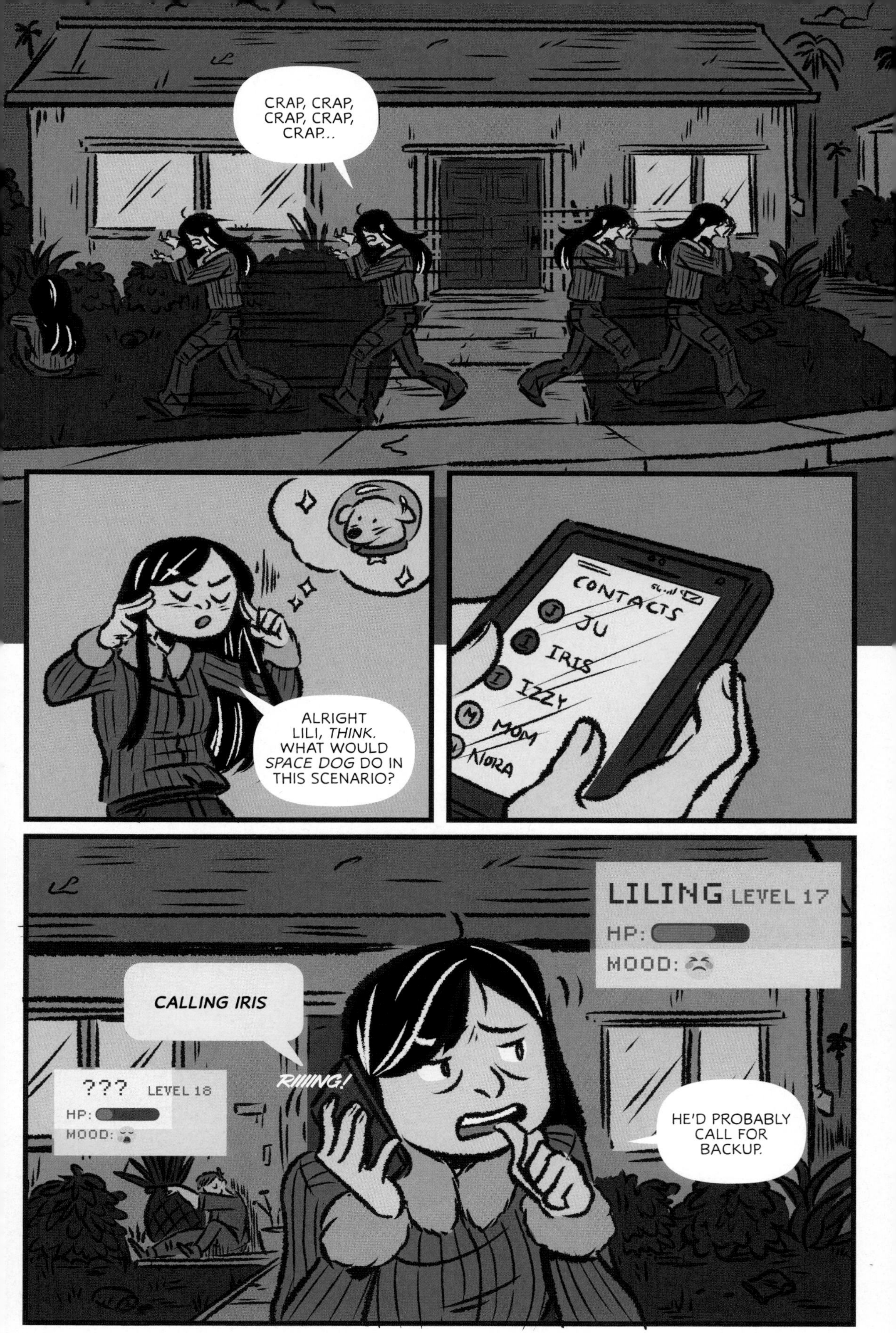
CRAP, CRAP, CRAP, CRAP, CRAP...
ALRIGHT LILI, *THINK.* WHAT WOULD *SPACE DOG* DO IN THIS SCENARIO?
CONTACTS
JU
IRIS
IZZY
MOM
NORA
LILING LEVEL 17
HP:
MOOD:
CALLING IRIS
RIIIING!
??? LEVEL 18
HP:
MOOD:
HE'D PROBABLY CALL FOR BACKUP.

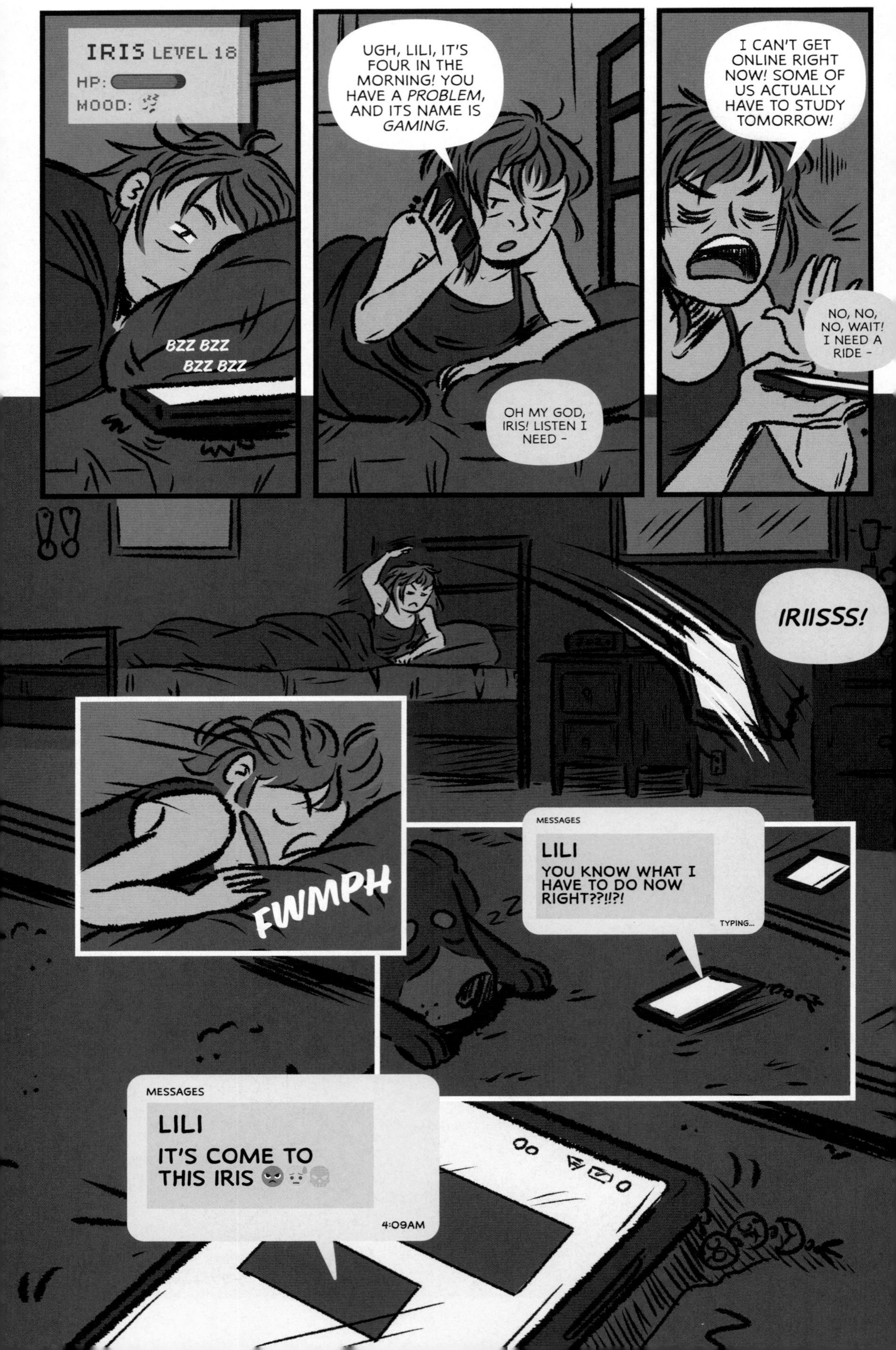
IRIS LEVEL 18
HP:
MOOD:
BZZ BZZ
BZZ BZZ
UGH, LILI, IT'S FOUR IN THE MORNING! YOU HAVE A *PROBLEM*, AND ITS NAME IS *GAMING.*
OH MY GOD, IRIS! LISTEN I NEED -
I CAN'T GET ONLINE RIGHT NOW! SOME OF US ACTUALLY HAVE TO STUDY TOMORROW!
NO, NO, NO, WAIT! I NEED A RIDE -
IRIISSS!
FWMPH
MESSAGES
LILI
YOU KNOW WHAT I HAVE TO DO NOW RIGHT??!!?!
TYPING...
MESSAGES
LILI
IT'S COME TO THIS IRIS
4:09AM

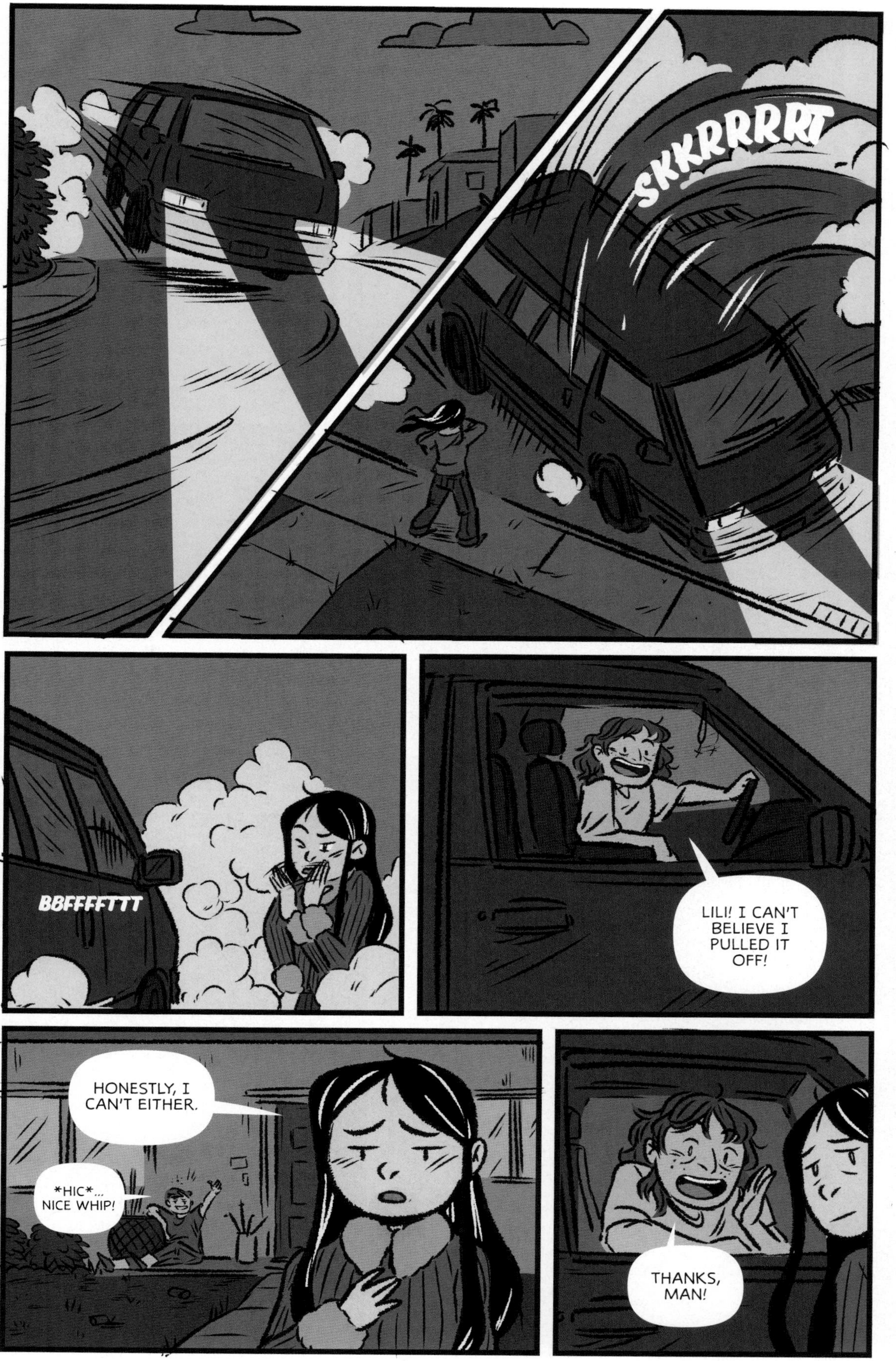
SKKRRRRT
BBFFFFTTT
LILI! I CAN'T BELIEVE I PULLED IT OFF!
HONESTLY, I CAN'T EITHER.
HIC... NICE WHIP!
THANKS, MAN!

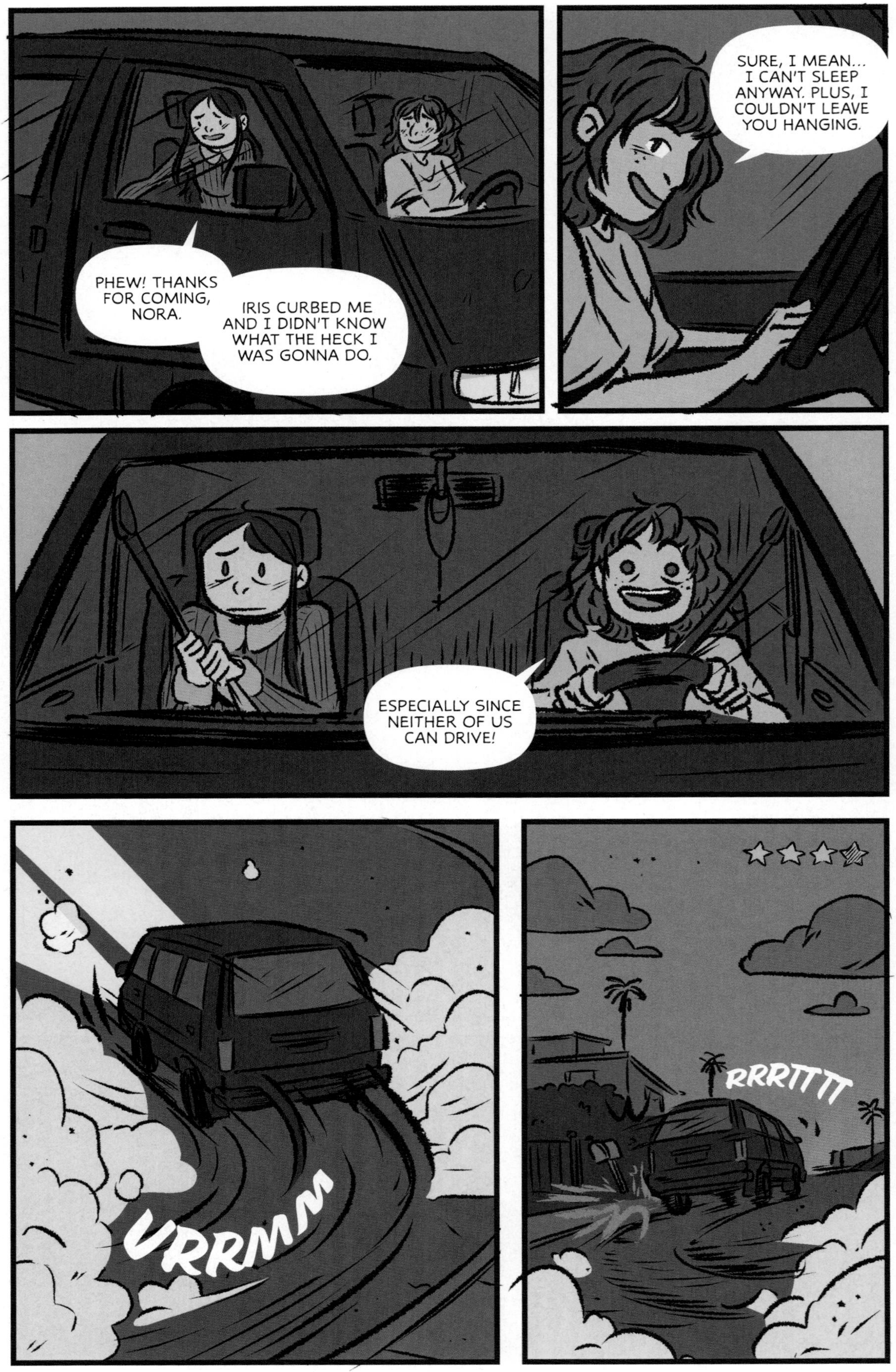
PHEW! THANKS FOR COMING, NORA.
IRIS CURBED ME AND I DIDN'T KNOW WHAT THE HECK I WAS GONNA DO.
SURE, I MEAN... I CAN'T SLEEP ANYWAY. PLUS, I COULDN'T LEAVE YOU HANGING.
ESPECIALLY SINCE NEITHER OF US CAN DRIVE!
URRMM
RRRTTTT

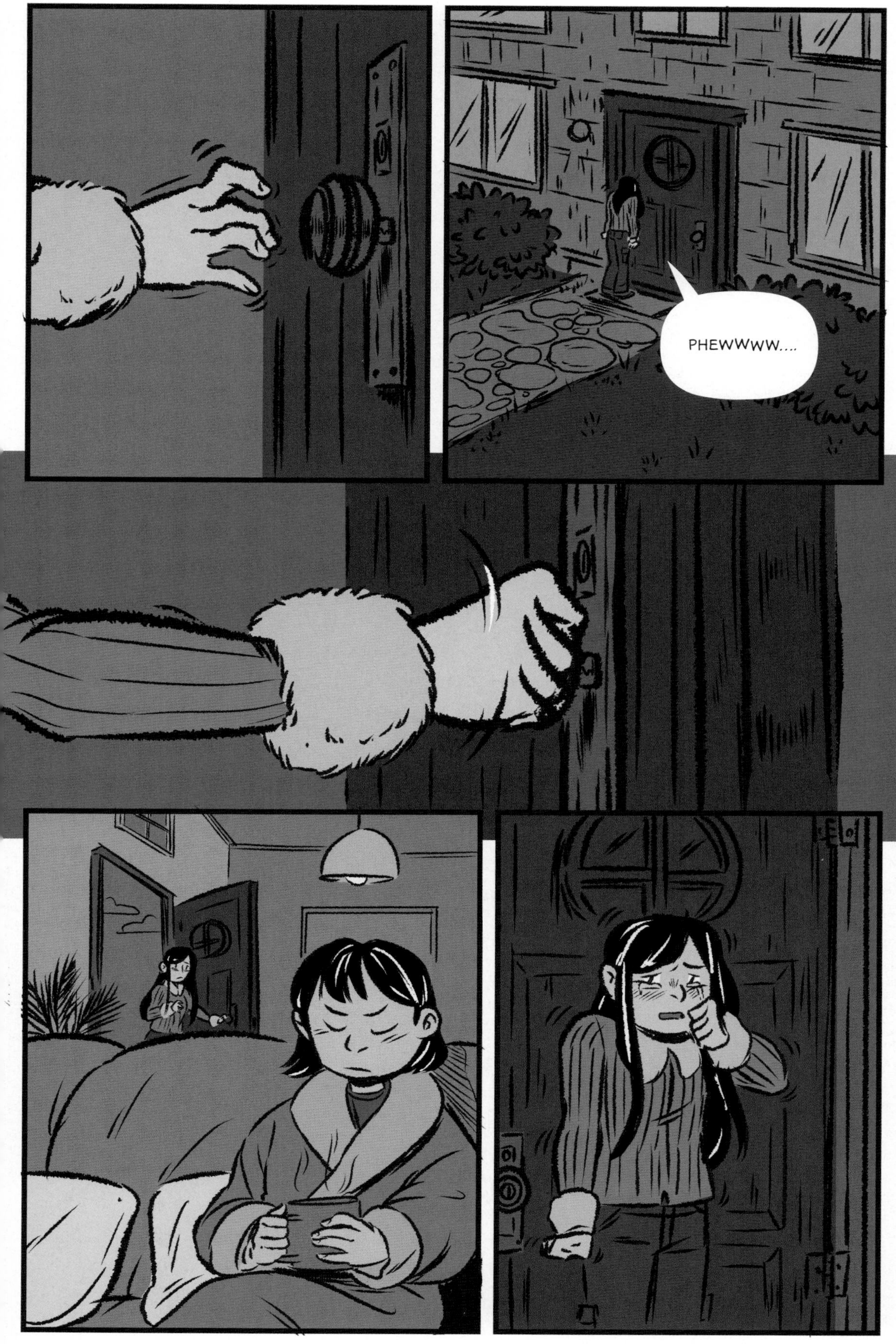
PHEWWWW....

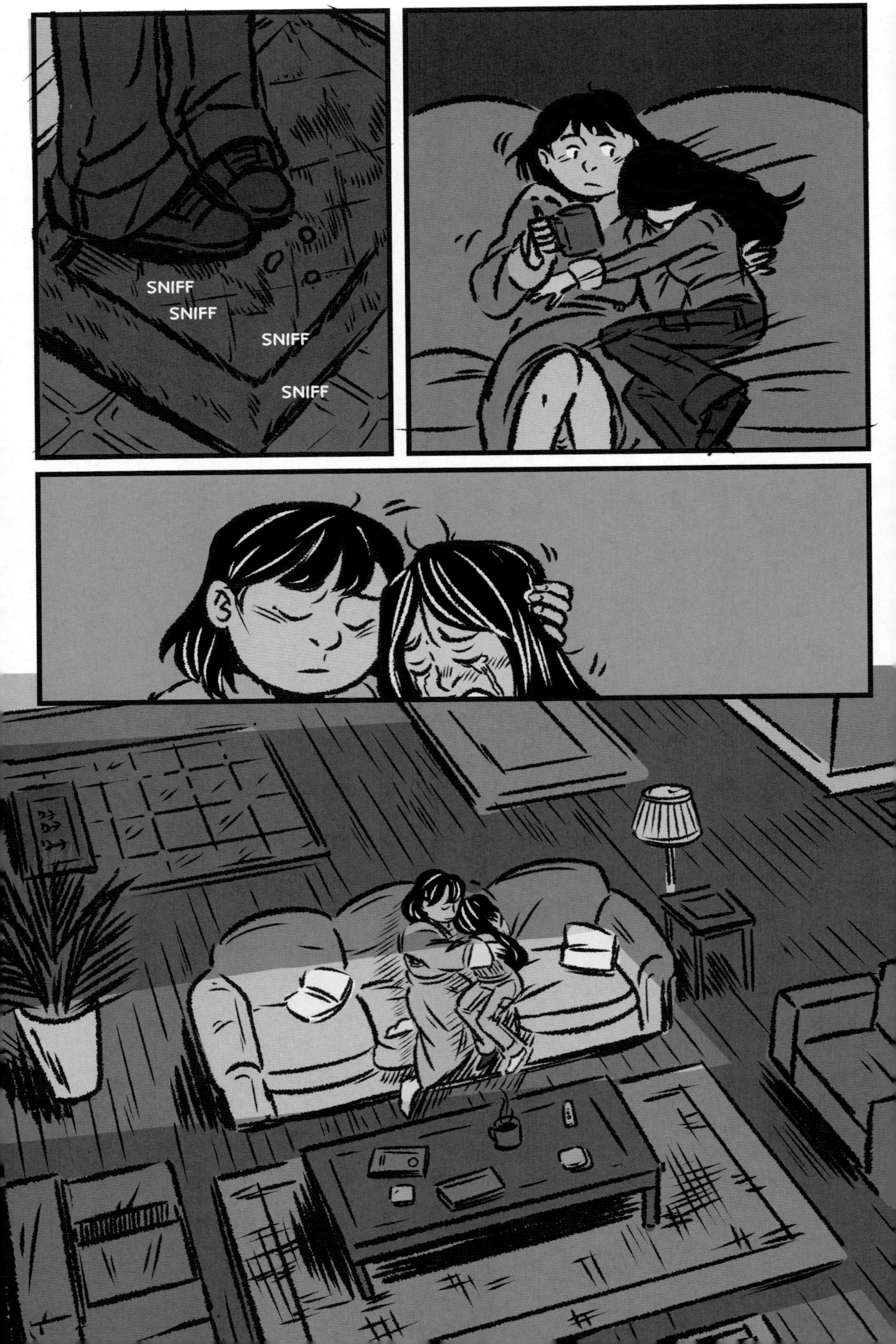
SNIFF
SNIFF
SNIFF
SNIFF

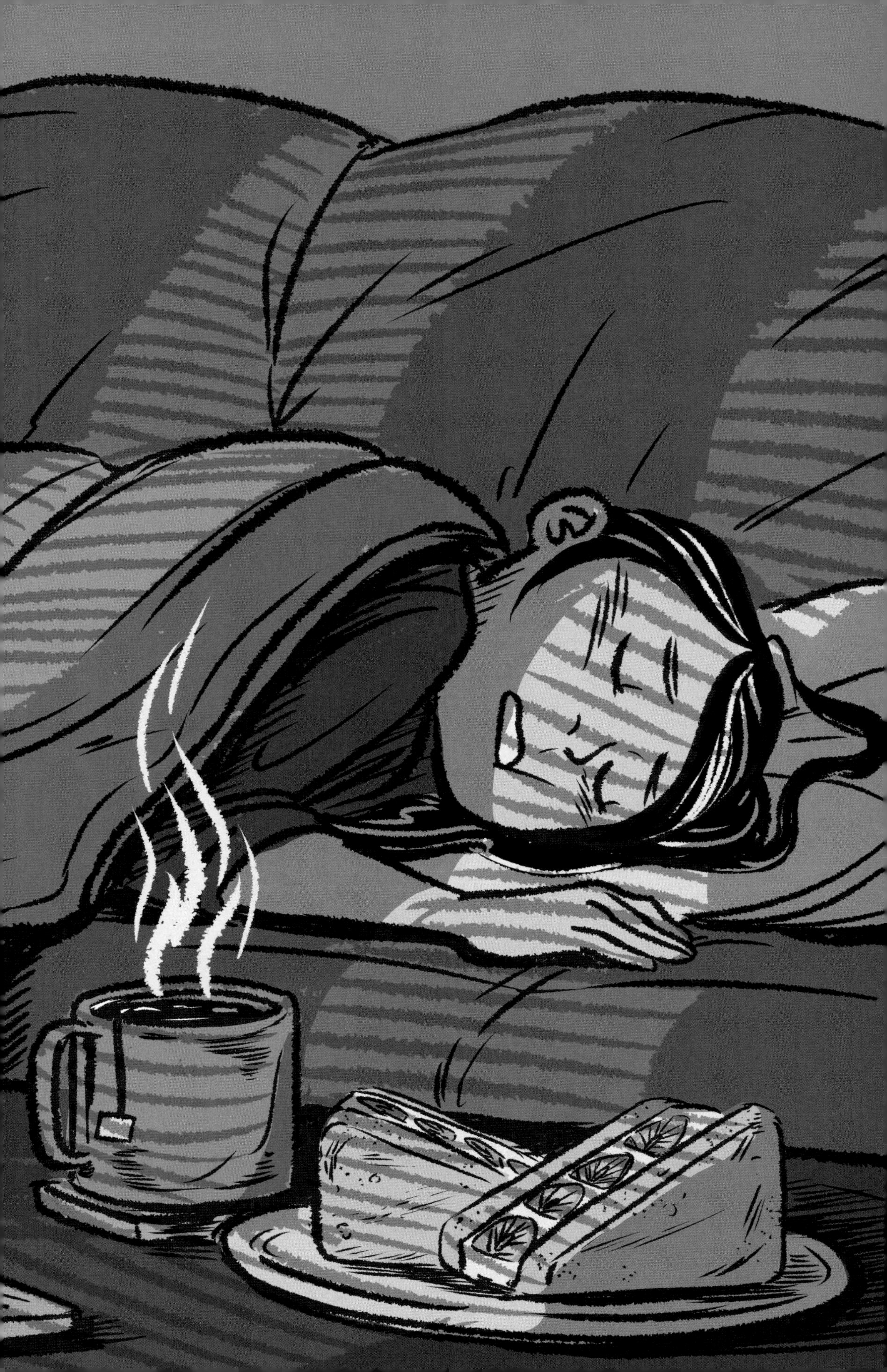

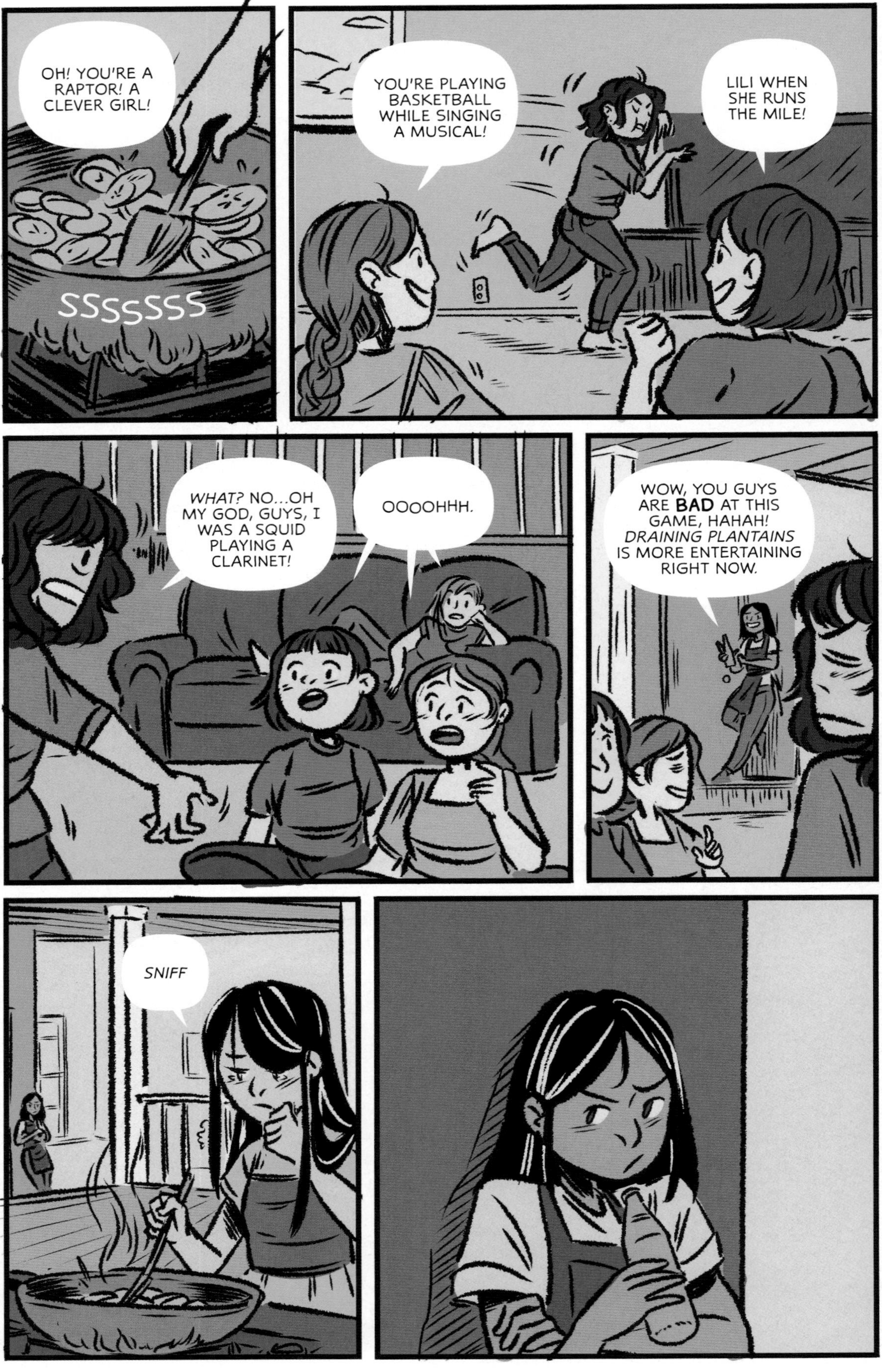
OH! YOU'RE A RAPTOR! A CLEVER GIRL!
SSSSSSS
YOU'RE PLAYING BASKETBALL WHILE SINGING A MUSICAL!
LILI WHEN SHE RUNS THE MILE!
WHAT? NO...OH MY GOD, GUYS, I WAS A SQUID PLAYING A CLARINET!
OOOOHHH.
WOW, YOU GUYS ARE BAD AT THIS GAME, HAHAH! DRAINING PLANTAINS IS MORE ENTERTAINING RIGHT NOW.
SNIFF

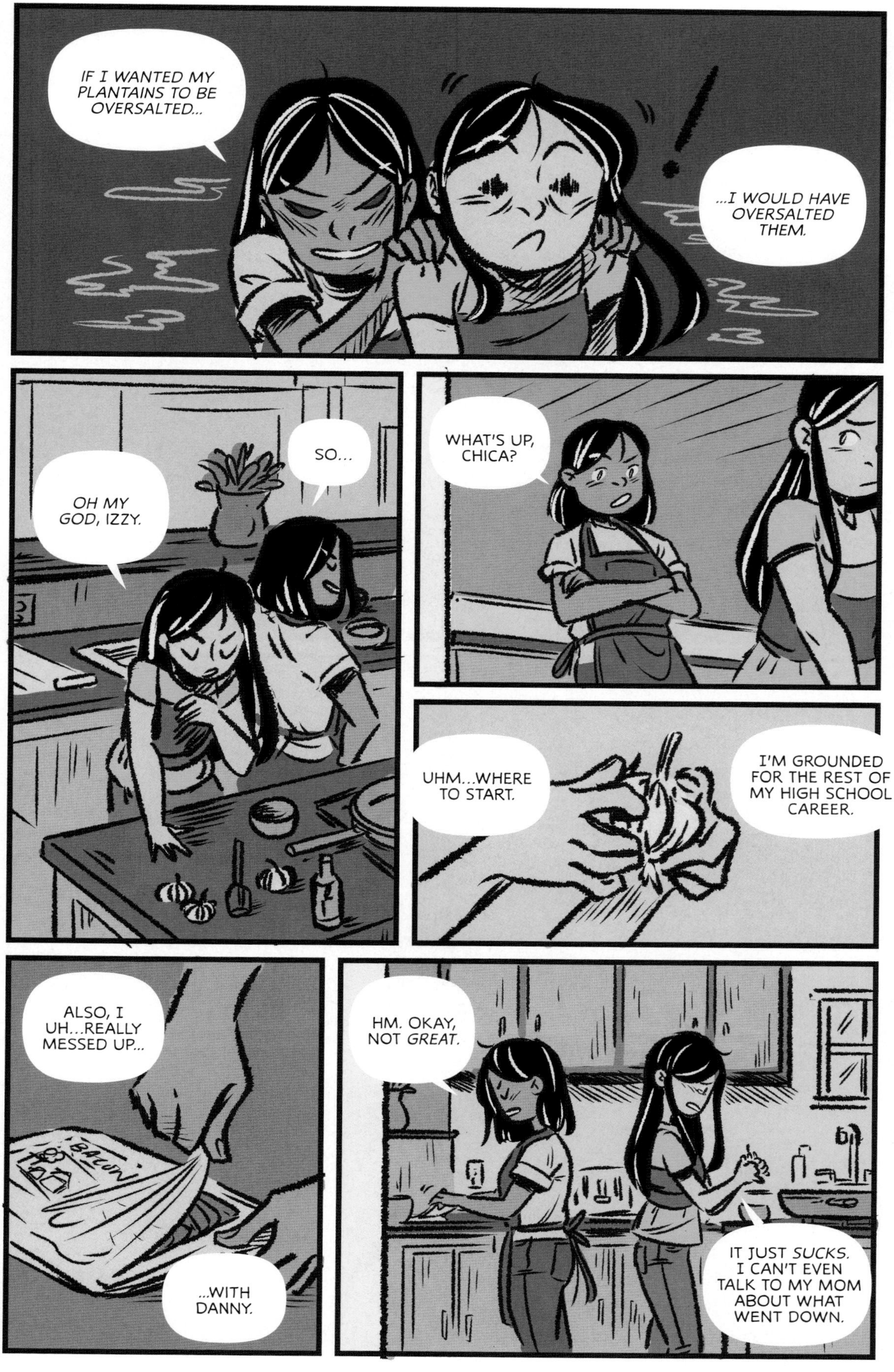
IF I WANTED MY PLANTAINS TO BE OVERSALTED...
...I WOULD HAVE OVERSALTED THEM.
SO...
OH MY GOD, IZZY.
WHAT'S UP, CHICA?
UHM...WHERE TO START.
I'M GROUNDED FOR THE REST OF MY HIGH SCHOOL CAREER.
ALSO, I UH...REALLY MESSED UP...
...WITH DANNY.
BACON
HM. OKAY, NOT GREAT.
IT JUST SUCKS. I CAN'T EVEN TALK TO MY MOM ABOUT WHAT WENT DOWN.

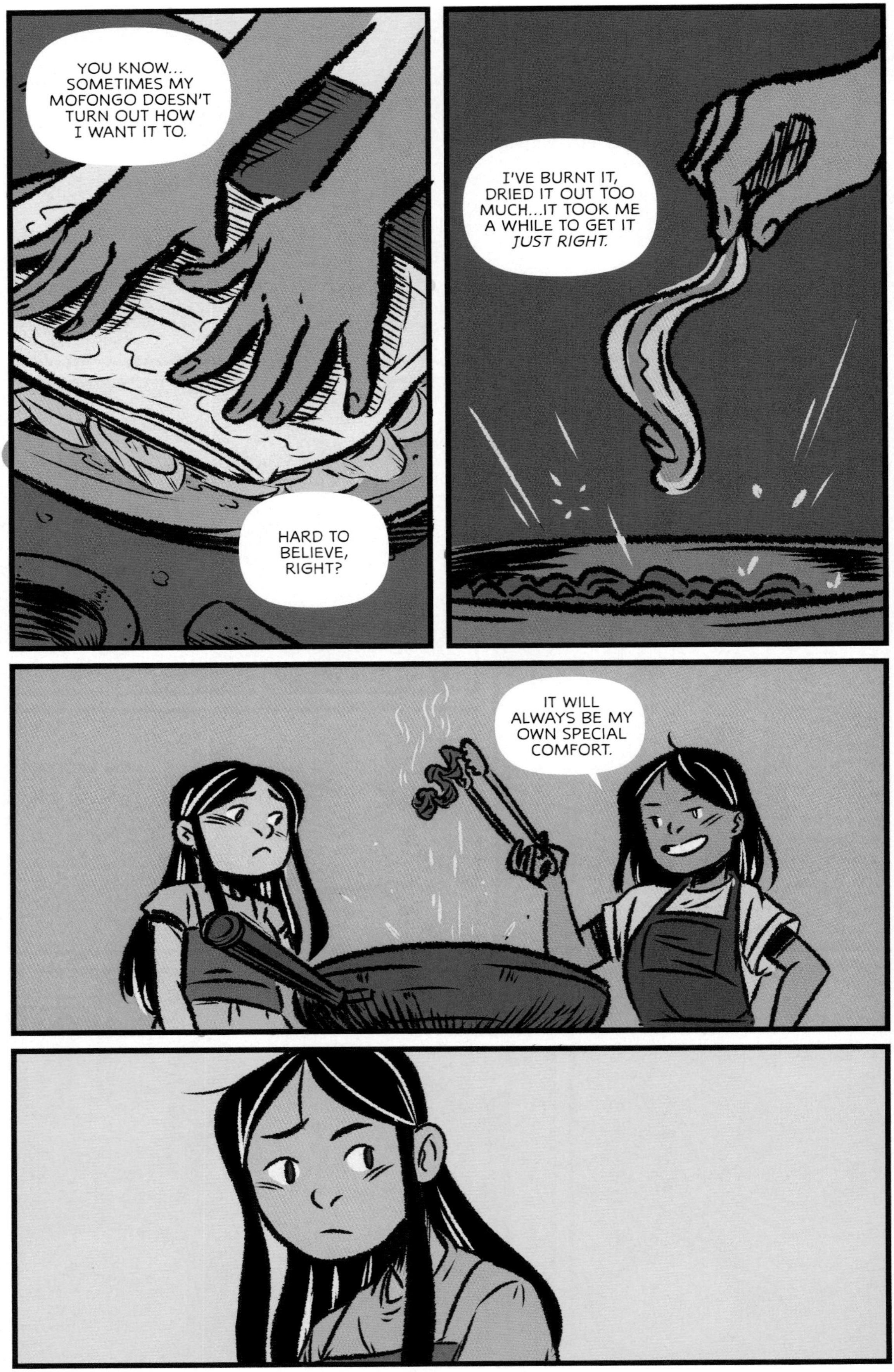

YOU KNOW... SOMETIMES MY MOFONGO DOESN'T TURN OUT HOW I WANT IT TO.
HARD TO BELIEVE, RIGHT?
I'VE BURNT IT, DRIED IT OUT TOO MUCH...IT TOOK ME A WHILE TO GET IT *JUST RIGHT.*
IT WILL ALWAYS BE MY OWN SPECIAL COMFORT.

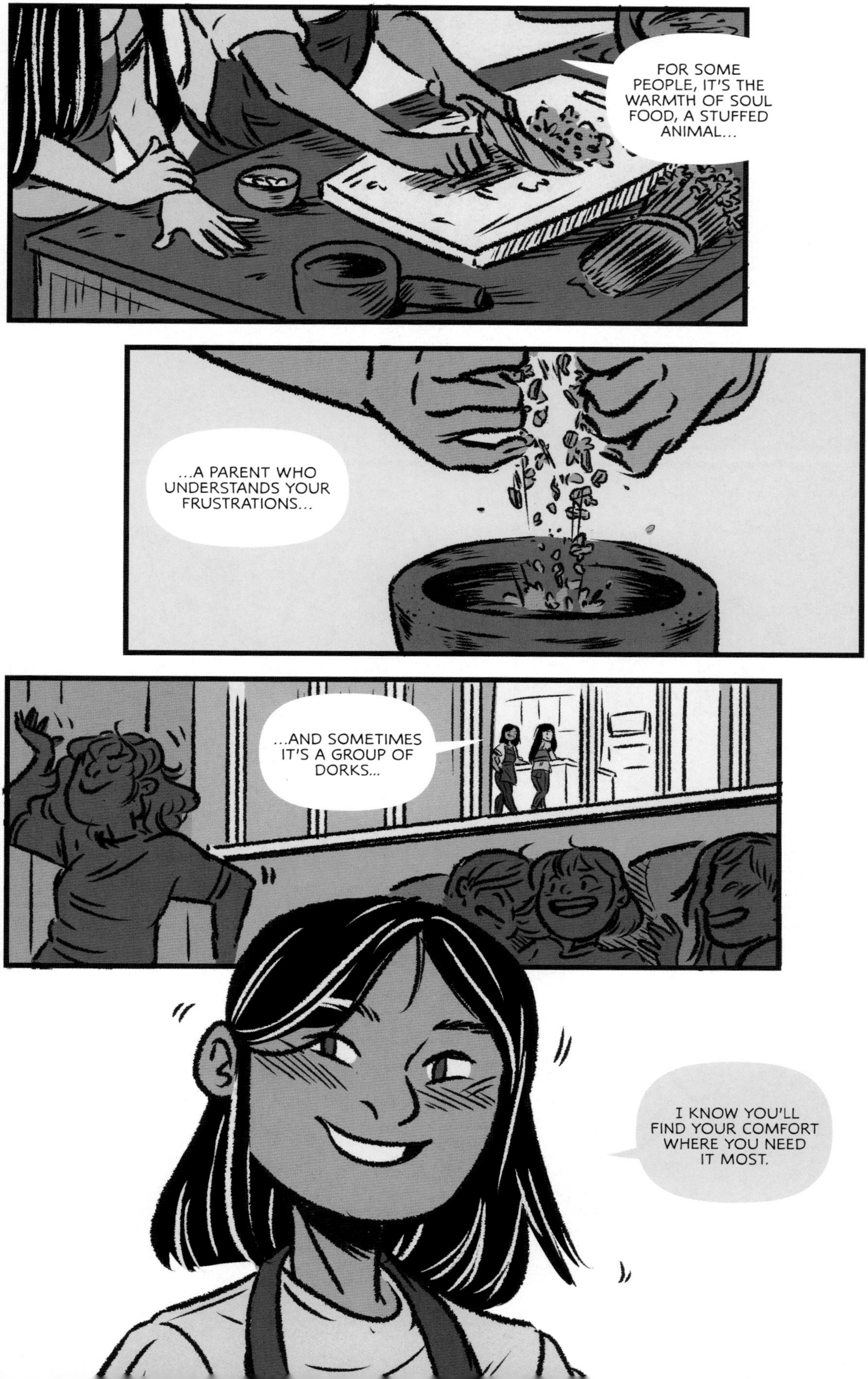
FOR SOME PEOPLE, IT'S THE WARMTH OF SOUL FOOD, A STUFFED ANIMAL...
...A PARENT WHO UNDERSTANDS YOUR FRUSTRATIONS...
...AND SOMETIMES IT'S A GROUP OF DORKS...
I KNOW YOU'LL FIND YOUR COMFORT WHERE YOU NEED IT MOST.

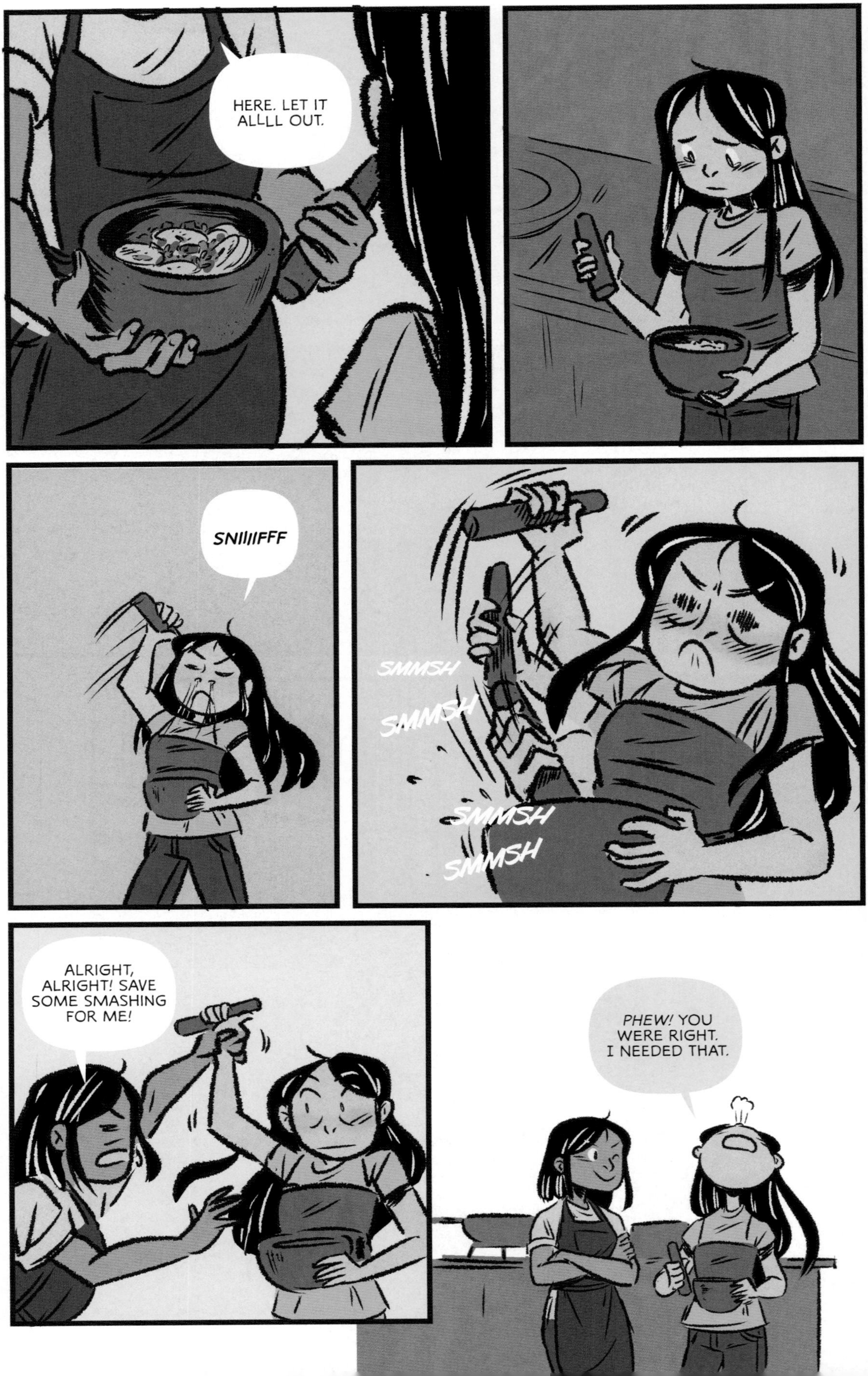
HERE. LET IT ALLLL OUT.
SNIIIIFFF
SMMSH
SMMSH
SMMSH
SMMSH
ALRIGHT, ALRIGHT! SAVE SOME SMASHING FOR ME!
PHEW! YOU WERE RIGHT. I NEEDED THAT.

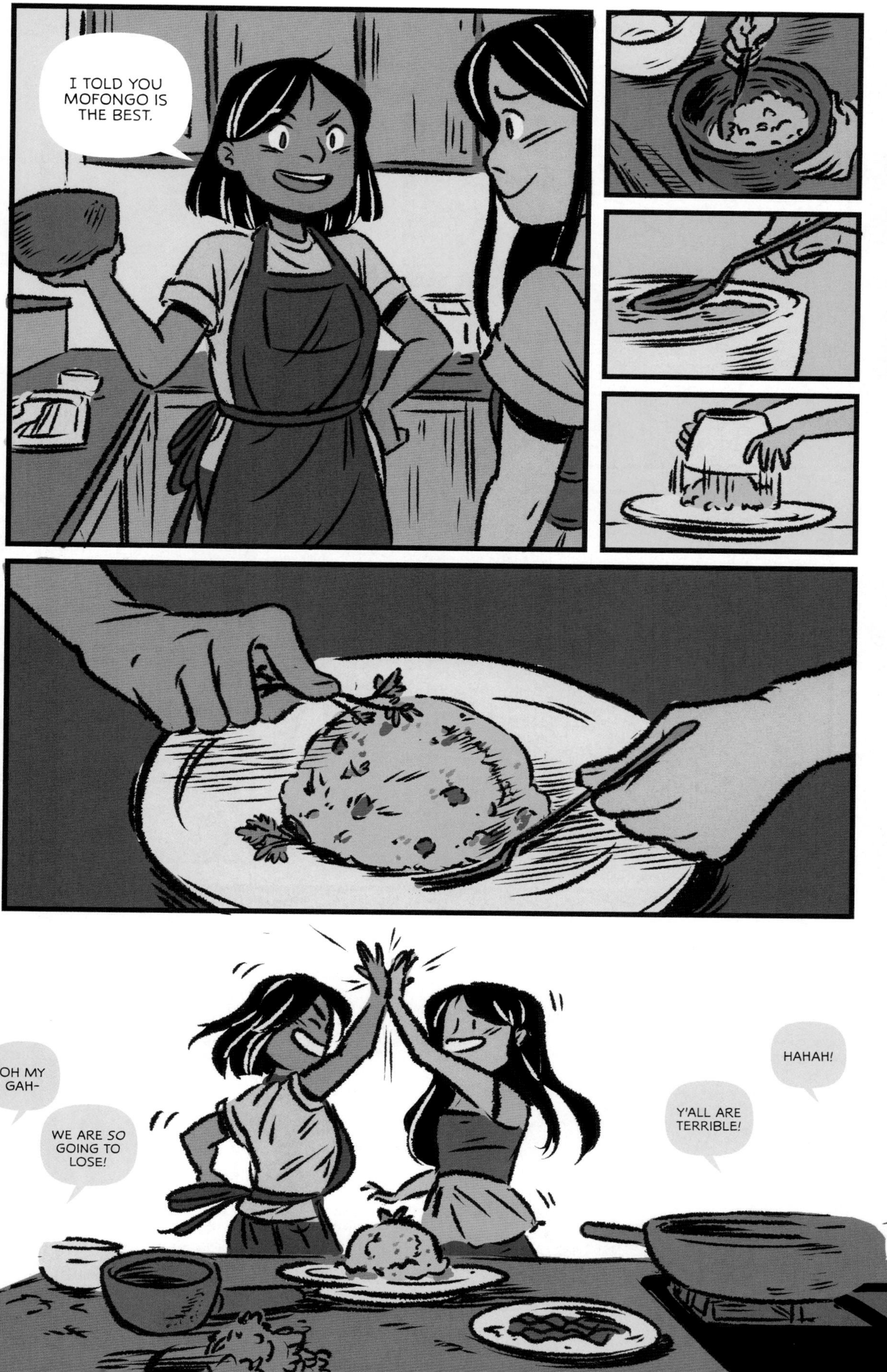
I TOLD YOU MOFONGO IS THE BEST.
OH MY GAH-
WE ARE *SO* GOING TO LOSE!
HAHAH!
Y'ALL ARE TERRIBLE!

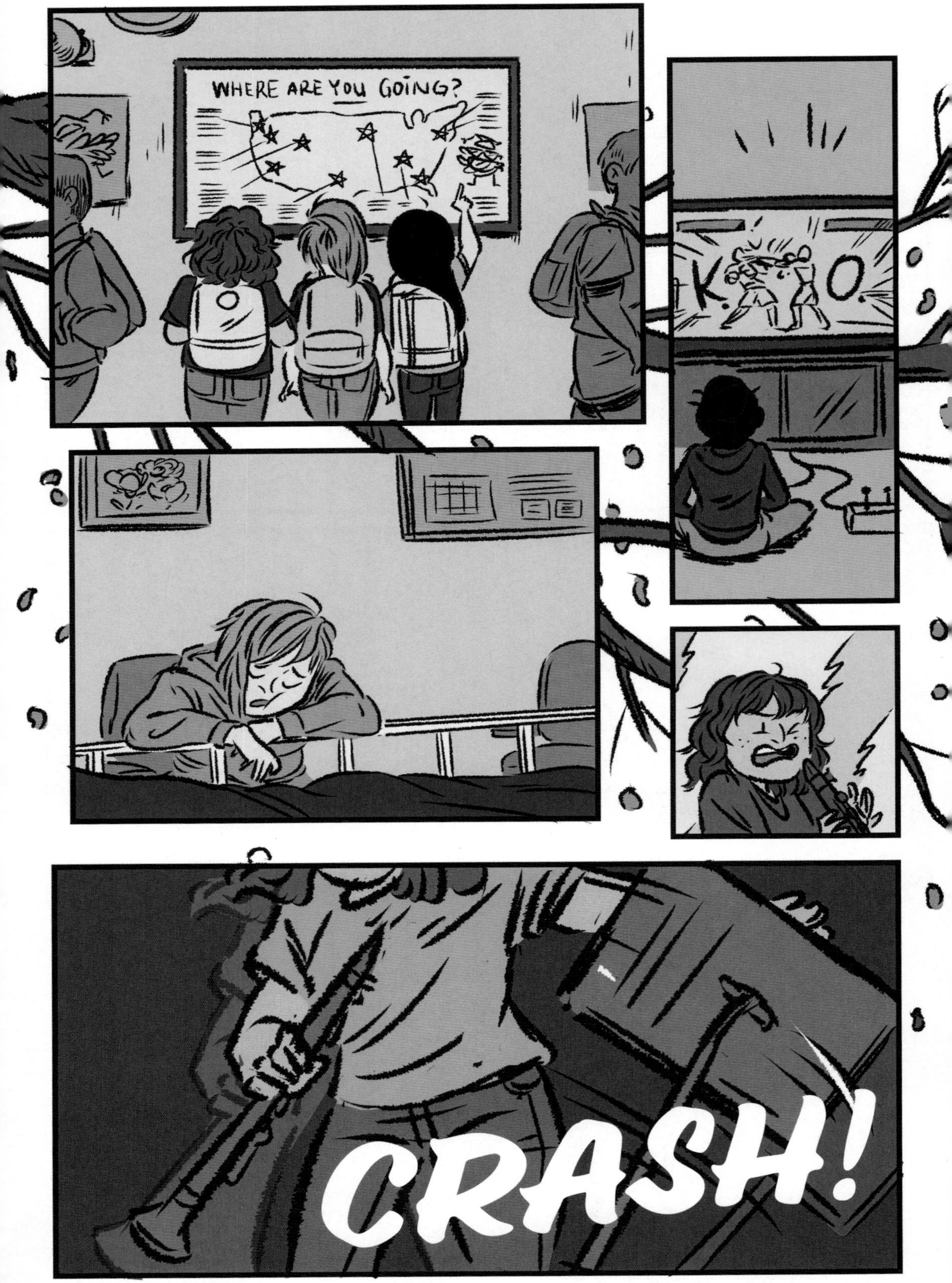
WHERE ARE YOU GOING?
K.O.
CRASH!

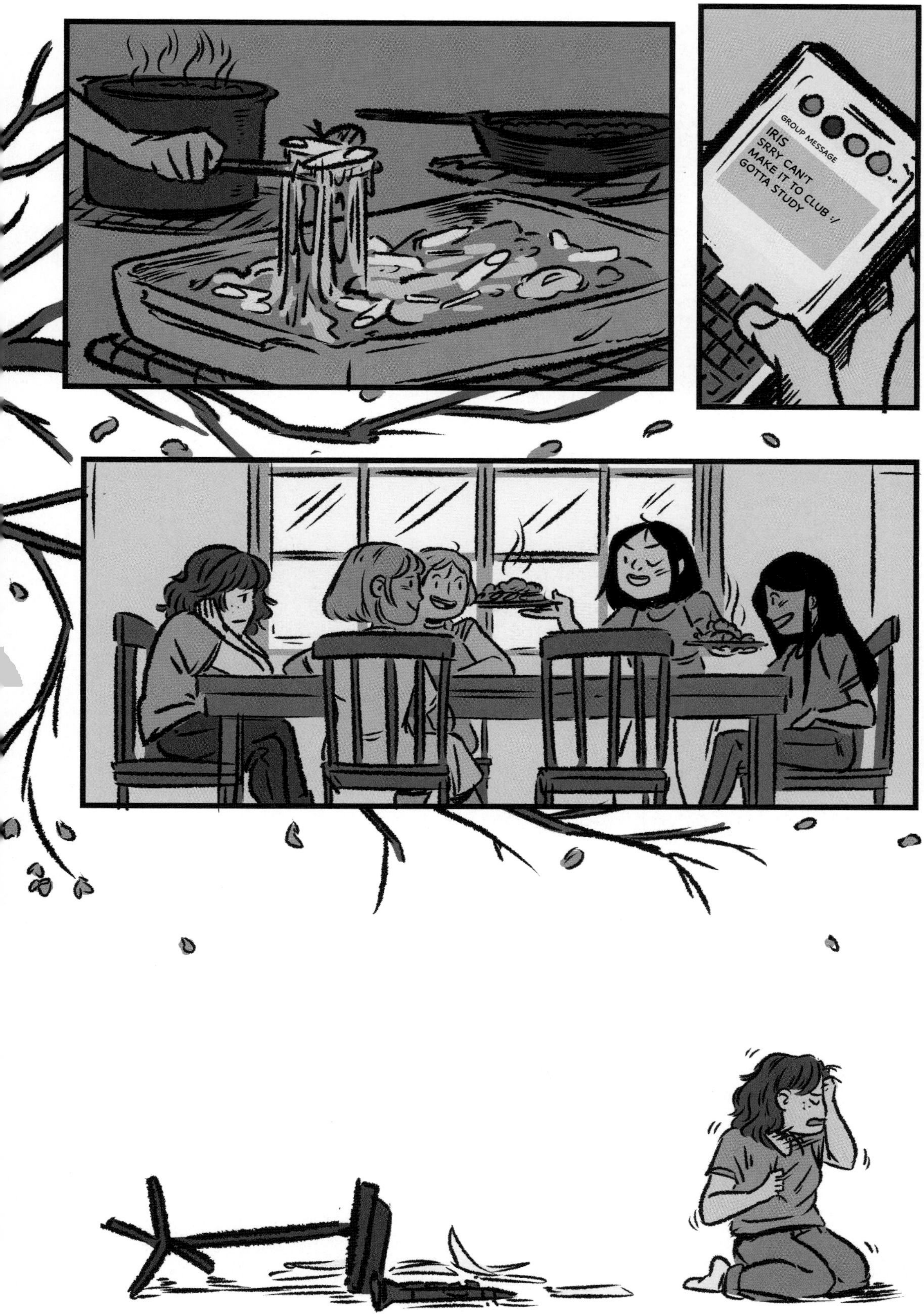
GROUP MESSAGE
IRIS
SRRY CAN'T
MAKE IT TO CLUB :/
GOTTA STUDY

Chapter Ten
black bean stew

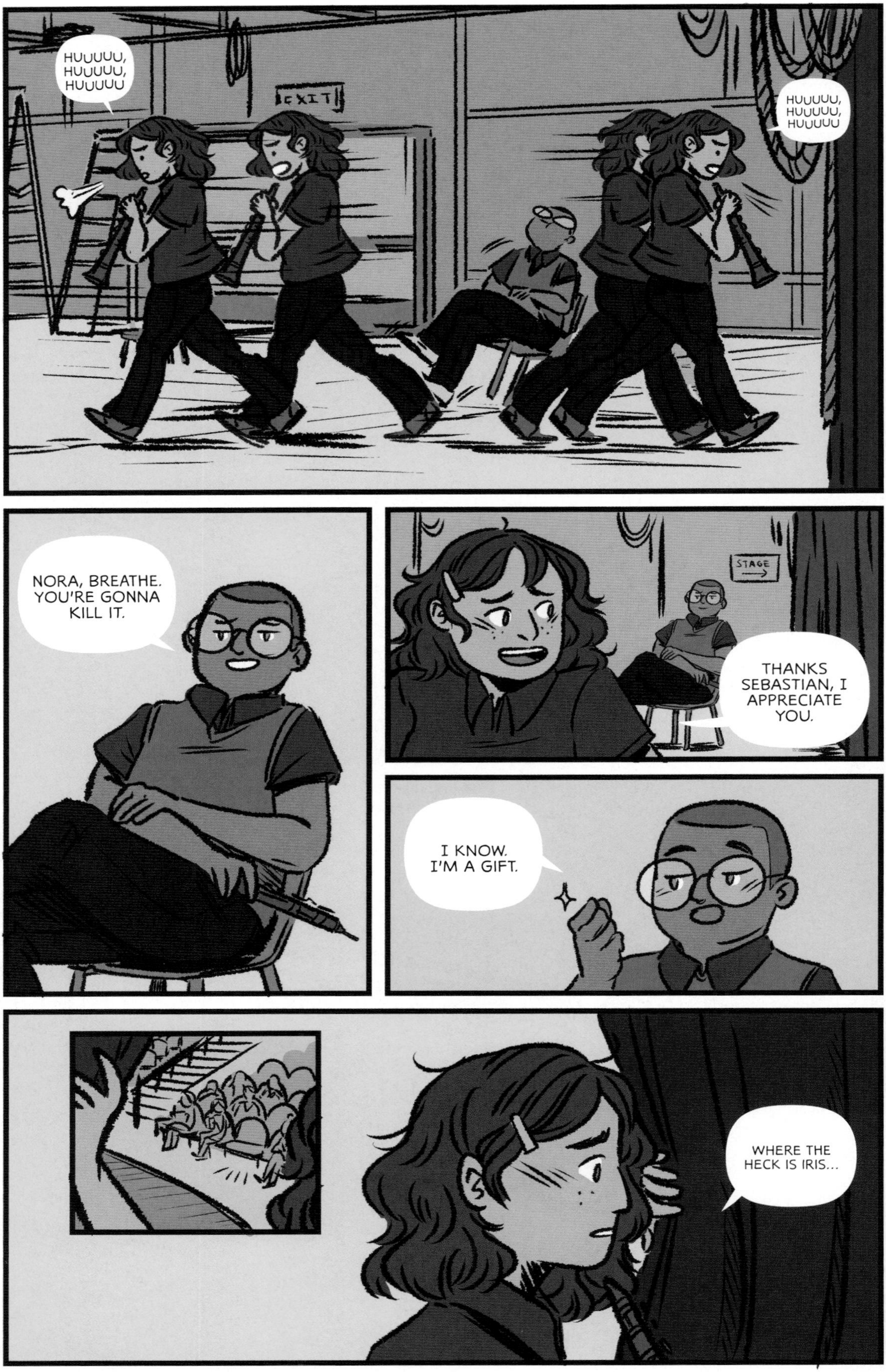
HUUUUU, HUUUUU, HUUUUU
EXIT
HUUUUU, HUUUUU, HUUUUU
NORA, BREATHE. YOU'RE GONNA KILL IT.
STAGE
THANKS SEBASTIAN, I APPRECIATE YOU.
I KNOW. I'M A GIFT.
WHERE THE HECK IS IRIS...

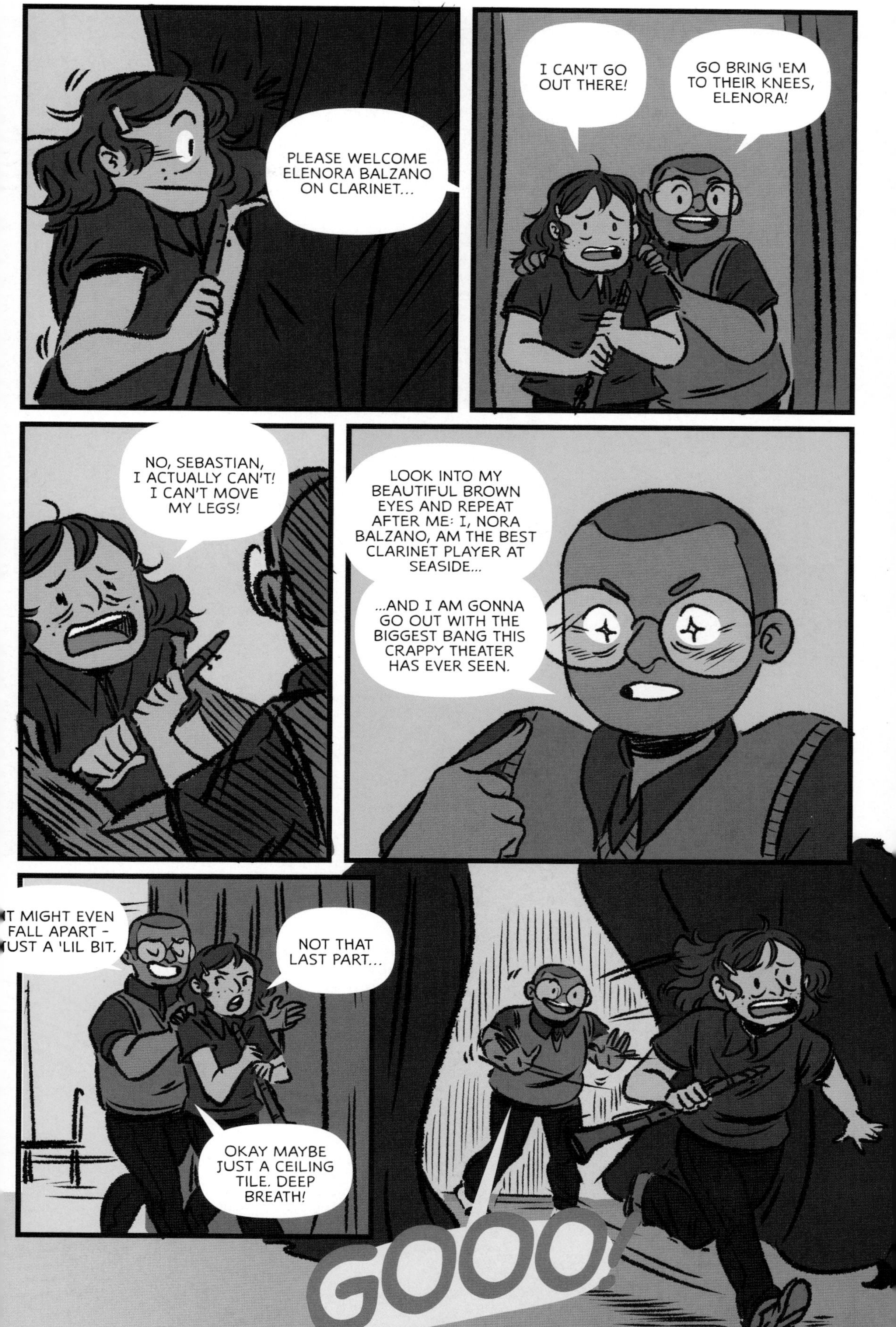
PLEASE WELCOME ELENORA BALZANO ON CLARINET...
I CAN'T GO OUT THERE!
GO BRING 'EM TO THEIR KNEES, ELENORA!
NO, SEBASTIAN, I ACTUALLY CAN'T! I CAN'T MOVE MY LEGS!
LOOK INTO MY BEAUTIFUL BROWN EYES AND REPEAT AFTER ME: I, NORA BALZANO, AM THE BEST CLARINET PLAYER AT SEASIDE...
...AND I AM GONNA GO OUT WITH THE BIGGEST BANG THIS CRAPPY THEATER HAS EVER SEEN.
T MIGHT EVEN FALL APART - UST A 'LIL BIT.
NOT THAT LAST PART...
OKAY MAYBE JUST A CEILING TILE. DEEP BREATH!
GOOO!

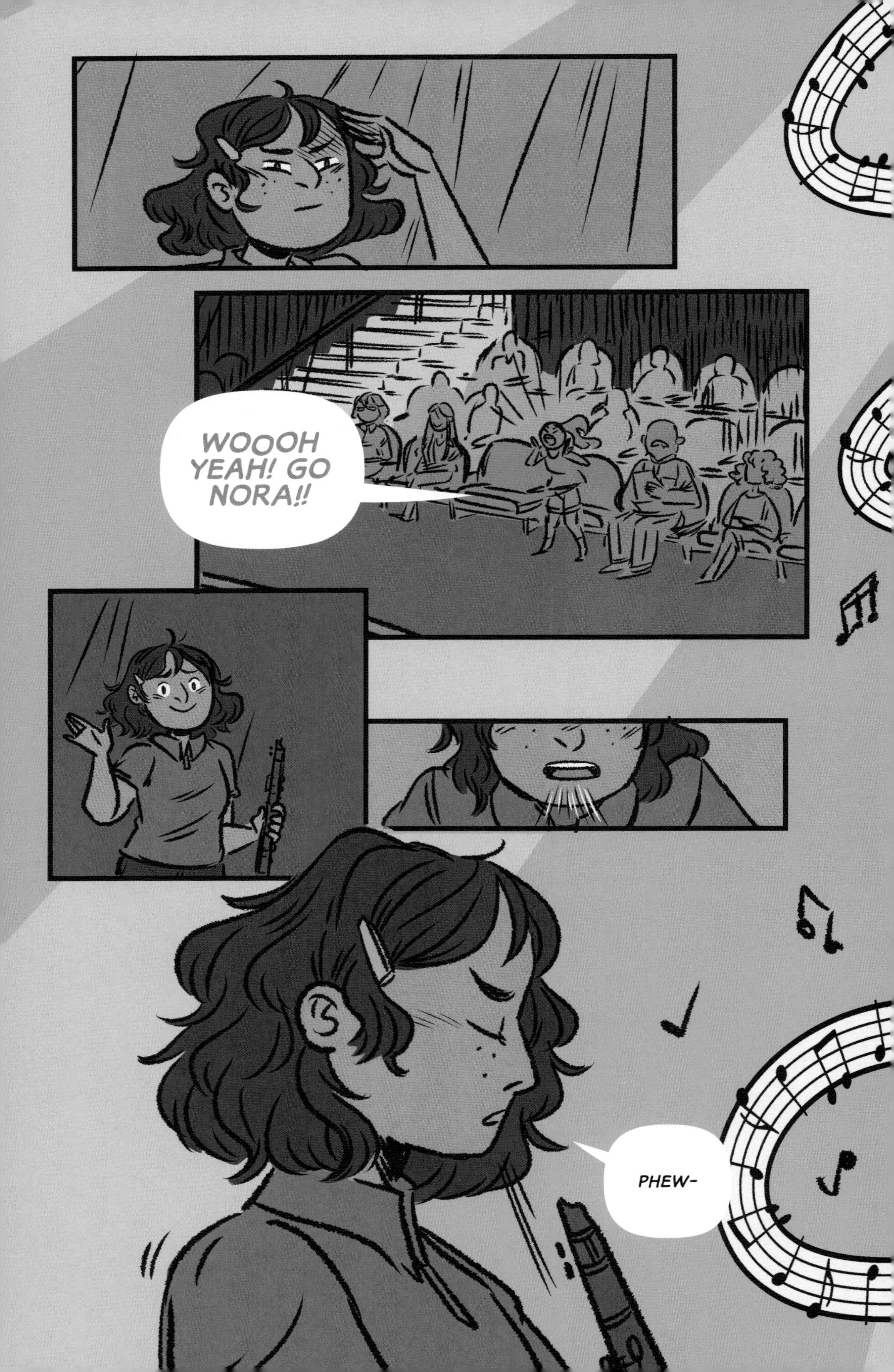
WOOOH YEAH! GO NORA!!
PHEW-

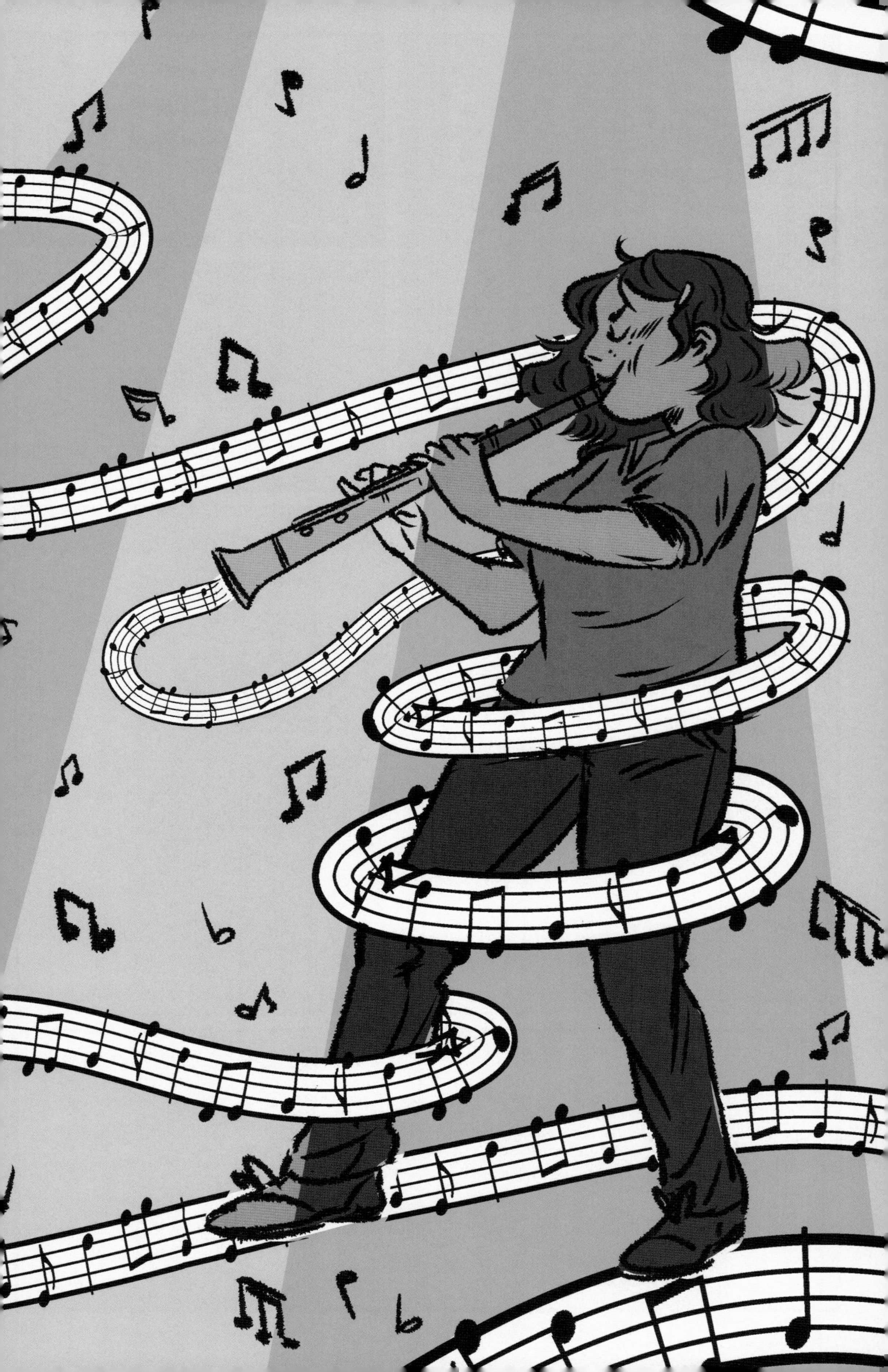

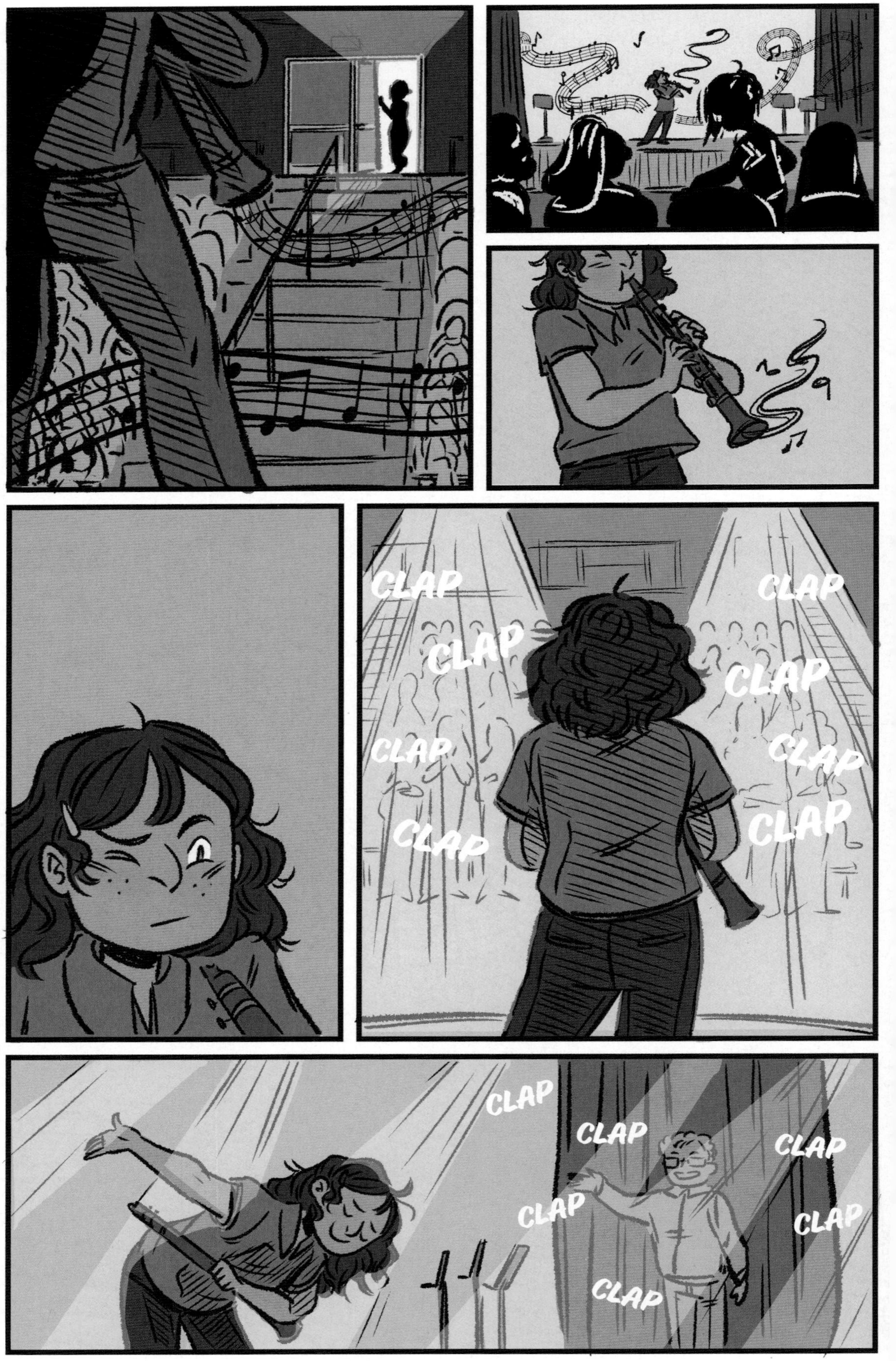
CLAP
CLAP
CLAP
CLAP
CLAP
CLAP
CLAP
CLAP
CLAP
CLAP
CLAP
CLAP
CLAP
CLAP

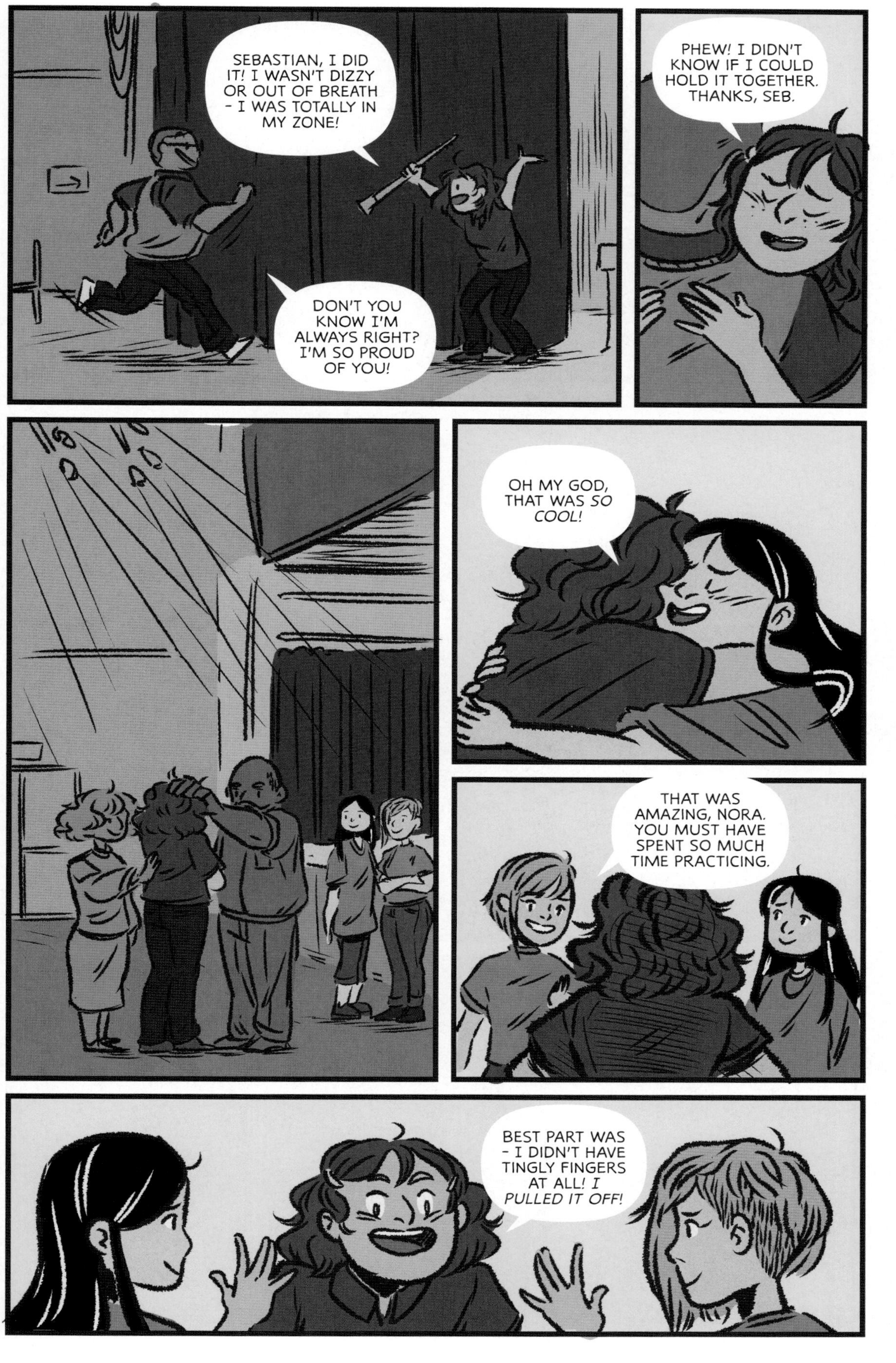
SEBASTIAN, I DID IT! I WASN'T DIZZY OR OUT OF BREATH - I WAS TOTALLY IN MY ZONE!
DON'T YOU KNOW I'M ALWAYS RIGHT? I'M SO PROUD OF YOU!
PHEW! I DIDN'T KNOW IF I COULD HOLD IT TOGETHER. THANKS, SEB.
OH MY GOD, THAT WAS *SO COOL!*
THAT WAS AMAZING, NORA. YOU MUST HAVE SPENT SO MUCH TIME PRACTICING.
BEST PART WAS - I DIDN'T HAVE TINGLY FINGERS AT ALL! *I PULLED IT OFF!*

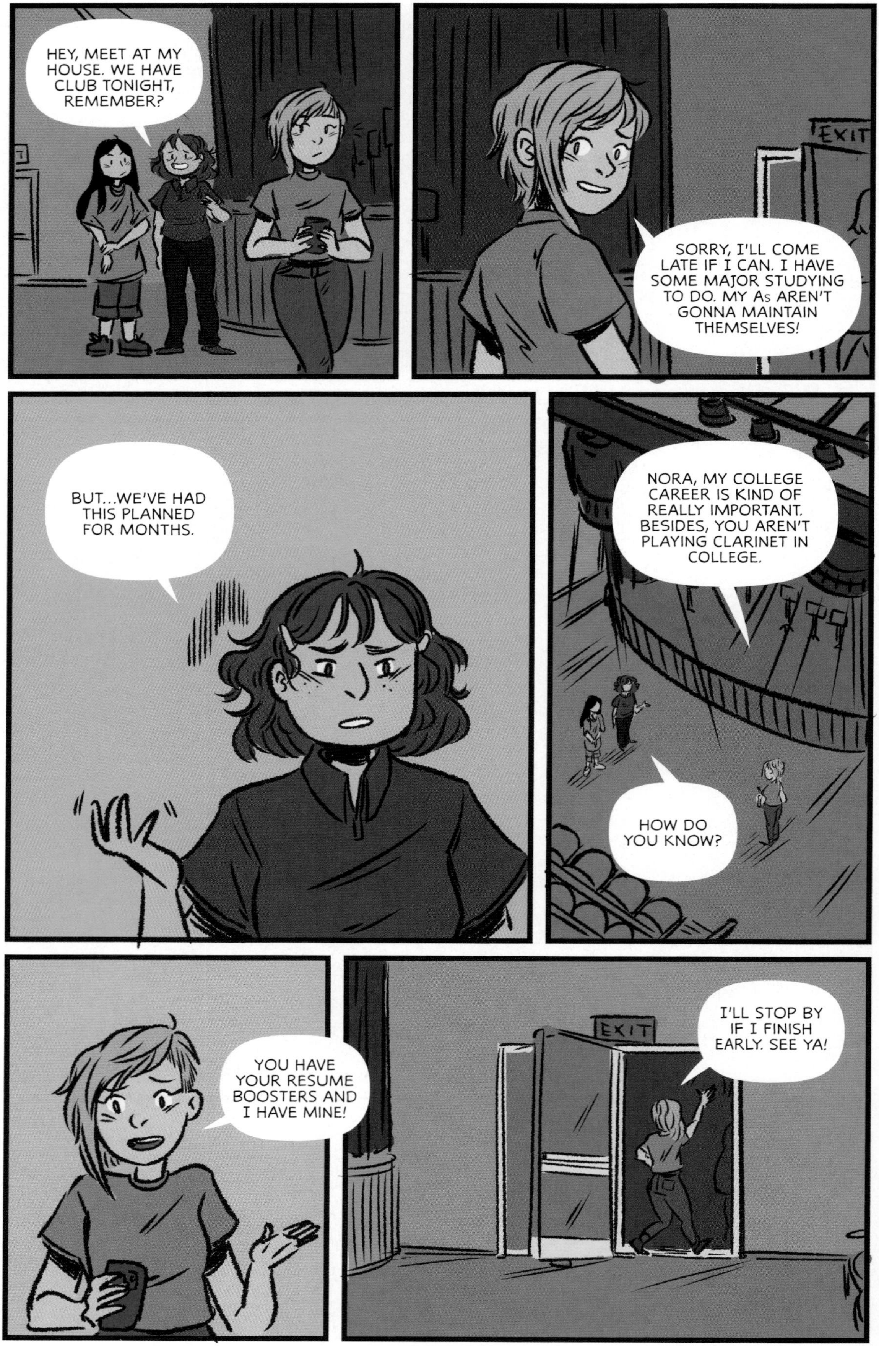
HEY, MEET AT MY HOUSE. WE HAVE CLUB TONIGHT, REMEMBER?
SORRY, I'LL COME LATE IF I CAN. I HAVE SOME MAJOR STUDYING TO DO. MY As AREN'T GONNA MAINTAIN THEMSELVES!
BUT...WE'VE HAD THIS PLANNED FOR MONTHS.
NORA, MY COLLEGE CAREER IS KIND OF REALLY IMPORTANT. BESIDES, YOU AREN'T PLAYING CLARINET IN COLLEGE.
HOW DO YOU KNOW?
YOU HAVE YOUR RESUME BOOSTERS AND I HAVE MINE!
EXIT
I'LL STOP BY IF I FINISH EARLY. SEE YA!

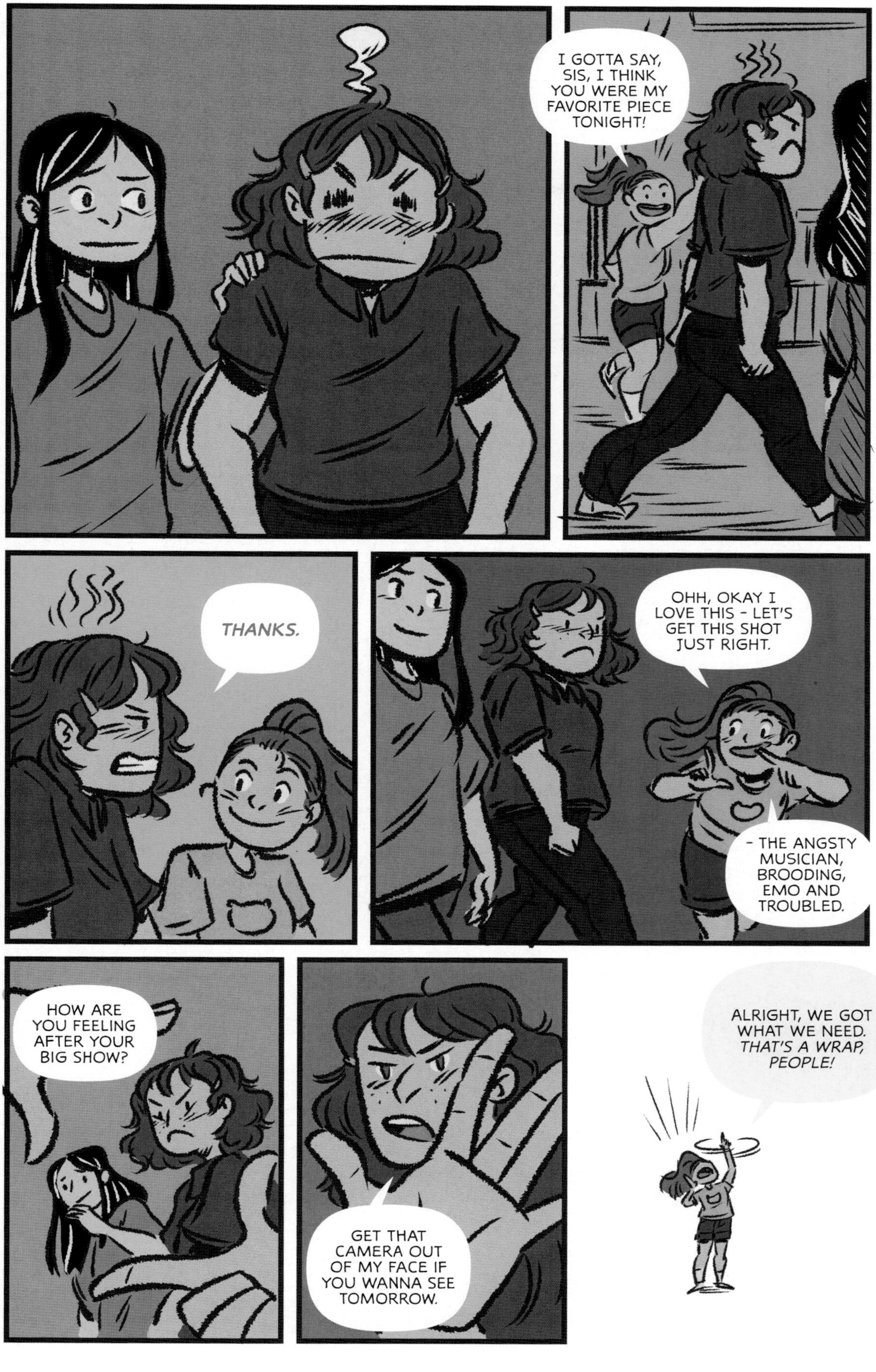
I GOTTA SAY, SIS, I THINK YOU WERE MY FAVORITE PIECE TONIGHT!
THANKS.
OHH, OKAY I LOVE THIS - LET'S GET THIS SHOT JUST RIGHT.
- THE ANGSTY MUSICIAN, BROODING, EMO AND TROUBLED.
HOW ARE YOU FEELING AFTER YOUR BIG SHOW?
GET THAT CAMERA OUT OF MY FACE IF YOU WANNA SEE TOMORROW.
ALRIGHT, WE GOT WHAT WE NEED. *THAT'S A WRAP, PEOPLE!*

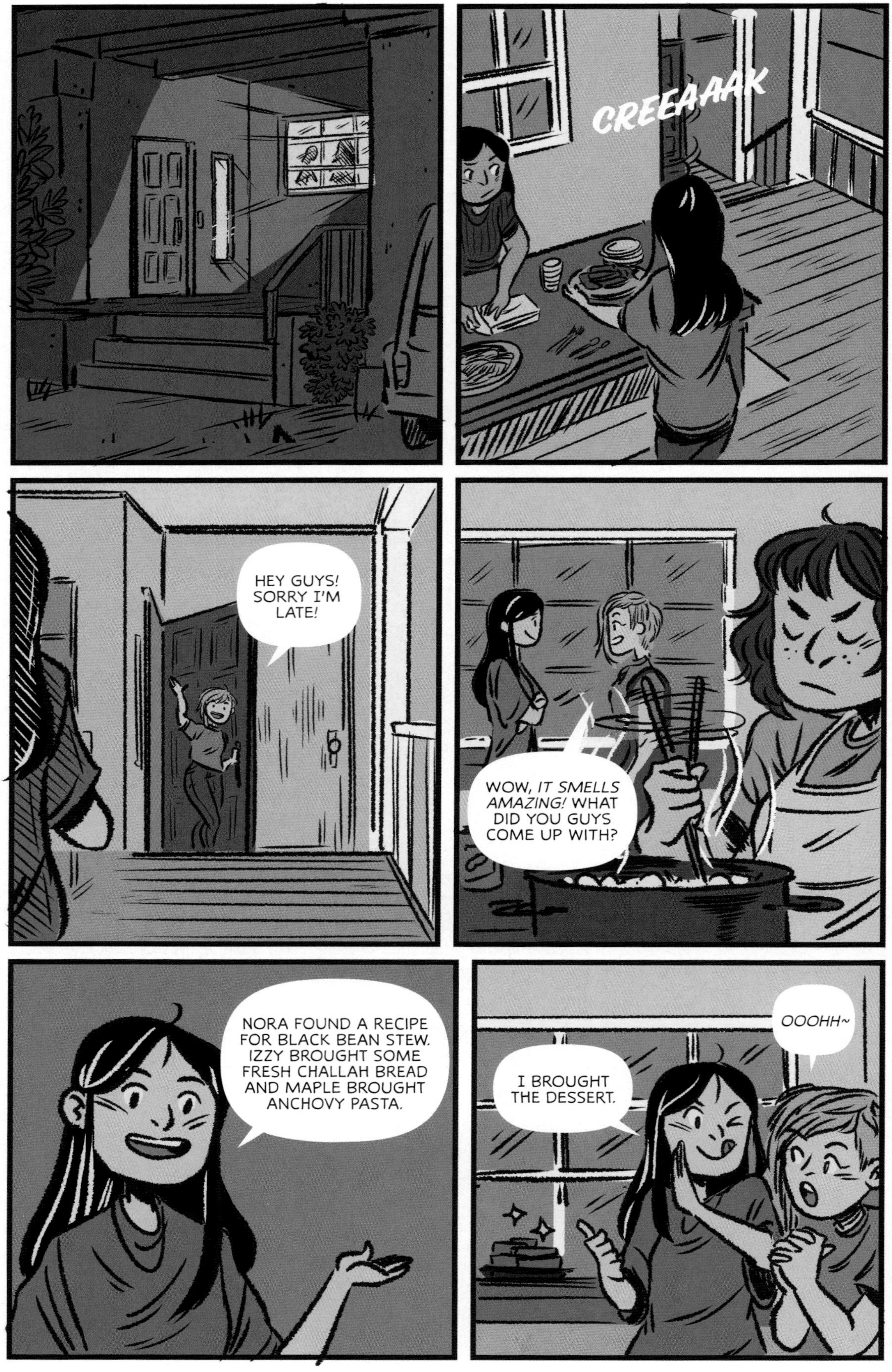
CREEAAAK
HEY GUYS! SORRY I'M LATE!
WOW, *IT SMELLS AMAZING!* WHAT DID YOU GUYS COME UP WITH?
NORA FOUND A RECIPE FOR BLACK BEAN STEW. IZZY BROUGHT SOME FRESH CHALLAH BREAD AND MAPLE BROUGHT ANCHOVY PASTA.
OOOHH~
I BROUGHT THE DESSERT.

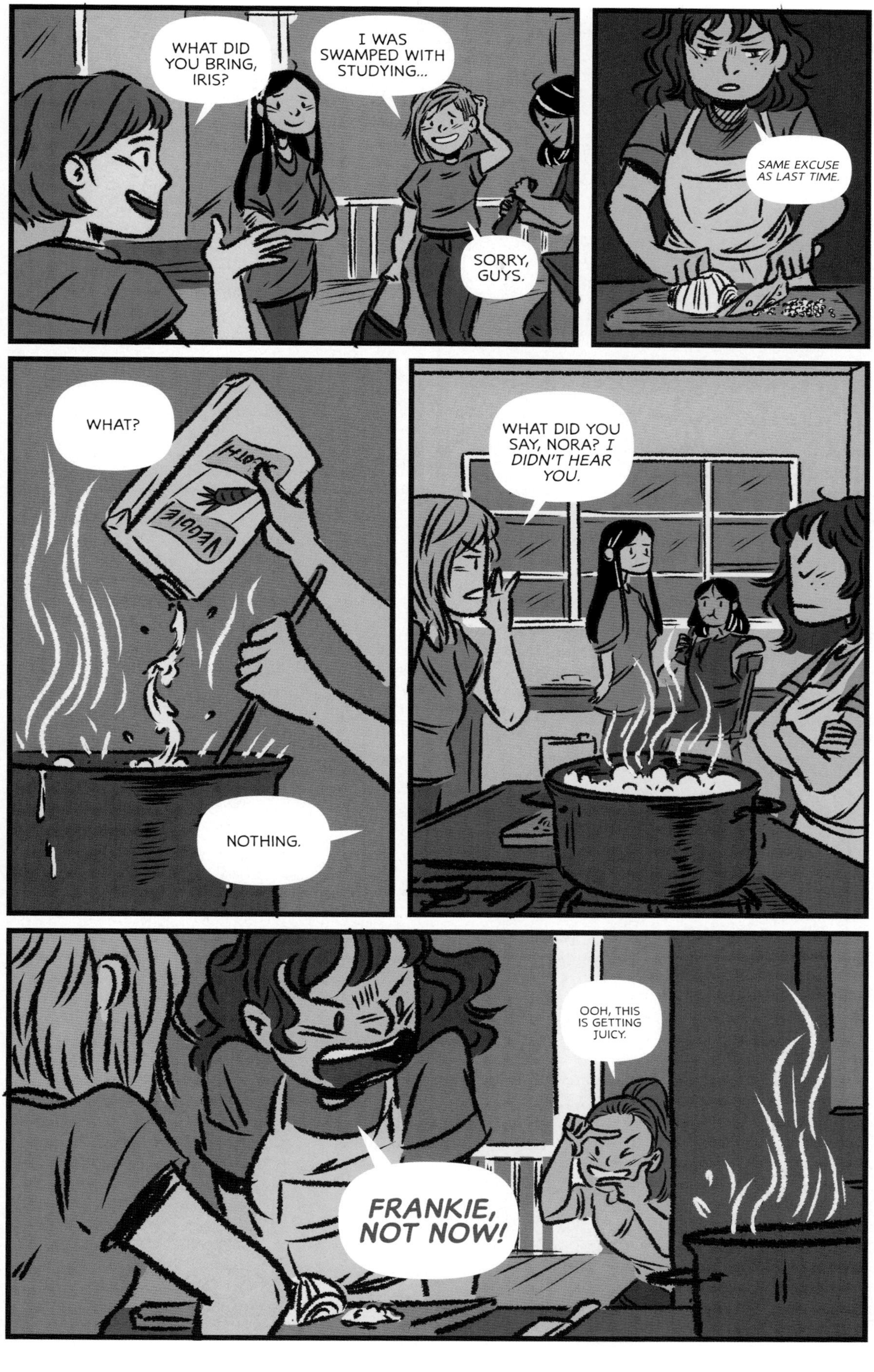
WHAT DID YOU BRING, IRIS?
I WAS SWAMPED WITH STUDYING...
SORRY, GUYS.
SAME EXCUSE AS LAST TIME.
WHAT?
NOTHING.
WHAT DID YOU SAY, NORA? I DIDN'T HEAR YOU.
FRANKIE, NOT NOW!
OOH, THIS IS GETTING JUICY.

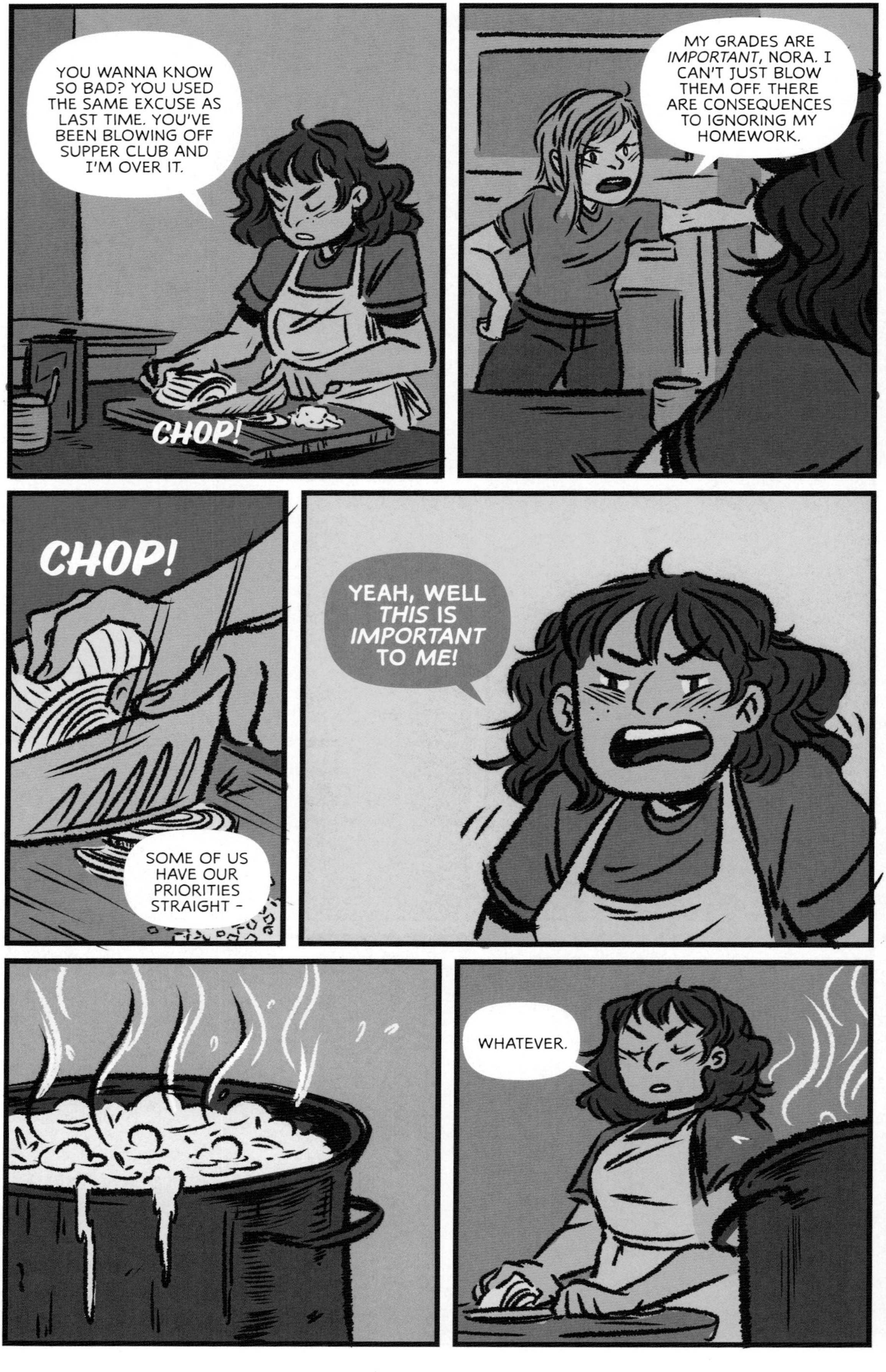
YOU WANNA KNOW SO BAD? YOU USED THE SAME EXCUSE AS LAST TIME. YOU'VE BEEN BLOWING OFF SUPPER CLUB AND I'M OVER IT.
CHOP!
MY GRADES ARE *IMPORTANT*, NORA. I CAN'T JUST BLOW THEM OFF. THERE ARE CONSEQUENCES TO IGNORING MY HOMEWORK.
CHOP!
SOME OF US HAVE OUR PRIORITIES STRAIGHT -
YEAH, WELL *THIS* IS IMPORTANT TO ME!
WHATEVER.

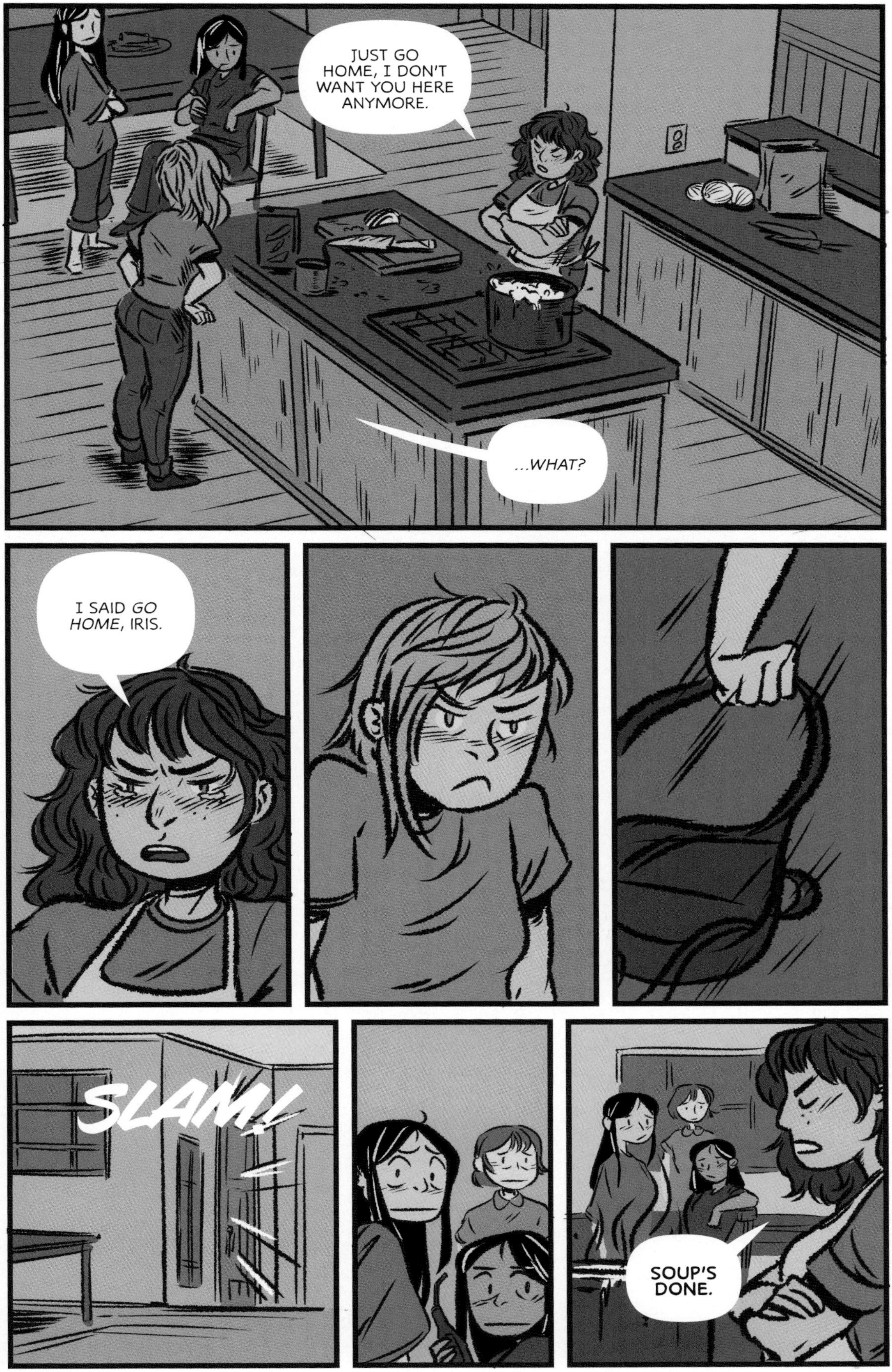
JUST GO HOME, I DON'T WANT YOU HERE ANYMORE.
...WHAT?
I SAID *GO HOME*, IRIS.
SLAM!
SOUP'S DONE.

Chapter Eleven

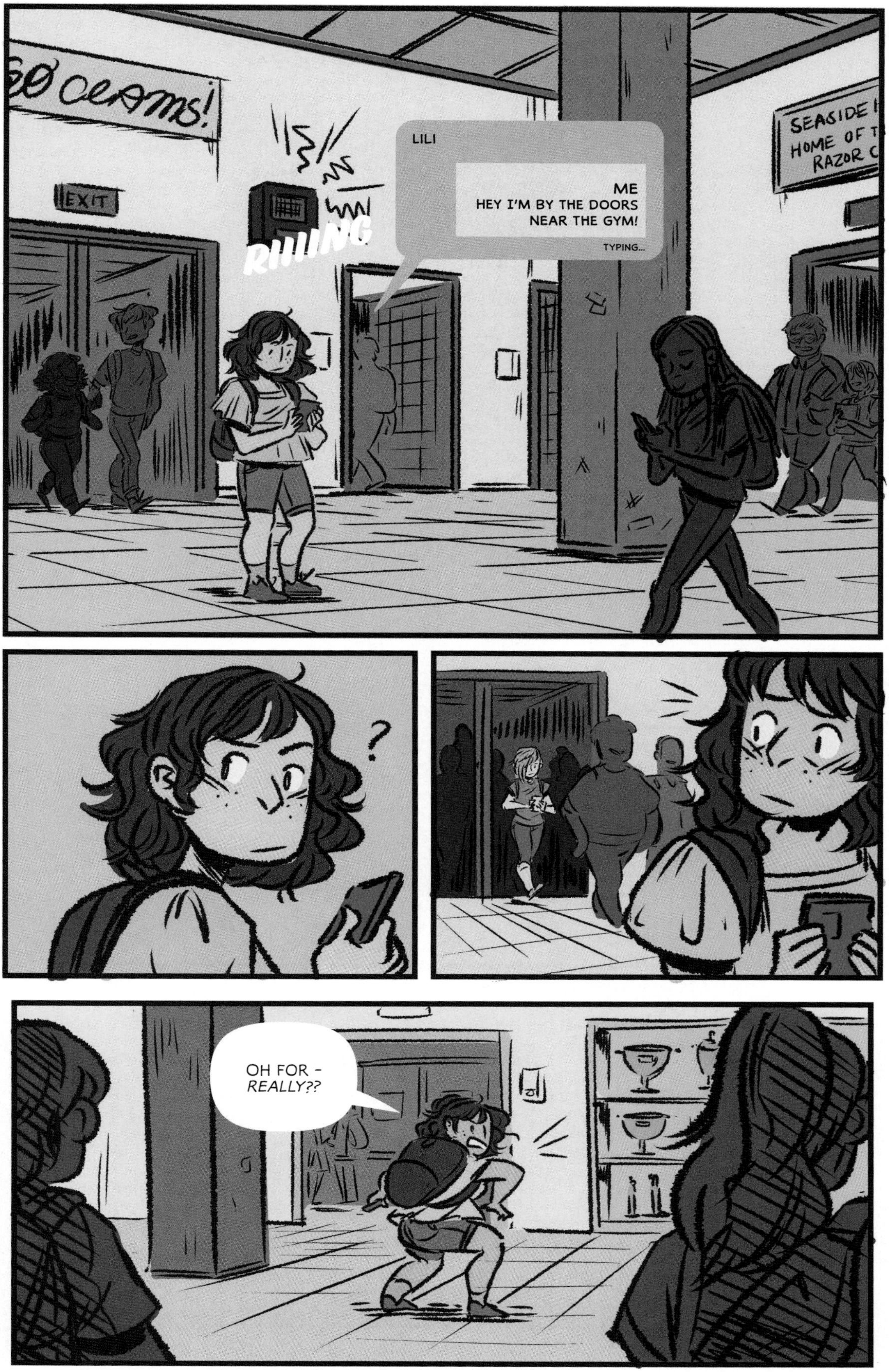
GO CLAMS!
EXIT
SEASIDE H
HOME OF T
RAZOR C
RIIIING
LILI
ME
HEY I'M BY THE DOORS
NEAR THE GYM!
TYPING...
?
OH FOR -
REALLY??

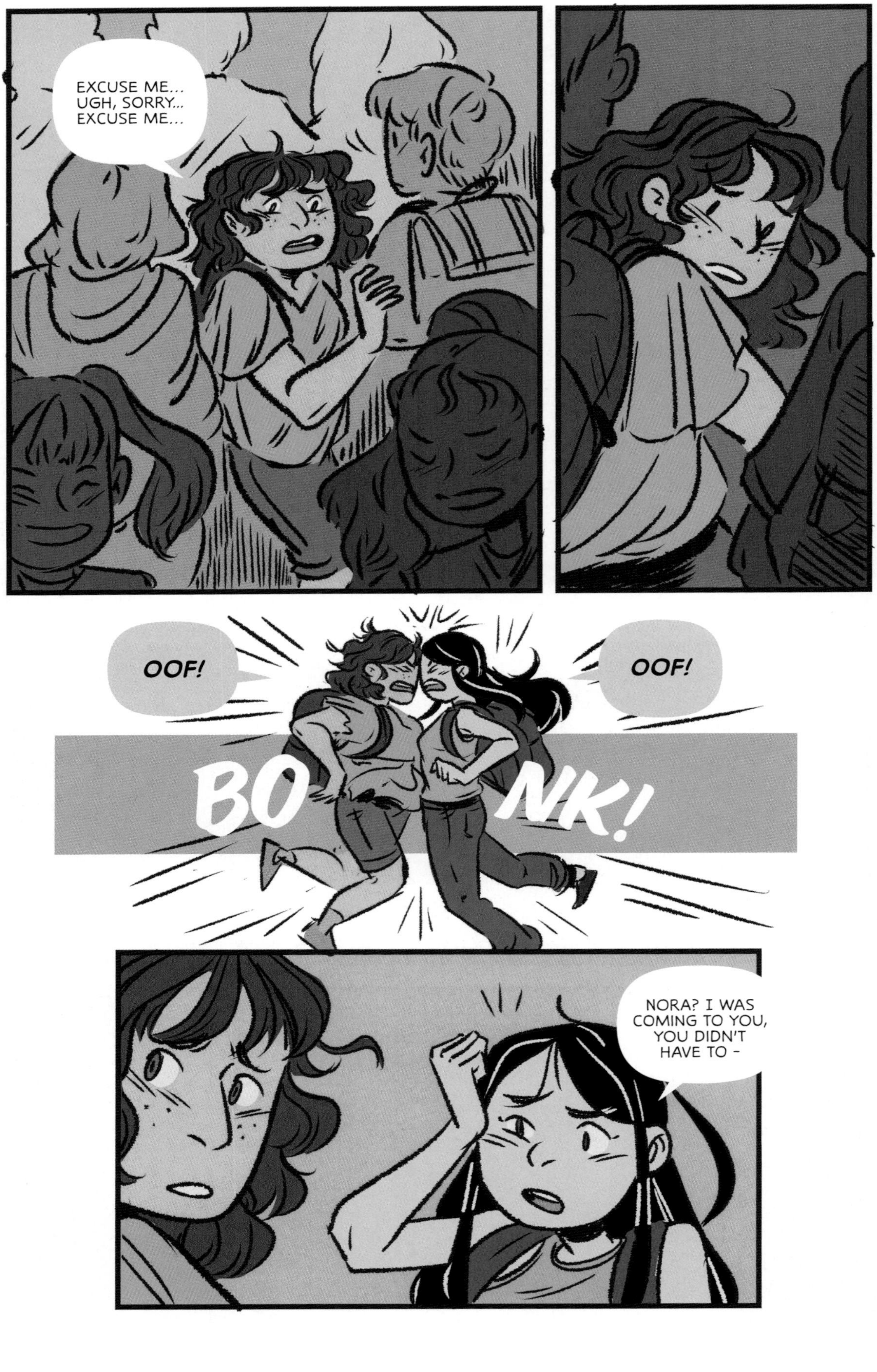
EXCUSE ME...
UGH, SORRY...
EXCUSE ME...
OOF!
OOF!
BONK!
NORA? I WAS COMING TO YOU, YOU DIDN'T HAVE TO -

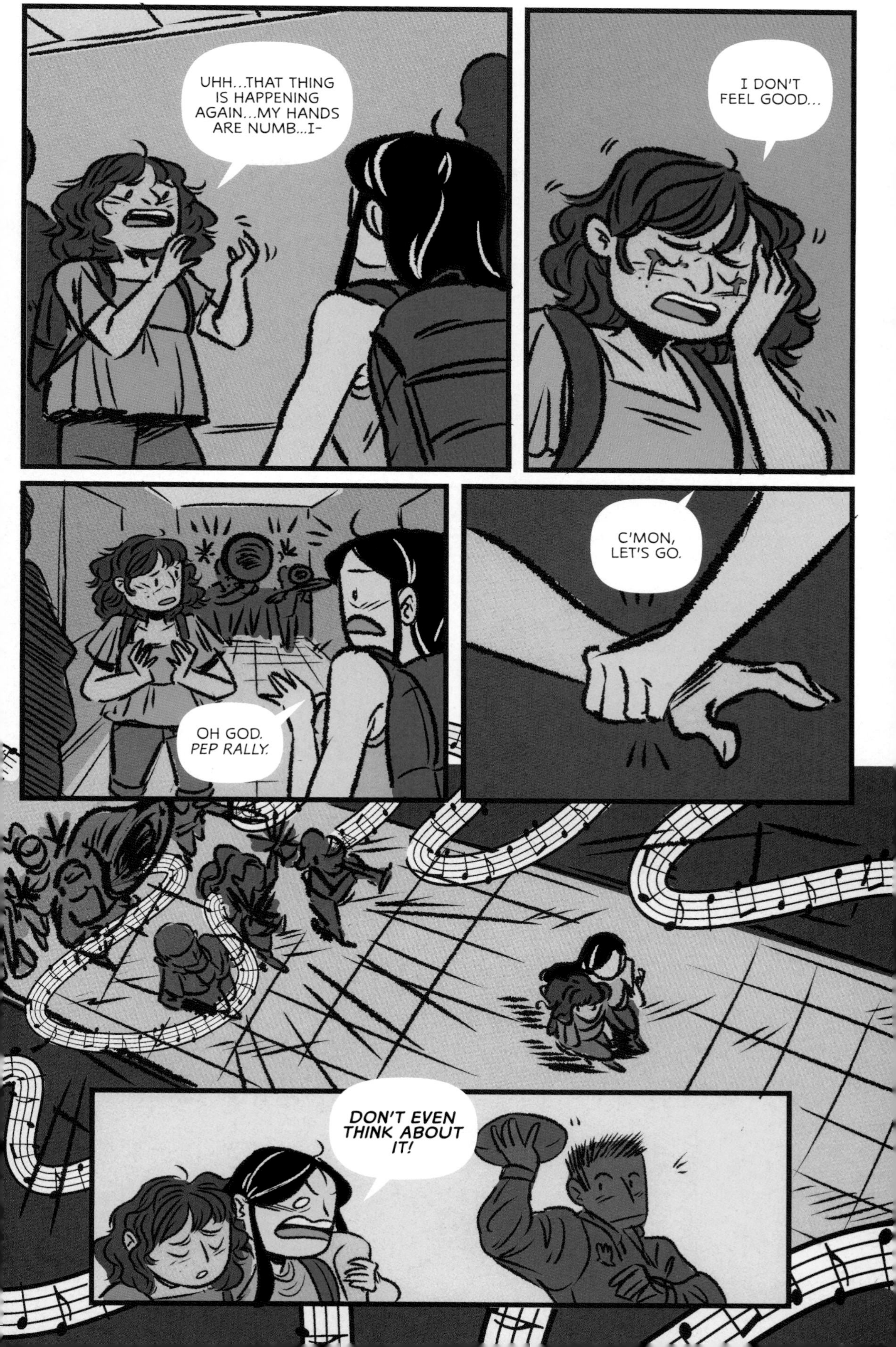
UHH...THAT THING IS HAPPENING AGAIN...MY HANDS ARE NUMB...I-
I DON'T FEEL GOOD...
OH GOD. *PEP RALLY.*
C'MON, LET'S GO.
DON'T EVEN THINK ABOUT IT!

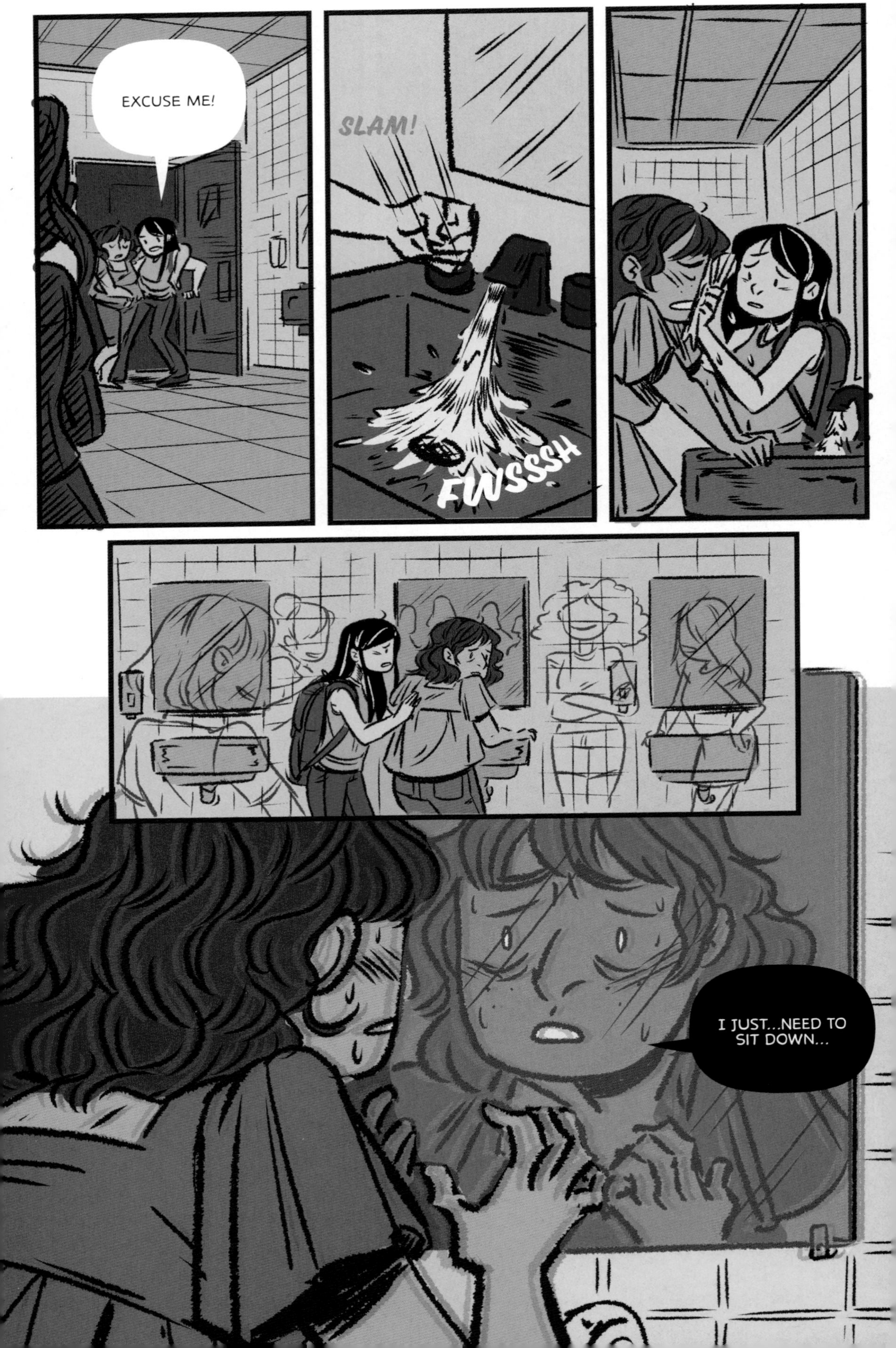
EXCUSE ME!
SLAM!
FWSSSH
I JUST...NEED TO SIT DOWN...

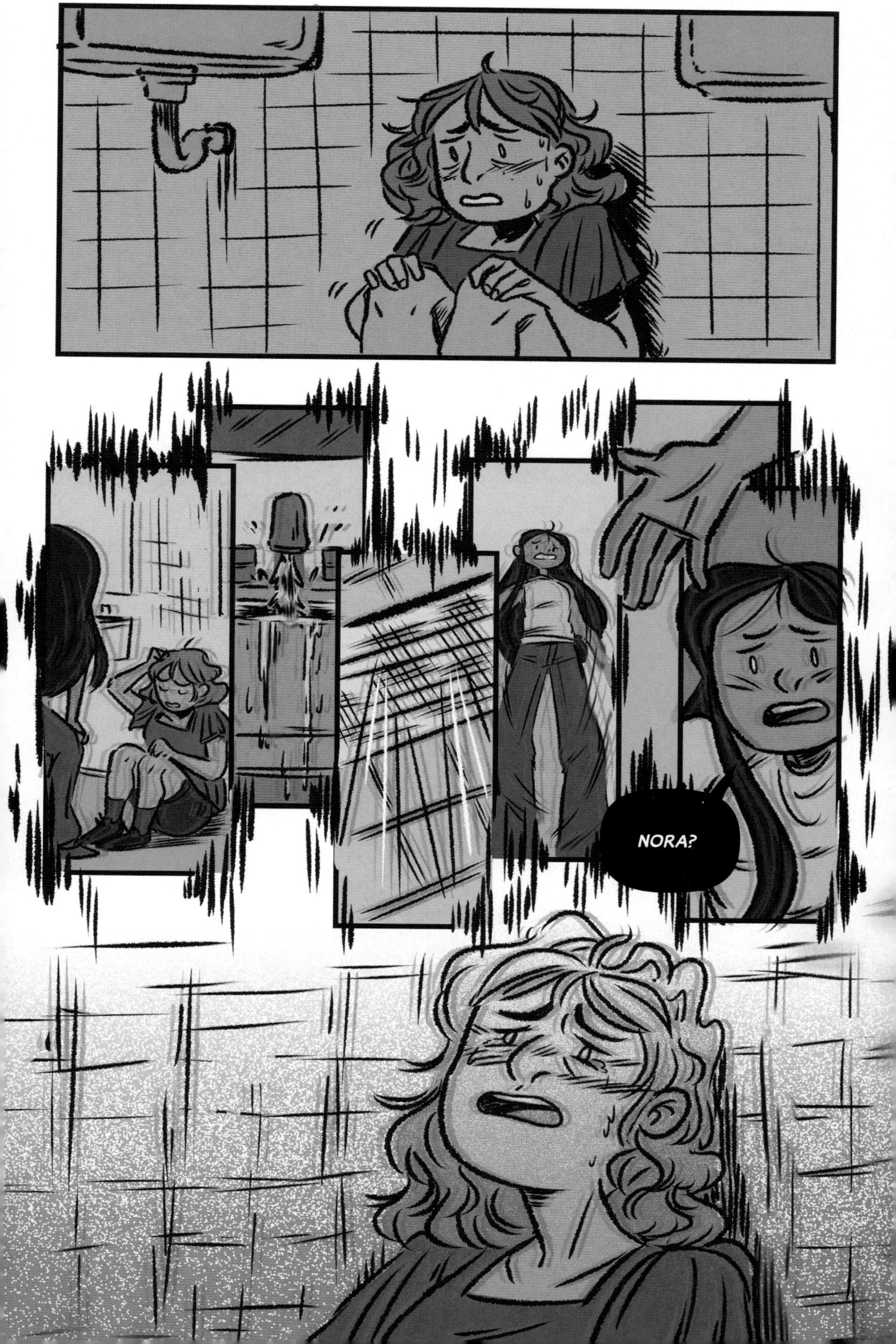
NORA?

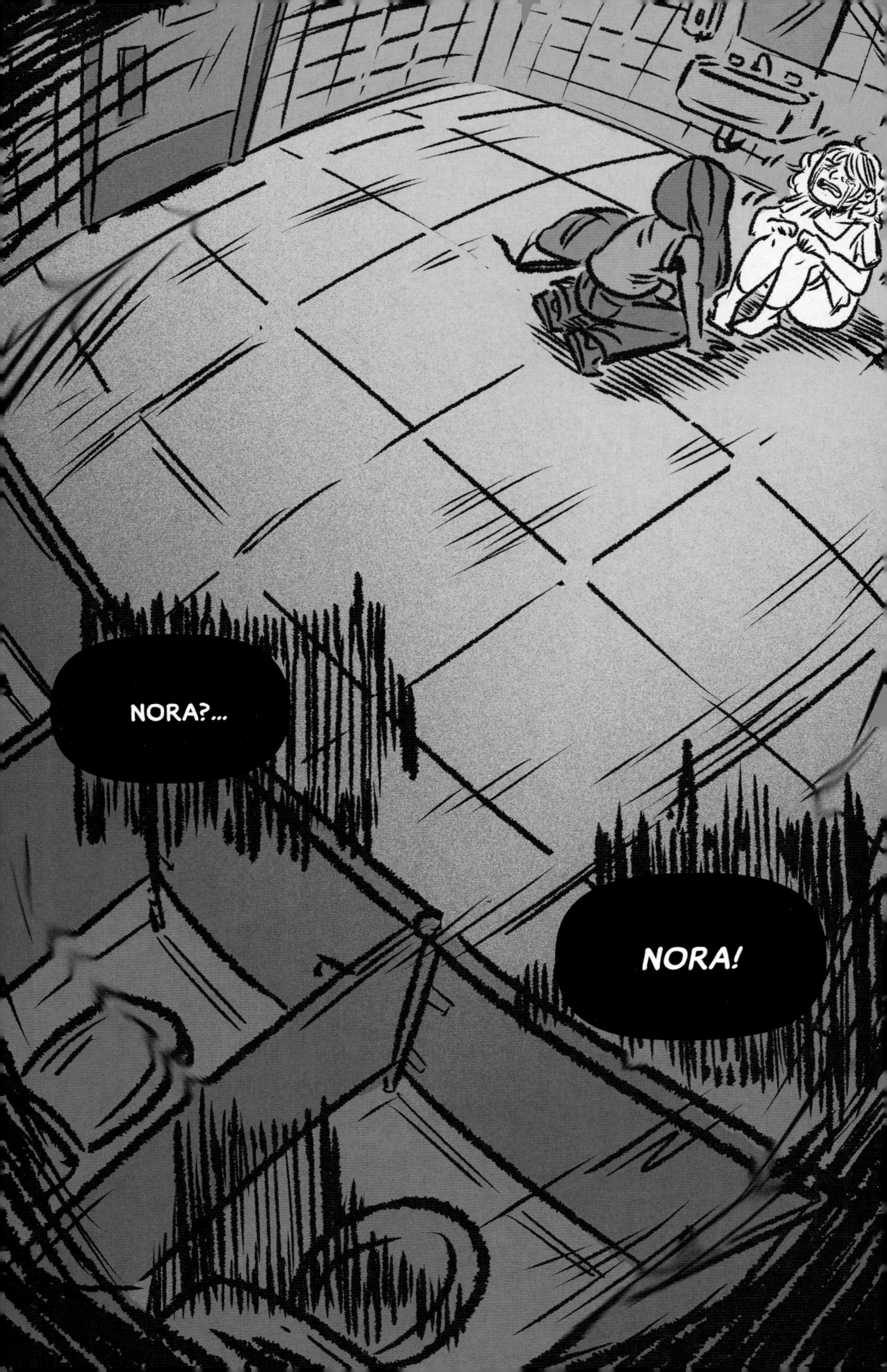
NORA?...
NORA!

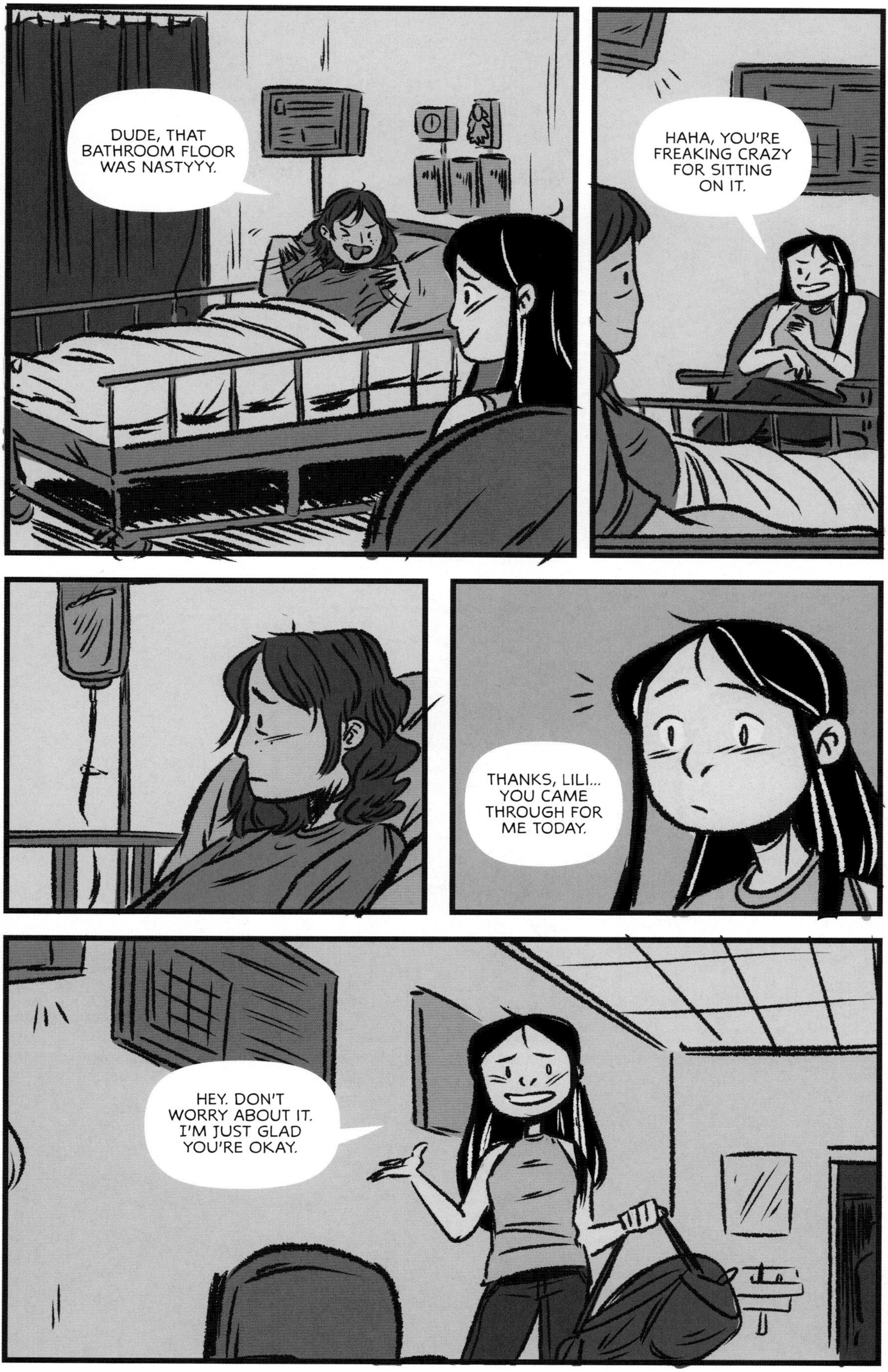
DUDE, THAT BATHROOM FLOOR WAS NASTYYY.
HAHA, YOU'RE FREAKING CRAZY FOR SITTING ON IT.
THANKS, LILI... YOU CAME THROUGH FOR ME TODAY.
HEY. DON'T WORRY ABOUT IT. I'M JUST GLAD YOU'RE OKAY.

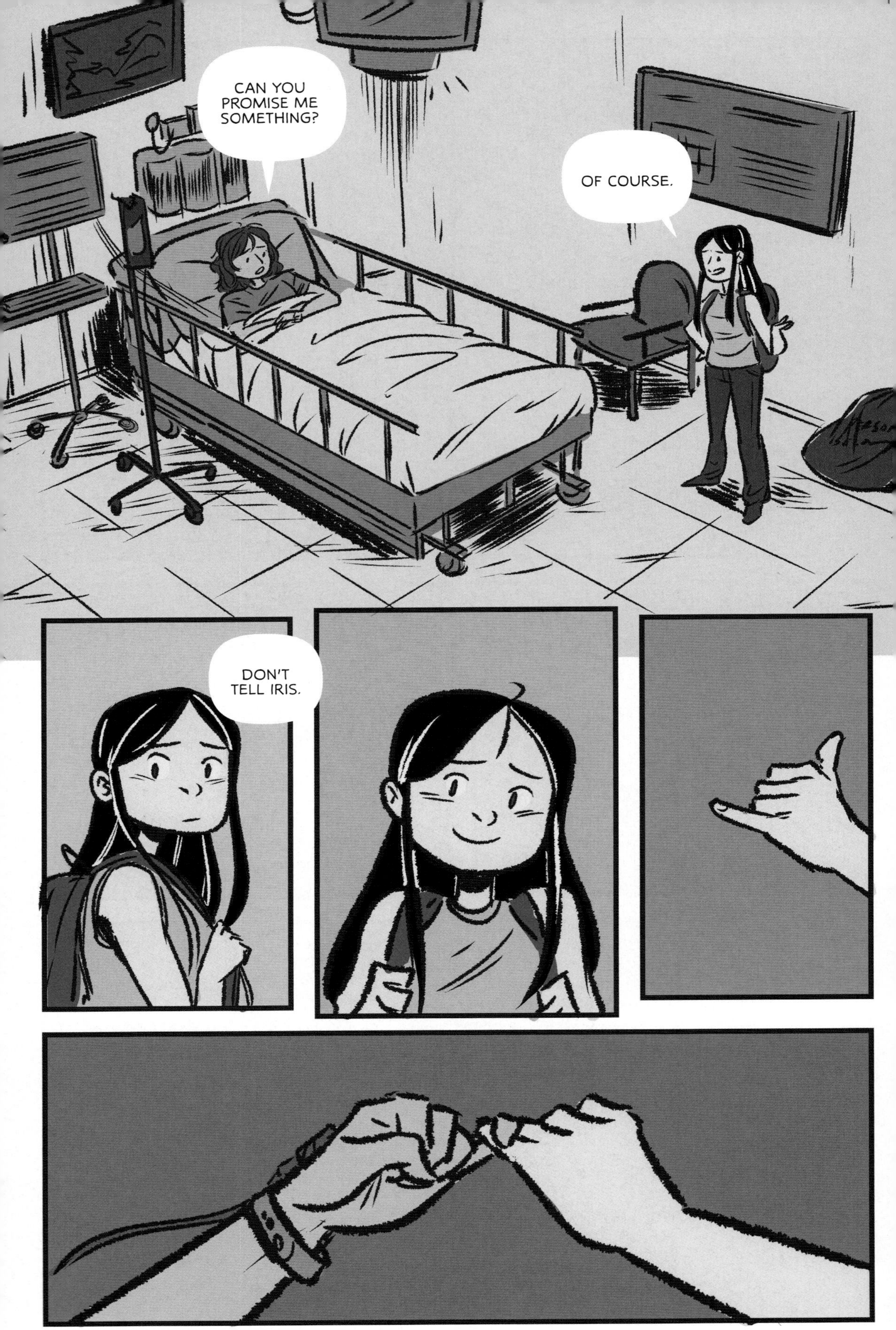
CAN YOU PROMISE ME SOMETHING?
OF COURSE.
DON'T TELL IRIS.

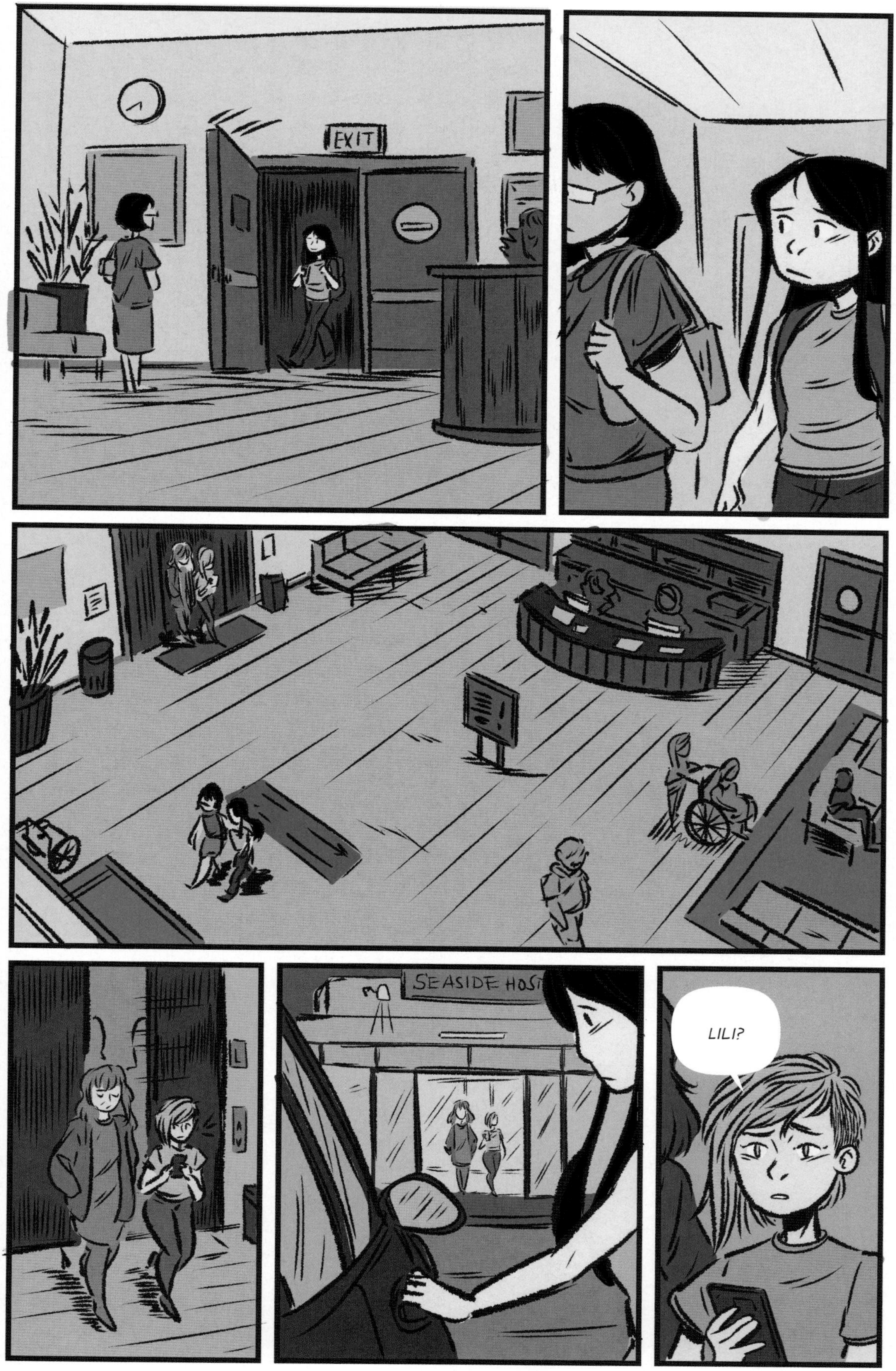
EXIT
SEASIDE HOS
LILI?

Chapter Twelve
challah french toast

BWMFPHH

PNNT

UGNH!

HUF...HUF...

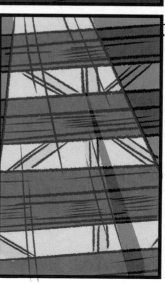

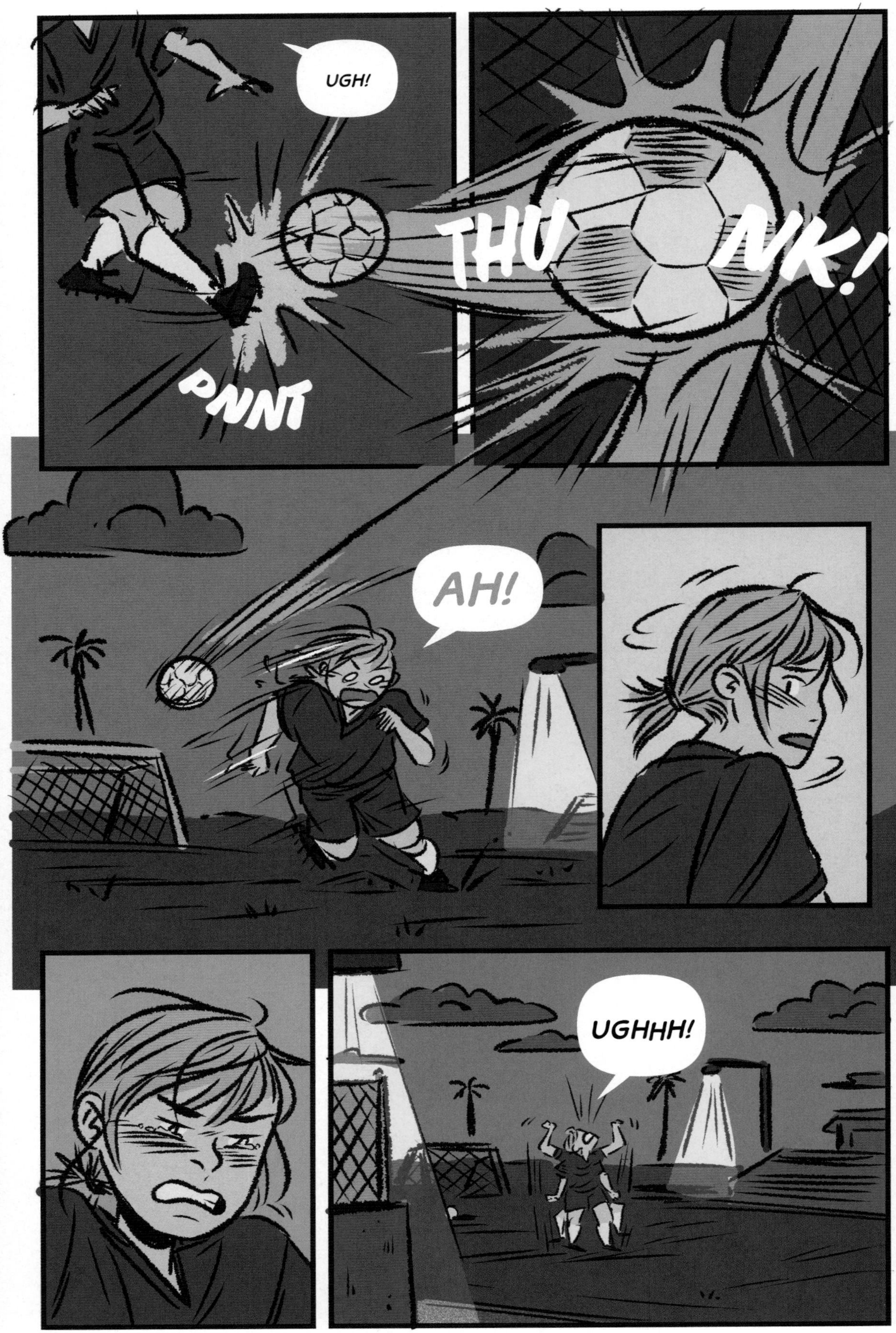
UGH!
PNNT
THU NK!
AH!
UGHHH!

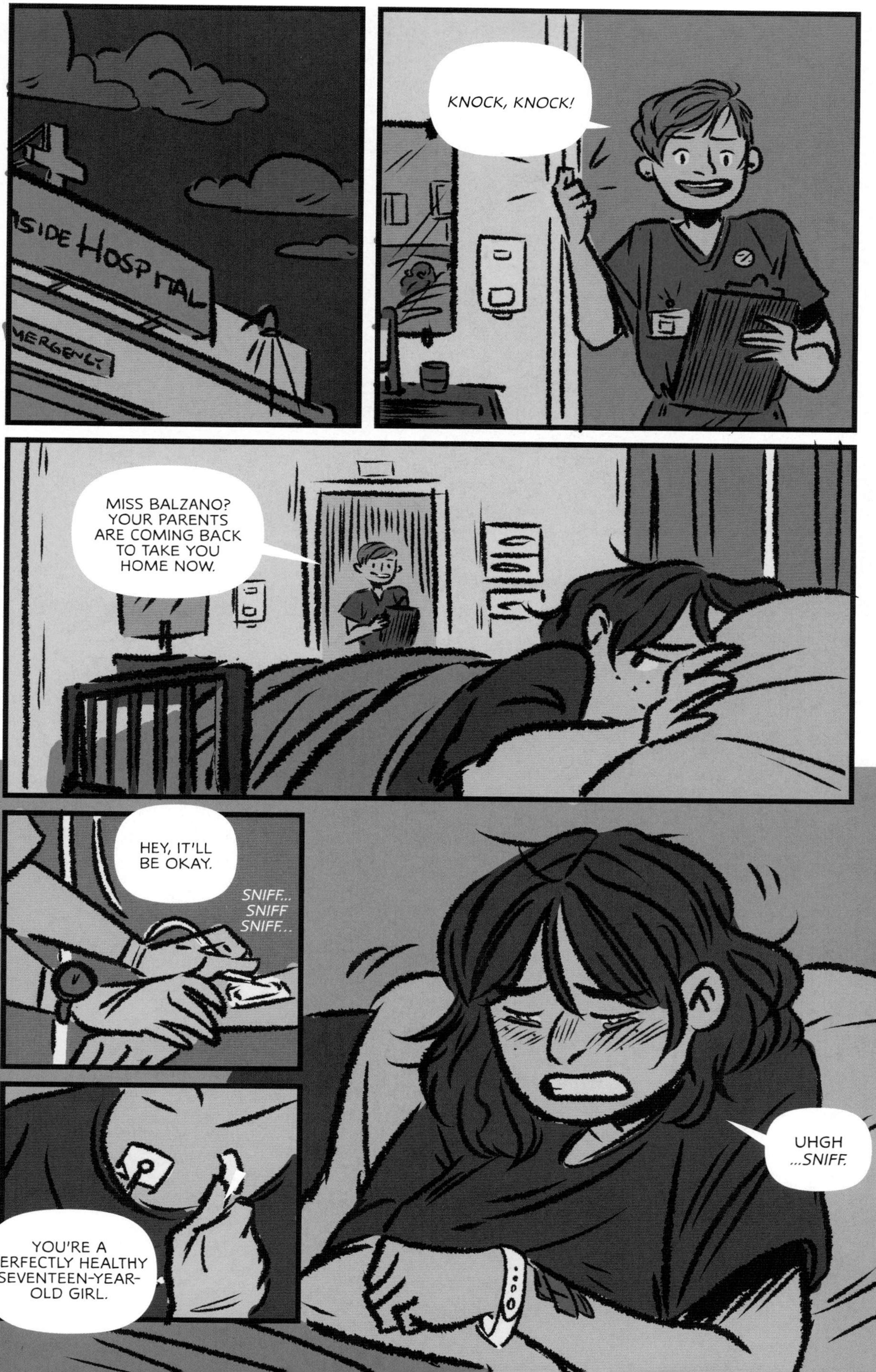

SIDE HOSPITAL
MERGENCY
KNOCK, KNOCK!
MISS BALZANO? YOUR PARENTS ARE COMING BACK TO TAKE YOU HOME NOW.
HEY, IT'LL BE OKAY.
SNIFF... SNIFF SNIFF...
UHGH ...SNIFF.
YOU'RE A PERFECTLY HEALTHY SEVENTEEN-YEAR-OLD GIRL.

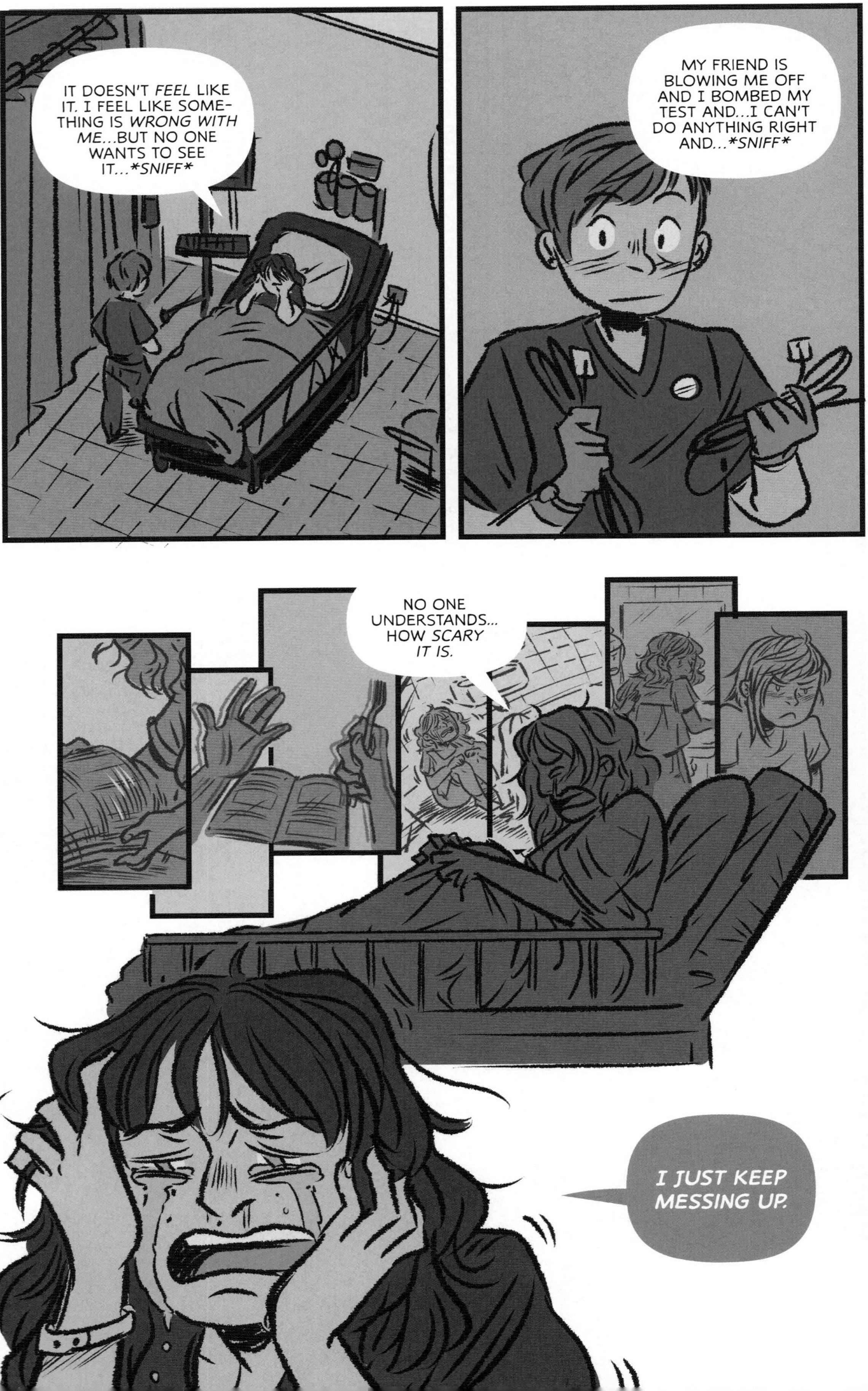
IT DOESN'T *FEEL* LIKE IT. I FEEL LIKE SOME-THING IS *WRONG WITH ME*...BUT NO ONE WANTS TO SEE IT...*SNIFF*
MY FRIEND IS BLOWING ME OFF AND I BOMBED MY TEST AND...I CAN'T DO ANYTHING RIGHT AND...*SNIFF*
NO ONE UNDERSTANDS... HOW *SCARY* IT IS.
I JUST KEEP MESSING UP.

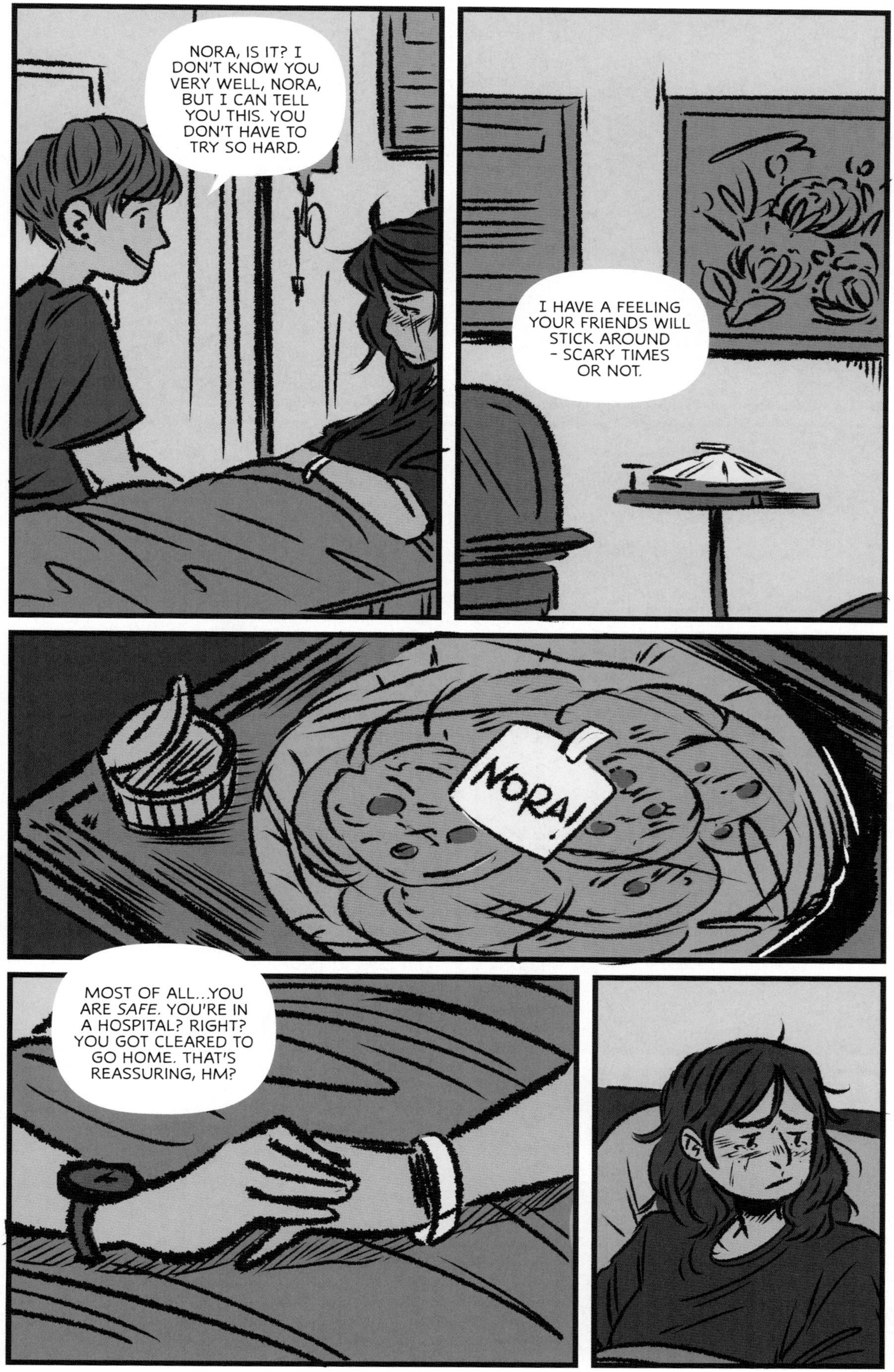
NORA, IS IT? I DON'T KNOW YOU VERY WELL, NORA, BUT I CAN TELL YOU THIS. YOU DON'T HAVE TO TRY SO HARD.
I HAVE A FEELING YOUR FRIENDS WILL STICK AROUND - SCARY TIMES OR NOT.
NORA!
MOST OF ALL...YOU ARE *SAFE*. YOU'RE IN A HOSPITAL? RIGHT? YOU GOT CLEARED TO GO HOME. THAT'S REASSURING, HM?

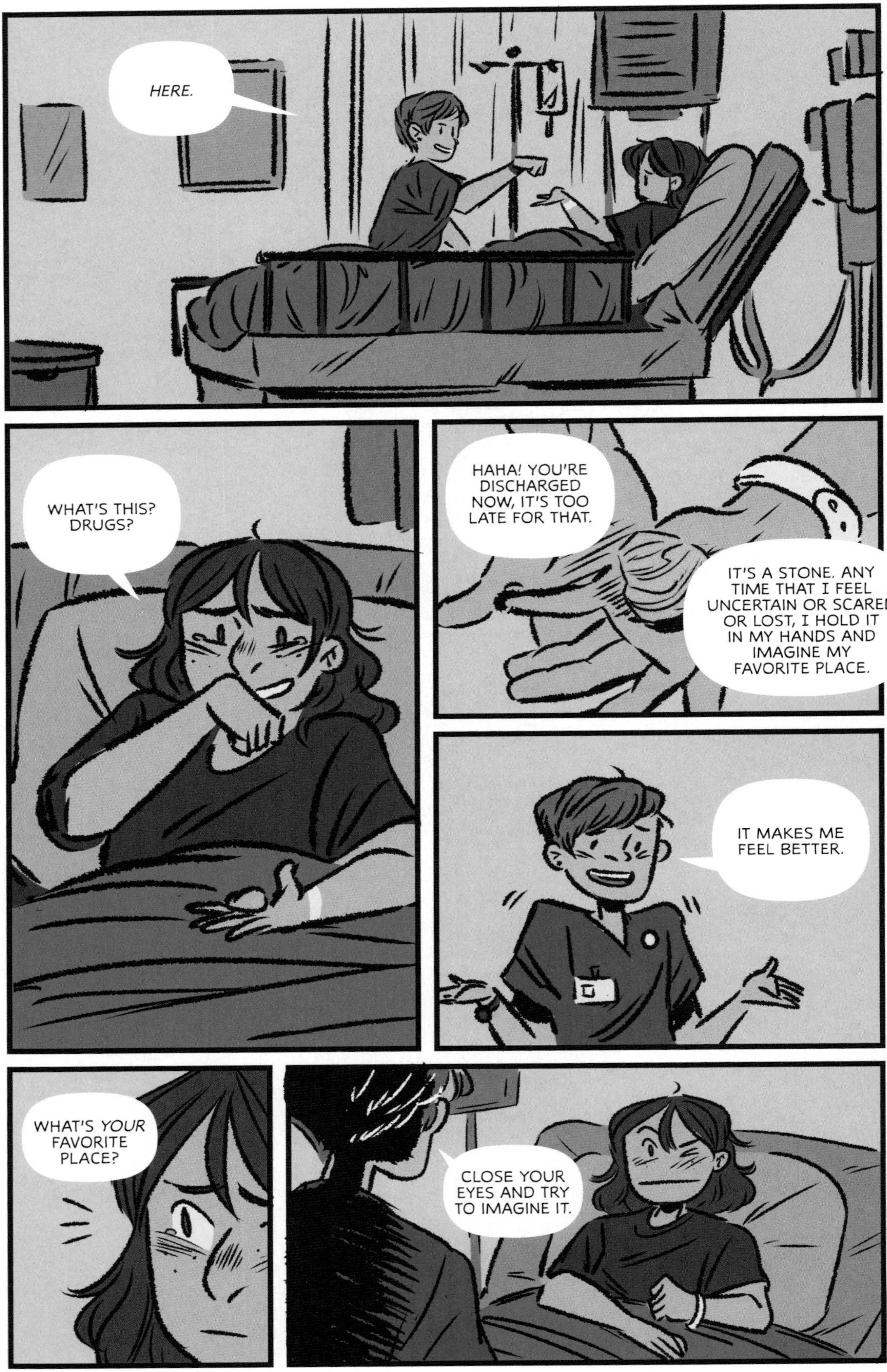
HERE.
WHAT'S THIS? DRUGS?
HAHA! YOU'RE DISCHARGED NOW, IT'S TOO LATE FOR THAT.
IT'S A STONE. ANY TIME THAT I FEEL UNCERTAIN OR SCARED OR LOST, I HOLD IT IN MY HANDS AND IMAGINE MY FAVORITE PLACE.
IT MAKES ME FEEL BETTER.
WHAT'S *YOUR* FAVORITE PLACE?
CLOSE YOUR EYES AND TRY TO IMAGINE IT.

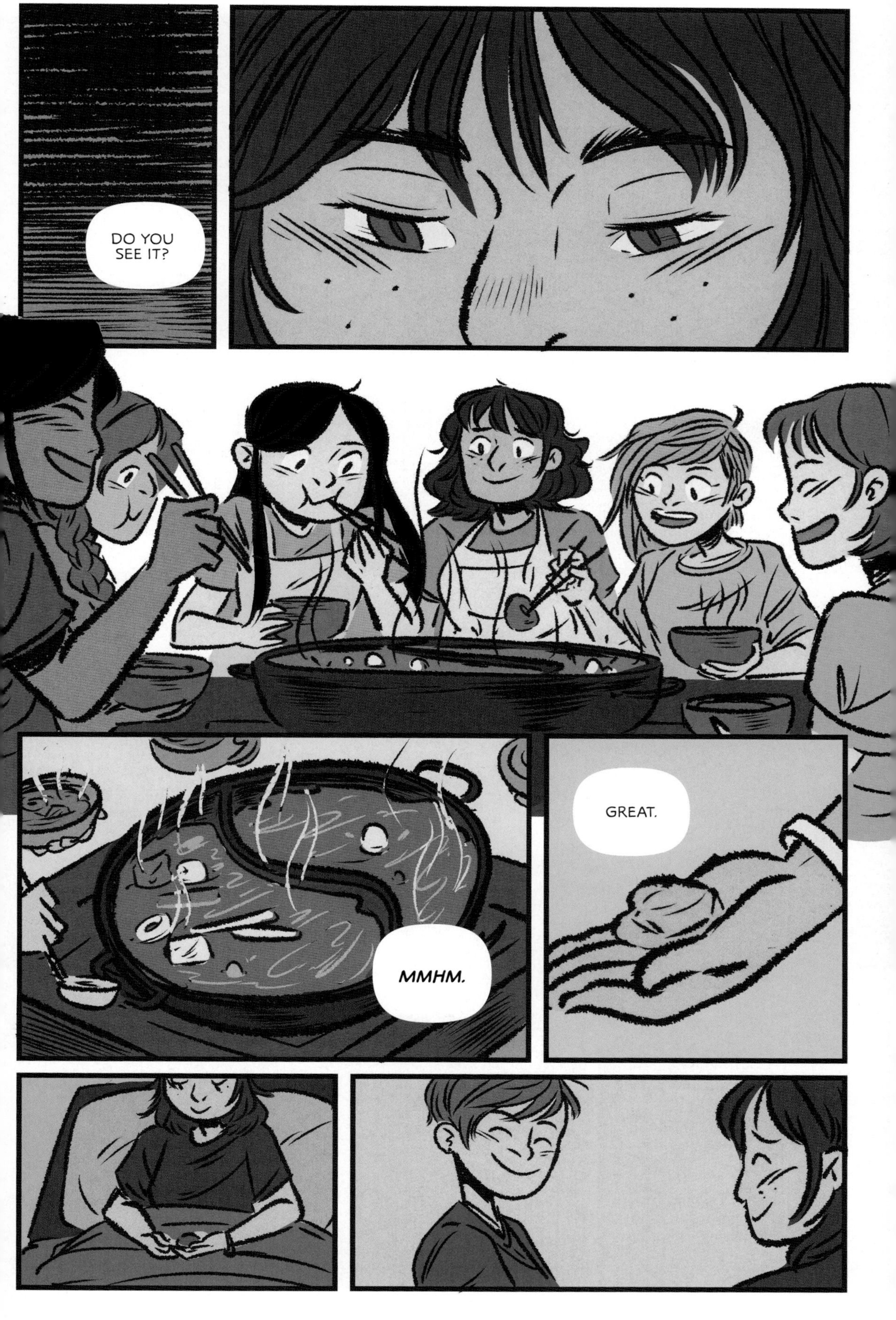
DO YOU SEE IT?
MMHM.
GREAT.

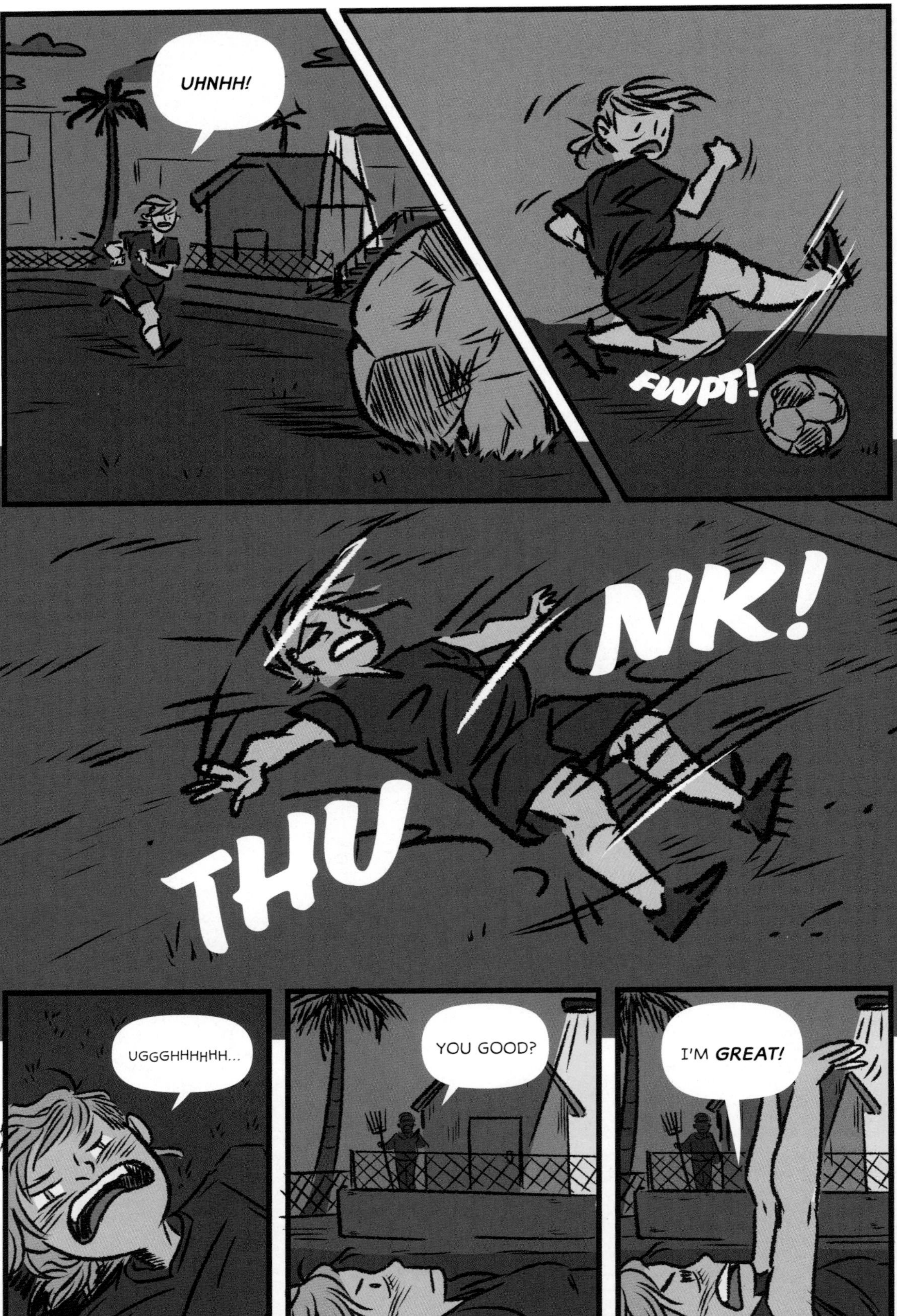
UHNHH!
FWPT!
THU
NK!
UGGGHHHHHH...
YOU GOOD?
I'M *GREAT!*

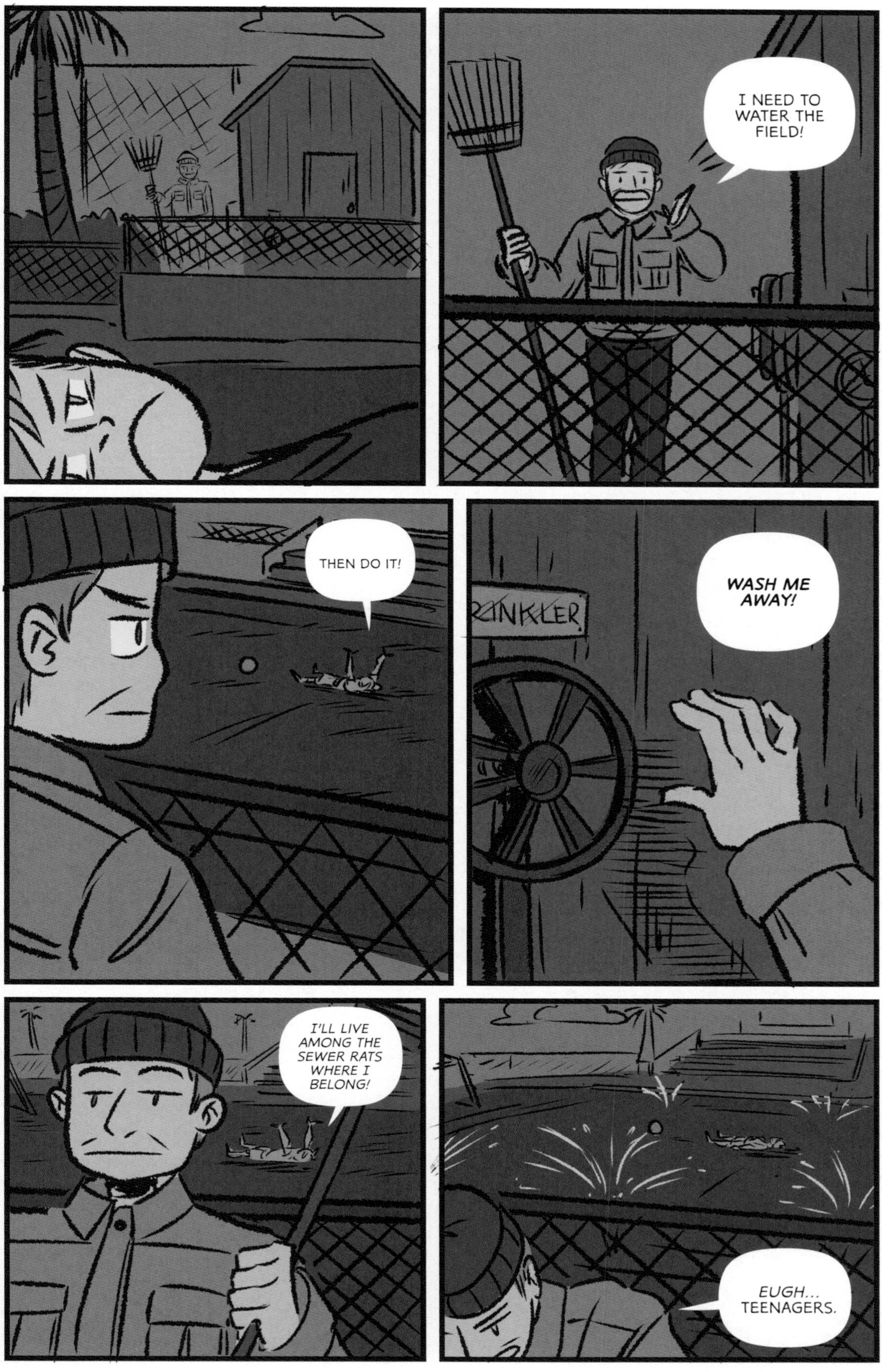
I NEED TO WATER THE FIELD!
THEN DO IT!
RINKLER
WASH ME AWAY!
I'LL LIVE AMONG THE SEWER RATS WHERE I BELONG!
EUGH... TEENAGERS.

Chapter Thirteen
spring bao

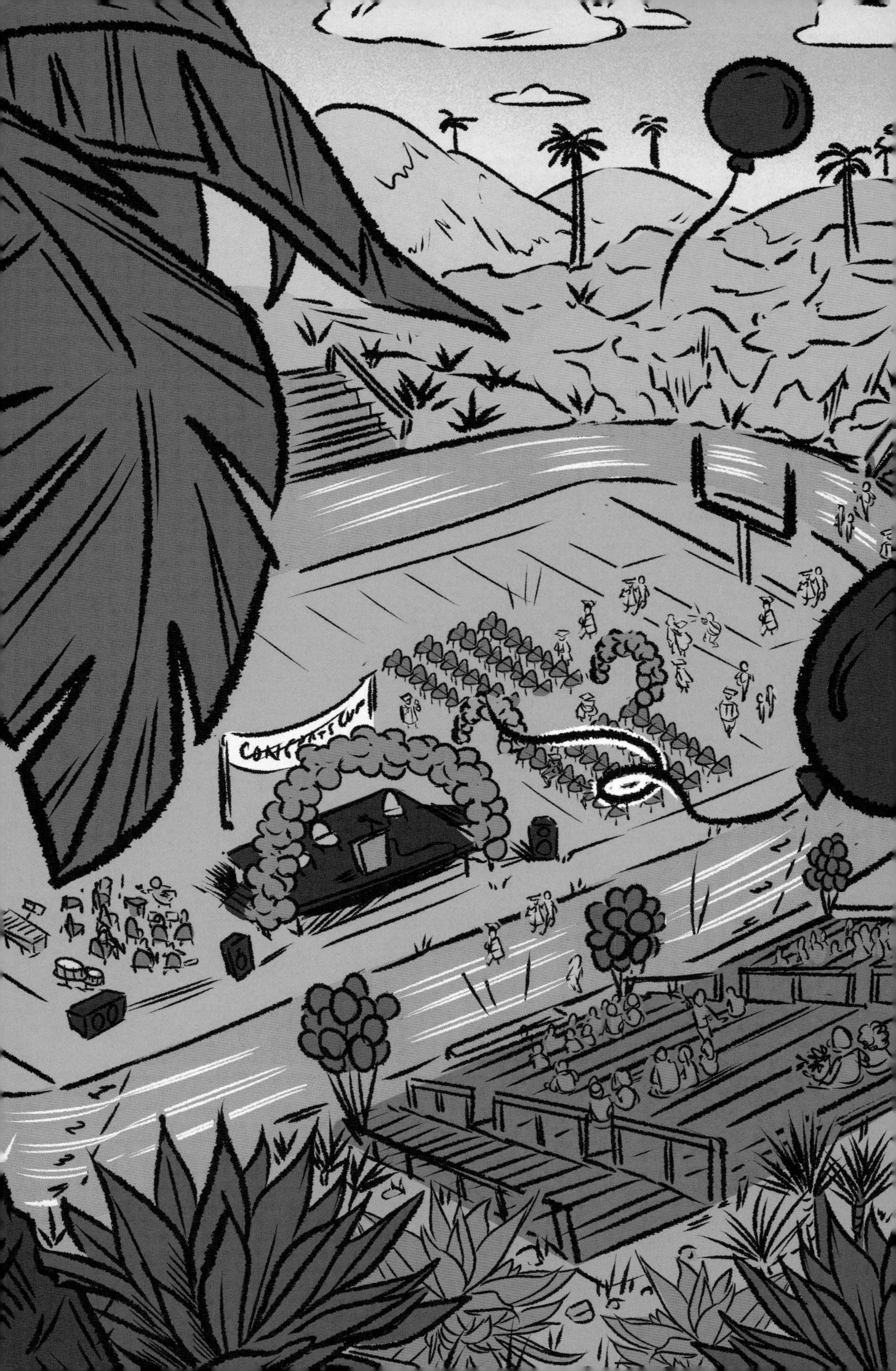

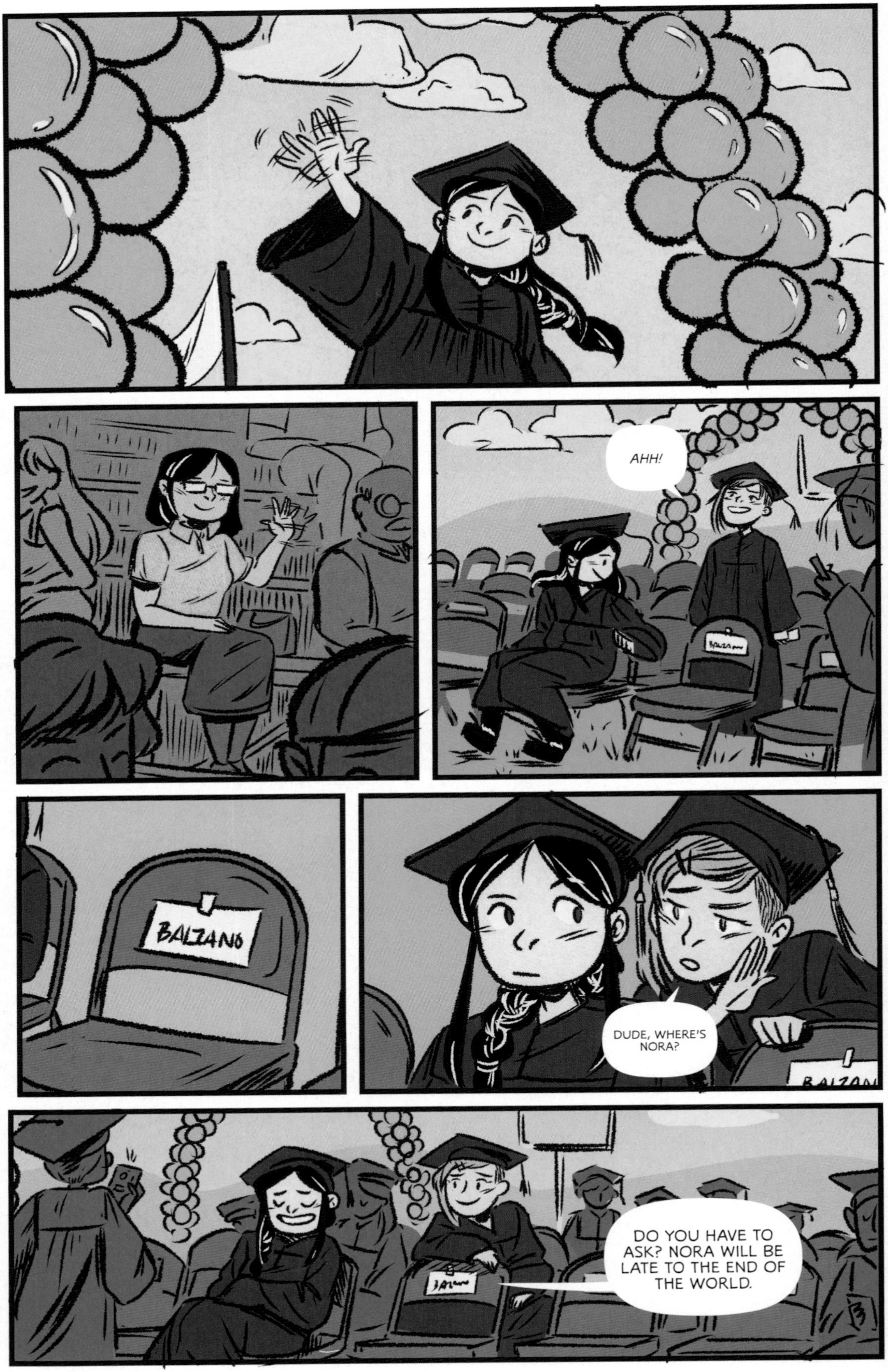
AHH!
BALZANO
DUDE, WHERE'S NORA?
DO YOU HAVE TO ASK? NORA WILL BE LATE TO THE END OF THE WORLD.

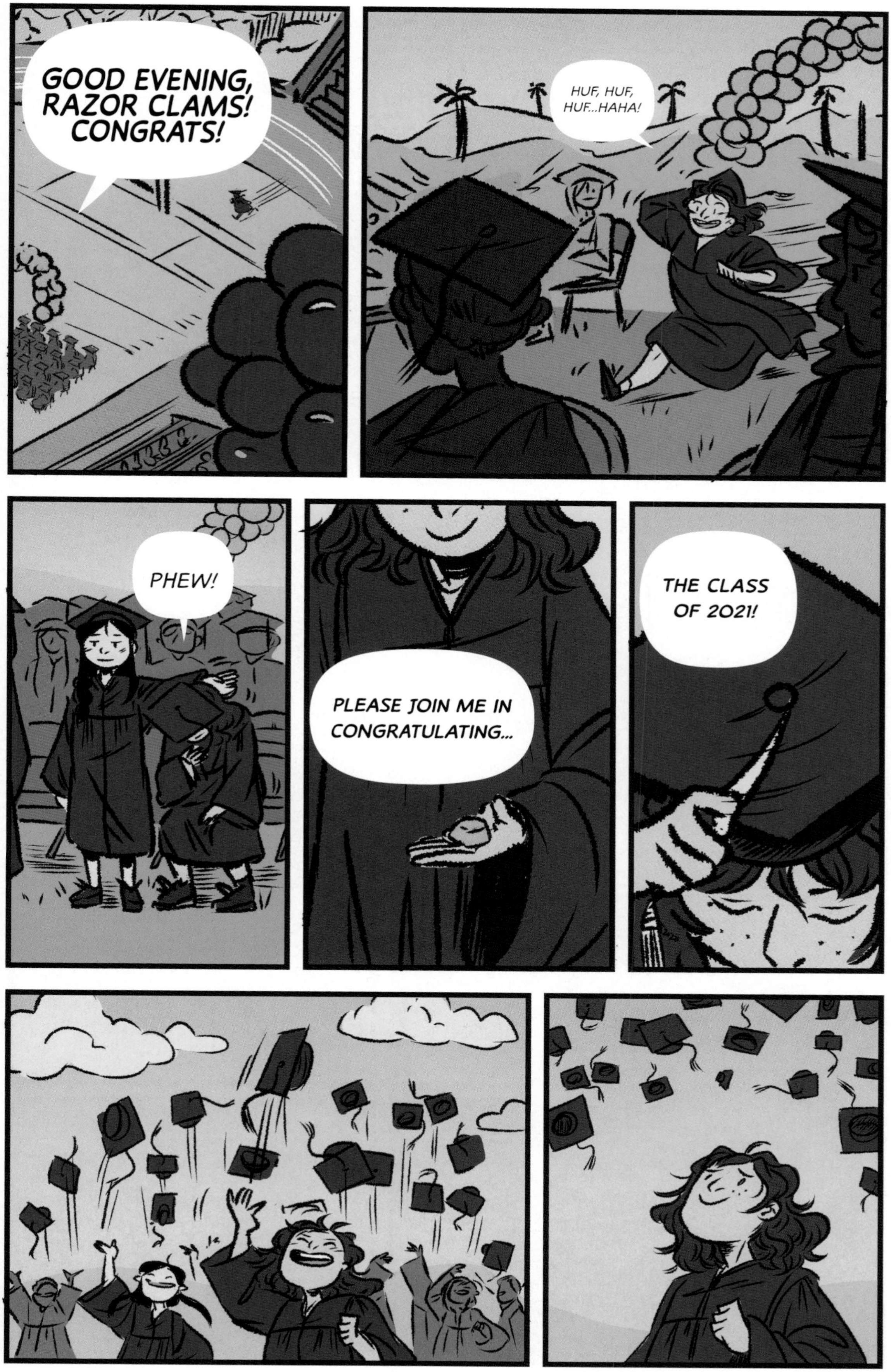
GOOD EVENING, RAZOR CLAMS! CONGRATS!
HUF, HUF, HUF...HAHA!
PHEW!
PLEASE JOIN ME IN CONGRATULATING...
THE CLASS OF 2021!

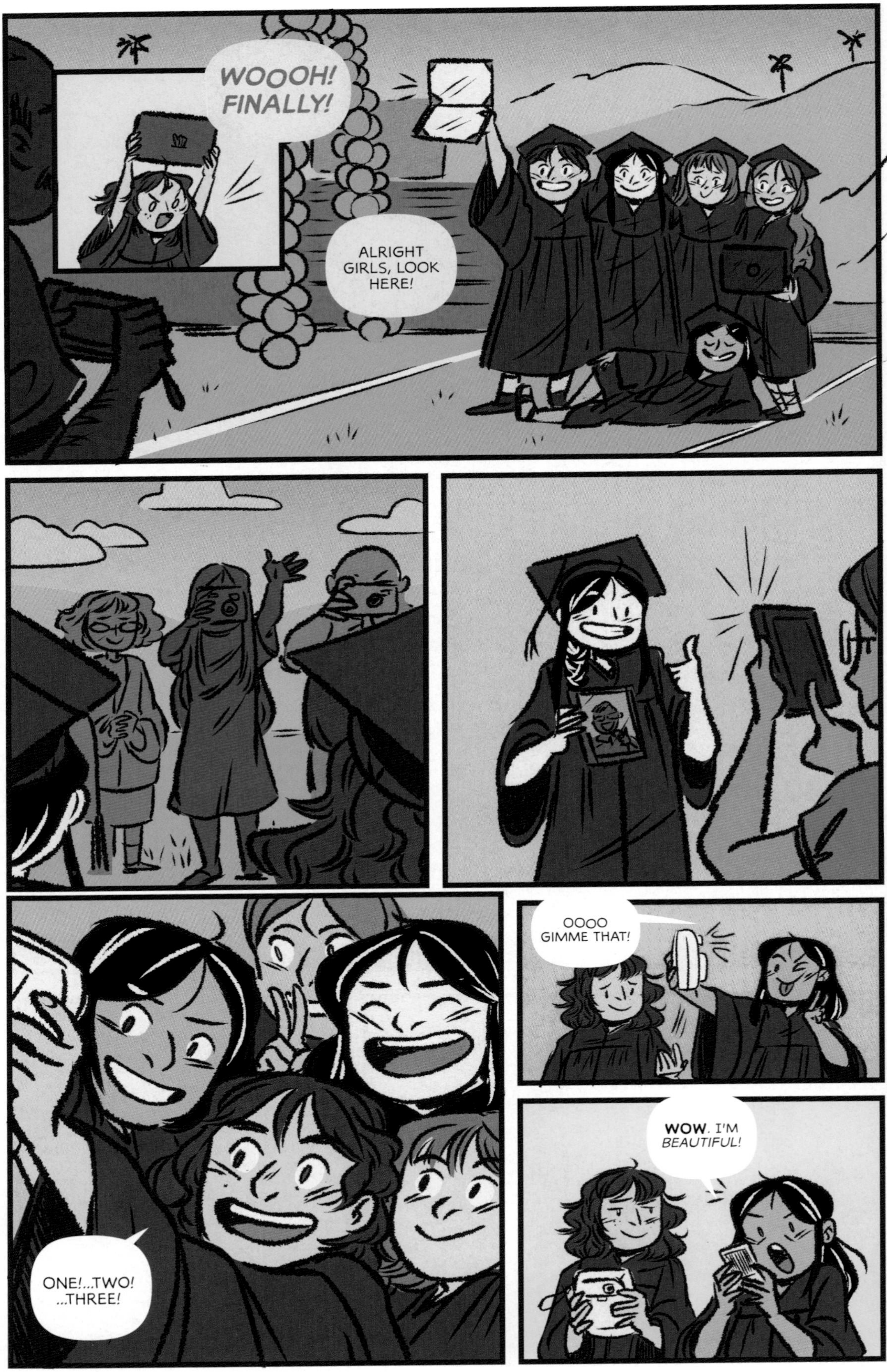
WOOOH! FINALLY!
ALRIGHT GIRLS, LOOK HERE!
ONE!...TWO! ...THREE!
OOOO GIMME THAT!
WOW. I'M BEAUTIFUL!

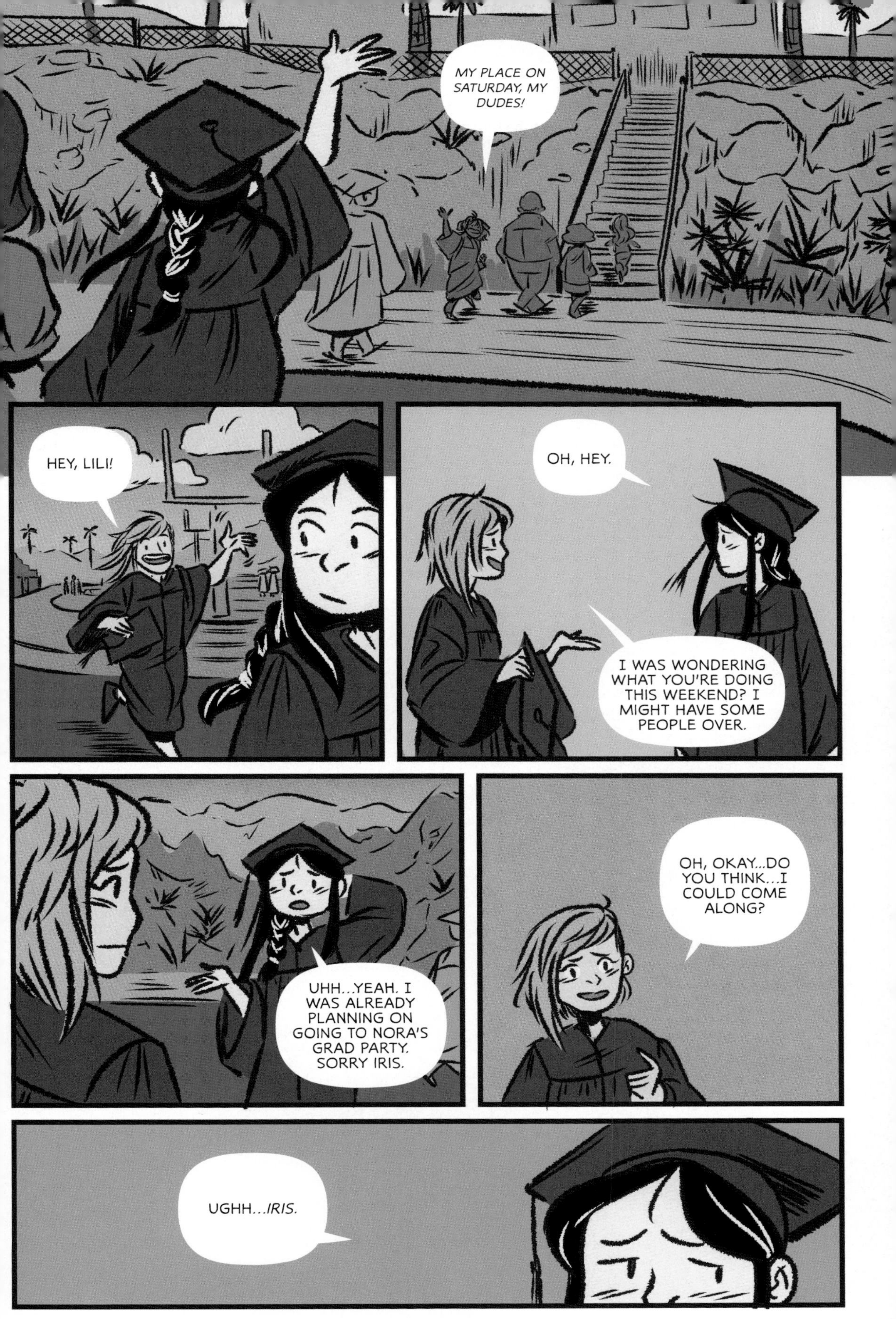
MY PLACE ON SATURDAY, MY DUDES!
HEY, LILI!
OH, HEY.
I WAS WONDERING WHAT YOU'RE DOING THIS WEEKEND? I MIGHT HAVE SOME PEOPLE OVER.
UHH...YEAH. I WAS ALREADY PLANNING ON GOING TO NORA'S GRAD PARTY. SORRY IRIS.
OH, OKAY...DO YOU THINK...I COULD COME ALONG?
UGHH...*IRIS.*

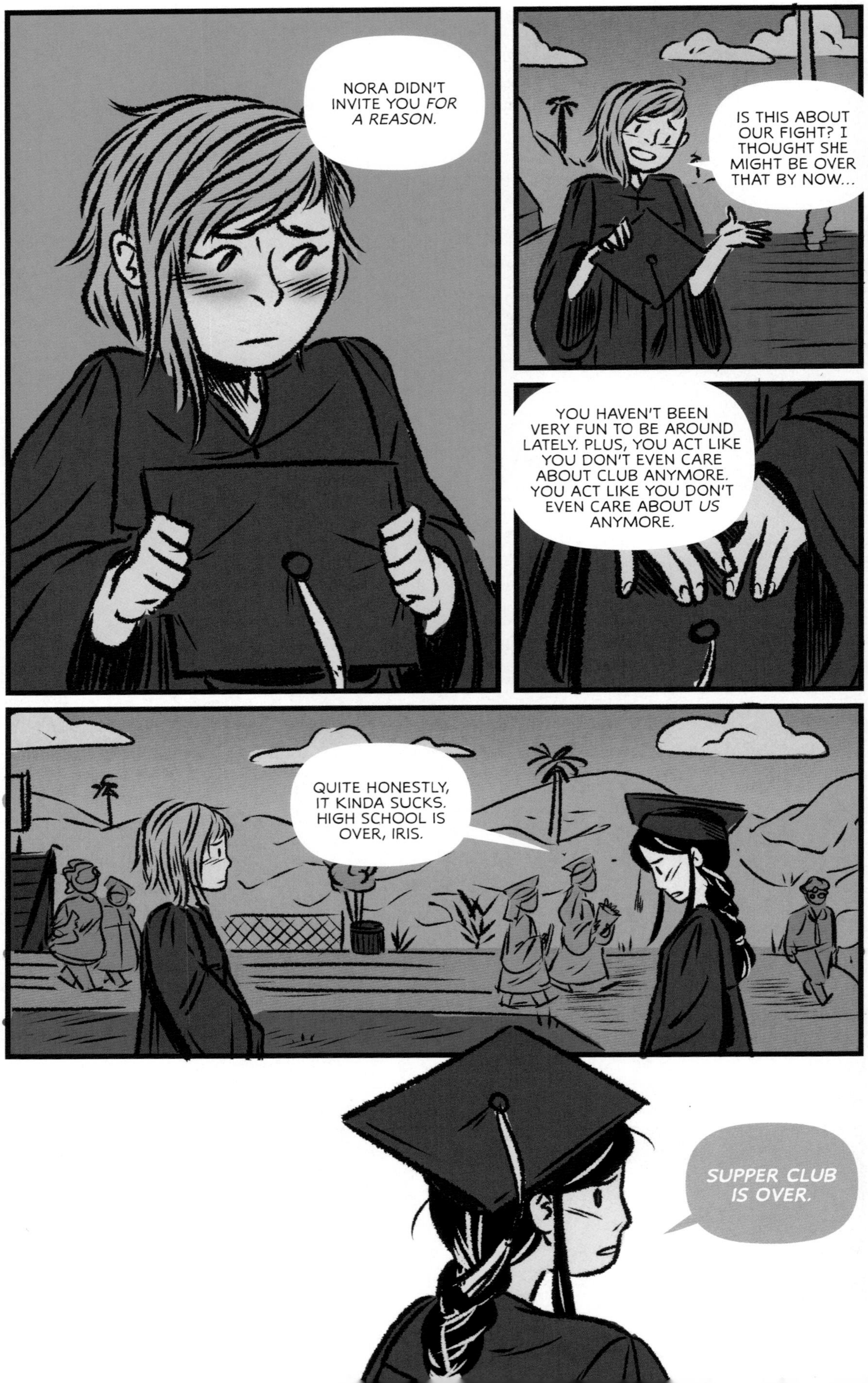
NORA DIDN'T INVITE YOU *FOR A REASON.*
IS THIS ABOUT OUR FIGHT? I THOUGHT SHE MIGHT BE OVER THAT BY NOW...
YOU HAVEN'T BEEN VERY FUN TO BE AROUND LATELY. PLUS, YOU ACT LIKE YOU DON'T EVEN CARE ABOUT CLUB ANYMORE. YOU ACT LIKE YOU DON'T EVEN CARE ABOUT *US* ANYMORE.
QUITE HONESTLY, IT KINDA SUCKS. HIGH SCHOOL IS OVER, IRIS.
SUPPER CLUB IS OVER.

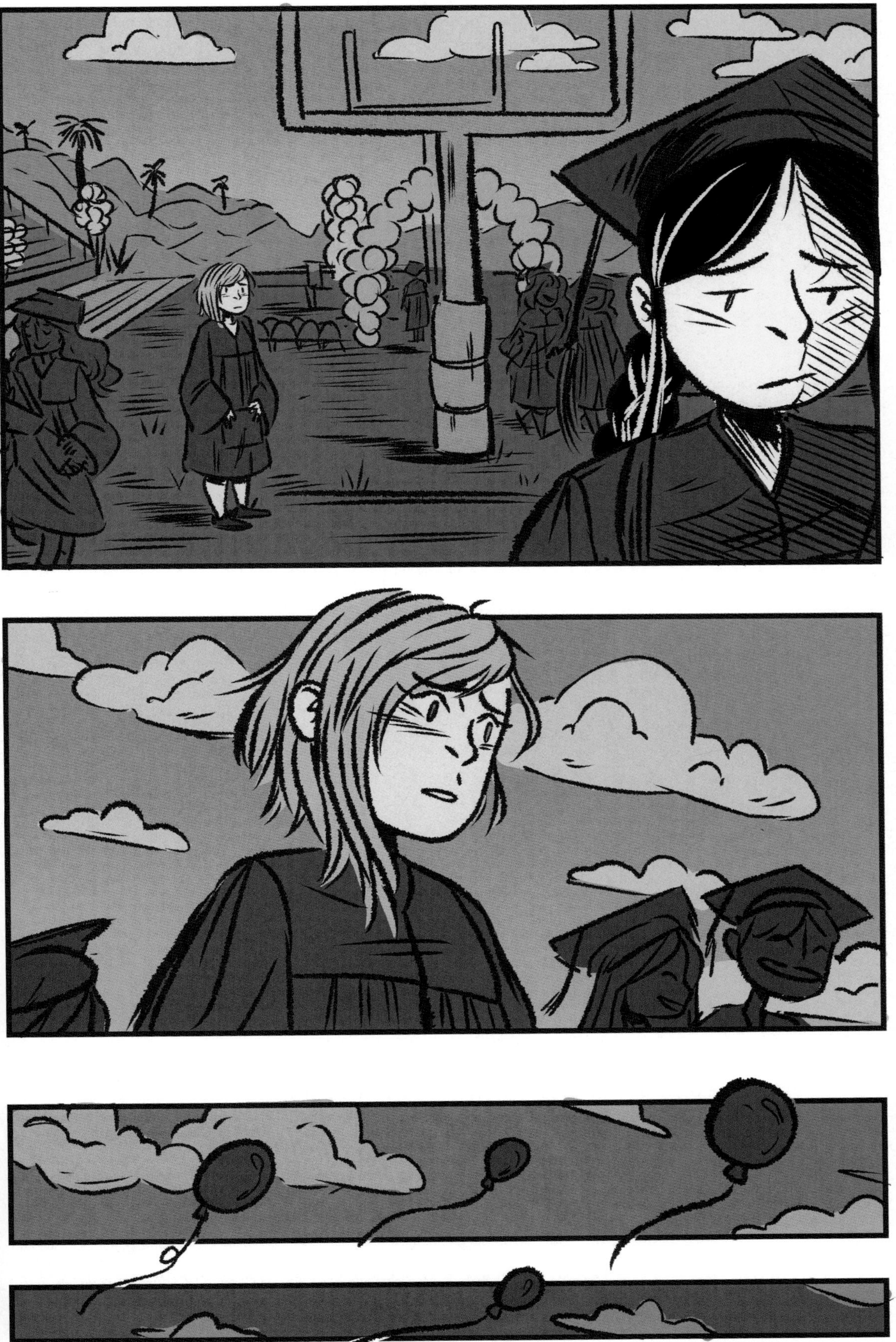

Chapter Fourteen
pork ribs

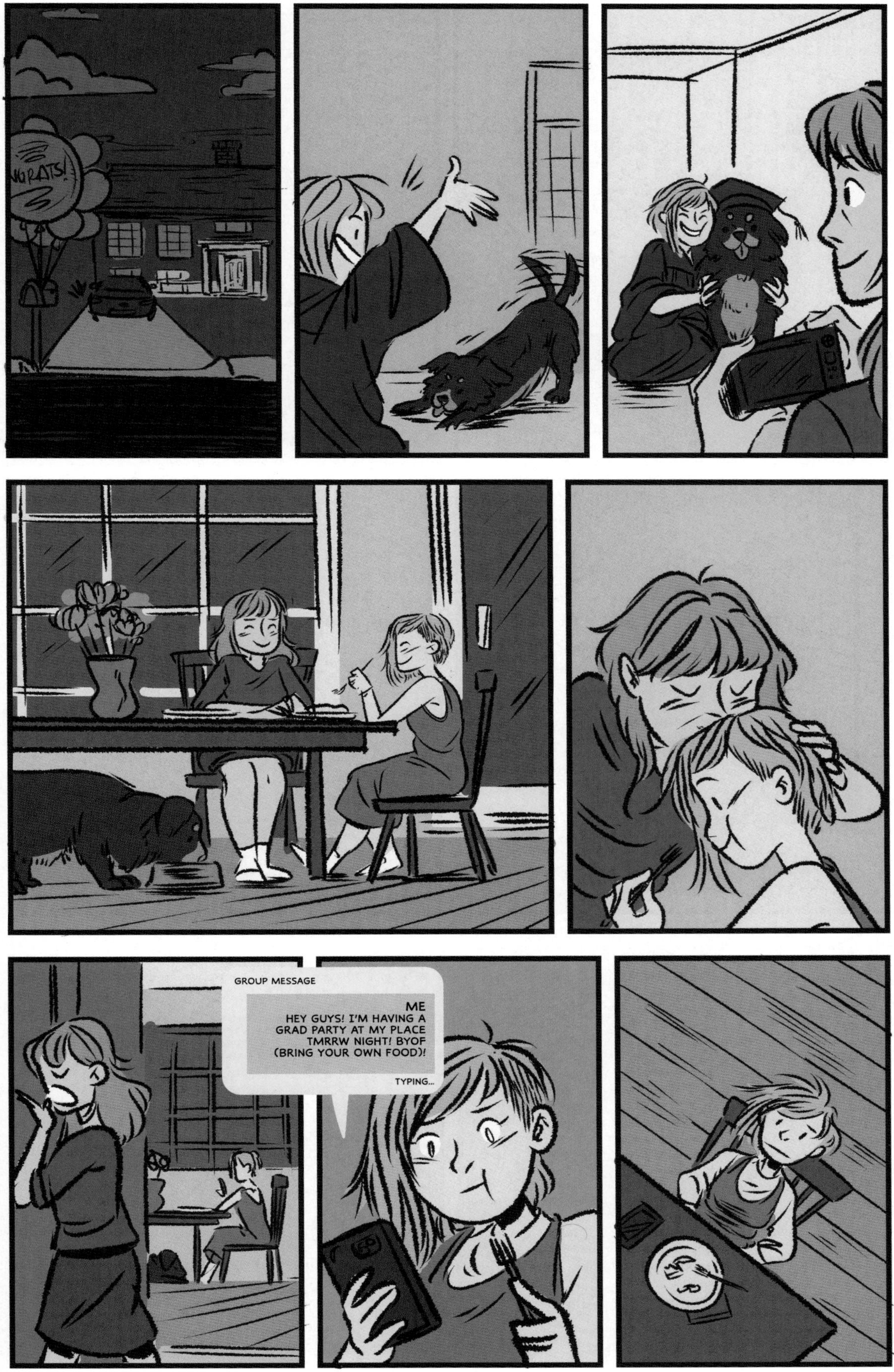

NGRATS!
GROUP MESSAGE
ME
HEY GUYS! I'M HAVING A GRAD PARTY AT MY PLACE TMRRW NIGHT! BYOF (BRING YOUR OWN FOOD)!
TYPING...

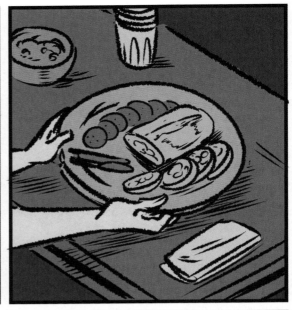

SNIFF!

CONGRATS!

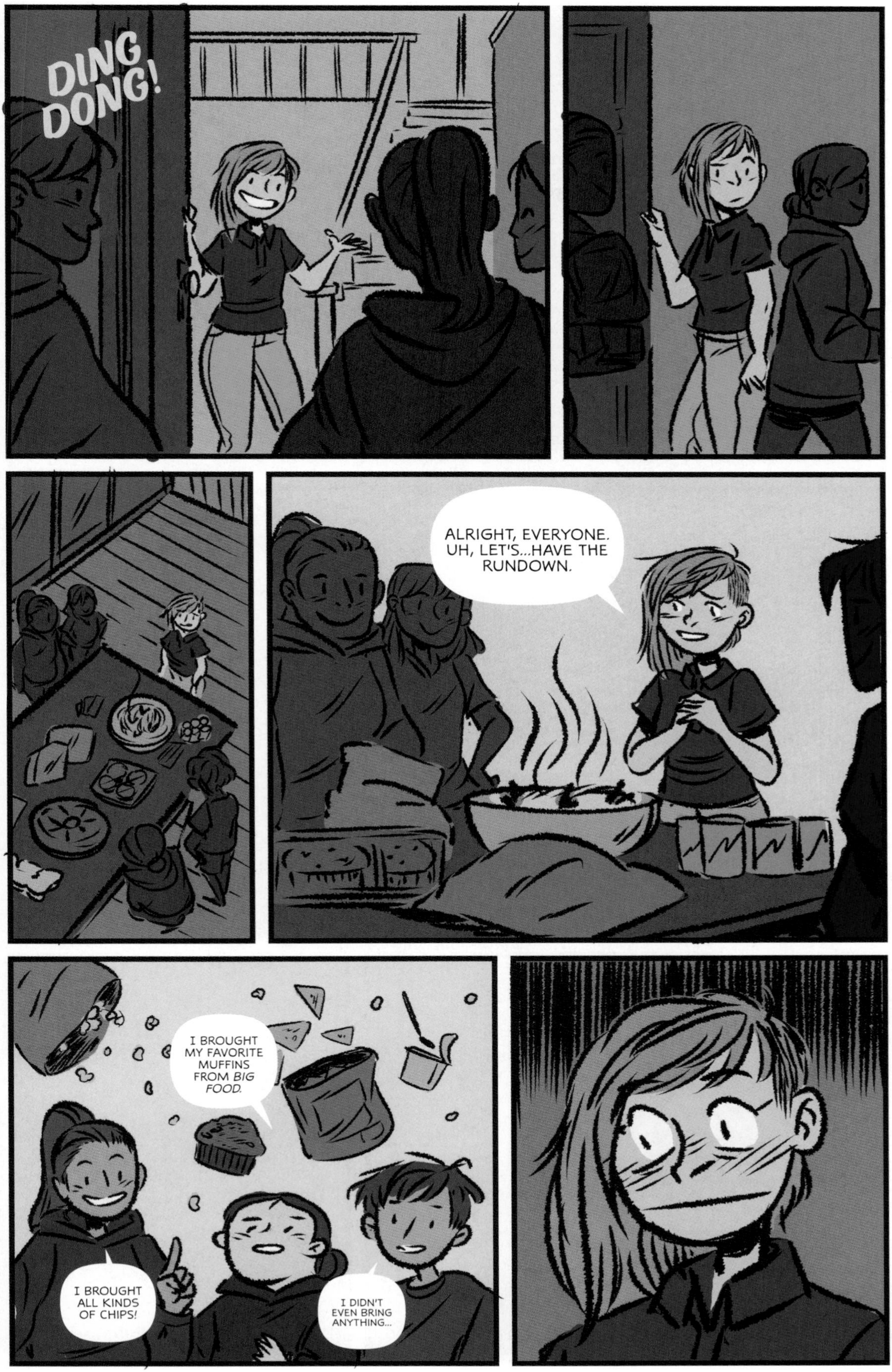
DING DONG!
ALRIGHT, EVERYONE. UH, LET'S...HAVE THE RUNDOWN.
I BROUGHT MY FAVORITE MUFFINS FROM *BIG FOOD.*
I BROUGHT ALL KINDS OF CHIPS!
I DIDN'T EVEN BRING ANYTHING...

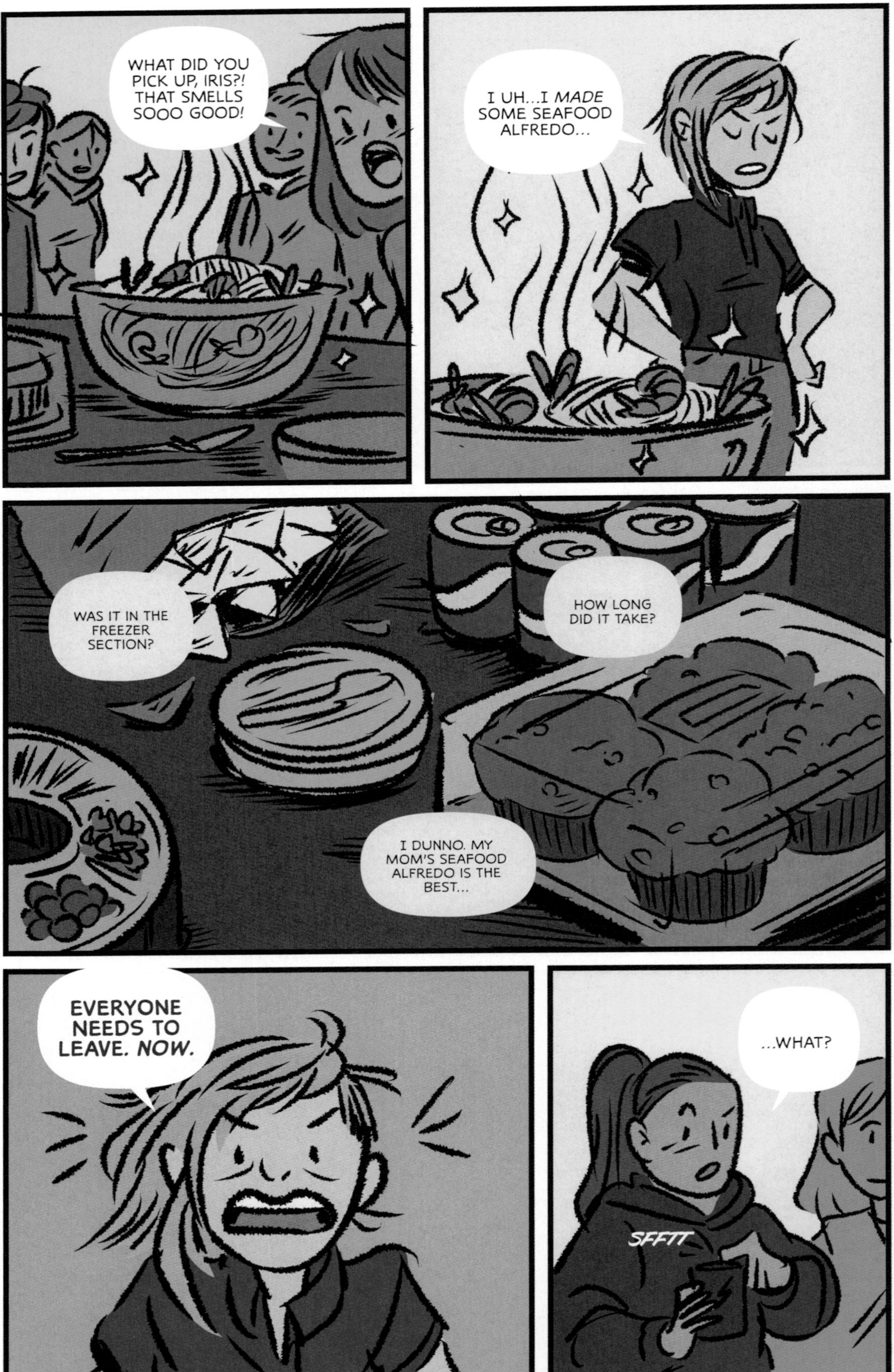
WHAT DID YOU PICK UP, IRIS?! THAT SMELLS SOOO GOOD!
I UH...I *MADE* SOME SEAFOOD ALFREDO...
WAS IT IN THE FREEZER SECTION?
HOW LONG DID IT TAKE?
I DUNNO. MY MOM'S SEAFOOD ALFREDO IS THE BEST...
EVERYONE NEEDS TO LEAVE. *NOW.*
...WHAT?
SFFTT

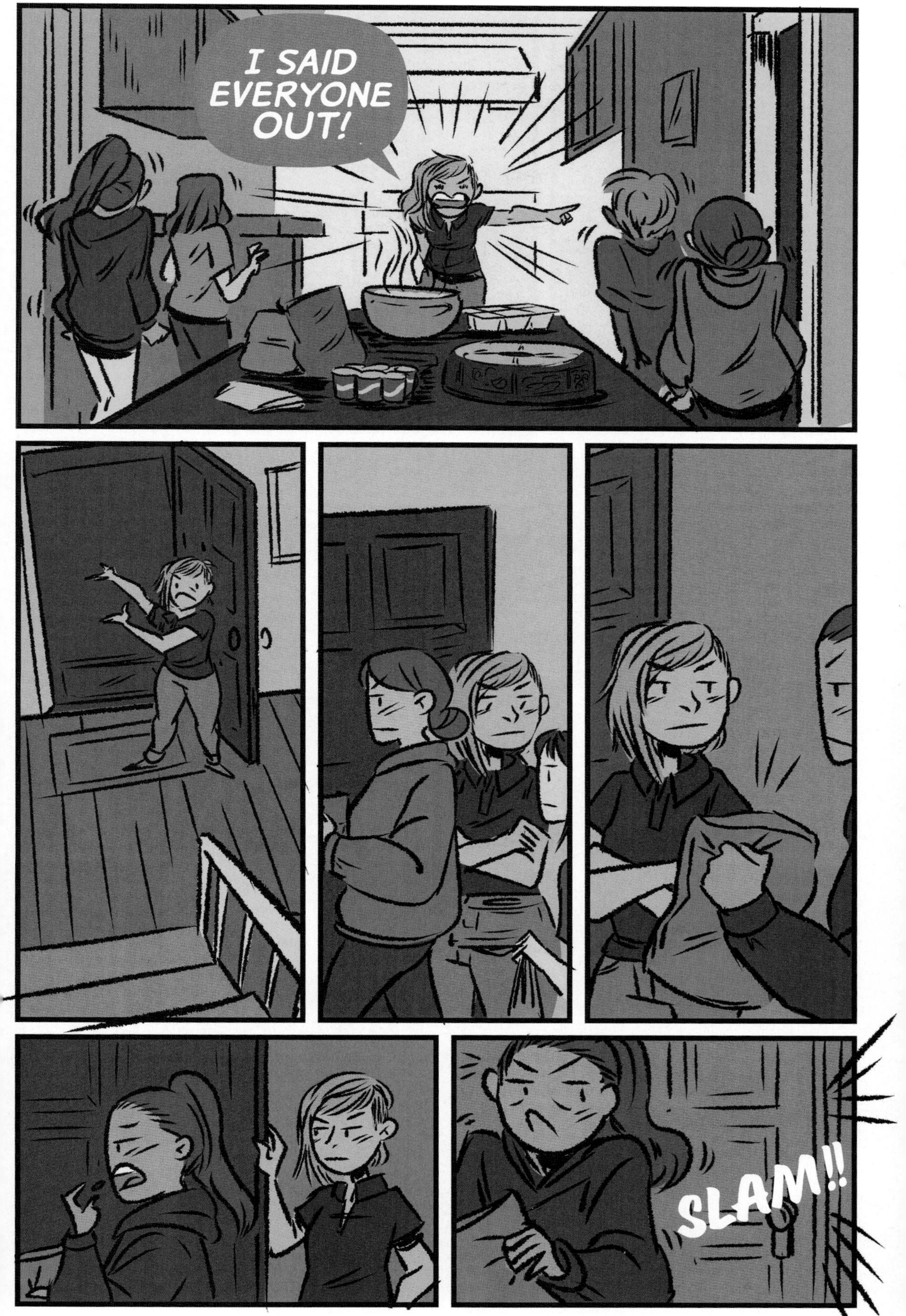
I SAID EVERYONE OUT!
SLAM!!

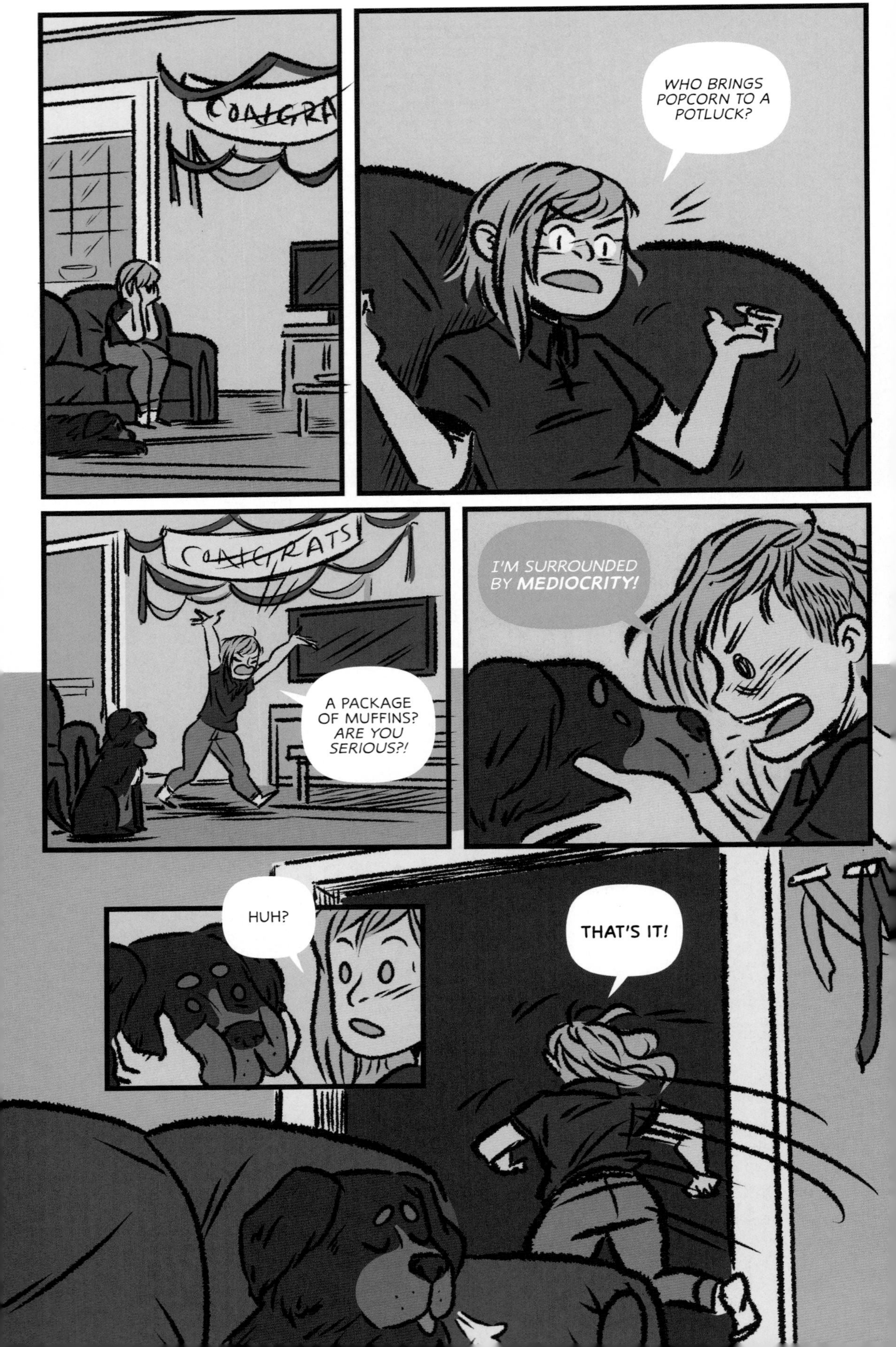
CONGRA
WHO BRINGS POPCORN TO A POTLUCK?
CONGRATS
A PACKAGE OF MUFFINS? ARE YOU SERIOUS?!
I'M SURROUNDED BY MEDIOCRITY!
HUH?
THAT'S IT!

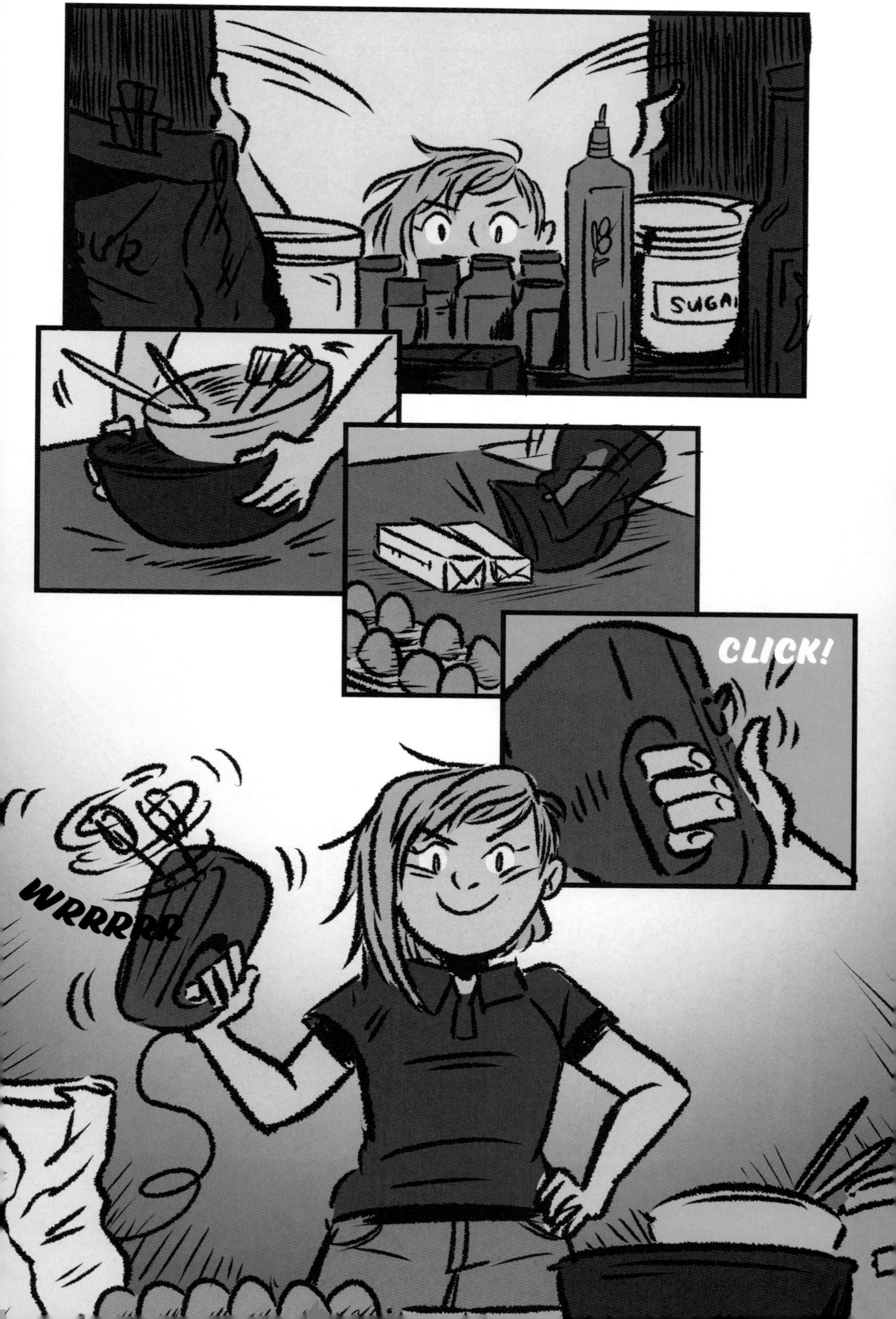
SUGA
CLICK!
WRRRRRR

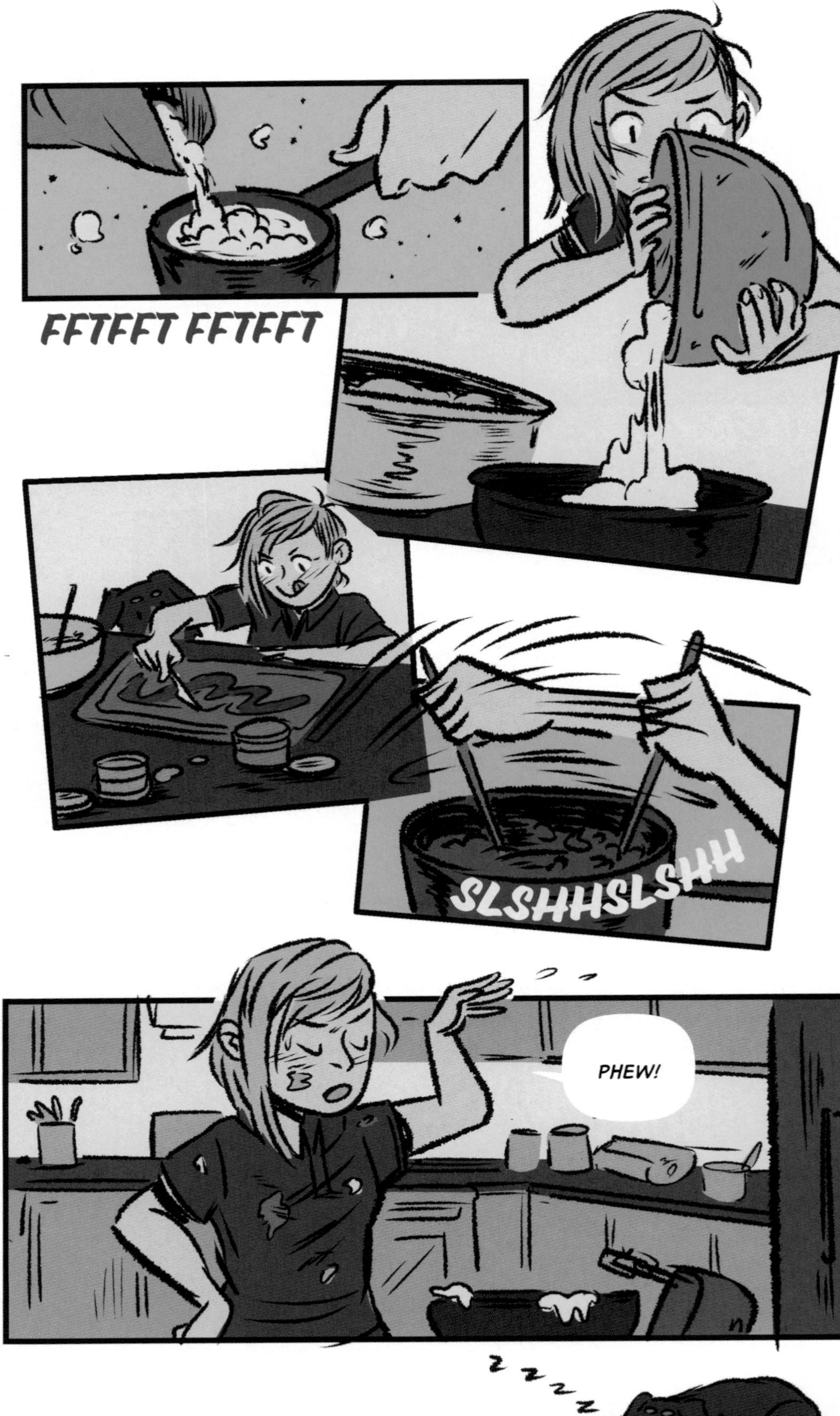
FFTFFT FFTFFT
SLSHHSLSHH
PHEW!
Z Z Z Z

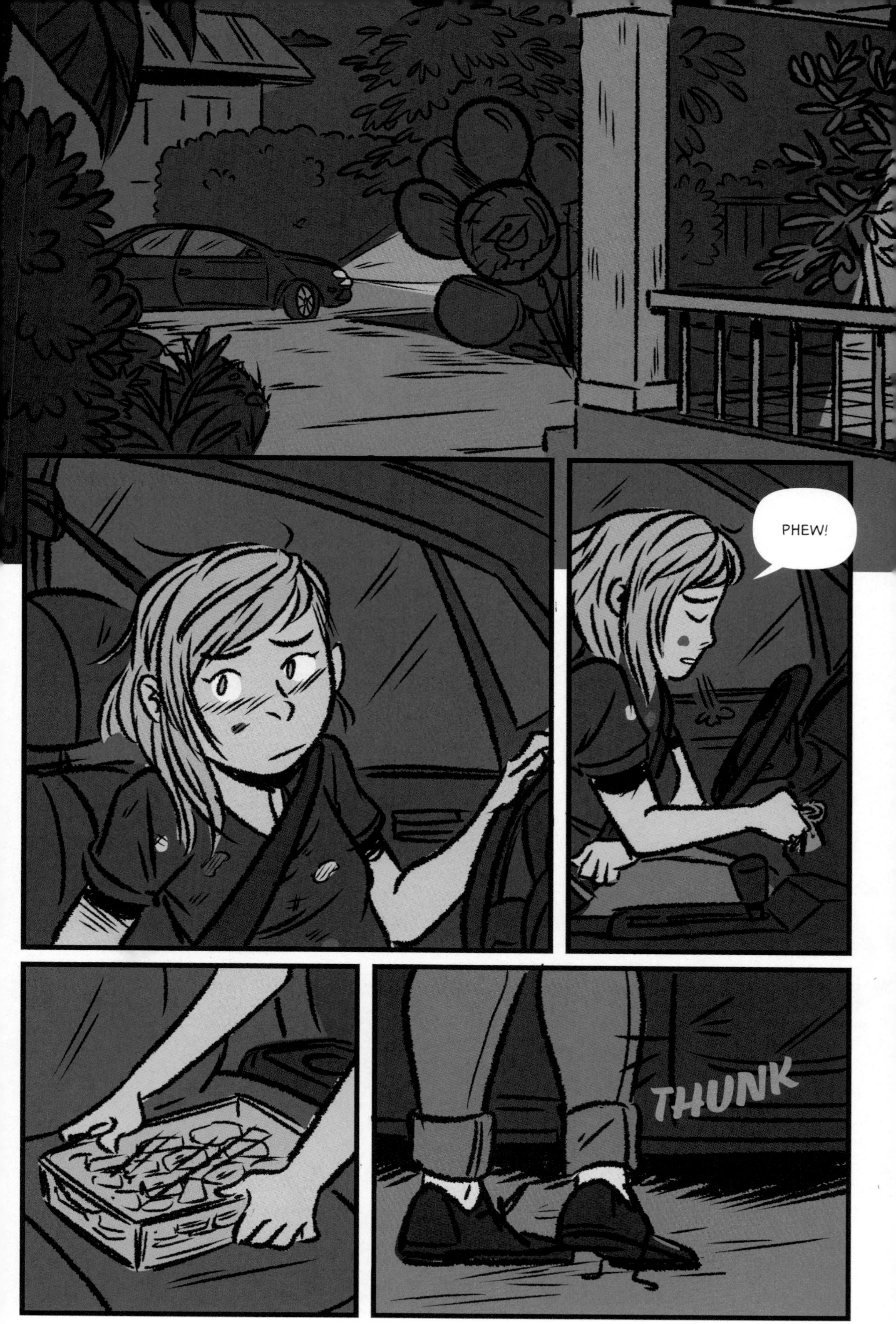
PHEW!
THUNK

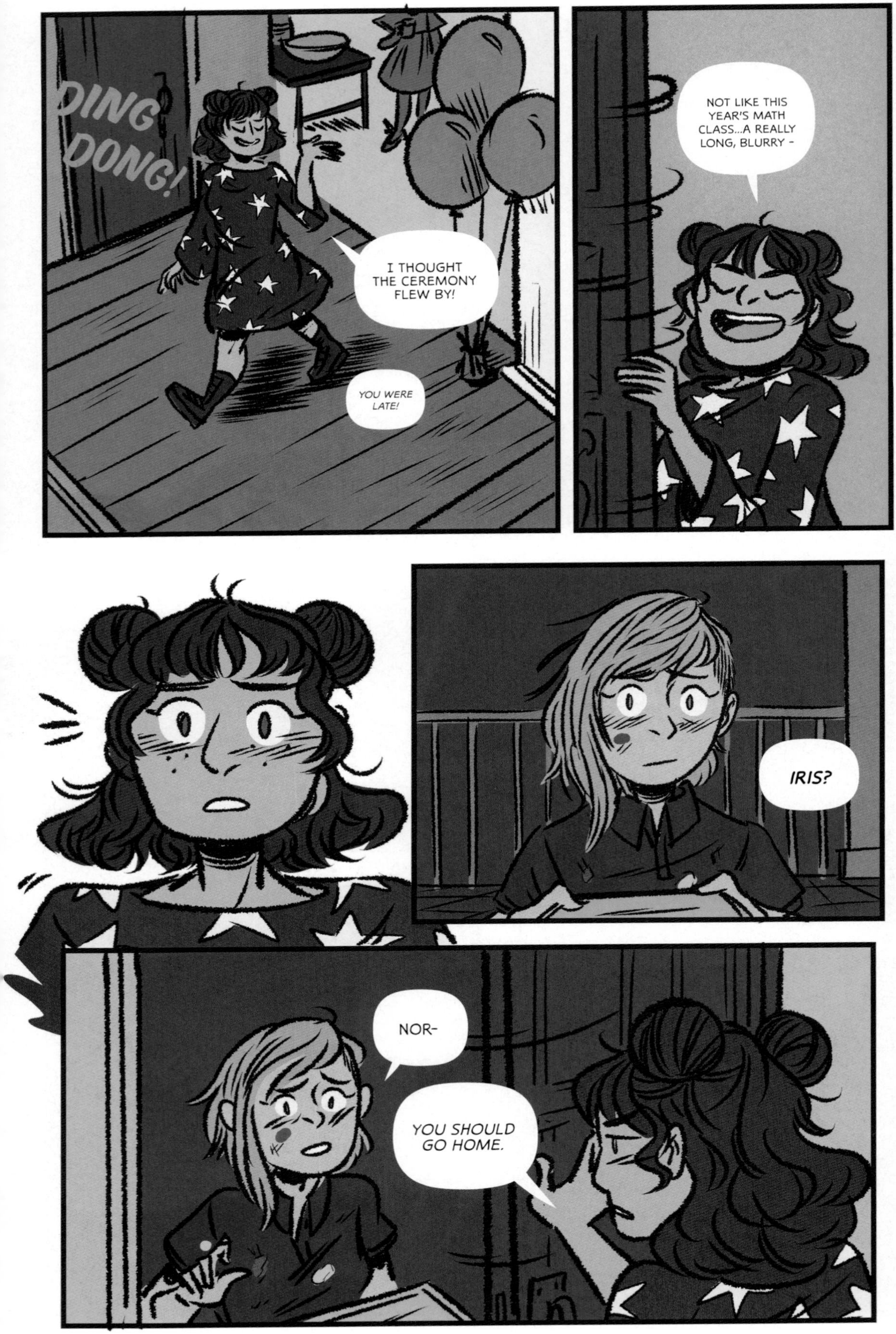
DING DONG!
I THOUGHT THE CEREMONY FLEW BY!
YOU WERE LATE!
NOT LIKE THIS YEAR'S MATH CLASS...A REALLY LONG, BLURRY -
IRIS?
NOR-
YOU SHOULD GO HOME.

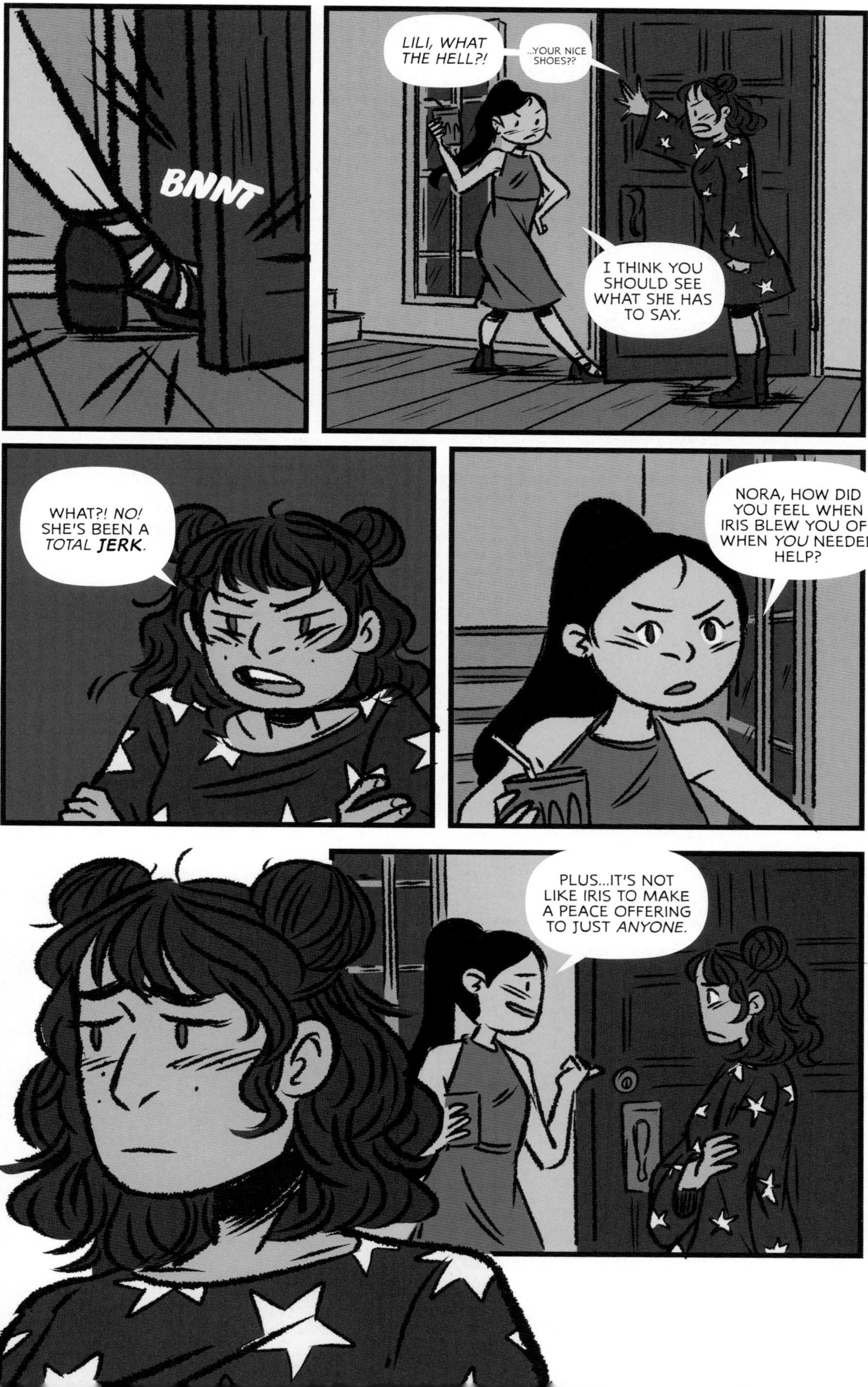
BNNT
LILI, WHAT THE HELL?!
...YOUR NICE SHOES??
I THINK YOU SHOULD SEE WHAT SHE HAS TO SAY.
WHAT?! NO! SHE'S BEEN A TOTAL JERK.
NORA, HOW DID YOU FEEL WHEN IRIS BLEW YOU OFF WHEN YOU NEEDED HELP?
PLUS...IT'S NOT LIKE IRIS TO MAKE A PEACE OFFERING TO JUST ANYONE.

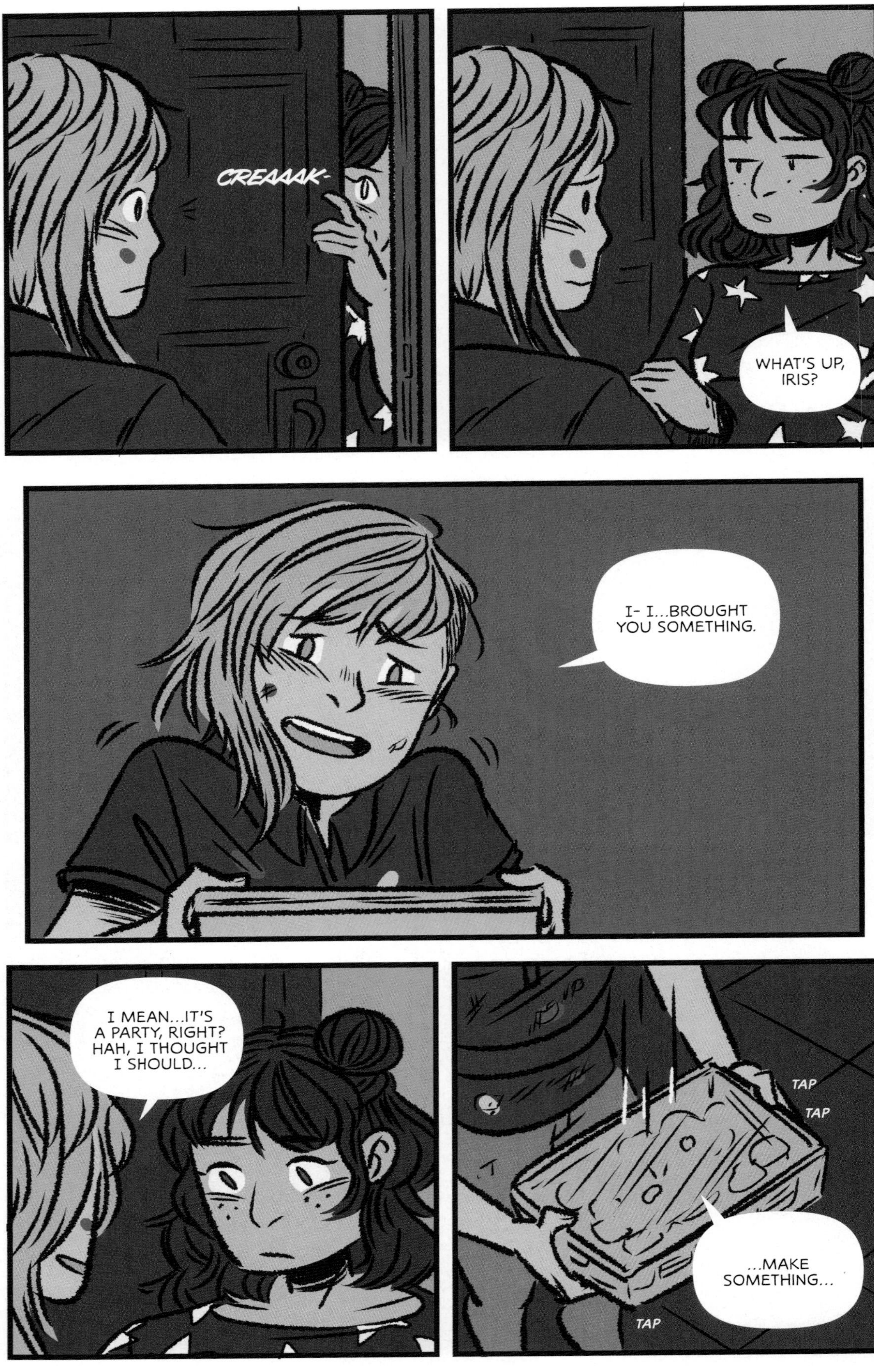
CREAAAK-
WHAT'S UP, IRIS?
I- I...BROUGHT YOU SOMETHING.
I MEAN...IT'S A PARTY, RIGHT? HAH, I THOUGHT I SHOULD...
TAP
TAP
...MAKE SOMETHING...
TAP

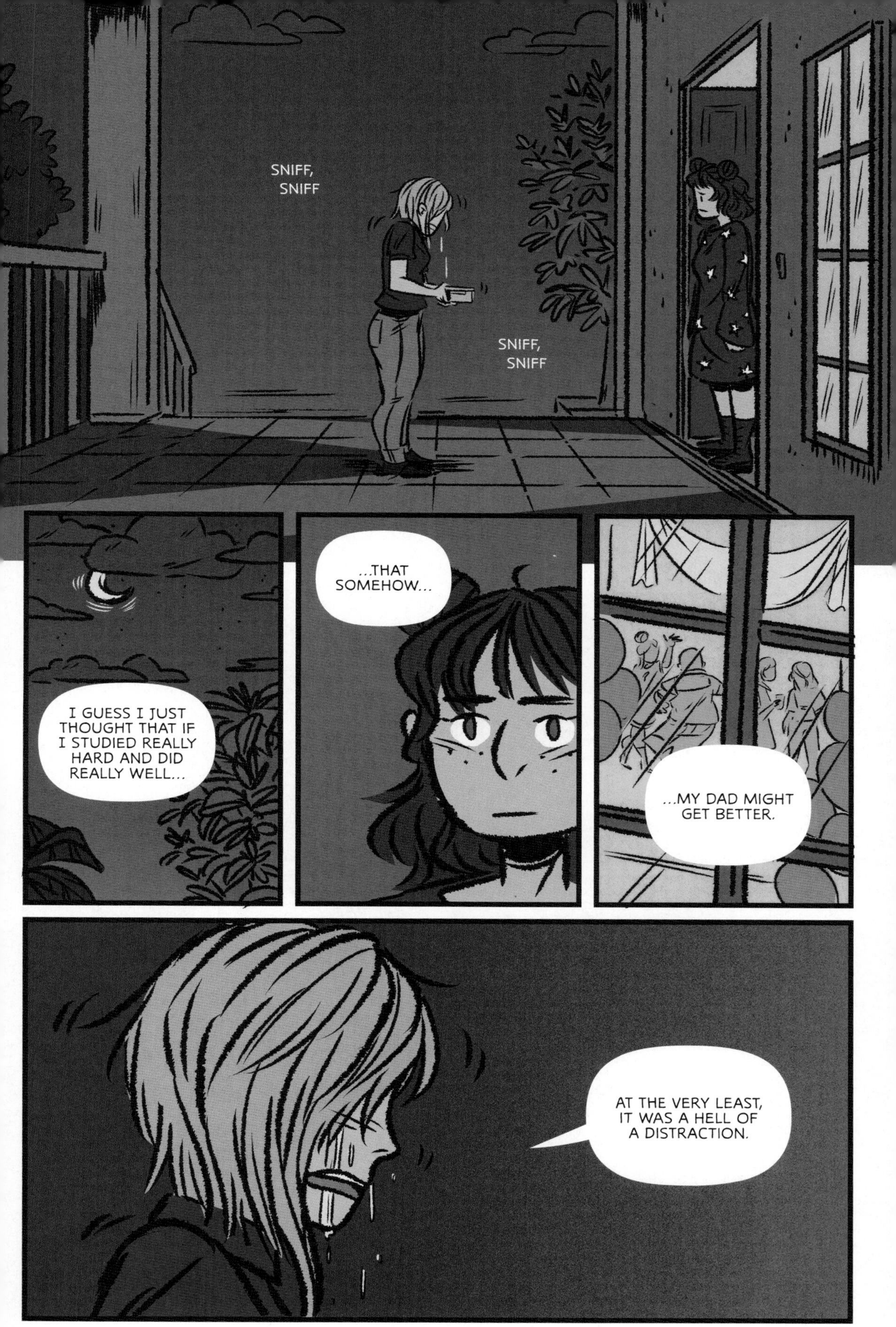
SNIFF, SNIFF
SNIFF, SNIFF
I GUESS I JUST THOUGHT THAT IF I STUDIED REALLY HARD AND DID REALLY WELL...
...THAT SOMEHOW...
...MY DAD MIGHT GET BETTER.
AT THE VERY LEAST, IT WAS A HELL OF A DISTRACTION.

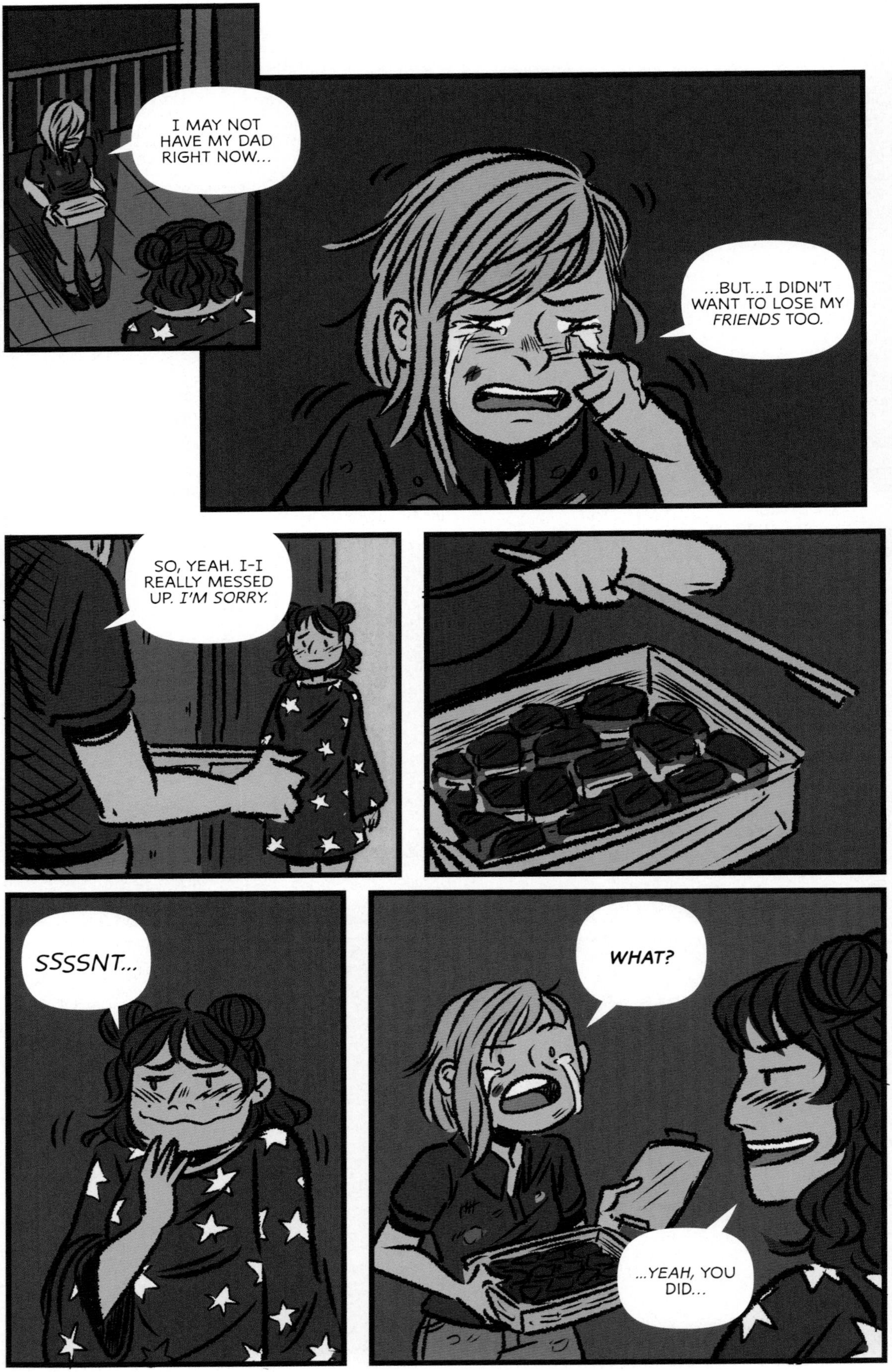
I MAY NOT HAVE MY DAD RIGHT NOW...
...BUT...I DIDN'T WANT TO LOSE MY *FRIENDS* TOO.
SO, YEAH. I-I REALLY MESSED UP. *I'M SORRY.*
SSSSNT...
WHAT?
...*YEAH,* YOU DID...

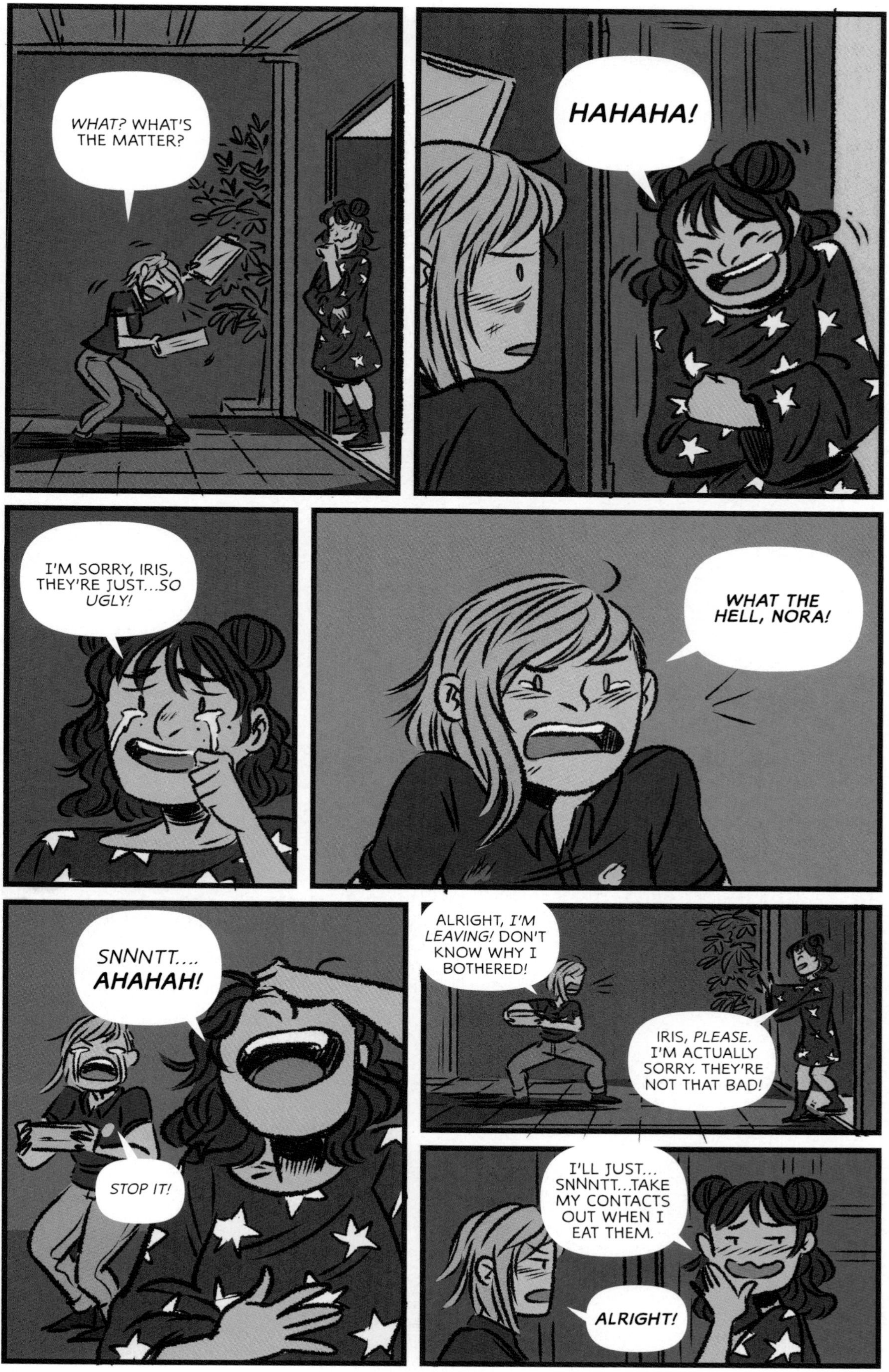
WHAT? WHAT'S THE MATTER?
HAHAHA!
I'M SORRY, IRIS, THEY'RE JUST...SO UGLY!
WHAT THE HELL, NORA!
SNNNTT.... AHAHAH!
STOP IT!
ALRIGHT, I'M LEAVING! DON'T KNOW WHY I BOTHERED!
IRIS, PLEASE. I'M ACTUALLY SORRY. THEY'RE NOT THAT BAD!
I'LL JUST... SNNNTT...TAKE MY CONTACTS OUT WHEN I EAT THEM.
ALRIGHT!

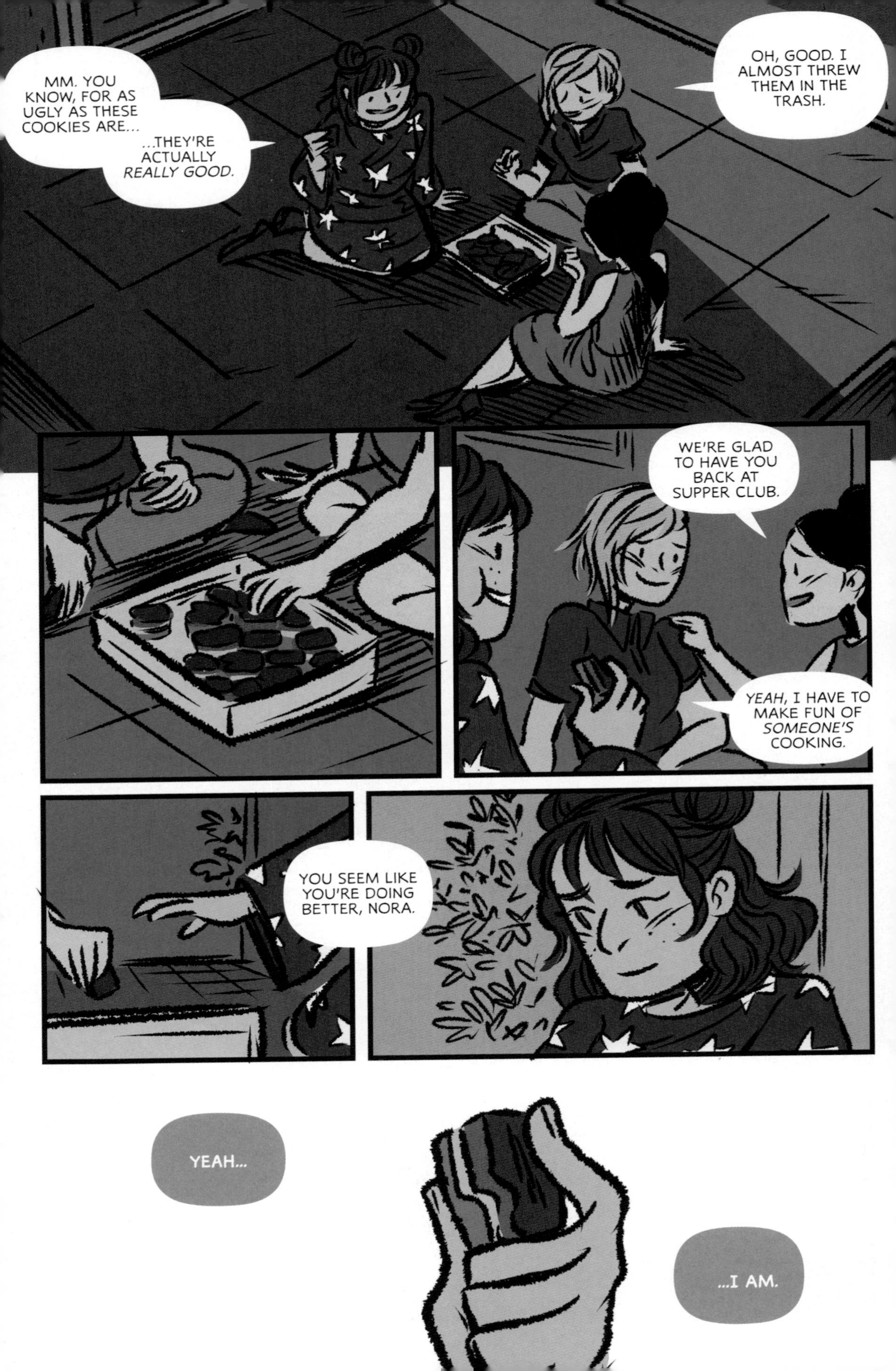
MM. YOU KNOW, FOR AS UGLY AS THESE COOKIES ARE...
...THEY'RE ACTUALLY *REALLY GOOD.*
OH, GOOD. I ALMOST THREW THEM IN THE TRASH.
WE'RE GLAD TO HAVE YOU BACK AT SUPPER CLUB.
YEAH, I HAVE TO MAKE FUN OF *SOMEONE'S* COOKING.
YOU SEEM LIKE YOU'RE DOING BETTER, NORA.
YEAH...
...I AM.

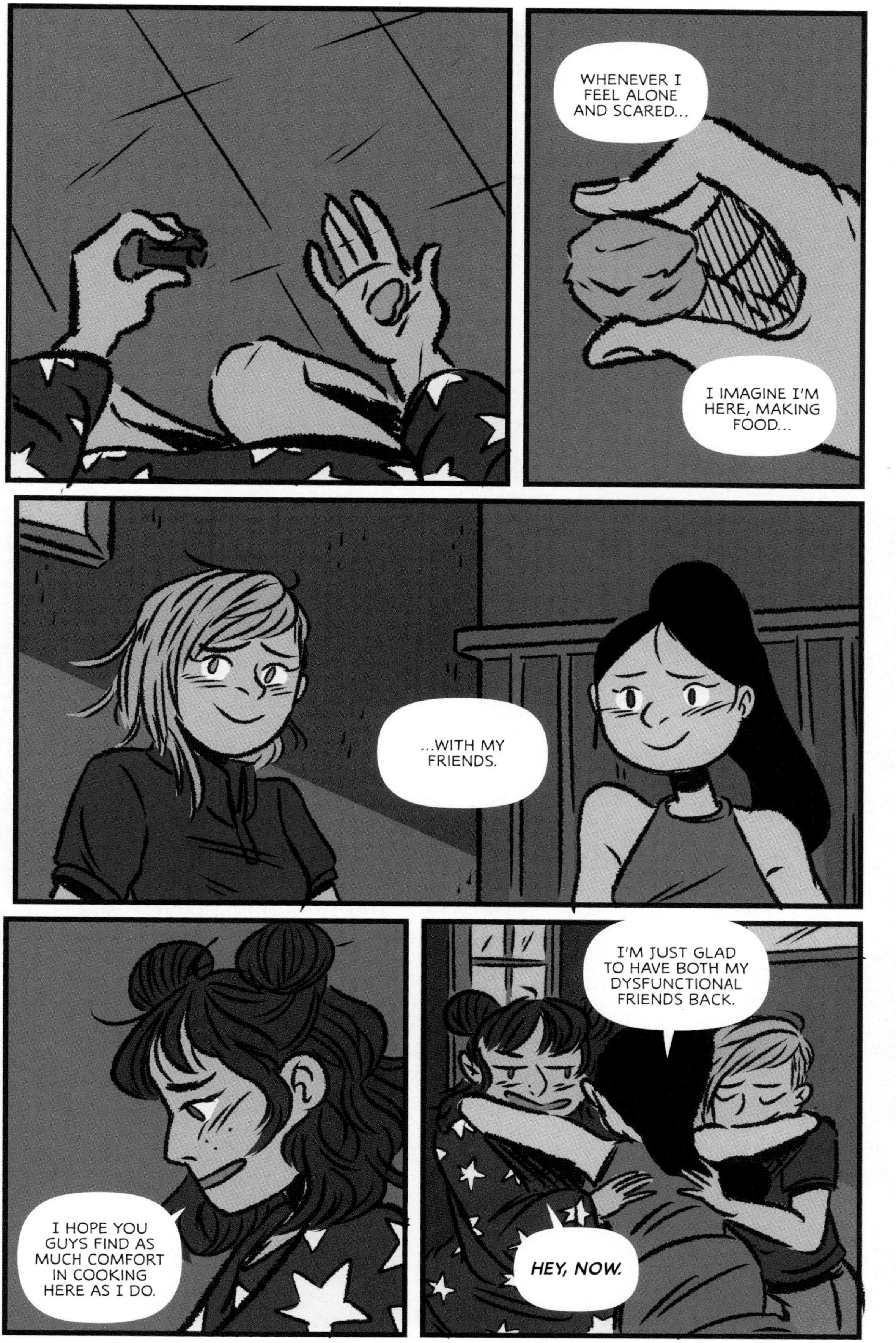
WHENEVER I FEEL ALONE AND SCARED...
I IMAGINE I'M HERE, MAKING FOOD...
...WITH MY FRIENDS.
I HOPE YOU GUYS FIND AS MUCH COMFORT IN COOKING HERE AS I DO.
I'M JUST GLAD TO HAVE BOTH MY DYSFUNCTIONAL FRIENDS BACK.
HEY, NOW.

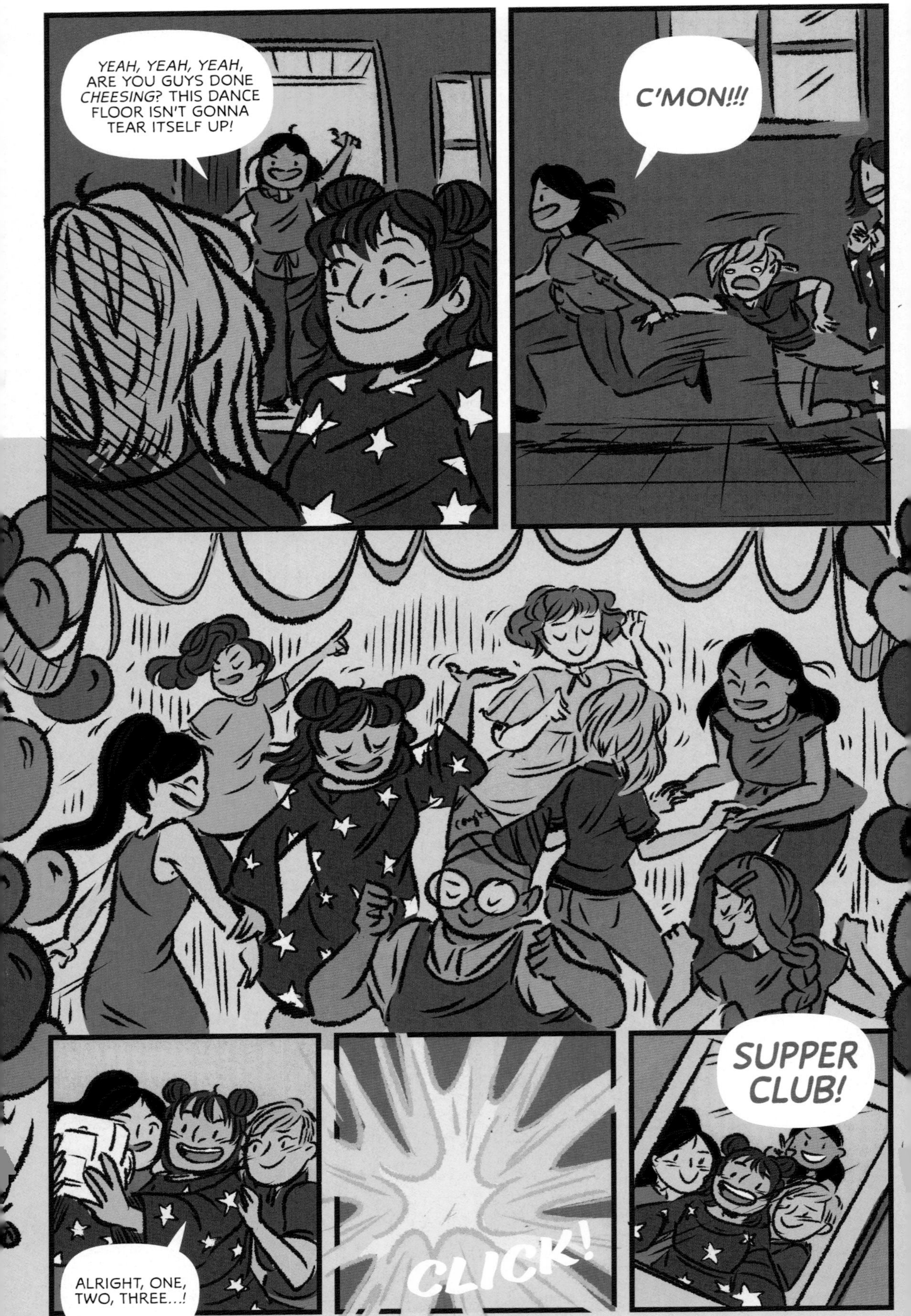
YEAH, YEAH, YEAH, ARE YOU GUYS DONE CHEESING? THIS DANCE FLOOR ISN'T GONNA TEAR ITSELF UP!
C'MON!!!
ALRIGHT, ONE, TWO, THREE...!
CLICK!
SUPPER CLUB!

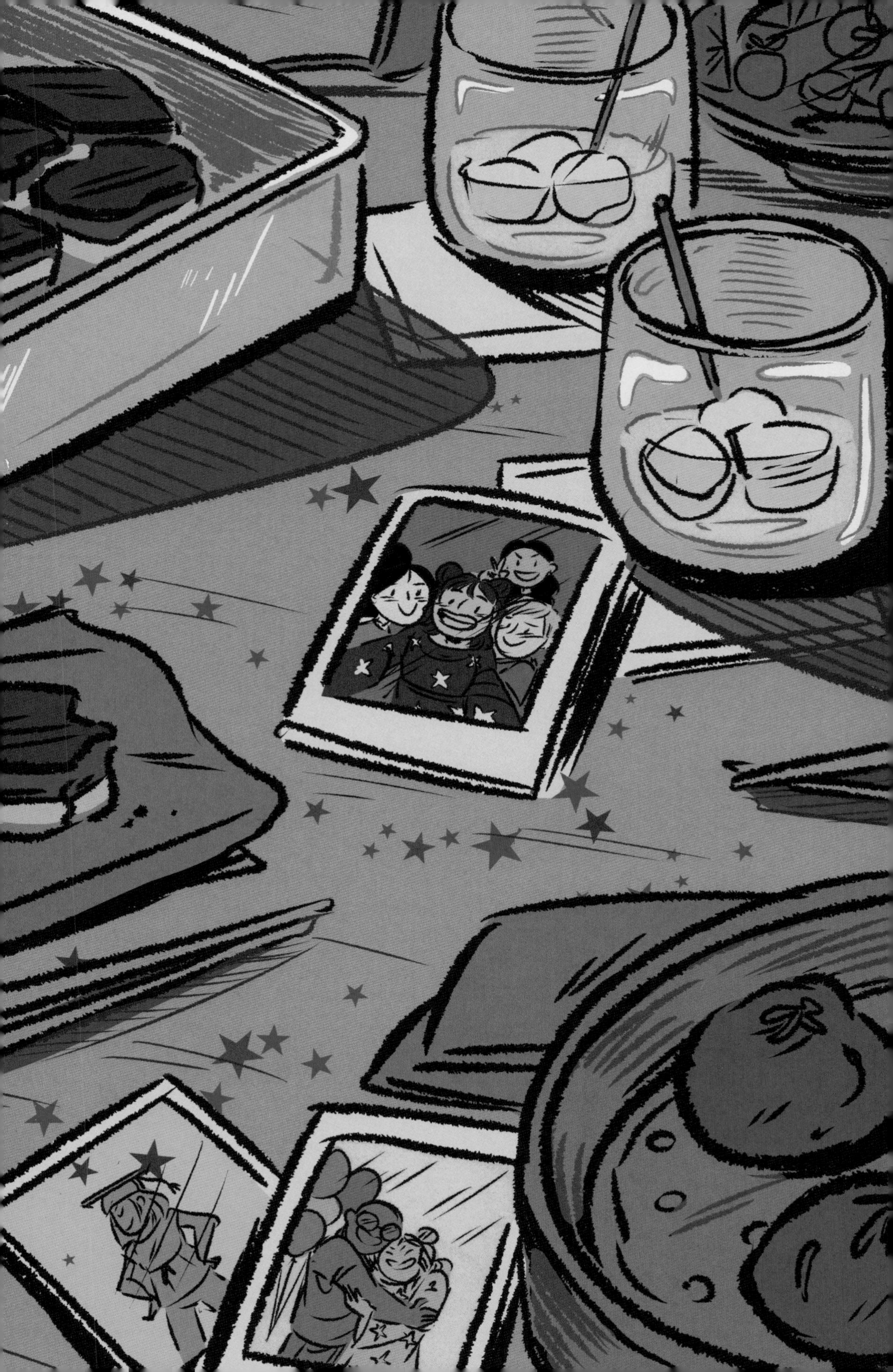

Italian Rainbow Cookies

INGREDIENTS

8 OUNCES ALMOND PASTE

1 CUP BUTTER, SOFTENED

1 CUP WHITE SUGAR

4 EGGS, SEPARATED

2 CUPS ALL-PURPOSE FLOUR

GREEN, YELLOW AND RED FOOD COLORING

¼ CUP SEEDLESS RED RASPBERRY JAM

¼ CUP APRICOT JAM

1 CUP SEMISWEET CHOCOLATE CHIPS, MELTED

DIRECTIONS

STEP 1:
PREHEAT OVEN TO 350 DEGREES F (175 DEGREES C). LINE THREE 9X13 INCH BAKING PANS WITH PARCHMENT PAPER.

STEP 2:
IN A LARGE BOWL, BREAK APART ALMOND PASTE WITH A FORK, AND CREAM TOGETHER WITH BUTTER, SUGAR, AND EGG YOLKS. WHEN MIXTURE IS FLUFFY AND SMOOTH, STIR IN FLOUR TO FORM A DOUGH.

STEP 3:
IN A SMALL BOWL, BEAT EGG WHITES UNTIL SOFT PEAKS FORM. FOLD EGG WHITES INTO THE DOUGH. DIVIDE DOUGH INTO 3 EQUAL PORTIONS. MIX ONE PORTION WITH RED FOOD COLORING, AND ONE WITH GREEN FOOD COLORING AND ONE WITH YELLOW. SPREAD EACH COLOR ONTO THE SEPARATE PARCHMENT PAPERS, CREATING A WIDE RECTANGLE ABOUT 3/4 INCH TALL.

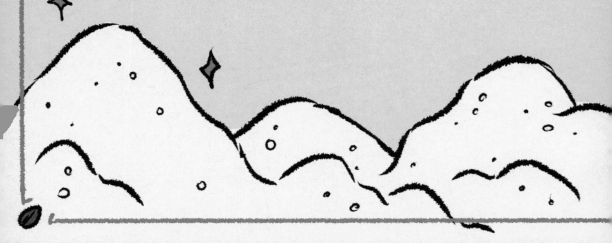

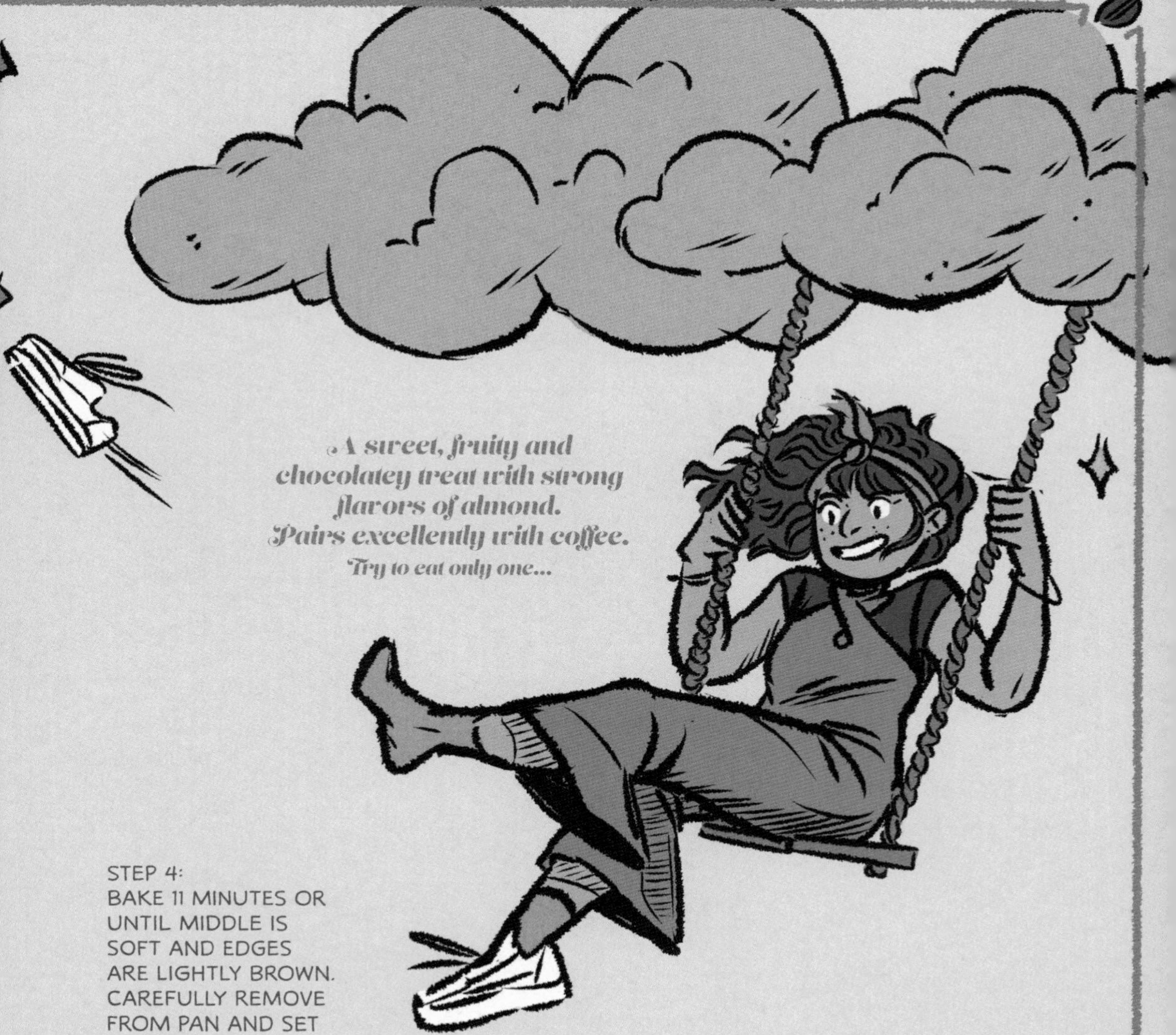

A sweet, fruity and chocolatey treat with strong flavors of almond. Pairs excellently with coffee.

Try to eat only one...

STEP 4:
BAKE 11 MINUTES OR UNTIL MIDDLE IS SOFT AND EDGES ARE LIGHTLY BROWN. CAREFULLY REMOVE FROM PAN AND SET ASIDE TO COOL.

STEP 5:
USE THE GREEN LAYER AS THE BASE FOR THE COOKIES. ON A PIECE OF PARCHMENT PAPER OR PLASTIC WRAP, SPREAD THE COOLED GREEN LAYER WITH RASPBERRY JAM. TOP WITH YELLOW LAYER. SPREAD WITH APRICOT JAM, AND TOP WITH RED LAYER. PLACE ANOTHER PIECE OF PARCHMENT PAPER OR PLASTIC WRAP ON TOP OF THE LAYERS. USE A HEAVY PAN OR CUTTING BOARD TO PRESS DOWN ON LAYERS, COMPRESSING THEM SLIGHTLY. CHILL IN THE REFRIGERATOR 2-4 HOURS.

STEP 6:
TOP WITH MELTED CHOCOLATE CHIPS, AND REFRIGERATE 30 MINUTES TO ONE HOUR, OR UNTIL CHOCOLATE IS SEMI-FIRM. SLICE INTO SMALL SQUARES. SERVE WHEN CHOCOLATE IS COMPLETELY FIRM.

STEP 7:
DIG IN!

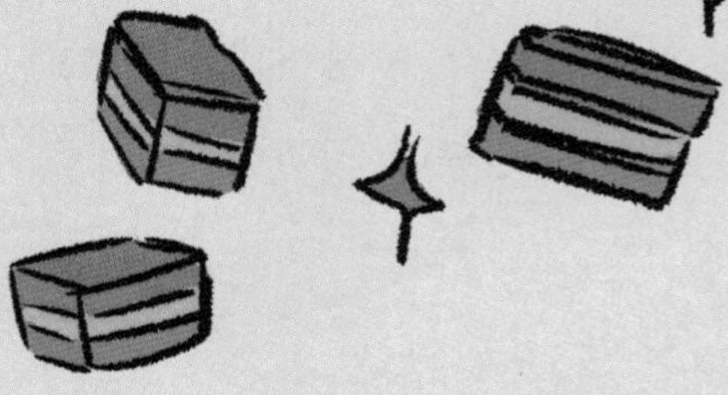

Braised Pork Ribs

BY TAN SHU

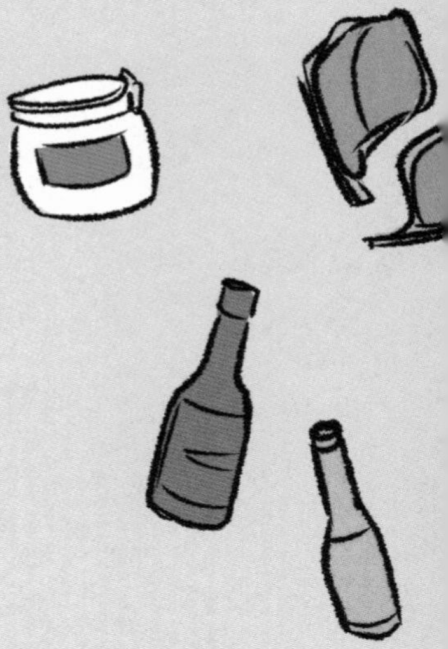

INGREDIENTS

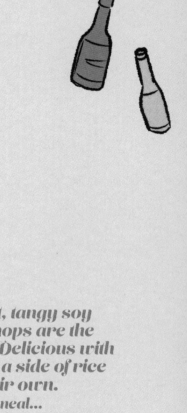

1 LB PORK CHOPS CUT INTO SMALL PIECES (OR YOU CAN BUY SOME PRE-CHOPPED)

4 TABLESPOONS OIL

3-4 PIECES OF GINGER, SLICED

2 TEASPOONS OF CHINESE VINEGAR

2 TABLESPOONS COOKING WINE

4 TABLESPOONS OF SOY SAUCE

6 TEASPOONS OF SUGAR

Robust with a sweet, tangy soy flavor, these pork chops are the ultimate comfort food. Delicious with crisp pickled veggies, a side of rice or simply on their own.

The star of any meal...

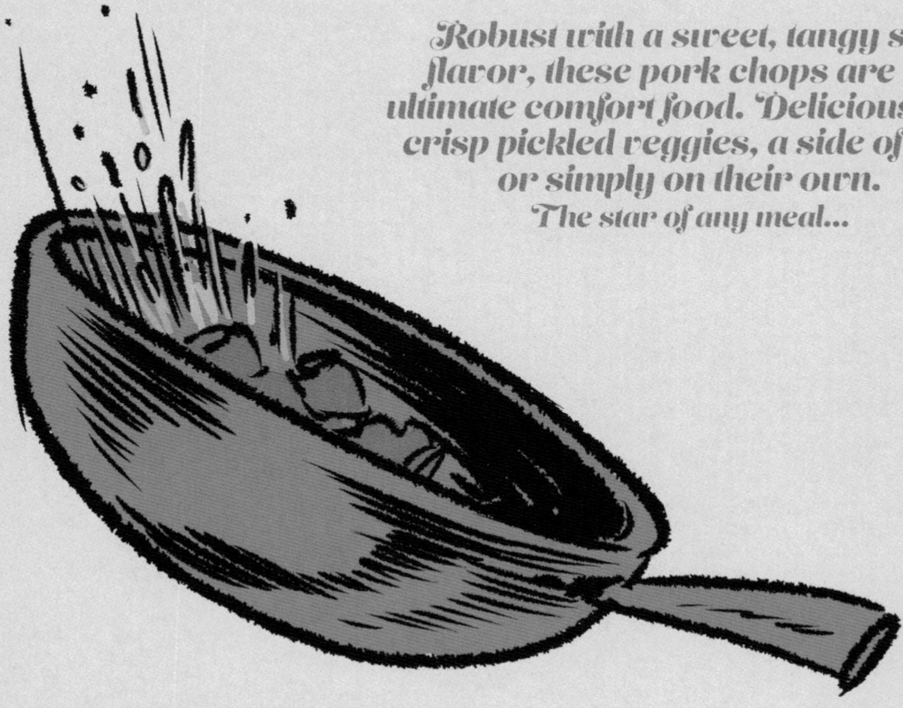

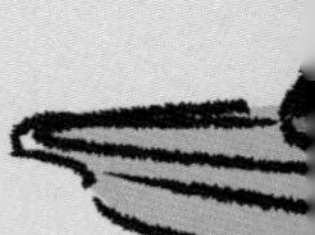

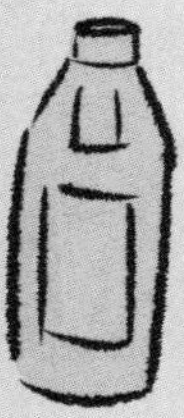

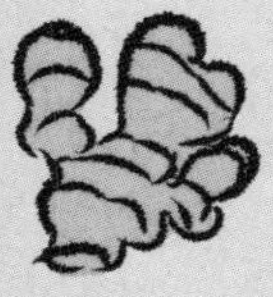

DIRECTIONS

STEP 1:
MAKE SURE YOU DON'T HAVE ANY WATER IN YOUR WOK, PREHEAT STOVE AND BOIL 2 TBSP OIL IN THE WOK. STIR GINGER SLICES IN THE HOT OIL FOR 10 SECONDS.

STEP 2:
ADD PORK CHOPS TO WOK WITH TWO TABLESPOONS OF COOKING WINE. STIR UNTIL THE PORK CHOPS ARE LIGHTLY BROWNED.

STEP 3:
ADD WATER TO THE WOK, ENOUGH TO COVER THE PORK CHOPS. ADD CHINESE VINEGAR, SOY SAUCE AND SUGAR. AFTER WATER HAS COME TO A BOIL, REDUCE HEAT TO LOW AND SIMMER FOR AT LEAST 40 MINUTES.

STEP 4:
WHEN IT'S ALMOST DONE, AND THE WATER HAS ALMOST EVAPORATED COMPLETELY, TURN BURNER ON HIGH TEMPERATURE AND STIR FOR 20-30 SECONDS.

STEP 5:
PLATE AND DEVOUR!

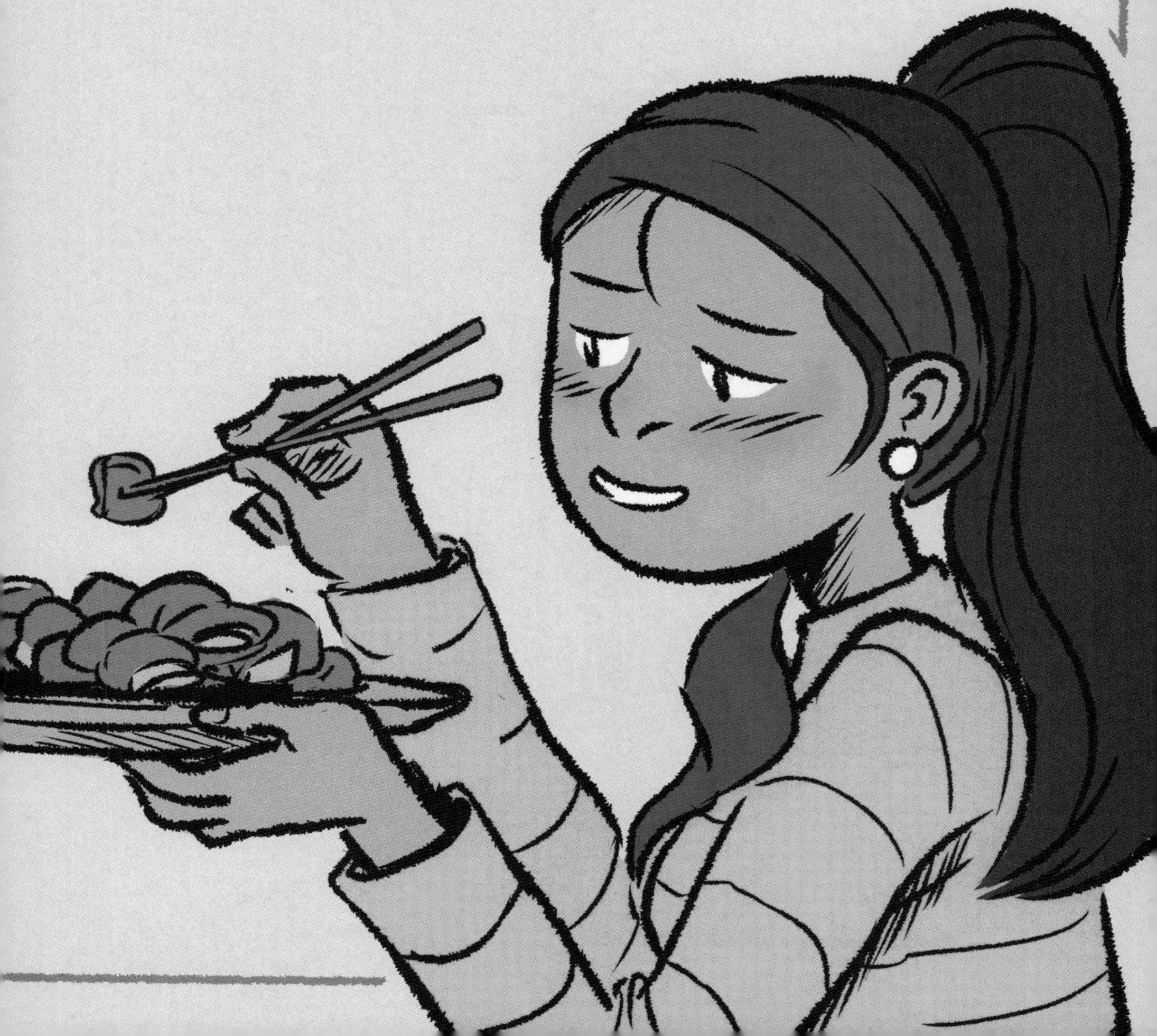

Three-Cheese Macaroni & Cheese

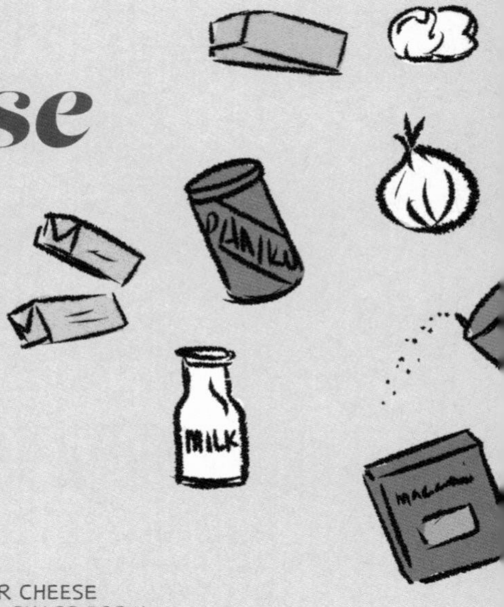
MILK

BY ALLIE PIPITONE

INGREDIENTS

1 TBSP MINCED WHITE ONION

4 TBSP (1/2 STICK) BUTTER OR MARGARINE

1/4 CUP ALL-PURPOSE FLOUR

2 CUPS MILK

4 OUNCES AMERICAN CHEESE, CUBED

1/4 CUP CUBED SHARP CHEESE (SUGGESTED: BLUE CHEESE)

1/4 CUP CUBED CHEDDAR CHEESE (MEDIUM, THOUGH ADD SHARP FOR A KICK)

1 TSP SALT

PINCH OF PEPPER

1/4 TSP DRY MUSTARD

4 OUNCES PASTA

PANKO BREAD CRUMBS TO TASTE (OPTIONAL)

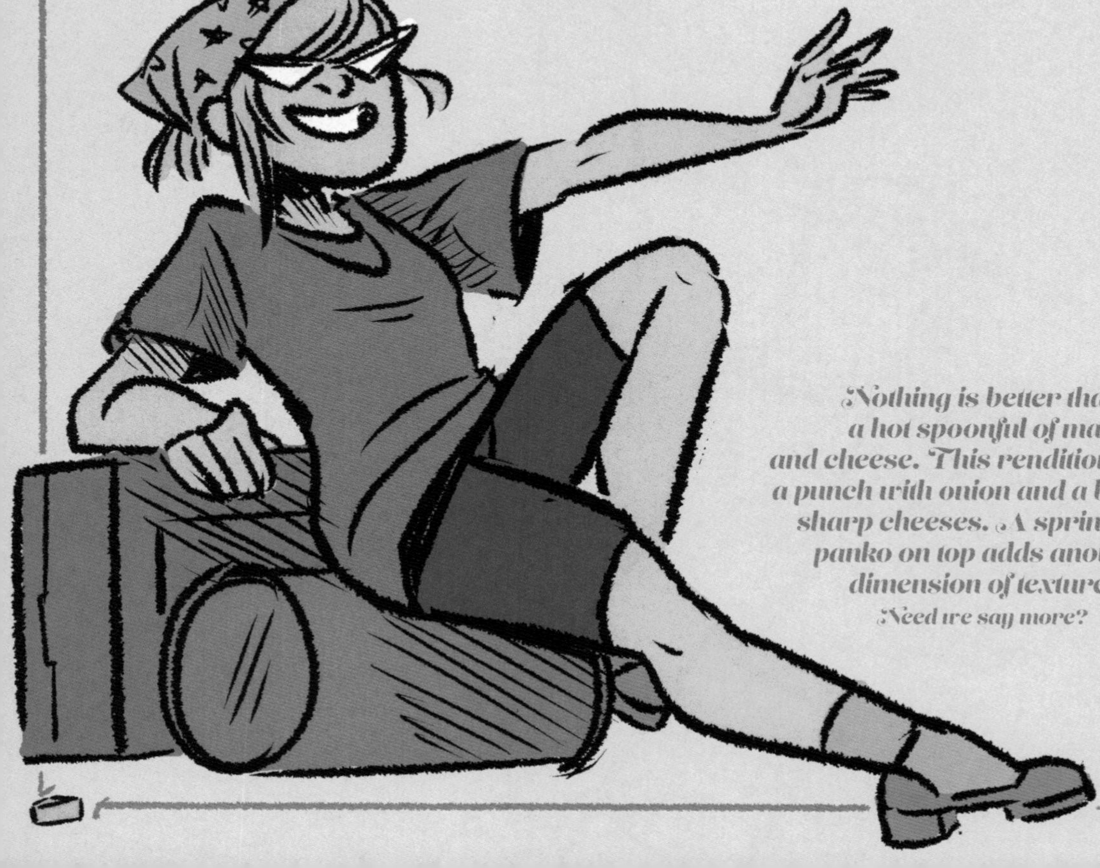

Nothing is better than a hot spoonful of mac and cheese. This rendition packs a punch with onion and a blend of sharp cheeses. A sprinkle of panko on top adds another dimension of texture.

Need we say more?

DIRECTIONS

STEP 1:
PREHEAT OVEN TO 400°F

STEP 2:
BOIL WATER FOR PASTA. WHEN BOILING, ADD PASTA
AND COOK TO AL-DENTE. DRAIN AND SET ASIDE.

STEP 3:
HEAT A FRYING PAN OVER MEDIUM-LOW HEAT. MELT
BUTTER AND ONCE MELTED, SAUTÉ THE ONION
UNTIL TRANSLUCENT.

STEP 4:
ONCE THE ONION IS TRANSLUCENT, SLOWLY STIR IN FLOUR AND THEN COOK FOR TWO
MINUTES. STIR CONTINUOUSLY FOR THE ENTIRE TWO MINUTES. MAKE SURE IT'S COATED IN THE
BUTTER EVENLY.

STEP 5:
SLOWLY STIR IN THE MILK.

STEP 6:
ONCE MILK IS ADDED IN, STIR IN THE CUBED CHEESES. THIS HELPS THEM MELT MORE EASILY
AND EVENLY. WHEN COMFORTABLE WITH THE RECIPE, TRY EXPERIMENTING WITH DIFFERENT
CHEESES!

STEP 7:
CONTINUE TO COOK OVER MEDIUM HEAT, STIRRING OCCASIONALLY UNTIL THICKENED. ONCE
THICKENED, ADD IN THE PASTA.

STEP 8:
LIGHTLY BUTTER A CASSEROLE DISH AND POUR THE MIXTURE INTO THE DISH. BAKE FOR 20
MINUTES. FOR AN ADDED CRUNCH, ADD BREAD CRUMBS TO THE TOP BEFORE BAKING.

Early Concept Work

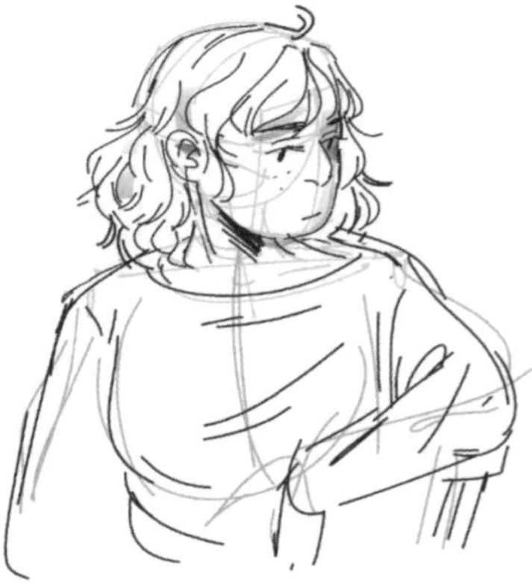

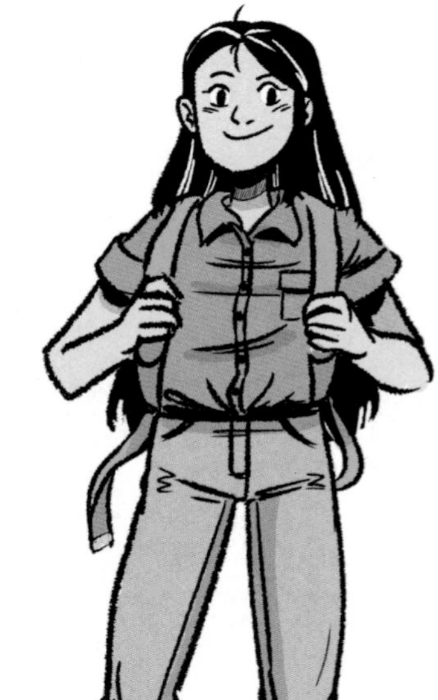

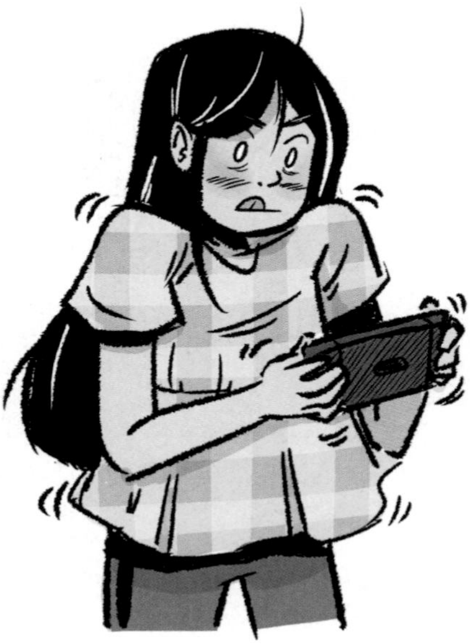

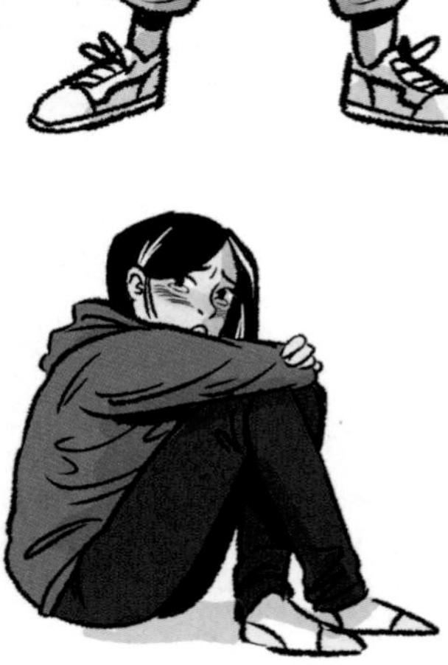

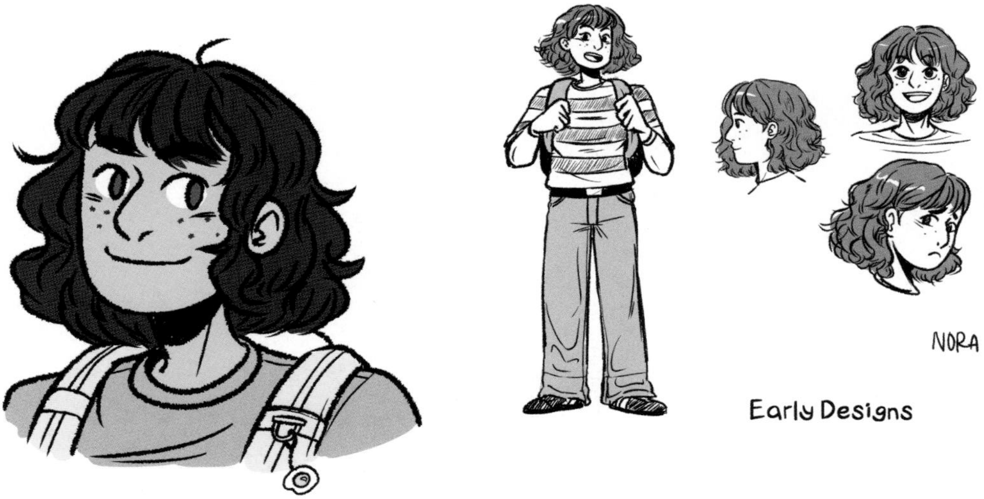
NORA
Early Designs

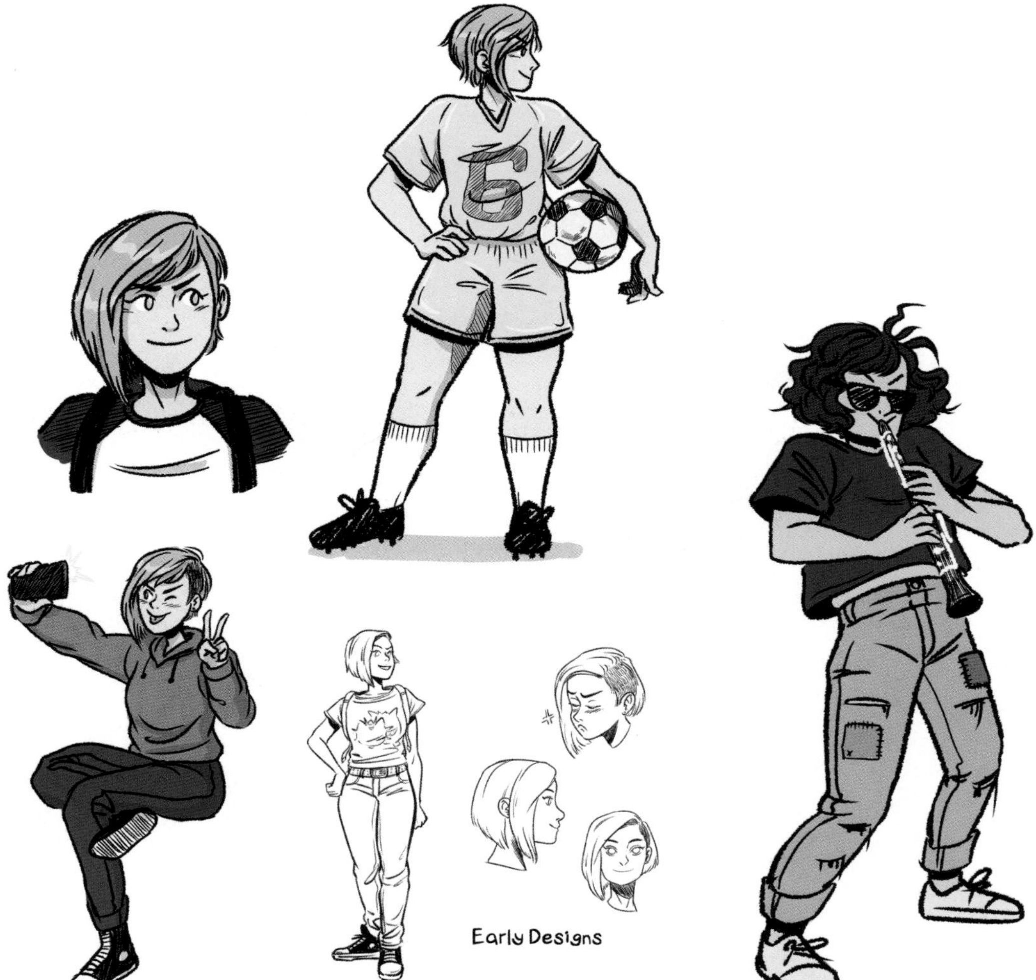
Early Designs

Keep on cooking!

Love,
Supper
Club